LAST CALL

LAST CALL

James Grippando

Doubleday Large Print
Home Library Edition

HARPER ● PERENNIAL

NEW YORK ● LONDON ● TORONTO ● SYDNEY

ISBN-978-0-7394-9062-4

For Tiffany. Better than ever.

LAST CALL

Prologue: 1986

In silent agreement, the Grove Lords selected their next victim.

All of Miami—or at least the bus-riding, project-dwelling population of the Coconut Grove ghetto—seemed to stop and admire the 1964 Chevy Impala cruising down Grand Avenue. The totally refurbished, twenty-year-old classic had all the trappings of the finest in gang wheels. Metallic blue paint job with a flaming red devil atop the hood. Bumpers, mirrors, and side strips in high-polished chrome that glistened in the sunset. Low-ride, hydraulic suspension that left barely enough ground clearance for a garden snake.

The most prized upgrades, of course, were the all-important rims—180-count spoke radials with 24-karat, gold-plate finish. Not bad for three punks from the 'hood. They'd stolen it from a Latino gang leader who had more flash than firepower. A pair of 9-millimeter bullet holes in the rear quarter panel marked the occasion.

Music blasted at ear-splitting decibels from a boom box in the trunk. The dark-tinted windows rattled with the deep-base vibes of "When Doves Cry," by Prince. Thirteen-year-old Theo Knight rode shotgun. He wore his Nike cap backward, the price tag still dangling from the bill. Sweat pasted an orange Miami Hurricanes football jersey to his back. A Mercedes-Benz hood ornament hung from a thick gold chain around his neck. It was the standard uniform of the Grove Lords, a gang of badass teenagers led by chief thief of the week Isaac Reems. Isaac was behind the wheel. Theo's older brother, Tatum, was sandwiched between them on the bench seat.

Isaac lowered the music so they could talk. "You seen him, right?"

"Uh-huh," said Tatum.

Theo didn't answer.

"Theo?" said Isaac. "You seen him, didn't ya?"

Theo knew exactly who he was talking about. The next white dude they spotted was their agreed-upon target. "Yeah, I seen him. Crazy man ridin' straight through nigguh town on a bicycle."

Coconut Grove was one of those mixed communities in south Florida. Long before the developers came with bulldozers and wrecking balls, the Grove was known as a bohemian enclave for tree lovers and flower children of the 1960s. Finding your way through the twisted, narrow residential streets beneath the green tropical canopy was a perennial right of passage in Miami. But to Theo—to any black kid who'd heard the gunshots outside the rundown bars and package stores on Douglas Road—the Grove was a world of extremes. Butting right up against Miami's most expensive real estate was a ghetto that could service just about anyone's bad habit, from gangs with their random hits, to doctors and lawyers who ventured out in obedience to their addictions. It was easy for affluent white folks to become careless and take a dangerous shortcut on their way home to paradise. And there were plenty of opportunists like the Grove Lords to make them pay for it.

"This one's all yours," said Tatum.

"I know," said Theo.

The cyclist turned on Grand Avenue. The Chevy followed. "Let's tail him for a while," said Isaac. "Make him shit his pants."

Tatum laughed and took a long swig from a half-empty bottle of vodka. He passed it to Theo, who pushed it away.

"What's wrong with you, pussy?" said Tatum.

"I ain't a pussy."

"We'll see," said Isaac. "Pop the glove box."

Theo opened it. Inside was a pearl-handled knife with a six-inch, serrated blade that shone like a mirror. It was an impressive weapon, a collector's item with serious pawn value. "What you want me to do with this?"

"Cut him," said Isaac.

"Say *what*? I thought I just had to take him down."

"What you think 'take him down' means?" said Isaac. "Show me some blood, brotha'. That's your ticket into the gang."

"I can knock his ass off his bike. That'll get him bloody."

"Fucking road rash?" said Tatum. "You think *that's* gonna make you a Grove Lord?"

The cyclist was pedaling faster, glancing nervously over his shoulder every few seconds, obviously sensing that he was being followed. "Nobody said nothin' about stabbin' nobody," said Theo.

"You want in the gang or don't you?" said Isaac.

"Yeah. I want in."

Tatum took another hit of vodka. "Then shut up and do your job."

Theo drew a deep breath and let it out. Compared to Tatum, Theo was the good kid in the family. Gang life seemed to come naturally to his older brother. Tatum was always in trouble, and Theo had inherited a bad-boy reputation and a slew of enemies without even trying. Not that Theo was a saint. Even with a thug for an older brother, Theo wouldn't have been considered for membership in the Grove Lords if he hadn't shown potential of his own. But his résumé was filled with petty stuff—smash-and-grabs from parked vehicles, some vandalism, that kind of thing. Theo had never really hurt anyone, at least not simply for the fun of it.

The cyclist made another quick left. The

Chevy was right behind him. A jerky hand signal told the driver to go around him.

Tatum nearly burst with laughter, slapping the dashboard. "Yeah, right. Like we need you to tell us what to do, white boy."

Isaac smiled. "He knows he's in trouble."

Theo was sullen. "I'm no good with knives."

"Man, why do I have such a pussy for a brother?" said Tatum, groaning.

Theo took a swing at him, but before it landed, Tatum had his younger brother's wrist in one hand and the knife in the other. "Don't you *ever* turn on me," said Tatum, showing him the tip of the blade.

The cyclist suddenly found a higher gear. He was racing through the green light, crossing six lanes of stopped traffic on U.S. 1.

"Got ourselves a flyer!" said Isaac. He hit the gas, and as the Chevy sped over the gentle crown in the highway, the chassis scraped on asphalt, sending sparks flying. *"Shee-it,"* said Isaac.

On the other side of the highway, the cyclist made a hard right onto the paved bicycle path.

"He's getting away," said Tatum.

"No, he ain't," said Isaac. The tires screeched as he steered the car onto the bike path in hot pursuit. Tatum howled, cheering on the chase.

The path was like a narrow, winding road beneath the elevated Metrorail tracks. A tall chain-link fence topped with spirals of razor wire bordered the left side, separating the public path from warehouses and auto-repair shops. To the right were the three southbound lanes of U.S. 1, an endless stream of traffic headed in the opposite direction at better than fifty miles per hour. The cyclist had nowhere to go but due north along the bicycle path. He swerved a few feet to the left, and the Chevy followed. The cyclist jerked to the right, and so did the Chevy. Isaac toyed with his prey, practically kissing the bicycle's rear tire with the Impala's big chrome bumper. The rider glanced back over his shoulder, terror on his face. He was inches away from being roadkill when they reached a cross street. The cyclist made a hard left turn.

"He's toast," said Isaac.

It was a side road of broken asphalt and rutted gravel. The rider hit a mud puddle and nearly fell, but he managed to right himself and keep going. He had to stand on the pedals to maintain his speed. The all-out sprint was taking its toll.

"Get ready," Tatum told his brother.

Dead ahead was a solid block wall. The paint-and-body shops on either side had closed hours earlier, their windows and doors protected by roll-down, metal security shutters. White boy had found himself a blind alley. He dropped his bicycle and ran, searching frantically for a way to scale the wall. It was like a sheer cliff. He turned and faced the music—literally—as the noisy low-rider raced toward him. His back was to the wall, his chest heaving, as he braced himself for the worst.

The Chevy skidded to a stop. Tatum reached across his brother's lap and pushed the door open. "Get him, Theo!"

Theo didn't move.

Tatum slapped the knife handle into the palm of Theo's hand. "Go on, do it!"

"Take the bike," shouted the rider, his voice quaking. "I paid over a thousand bucks for it. Really. You can have it."

"Now!" Tatum said to his brother.

"Why don't we just take the bike?" said Theo.

"We ain't here for no bike. You gonna cut him or not?"

The rider was ash white with fear, pleading. "Come on, guys. Please. Don't do this. I have a two-year-old daughter."

Tatum had lost all patience. "Cut him, damn it! Cut him good!"

Theo's gaze shifted back to the rider, who was trying to adopt a goofy martial-arts, self-defense pose. Theo could have kicked his ass so easily. It wasn't fear that was holding him back. In fact, there was strange satisfaction in walking up to a Bruce Lee wannabe and laying him out on the sidewalk—but only if there was a good reason to do it, like payback or protection. If Theo was going to turn some random Joe into a noisy amusement for a knife, it was important that he stand to gain something more than acceptance by a couple of punks who called themselves the Grove Lords.

Theo handed the knife to his brother. "You cut him."

"Pussy!" shouted Tatum. He reached across for the handle and slammed the door shut.

Isaac shook his head with disapproval as he hit the gas. The tires spun and gravel flew. Theo looked back and saw white boy fall to his knees, relieved and exhausted.

Tatum shoved the knife back into the glove compartment. Theo thought he heard him say "pussy" again, but the boom box was way too loud. Isaac was singing along to Prince again, changing the words: "This is what it sounds like / when Theo Knight cries."

Twilight turned into night as they drove back into Coconut Grove. Theo retreated into thought. He was no pussy. He just wasn't as stupid as his older brother. Even so, Tatum would pound him when they got home, no question about it. Or at least he would try. Theo grew bigger and stronger with each passing month, and everyone knew that before long the younger brother would have the upper hand.

"Something's goin' down over there," said Isaac.

At the south end of Grand Avenue, right outside Homeboy's Tavern, a crowd had gathered in the street. A line of cars in the right lane was blocking traffic. The Chevy stopped a block away at the red light. Isaac rolled down the window and shouted to another Grove Lord who was standing on the corner.

"Hey, Switch," said Isaac. Switch (short for "switchblade") sauntered up to the driver's side of the Impala. Isaac said, "Hey, what's happenin', bro'?"

"You mean over there?" he said, indicating the crowd.

"I sure don't mean in your shitty little life."

Switch smiled, too dumb to know when he was being insulted. "Some bitch got her throat slit."

"Who?"

"I dunno."

"She still there?"

"Yeah. Blood everywhere. And she's wearing this short skirt with nothin' underneath. You can see it all, dude. Definitely worth a look."

"Cops there yet?"

"Uh-uh. Just happened."

"Let's go see," said Tatum.

Isaac raised the window. The traffic light changed, and the car started slowly down the street. Isaac looked at Theo and said, "Here's the deal, bro'. I'm giving you one more chance to make it."

"I ain't cuttin' no dead woman."

"Forget the knife. All you gotta do is walk up to the body in front of all these people. Make sure everyone sees you. And then I want you to steal something off her."

"That's too easy," said Tatum.

"I make the rules," said Isaac. "This is Theo's gig. You up for it?"

"Shit, yeah. No problem."

Isaac steered the Chevy into Homeboy's parking lot and killed the engine. "All right. Go for it, dude."

Theo climbed down from the low-rider and started toward the crowd. About fifty black folks had gathered, most of the adults with drinks in their hands from Homeboy's. The front door to the bar was wide open. The latest hit song from Kool and the Gang filled the warm night air. The nearest street lamp had been shot out by the Grove Lords weeks earlier, so the only source of light was the half-moon and the blinking Budweiser sign above the entrance to Homeboy's. The main crowd formed a semicircle that blocked Theo's view of the fallen victim. Several shirtless teenage boys were on their bellies, getting the X-rated up-skirt view that Switch had mentioned. Not a cop was in sight, but sirens could be heard in the distance. Theo needed to move quickly. He was about to break through the crowd when someone grabbed him by the arm, halting him.

"Don't go there," the man said.

Theo nearly slugged him in the darkness, but at the last moment he recognized his great-uncle. "Uncle Cy, what are you doing here?"

"That don't make no never mind. Just do as I tell ya. Don't go there."

Theo glanced back toward his brother in the Chevy. "I gotta go."

"No, you don't want to do that." Uncle Cy tightened his grip. Theo noticed that the old man's hand was shaking. At six foot two he was taller than Theo, but he was a thin reed who lived on gin and cigarettes and God only knew what else. Theo could have shaken him off like a fly, but Uncle Cy with all his flaws was the closest thing he had to a father.

"You're messing me up here," said Theo.

"I ain't gonna let you do this."

Theo had no idea how the old man knew he was on a Grove Lord mission. He must have just figured that if Theo was out cruising with Tatum and Isaac, they had to be up to no good. "You need to let go."

"No can do, boy."

"Take you hands off me."

"Not tonight I won't."

"Get out of the way."

"It's for your own good."

"Don't make me knock you on your ass."

"You're gonna have to. 'Cuz I ain't lettin' you through here, boy."

Theo shoved him, and Uncle Cy went down like a bowling pin. Theo started through the crowd.

"Theo, stop!"

He kept going.

"Come back, boy!"

Theo ignored him.

"Theo, it's your momma!"

Theo froze. There was blood on the street, on her dress, in her hair—so much blood, the color of her long crimson nails dotted with cheap rhinestones. Flies buzzed with interest around the deep gash across her throat. The wound was just below the white leather choker around her neck, a few inches above the rose tattoo on her right breast. Theo didn't want to see her face, but some inner curiosity made him take a good long look. He saw the open mouth, the painted lips, the vacant eyes staring into the night— two black pools behind a hooker's false lashes and enough sparkling purple shadow to let the johns know exactly what she was.

And he saw a leopard-print shoulder bag on the ground, beside the lifeless body.

Sirens in the distance grew louder. Theo stood silent and stared, as if searching for the right emotions. He didn't let his eyes go there, but he knew Switch was right: you could see right up her skirt. The view would have been only slightly less revealing had she been standing in her usual spot on the corner.

"Theo," his uncle said, but Theo ignored him.

He stepped toward his mother, bent down on one knee, and checked to make sure that everyone was watching.

Then he grabbed the purse and ran back to the Chevy.

Twenty years later

Chapter 1

Jack Swyteck woke after midnight. The television was playing, but the sound was still on mute. Rene didn't like sex in total darkness. Leno the night-light.

Jack stole a glimpse of the gorgeous woman in bed next to him. He was a lucky guy, he supposed, on many different levels. He was a respected criminal defense lawyer with his own practice. He had an unlikely best friend in Theo Knight, an ex-con and former client who would do anything for Jack. His beloved *abuela* was healthy, and it had been ages since he and his famous father had argued the way they used to. With Rene

in town, there was plenty to be happy about—
so long as he didn't overanalyze things.

But he *always* overanalyzed things. Last
month's draw had fallen short of what some
lawyers paid their personal trainers. His ex-
wife was a fruitcake, and his post-divorce
love life could have filled an entire volume of
Cupid's Rules of Love and War (Idiot's Edition). To add insult to injury, twice a week
Abuela called Spanish talk radio to find her
thirty-nine-year-old grandson "a nice Cuban
girl." Sometimes Jack felt as if he had used
up his lifetime allotment of luck getting Theo
off death row for a murder he didn't commit—whose death warrant had been signed
by the law-and-order governor of Florida,
Jack's father.

And then there was Rene.

She lay on her side, sound asleep, the soft
cotton sheet hugging the curve of her hip.
Her flight from West Africa had landed that
afternoon. She'd finally succumbed to jet lag,
though not before taking Jack for a ride that
seemed to have been propelled by rocket
fuel. They had planned to hit South Beach
for dinner. They never made it out of Jack's
bedroom. Typical for her first night in town.
Unfortunately, she would be gone in two

days, three at the most. Some emergency would undoubtedly come up and force her to cut the trip short. That would also be "typical."

The first time Jack had laid eyes on Rene, she was covered in dust, caught in the midst of the Senoufo country's equivalent of a sandstorm. It was hard not to be impressed by a Harvard Med School grad who had given up the financial rewards of private practice to be a one-doc operation in a clinic near the cocoa region of Côte d'Ivoire. Many of her patients were young children escaping forced servitude on the plantations, mere innocents who had been snatched by kidnappers, lured away by liars, or sold into slavery by their own families for as little as fifteen dollars. Rene saw all that and more—malnutrition, AIDS, infant mortality, even genital mutilation among some migrant tribes. Perhaps it was a stretch, but Jack felt an immediate connection to Rene, having passed up offers himself from prestigious firms right out of law school to defend death-row inmates. For whatever reason, they hit it off. *Really* hit it off.

Passion, however, was a tricky thing. On the emotional EKG, Jack and Rene resembled a couple of flat-liners with occasional bursts of tachycardia. She flew into Miami to see him every three months or so. Sometimes she didn't even tell Jack she was coming. Smart, funny, sexy, and spontaneous, she could have been everything Jack thought he wanted in a woman—except that she was hardly ever around. On one of these visits she was going to put away the passport and announce that she was moving to Miami. At least that was what Jack told himself. A little optimism kept him in the game.

"Rene?" he whispered. She didn't move. He nudged her.

"What?" she muttered.

"Where's the remote?"

Only one eye opened, which was a good thing. A two-eyed glare of that caliber would have killed him, for sure. She swung her arm around and jabbed the remote control into Jack's elbow.

Jack punched the button, but nothing happened. "Damn it. How are you supposed to get this thing turned on?"

"Talk dirty to it," she said into her pillow.

"Thanks."

"Go to hell."

I love you, too, he started to say, but thought better of a joke like that. On her last visit, he'd used the three operative words in a serious way. Her response was not what he'd hoped for. It left him resolved never to say "I love you" again—unless followed by the word "too."

Waves of colored light flickered across the bedroom as Jack channel-surfed. He skipped through the reruns and infomercials, pausing only for a moment at yet another forensic drama that looked like *CSI: Mars*, or some such remote geographic rip-off of the original hit series. At the bottom of the hour, a local news headline caught his eye. He raised the volume. This time, it worked.

"No sound," said Rene.

"It's still on mute."

"Liar. I can hear it."

"That's because you're dreaming. In real life, I'm perfect. Only in dreams am I a total pain in the ass."

She was too tired to argue, or maybe it was his sense of humor that sent her back to sleep. Jack turned his attention to the television newscast. At such a low volume he could pick up only a few words here and there, but the image on screen was familiar. Jack had visited plenty of clients at the Turner Guilford Knight Correctional Center. A young and attractive reporter with ambition in her eyes and an Action News microphone in her hand was doing a live broadcast from outside the jail's main entrance. Helicopters circled in the night sky behind her, powerful white search-lights sweeping the landscape. Those defi-nitely weren't media choppers.

The words "Breaking News" and "Prison Escape" flashed in white letters against a bright red banner on the bottom of the screen.

Jack glanced at Rene—still sleeping—and decided to risk a little added volume. With the press of a button, he immediately heard the excitement in the reporter's voice, catch-ing her in mid-sentence.

"—the second escape from TGK Correc-tional Center in the past twelve months, and the first ever from the second floor, which is reserved for convicted or suspected sex of-fenders. TGK is operated by the Miami-Dade Corrections and Rehabilitation Department, which countywide houses approximately seven thousand inmates in the nation's sixth-largest jail system. Last April, the depart-ment's director resigned after a police and fire task force found that jail buildings were severely outdated, officer training was poor, and 134 positions were unfilled. Department officials say that last night's escape occurred sometime after—"

The air conditioner kicked on, and the hum completely drowned out the television. Jack increased the volume a few bars too many, which had Rene grumbling.

"I'm going to kill you."

"You can't. Hippocratic oath, remember?"

"Sue me!" she said as she sprang to life like a lioness. A wrestling match ensued. Rene was on top, then Jack, then Rene. The sheets ended up on the floor, right beside the clothes that had fallen there four hours earlier. Jack was about to retake control of the situation when she grabbed him where it counted, the sparkle back in her eyes.

Jack froze, raising his hands in playful surrender. "Put the gun down, Rene. Unless you intend to use it."

She didn't let go. "I'm wide awake now, thanks to you. Come on. We have some serious catching up to do."

"Slow down. We've got all week."

She kissed him gently, so lightly that it was difficult to tell whether she'd actually made contact—a kind of sensual ambiguity that Rene had perfected and that could drive Jack crazy. Her lips drifted toward his ear as she whispered, "I have to fly back to Abidjan on Monday."

This time, her words barely tugged at his heartstrings. "It's okay," he said flatly. "I knew you did."

IT WAS LAST CALL at Sparky's Tavern.

Theo Knight made the announcement from behind the long, crowded bar. He was smiling widely, and with good reason. Sparky's was an old gas station that he'd converted into the last watering hole between the mainland and the Florida Keys. It was a true dive, but it was *his* dive. And business was better than ever. At this rate, it wouldn't be long before he could say good-bye to the bikers, the rednecks, and the electric slide and open Sparky's II, a true jazz bar in Coconut Grove. The mere thought blew his mind. Talk about beating the odds.

Theo had never actually made it into the Grove Lords—stealing his own mother's purse didn't cut it—but life didn't offer many choices to the illegitimate son of a drug-addicted prostitute. The cops never did catch the guy who'd slit his mother's throat. The word on the street was that it was "some john who didn't think her blow job was worth the ten bucks." Theo and his older brother went to live with their mother's sister in Liberty City, one of Miami's roughest hardscrabble neighborhoods. Aunt Teesha did her best to raise them, but with five children of her own, it wasn't easy. The Knight brothers were soon on every crime-watch list in the area, thanks mostly to Tatum, but Theo did his part too. He dropped out of high school, stuck his hand in the wrong cash register, and got tagged with the brutal murder of a convenience store clerk. At age fifteen he was the youngest inmate on Florida's death row. The Grove Lords finally thought he rocked. Theo didn't find the irony amusing.

Especially since he was innocent.

"Hey, look who's here," said one of his barmaids.

Theo looked up from a sink full of cocktail glasses and saw Trina entering the bar. She was the closest he'd ever come to having a steady. He'd met her through his buddy Jack Swyteck, but only after circumstances had forced her to lay Jack out on the sidewalk with a martial arts kick. Almost immediately, Theo knew he had to have this sexy brunette with the olive skin of a Latina supermodel and the mysterious accent of a Russian spy.

Trina walked straight to the bar and took a seat on a stool opposite Theo. She wasn't smiling.

"Hey, baby," he said.

"Don't call me baby."

"You still mad at me? It ain't nice to hold a grudge."

She laid her purse on the bar top and crossed her legs. She had great legs. Strong, too. She'd kicked him in the ass enough for him to know.

"You bought me a bug for my birthday," she said.

"It's not a bug. It's a roach brooch."

"It was a *live* insect."

"Bred by a jeweler who happens to be an etymological genius."

"Ety-what?"

"Etygomical."

"See, you can't even say it twice. You have no idea what you're talking about."

"The man is still a genius."

"He's an *idiot* who glued diamond chips and sapphires onto a live cockroach and then figured out a way to attach it to a thin gold chain without killing it. You think I'm going to wear that thing around my neck and let a living, breathing insect crawl in and out of my cleavage?"

Mere mention of her cleavage set Theo's mind to wandering, but he reeled himself in. "It's a one-of-a-kind piece."

"Thank God for small favors."

"Baby—"

"I'm not your baby. Stop calling me that."

"Okay, fine. You don't like the roach brooch. Let me make it up to you."

"How?"

"I don't know. You name it."

She arched an eyebrow, obviously intrigued. "Do you mean that?"

"Sure. It was your birthday, and I blew it. Tell me how I can make good."

"Wow, that's really sweet of you. Anything I want?"

"Yeah. But don't get crazy on me."

She pondered it, then flashed a mischievous smile. "I know. This will be perfect. I want you to get . . ."

"Get you what?"

"No," she said coyly. "I don't think I should tell you tonight. I'll let you squirm a little. Like that cockroach you hung around my neck."

"You're just not gonna let that go, are you?"

She leaned across the bar, grabbed his shirt, and pulled him in for a kiss. "Keep your promise—*anything* I want—and we're square."

"You know me. I'm a man of my word."

"You'd better be. See you tomorrow."

Theo enjoyed the view as she turned and walked toward the door with a little attitude, all for his benefit. Then in a raised voice he announced, "That's it, you scumbags. Bar's closed."

A few groans rolled in from the crowd, but as soon as the bright lights went up, they scurried for the door like cockroaches—sans jewels.

The time was 2:10 A.M. when the last patron found the parking lot. Theo and two of his employees stayed behind for clean up and closing. He took the cash drawer into the stockroom, locked the door, and set himself up at the card table with a cup of coffee, a calculator, and his ledger book. Numbers were not his strong suit, but he didn't mind math as long as it involved money. He was up to $216 in cash receipts when he heard a noise from behind a wall of stacked beer kegs.

He put down the money and listened. Over the hum of the fluorescent lighting, he thought he heard breathing. Slowly, silently, he slid open the drawer. He always kept a loaded .38-caliber revolver in his desk, and he knew how to use it.

The gun wasn't there.

"Looking for this?"

The voice had come from across the room. Theo looked up and froze. The man was leaning against the tower of beer kegs, showing Theo the business end of his own Smith & Wesson.

"Be cool," said Theo. "Just take the money and go."

The man was dressed like a bum—pants with grease stains around the pockets and holes in the knees, and an old shirt with frayed cuffs and buttons that didn't match. But his demeanor was oddly cool for a robbery. "Don't you recognize me?"

"I ain't even seen your face, okay? No need to worry about me telling the cops what you look like. So grab the cash and get lost."

"Dude, look at me. Don't you know who I am?"

Theo let his eyes meet the gunman's, and recognition kicked in. "Isaac?"

He flashed a big smile. "How you doin', my man?"

Theo hadn't seen him in almost twenty years. He would have been happy to go another twenty. "How did you get in here?"

"Come on, dude. It's me, Isaac. The leader of the Grove Lords."

This was no overstatement. The Grove Lords had once ruled Miami—until every cop in the city made it a priority to land Isaac in prison. Theo searched his memory for old scores that Isaac might want to settle with him—anything that might explain his sudden reappearance after all this time.

Theo said, "Let's talk about this, all right? Put my gun down."

"Ain't your gun no more, bro'."

"What do you want?" said Theo.

"Can't I come see an old brotha'? Especially one as rich and famous as you?"

"Cut the crap."

"Serious, dude. The whole world knows about Theo Knight and Sparky's. Even the homeboys in the can."

It wasn't exactly the clientele Theo was looking for. "That's where I thought you was. In jail."

"You got that right." Isaac stepped out from

around the tower of beer kegs. He was a
good five inches shorter than Theo, but that
still put him at almost six feet tall and solid
muscle. He'd obviously made good use of the
prison weight room. The clothes were definitely fresh off the back of a homeless person, though apparently not without a struggle.
Theo noticed a fresh bloodstain on the left
pants leg.

"When did you get out?"

"About six hours ago," said Isaac.

"Your first night out of prison, and you got
nothin' better to do than to stick a gun in my
face?"

"I guess you ain't seen the news yet tonight."

"All I watch is ESPN when I'm working."

"Too bad. You would have seen me all
over the local stations, for sure. I bet I'm more
famous than you now. Another kid from the
'hood makes good."

"What did you do?"

"Nothin'," said Isaac, smiling thinly. "Let's
just say I had enough of those jerk-offs at
TGK. I put myself on the early-release plan."

Theo didn't share the smile. A fugitive in
his stockroom wearing the dirty and bloody
clothes he'd obviously stolen from a homeless

guy as a disguise—it was the last thing he needed.

"What do you want from me?" said Theo.

Isaac's expression turned very serious. "I had the perfect plan, see? New clothes, fake ID, cash, car, gun—it was all supposed to be waiting for me at the 7-Eleven on Eighth Street when I busted out. That was the deal. I show up exactly on time, but it ain't there. I got screwed, bro'!"

Theo glanced at the gun. "I got nothin' to do with that."

"I ain't blamin' you," he said, his voice calming. "But you know Isaac Reems. He always got hisself a plan B."

"Should have just robbed the 7-Eleven. That seems about your speed."

"You think you're the only one who's moved up in the world? The small time is way behind me. And even if it wasn't, I did my homework behind bars. A guy busts out of prison, the first thing cops watch is recent crime reports—stolen guns, cash, cars. Crimes like that leave a trail. I can't be leavin' no trails. So I asks myself: how can I get my hands on everything I need and be sure the cops don't find out about it? Then it hits me. I'll go see Theo Knight. I *know* he won't report it."

"You should have called a friend."

"Fugitives ain't got friends. You know how they caught the last dude who escaped from prison in Florida? His own momma turned him in."

"I don't want no part of this."

Isaac tipped the gun for emphasis. "It ain't exactly a choice."

"You think I'm still some teenage punk who wants into your gang?"

"Uh-uh. You ain't no gangster, my main man, my brotha'. You ain't nothin' to me. You's just Theo Knight—Mr. Respectable Member of the Community. Which is exactly why you can't report this gun stolen. Or the money. You can't even call the cops and tell 'em I was here."

"You don't know me no more," said Theo.

All trace of a smile vanished. "I know this much, bro'. If I get caught, I'm gonna say it was you who helped me escape from TGK. We had a nice little understanding, you and me. The two of us met up after hours in your bar. You gave me money, a gun. Then you tried to change our deal and pinch me for way more than your help was worth. I said 'Eat me' and left. That's when you lost your cool and called the cops on me."

Theo didn't respond.

Smugness was all over Isaac's face. "You know they'll believe me. You like to think you're a new man. You keep your nose clean now that you're outta prison, got yourself a fine tavern. But to the cops, you're still just a homeboy from the 'hood who's stupid enough to help his old buddy Isaac blow the joint and skip town."

Theo glared, but he didn't argue. Four years on death row for a crime he didn't commit made it tough to trust cops, and Isaac was smart enough to exploit that. "Just take what you want and go," said Theo.

He pointed with the gun. "The cash. All of it."

Theo scooped it up and started toward Isaac.

"Just leave it right there on the edge of the desk," said Isaac. "Then back your ass up against the wall."

Theo complied. Isaac stepped forward, took the cash, and stuffed it into his pocket. "Got more bullets?"

"Uh-uh," said Theo.

Isaac rifled through the other desk drawers, found the extra ammunition, and filled his other pocket. "You never was the liar your brother Tatum was. Now, where's the car keys?"

Theo pointed with a nod toward the hook on the wall.

Isaac said, "On second thought, I'll leave 'em right there."

"Suit yourself."

"Be nice to have wheels. And I'm pretty sure you ain't gonna call the cops. But if you get weak on me and dial 911, that's too easy a mark, me drivin' around in your car."

Theo watched as he started toward the door. Isaac opened it, then stopped in the open doorway. "For what it's worth, that was a shitty thing that happened to your momma. Even shittier that they never caught the guy who done it."

Theo didn't answer. He simply wanted to strangle him.

Isaac said, "See you around, Mr. Respectable."

He closed the door quietly, the sound of his footsteps fading into the night.

Chapter 2

Theo drove home alone and angry. Really angry. There were two things you just didn't talk about with Theo Knight.

His father.

And his mother.

Isaac had thought he was so clever, the way he'd ventured into the maternal half of the forbidden territory. Theo knew he didn't give a rat's ass about him or his mother. Isaac brought her up only as a reminder that the cops hadn't lifted a finger to catch the guy who'd slit her throat—yet another reason Theo shouldn't turn to the police. Little did Isaac know that Theo had shipped off those demons to a place that Trina called the gulag of Theo's mind.

Theo's Coconut Grove town house wasn't in the ghetto, where he'd once lived with Tatum and their mother, but his little hovel wasn't exactly the poster property for Miami's real estate nirvana, either. In many ways, Theo was a man in transition.

The porch light was out. He fumbled for his key in the darkness, but the blue-green glow of the television screen greeted him as he opened the front door.

"Cy?" he said. "You up?"

The old man rose from the E-Z chair. He was technically Theo's great-uncle, and just about everyone called him "Uncle Cy," but Theo just called him Cy. "'Course I'm up," he said.

"It's three-thirty in the morning."

"When you're my age, that's almost lunchtime."

The old man chuckled, and Theo smiled, even though he'd heard the joke many times before. His great-uncle had suffered a mild stroke over the summer. He was almost completely recovered, save for a slight loss of motion in his right leg and occasional short-term memory issues. The doctors thought it was better that he not live alone until he finished his rehab. He'd been staying with Theo for the past three months. It was the least Theo could do for the man who'd taught him to play the saxophone.

"Sit with me for a minute," said Cy as he cleared away the clutter of newspapers on the couch.

Theo tried not to groan. "I'm really beat."

The old man shot him one of those lonely hound-dog looks. All his life, he'd been tall and thin, and he had a saxophone player's stoop even when he wasn't playing, as if his chin were glued to his sternum. He could cut to the soul when he looked at you, head down, through the top of those sad eyes. The man just didn't play fair.

"All right," said Theo as he flopped onto the sofa.

Cy lowered himself into the chair and flipped through the channels with the remote. "I wanted you to see this," he said.

"See what?"

"It's been all over the news. There was a prison break last night. A guy named Isaac Reems escaped. There it is," he said, stopping on Action News.

Isaac's inmate photograph was on-screen

staring back at Theo. The orange jumpsuit, the prison haircut, the mad-at-the-world scowl. For a fleeting moment, Theo saw himself—what he once was, the way he could have ended up. Thankfully, the anchorwoman was at the end of her three-minute update.

"Reems is assumed to be armed and dangerous," she said to her television audience. "Anyone with information as to his whereabouts should immediately contact the Miami-Dade Department of Corrections." A telephone number flashed on the screen, and then the newscast broke for a commercial.

Cy hit the mute button. "Isn't that the boy you and your brother used to hang out with?"

"Yeah, that's him."

His uncle shook his head. "I knew he'd never amount to nothing. The other newsman said he's been in and out of prison since he was seventeen."

"Almost as bad as Tatum," said Theo.

Almost. His older brother had grown up to be a contract killer.

Cy said, "I just thank God one of y'all made something of hisself."

"Yup, that's me, all right. Saint Theo."

"Don't you go puttin' yourself down. Ain't no comparison between you and those two thugs. You should be proud of yourself."

"Must have been the music that turned me around," said Theo.

He meant that. In his prime, Cyrus Knight had been a nightclub star in old Overtown, Miami's Harlem. He played all the best joints. At his peak, in the 1960s, he even did orchestra gigs for Sammy Davis Jr. and other stars in the big hotels on Miami Beach. When Theo was released from prison, Cy gave him his old saxophone, a classic Buescher 400. "You might be happy to be out of prison," his uncle had told him, "or you might be pissed off that they locked you up in the first place. It don't make no never mind. You just put all those feelings right here." Theo took the sax and the advice.

"Tell me something about my momma," said Theo.

His uncle did a double take. It might have amazed an outsider, but this was a conversation they'd never had before. Never. Theo was that adamant about it.

"Where did that question come from?" said Cy.

"Isaac was there the night we found her. I

guess it got me to wondering, seeing him to-night. I mean on the TV," he said, quick to correct himself.

Cy didn't seem at all comfortable with the chosen topic of conversation. "What do you want to know?"

"Something good. Tell me something good about her."

The old man was silent, as if searching. He answered without looking at Theo, his gaze drifting off toward the middle distance. "Ain't nothin' good to tell, Theo. Nothin' good at all."

Theo nodded, more in resignation than agreement. "I'm going to bed." He rose and headed toward the bedroom.

Cy called his name, stopping him. "Are you okay, boy? You seem a little bit off."

Theo shrugged. "Tough night."

"Trina giving you heartache again?"

"No, it's not that. We talked right before closing. I think we're gonna be okay."

"Good. I like that girl. But something's eatin' at you. What is it?"

Theo sighed, burying his hands in his pockets. "I just don't like feeling ripped off, that's all."

"Not again. You was robbed?"

He weighed the word's every connotation. "Comes with the turf, I guess."

"Did you call the cops?"

Theo harrumphed, as if to say, "What the hell good would that do?" He suddenly felt much the same way about this conversation. Absolutely no good could come of telling Cy about his surprise visit from Isaac. "I really don't feel like talking about it."

"That's all right. You get some rest."

"'Night, old man."

"Good night, boy."

Theo continued down the dark hallway and didn't even bother turning on the bedroom light. He practically fell on the bed, dead tired, emotionally exhausted, drained in every sense of the word—and completely unable to sleep. He could have lain there till dawn, staring at the ceiling as all of Miami woke. Or . . .

He knew Rene was in town, but this couldn't wait till morning. He reached for the phone on his nightstand and dialed Jack. His friend.

His lawyer.

Chapter 3

Most days, Jack was simply a criminal defense lawyer. At 3:30 A.M., when calling the Miami-Dade state attorney at home, he donned his former-prosecutor hat. There were times when it paid to be part of the club.

"This had better be good, Swyteck," she said with a grumble into the telephone.

"I can help you find Isaac Reems."

He sensed that she was suddenly wide awake.

Jack's talk with Theo had raised a serious dilemma. An old robbery conviction made Theo's possession of a firearm a second-degree felony in Florida. Theo was willing to tell all about Reems, but Jack insisted that it be done through his lawyer—with an agreement from the state attorney that there would be no flack about the illegal firearm.

"Deal," she said. "What do you have?"

"One other thing," said Jack. "I want this information disseminated to law enforcement without attribution. My client's name stays out of this."

"Why? He's doing the right thing."

"He's turning in the former leader of the Grove Lords. They ruled this city once upon a time. Gangsters have long memories and they don't like rats."

"I see your point, but I hate making deals with these kinds of conditions."

"It's not negotiable. I gave him strict orders not to tell anyone—not even his uncle, who lives with him."

The line was silent. She seemed to be considering it. "All right. The source isn't important, as long as I'm able to vouch for the fact that the information is reliable."

"It's totally reliable," said Jack. He was speaking in his former-prosecutor voice again.

"Then we understand each other. Talk to me."

ANDIE HENNING WAS IN a downward-facing dog pose, wearing only a black exercise leotard, struggling to get her breathing under control. It was her Saturday morning routine: yoga class to the soothing sound of breaking waves on Miami Beach. Watching the sun climb up above the Atlantic was totally invigorating, and if you could do it with your ankles up around your ears, you were among a privileged few.

The class ended by 7:30 A.M., and even though it was early May, Andie could feel summer in the air. She pulled on sweatpants, more out of modesty than necessity, and then packed up her workout bag and slung it over her shoulder. Inside were the standard yoga props, her cell phone, and her Sig Sauer 9-millimeter pistol.

Andie was in her ninth year with the FBI; she'd spent the first six in Seattle and the balance in the Miami field office. Hardly a lifelong dream of hers, the bureau had been more of a safe landing for a self-assured thrill seeker. At the training academy, she became only the twentieth woman in bureau history to make the Possible Club, a 98 percent male honorary fraternity for agents who shoot perfect scores on one of the toughest firearms courses in law enforcement. Her supervisor in Seattle saw her potential, and she didn't disappoint him—at least not until personal reasons prompted her to put in for a transfer to Miami, about as far away from Seattle as she could get.

"Nice look, babe," said the jogger as he passed her on the sidewalk.

Dumb-ass remarks were one thing she didn't like about South Beach. At least they came in about nine different languages—part of the panoply of contradictions that made for the crude-cosmopolitan, chic-chauvinist ambience of Ocean Drive.

Lincoln Road Mall was her destination, a pedestrian-only thoroughfare lined with eclectic shops, restaurants, bars, and galleries. Andie had a breakfast meeting with an acquaintance who fancied herself an expert on computer dating. With such a busy career, Andie had resigned herself to trying something new. At one of the many outdoor cafés on the mall she found Maria Cortina smoking a cigarette at a small table beneath the shade of a Cinzano umbrella. Maria was wearing a tight red dress and evening makeup that needed to be refreshed or removed. Either she hadn't made it to bed at all last night or she hadn't made it to her own bed.

Maria borrowed a pen from the waiter and took notes on a napkin while slurping highly caffeinated coffee.

"So, what was your last serious relationship?" Maria asked.

"Not exactly my favorite subject," said Andie. "I was engaged when I lived in Seattle. He slept with my sister."

"Ouch." Maria took a drag from her cigarette. "Have you dated at all since coming to Miami?"

"Some."

"Anyone you really liked?"

"Is this personal dating history really important?"

"Absolutely," she said, smoke pouring out with her words. "I'm trying to get a feel for your target mate. Juicy details aren't necessary. But if there's a guy in your recent past who you thought had some promise, tell me about him."

Andie considered it. "I guess that would be Jack Swyteck."

"The former governor's son?"

"Yeah. We met while I was working a big kidnapping case out of central Florida, and we ended up going out a couple times after it wrapped up. Believe me, my expectations were extremely low. An FBI agent dating a criminal defense lawyer—what chance does that have? But to my surprise, I was feeling some major sparks."

"What happened?"

"Bam! I said something stupid and it was over."

"How stupid?"

"I'd really rather not get into it, if that's okay."

Andie got the impression that Maria would have persevered on any other morning, but the coffee and cigarettes didn't seem to be doing the trick on her hangover. Maria glanced at Andie's résumé and frowned almost immediately.

"Is something the matter?" said Andie.

"Your photograph. You're beautiful in person. Those high cheekbones, the raven black hair."

"My biological mother was American Indian."

"I presume it was an Anglo father who gave you the amazing green eyes. The mix makes for an exotic, captivating look. But . . ." Maria crushed out her cigarette and savored her last lungful. "You should be blonde."

"Blonde? But I get a lot of compliments about my hair."

"I know computer dating. Blonde women get twice the calls."

"And I'm sure naked women get three times the calls. I'm not changing my hair."

"Okeydoke." She read on. Another frown. "I see you put the FBI right up top."

"You say that like it's a bad thing."

"For a job application, it's great. But in the world of online romance, women in law enforcement don't get callbacks. You need to hold that info for the actual date. What else are you trained to do?"

"Well, I went to law school, but I never practiced."

"Excellent. Men will adore you: smart but nonthreatening. How about other jobs? What did you do before the FBI?"

"Waited tables in college. I actually drove a truck one summer in law schooi."

"Hmmm. What kind of truck?"

"Delivery truck. I worked for UPS."

"Perfect!" she said, thinking aloud as she scribbled on a napkin. "Educated at Brown."

"Hold on. That is *so* misleading."

"Half your callbacks will be from married men who keep a credit card and a cell phone in the name of an unmarried friend so that the wife won't see the paper trail. *That's* misleading."

Andie retrieved her résumé. "You know, maybe this online stuff isn't for me."

Her cell phone rang. It was Guy Schwartz, the assistant special agent in charge of the Miami field office. Her boss. She excused herself and took the call, finding a more private spot a little farther down the mall. She talked while standing in the recessed entranceway to a closed gallery.

"The feds are getting into the Isaac Reems manhunt," Schwartz said.

"We clearly have jurisdiction. Reems was in federal custody before we released him to TGK for trial on the state charges."

"Yeah. Apparently life in federal prison for kidnapping wasn't enough for the state attorney. She had to tack on sexual assault under Florida law."

"Hard to argue with that if you look through the victim's eyes," said Andie.

"Sure. But now look where we are. Miami-Dade Corrections let him slip out the window on a rope made from bedsheets. *Bedsheets.* How the hell does that happen in the twenty-first century?"

"He won't get far."

"That's where you come in. I just got off the phone with the commander of the Violent Offenders and Fugitive Task Force. He's bringing in every resource—the state and locals, the U.S. Marshals, and the FBI. I need an agent I can count on to coordinate our office's involvement. You've done excellent work with the kidnapping joint task forces. I would expect nothing less here."

"When do I start?"

"How soon can you be here?"

She checked her appearance. Sweatpants and a leotard weren't exactly office attire. Good thing she kept a clean set of clothes at work. She could shower there, too. "See you in twenty minutes," she said.

Chapter 4

The search was on. With the help of Uncle Cy, Theo was determined to find the perfect location for Sparky's II.

They checked out three locations before lunch. Theo saved the best for last.

"Holy crap," said Cy. He was dressed like Johnny Cash—black shirt, black shoes, and black pants. It was his serious jazz club attire, but he had a smile that brought the look to life.

They were standing in a vacant restaurant with old wood floors, redbrick walls, and high ceilings. On one side of the room was a huge U-shaped bar that would allow the bartender to work three sides; the top of the U was closed off by café doors that led to the kitchen. The bar stools had been sold off in the previous tenant's liquidation, but Theo could pick up some used ones on the cheap. The chandeliers were also gone, but it didn't take much to imagine a big brass antique casting its moody glow as Theo served up drinks till the wee hours of the morning. The previous tenant had obviously overimproved, the cost of the build-out making profit impossible. The restaurant owner's downfall was the bar owner's windfall. Capitalism, 100 proof.

"You like it?" said Theo.

"Holy crap," he said again.

Theo crossed the room. "This is where the dinner tables used to be. We could put cocktail tables here, and the ceiling is plenty high for us to build a little stage against the back wall for the band."

"I can hear that beautiful sax already," said Cy.

"I was thinking maybe fifteen tables or so."

"Twenty," said Cy. "You need that crowded jazz bar feelin' with the lights dimmed and the smoke risin' up—"

"No smoking," said Theo. "It's against the law if we're gonna serve food."

"No smoke in a jazz bar? That's like no blue in the Blue Note."

"Things change," said Theo.

"Yeah," he said wistfully, "they sure do." Then his face lit up. "Hey, here's an idea. Why don't I take you on a tour? Overtown, old Miami, Miami Beach. I'll show you all the joints I used to play."

"Are they still around?"

"Yeah, every last one of them is still right here," he said, as he pointed to his heart. "Don't make no difference if they've been turned into parking lots or fancy office buildings. It's like visiting hallowed ground. It'll all come back to me when we walk the old streets. Maybe you'll even pick up some vibes of inspiration for this joint."

"I'd like that," said Theo. "We should have done it a long time ago."

Together, they fell into silence, remembering when Uncle Cy had made that very suggestion years earlier—before Theo got mixed up with the Grove Lords and ended up in prison.

His cell phone rang. He checked the number, and it was Trina. "Gotta take this."

"You go ahead. I'll just keep on dreamin'."

Theo wandered toward the bar and took the call. He could hear the excitement in Trina's voice.

"I figured out what I want," she said.

"Huh?"

"For my birthday. The replacement for the roach brooch. You said I could have whatever I wanted."

"Oh, yeah," he said. *She's actually holding me to this.*

"This may be asking too much," she said. "But would you even consider getting a Prince Albert for me?"

Theo leaned against the bar. "A what?"

"A Prince Albert. You know what it is, right?"

"Uh . . . yeah. 'Course I know what it is."

"Can you get one?"

He ran his finger over the bar top and collected a good six months' worth of dust—a long time for commercial property to sit idle. *Room to negotiate on the rent.* "Sure. If a Prince Albert is what you want, I'll get it for you."

"Really? Oh, Theo, you are the absolute best."

"True. But we already knew that."

"Do you know where to go?"

"I'll figure it out."

"Be careful. There are good ones and bad ones. You can't just go anywhere."

"You think I don't know that?"

"Okay. But I've researched this. For people who are serious and don't mind paying a little extra, the go-to guy is down in Marathon. His name's Manny Ochoa."

"Okay. I've got a few sources of my own. But I'll check out this Manny."

"Thank you. I can't wait to see it. This is the best birthday present this girl has ever gotten."

"I aim to please."

"And your aim is getting better all the time."

They shared a laugh and said good-bye. Theo closed his flip phone slowly, then reached inside his pocket and clutched his wallet. It gave him an uneasy feeling. He had no idea what he'd just promised to get her.

"Everything okay?" asked Cy.

"Yeah, same old bullshit. Where do we start on this tour of yours?"

"I thought we'd head on over to—"

The ring of Theo's cell interrupted again.

He left it in his pocket, not even checking the number. "Head over to where?" said Theo.

The phone continued to ring. "Don't you need to get that?" said his uncle.

"I'm sure it's Trina calling back."

"Then take it."

"I don't feel like it. I swear she's always changing her mind."

"You want her to change her mind *about you*? Take the call, fool."

Uncle Cy was the only man besides Jack who could talk like that to Theo. But at least the old man made sense. Theo dug the phone out of his pocket and flipped it open. "Whassup, baby?"

"Whassup, baby yourself." It was Isaac's voice.

Theo struggled to show no reaction, but his uncle seemed to pick up his sudden annoyance. He drifted in the general direction of Theo's future stage, pretending to act busy by pacing off the room's dimensions.

"I thought we were done," Theo said through clenched teeth.

"We would be if you hadn't tried to change our deal."

"What the hell do you mean?"

"Come on, dude. If I didn't know you so well, I'd think you got your phone calls open to the cops or somethin'. Quit playing games and stop talkin' like it wasn't you who helped me blow TGK in the first place."

Theo was on to him immediately. Isaac was making good on his threat: If Theo went to the police, he was going to convince them that Theo had "come to Jesus" only *after* he'd helped Isaac escape. Thank God he and Jack had decided not to let the cops monitor his phones.

Theo said, "I got nothin' to say to you."

"Hey, I know it didn't go exactly as we planned, but—"

"We never had no plan, you son of a bitch."

"I ain't askin' for freebies here. There's something in it for you, too."

"I already called the cops, all right? Don't bother me no more."

"You *what*? You motha'—"

"Don't call me." He ended the call and drew a deep breath as he rolled his head from one shoulder to the other, trying to release the anger. He opened the flip phone again, but the sound of his uncle's voice kept him from hitting Jack's speed-dial digit.

"What's wrong?" said Cy.

Theo closed the cell phone. The old man had always been good about not butting into Theo's business, but he seemed to have a nose for real trouble.

"That definitely wasn't Trina," his uncle said. "Who was it?"

Theo slipped the phone back into his pocket. He'd already done the right thing. He'd called the cops. Like Jack had said: It was best to keep that between him and his lawyer. No point spoiling his afternoon with his uncle.

"Nobody," said Theo. "A real nobody."

Chapter 5

Jack felt naked when he opened his front door. He was wearing only a swimsuit, and an FBI agent standing on his doorstep made him want to run for cover. Especially when it was Special Agent Andie Henning—with the emphasis on "special."

"Hey, Andie." He didn't know what else to say. It had been almost three months since their last date, which hadn't ended on the best of terms.

"Sorry to drop by unannounced," she said. "I was afraid you might blow me off if I called. But I knew you'd be professional if I showed up on official business. It's about—"

"Jack, did you hide my cover-up?" said Rene. She was suddenly standing right behind him, wearing a white string bikini that showcased every square inch of her suntan.

"Your what?" he said.

"My swimsuit cover-up. It's a tunic-style wrap, Hawaiian-print. Keeps the sun from turning me into a lobster."

He'd last seen it on the floor. Next to the bed. Jack looked at Andie and said, "We were just getting ready to take the boat out."

Andie was caught staring. Funny, Jack thought. If a man checks out another man in a bathing suit like that, he's gay. If a woman checks out another woman, she's—well, a woman.

"Sorry," said Andie, "but this is important."

"I'm sure it is," said Rene. She was speaking to Jack but looking at Andie.

Jack said, "I'll catch up with you on the boat."

"How long are you going to be?" said Rene, as she slipped her arms around his torso and hugged him from behind.

The affection wasn't overdone, but it was still uncomfortable for Jack in front of Andie. "I'll be quick. Just, uh . . . how about picking out some CDs?"

Rene let go of him. "You two have any favorites?"

For a split second he wondered how Rene could possibly have known, but how stupid was that? *They always know.*

"Anything you like is fine," said Jack, though he actually would have been more comfortable giving carte blanche to Andie. Weird, but Andie's tastes were more in line with Jack's than were Rene's.

"Leave it to me," said Rene, as she left the living room and headed for the back patio. It wasn't until he heard the California door slide open and then close that Jack realized he was being rude to Andie. "Would you like to come inside?" he said.

"That's okay. I can see you're in a hurry."

"What's the official business?"

"Isaac Reems. There's a joint task force led by the U.S. Marshals Service. I'm the bureau's point person for the Miami field office."

Jack couldn't hide his surprise. When he'd cut a deal with the state attorney to keep Theo's name out of the manhunt, he would have thought that had also covered the name of his attorney. "And what brings you here?" said Jack.

"You were Reems's attorney of record during his first federal incarceration."

Jack reeled in his anger against the prosecutor. Suddenly, he—not Theo—was the tie to Isaac, but there was an even more surprising part of the equation. "The FBI chose *you* to come and talk to me?"

"Uh, yeah," she said. "My ASAC remembered that you and I got to know each other on that kidnapping case I headed when I first moved here from Seattle."

"So you didn't tell them that after the case was over we . . ."

"No. I didn't tell anyone."

Jack understood. That kind of personal history didn't exactly spell career advancement at the bureau—an FBI agent crazy enough to date a criminal defense lawyer.

Andie said, "So, you weren't Mr. Reems's lawyer?"

"No."

"But your name was on his list of approved visitors when he was serving time in the early nineties."

"I'm sure he put it there when he heard that I got Theo Knight off death row. Half the inmates in Florida wanted me as their lawyer after that. The innocent half, anyway," he said with a defense lawyer's grin.

"Did he know Theo?"

Jack reeled in his smile, reluctant to involve Theo in anything that had to do with the FBI.

"Did he?" she pressed.

"They knew each other as teenagers. Basically, just two guys who grew up in the same neighborhood."

Andie pulled a pen and notepad from her pocket and jotted something down.

Jack nearly groaned. "You're not going to drag Theo into this, are you?"

"I'm just following every lead."

Jack tried to fight it, but he could feel the personal emotions taking over the business profile. "When are you going to get off Theo's back?"

"I'm not riding anybody's back."

"So it's all in my head, is that it? It's always been just my imagination."

"Jack, please. Before . . ." She paused, as if wary of their immediate past. "When you and I were . . . you know, together, I wasn't forcing you to choose between me and Theo."

"You said if I stayed friends with him, he was going to get me disbarred someday."

"I wasn't even serious. Give me a little credit. I fully understand that Theo's your friend."

"Best friend."

"Okay. Best friend. And I like Theo too. Really I do. I just made a stupid joke."

"That's the funny thing about stupid jokes. They're loaded with truth."

"Not this one."

"Is that what you came here to tell me?"

She made a face, as if trying to stave off a migraine. "No. I came here to talk about Isaac Reems, and now I've bumbled the whole thing. I'm sorry."

"I am too. But you know what I'm most sorry about? Every time something goes wrong in this city, it seems like Theo's on somebody's list of suspects."

"You know that's not true."

"Then why did you write his name in your notepad?"

"There's been a prison break, and the latest advisory said that Reems was last seen at Sparky's around two thirty in the morning."

"Oh, I see. So you put two and two together and figure that—"

"I'm not figuring anything, Jack. Can we please just drop the whole Theo thing?"

Behind him, in the kitchen, the California door slid open. Rene stuck her head inside and called to him from the other side of the house. "Are you almost ready?"

"I'll be right there."

Rene turned and walked toward the dock behind the house, but she left the sliding door open. Jack looked at Andie and said, "Anything else?"

"No. You go ahead. I think we're done."

We're done. The awkward choice of words registered on his face as well as hers.

"Okay, I'll see you," he said.

"See ya." For a moment she seemed to wonder if they should shake hands. They didn't. She just thanked him the way she would have thanked any witness for his time and headed for her car.

He called to her as she reached his driveway.

She stopped. "Yeah?"

"Take care of yourself, all right?" he said.

She shrugged, gave a halfhearted smile, and said, "You know I will."

Jack watched as she opened the car door. "Hey, Andie," he said before she could climb behind the wheel.

"What?"

Jack paused, summoning the right tone of voice. "If you're thinking about talking to Theo, don't. He has a lawyer."

Andie didn't answer, but she seemed to understand that it wasn't anything personal—that Jack was simply tired of the cops harassing his friend, and that Theo deserved better. She got in her car and drove away.

Jack shut the door and leaned against it, thinking for moment, and finally chastising himself for thinking way too much. *Stop over-analyzing everything, already.*

He grabbed the boat keys from the kitchen counter and went to find Rene, curious to know which CDs she'd chosen—and wondering if, by chance, she had chosen his and Andie's favorite.

UNCLE CY FELT LIKE he owned the place.

It sounded like an oxymoron, but Theo said he had "personal business" in the upper Keys, so he left his uncle in charge of Sparky's Tavern until his return. Cy was all over the chance to live out this fantasy—even if the bikers and rednecks did outnumber the brothas and jazz lovers by about fifty to one.

"Hey, Lenny," said Cy. "Can you replace the number two keg for me?"

Theo's assistant was at the other end of the bar, setting up for the Saturday night crowd. If the rum he was stocking was 80 proof, it posted a bigger number than Lenny's IQ. "Sure thing, boss."

Boss. The very ring of it made the old man smile.

The day had been absolutely perfect, just him and Theo, the old sax and the new sax. They'd made it to only one of the old bars Cy had played in his youth—Tobacco Road, which Theo also played on occasion—but they vowed to hit all of his old spots eventually, one at a time, a regular outing. More important, they also agreed that the vacant restaurant with the U-shaped bar was *the* spot for Sparky's II. He sure hoped Theo could nail it down. Hell, was there really anything to worry about? This was Theo Knight, his nephew, a punk from the ghetto who'd survived death row and then named his first bar Sparky's—a double-barreled flip of the bird to Florida's old electric chair, nicknamed "Old Sparky." Theo often said that his uncle was his hero. In truth, Theo was Cy's hero.

"Lenny, the keg, please."

Cyrus Knight didn't have many perfect days in his life story. At least not that he remembered. The culprit was drugs. From the very beginning, friends had begged him not to let customers buy him drinks. Take the tips in cash, they warned him, not liquor. But it seemed rude to refuse a gin-and-tonic from a good-natured guy who swears you're the next Charlie Parker. So he drank. All night. While he played. On his breaks. After his gig. He drank before he went to bed at 5 A.M., and he drank some more when he woke the following afternoon. Before he knew it, he'd burned through the best years of his life as a full-blown alcoholic. Then a pothead. Then a coke fiend. And it only got worse. His arms still bore traces of the track marks to prove it.

It was no wonder that he threatened to kill Theo if ever he caught him drinking when he played.

"Lenny! The keg already."

"I'm getting to it, boss."

Nice kid, but he had the work ethic of a sloth. "Hell, I'll do it myself."

Cy untapped the spent keg first. As he rose from his crouch, however, a sudden wave of nausea sent the room spinning. He leaned on the edge of the sink behind the bar to support his weight. It would pass in a minute, for sure. He was actually getting used

to these spells. Damn blood pressure medicine didn't agree with him one bit.

Getting old sucks.

He splashed cold water on his face and
breathed in and out, slowly and deeply. Better already. He drew a breath and headed
toward the stockroom.

Lenny looked up from behind the cash
register. "Boss, I said I'd get it."

"Right. Just like the check's in her mouth,
and I won't come in the mail."

"Huh?"

"Never mind."

He found a handcart near the door, but it
was plain to see that the full-sized keg was
beyond his strength. He went behind the
tower of stacked kegs in search of a pony
keg, something more his size. There he found
just about everything except what he was
looking for. He saw plastic bags filled with
trash that needed to be taken out and doz-
ens of crushed boxes. There were cans of
beer that had broken loose from the twenty-
four-pack, an assortment of liquor bottles,
and some empty cigarette packages. He
spotted several broken cocktail glasses, a
cockroach or two, a rat trap.

And an orange jumpsuit.

He stooped down and tugged at the hem, pulling the garment toward him slowly, his heart thumping, though deep inside he already knew what it was. The name and number printed on the left breast pocket confirmed his fears.

REEMS 007516.

The nausea was back, but it had nothing to do with the medication. All perfect days had to end. This one had just ended a little sooner than he thought it would.

Damn it, Theo. Damn it all to hell, boy.

Chapter 6

Isaac Reems needed a girlfriend.

He'd studied other prison breaks as part of his monthslong preparation, mostly by trading stories with inmates. There was no single formula for success. But the smart guys always had a girlfriend—it was never a wife—waiting on the outside to help them evade law enforcement and melt back into society. With the girlfriend came a fast car, plenty of cash, new clothes, disguises, phony identification, guns and ammunition, food and liquor, a place to hide, and—chicks just dig fugitives—great sex galore. But Isaac figured out a way to get all he needed without a woman, and so long as he had money, even the pussy would follow.

Eighteen hours on the run proved him dead wrong. Sad to say, but in situations like these, girlfriends were the only friends a man could count on.

Thanks for nothin', brothas.

Isaac was laying flat on a hard tile floor, staring up at the kitchen ceiling. He'd actually dozed off, probably hadn't moved in at least two hours. A realtor's FOR SALE sign posted in the yard had lured him inside. The modest house, a three-bedroom, two-bath concrete shoebox in a middle-class neighborhood, was completely empty, not a stick of furniture anywhere. The REDUCED sign out front suggested that the owners had packed up their belongings long ago and moved everything to their new house. It took Isaac all of three minutes to bypass the cheap home alarm system, and the lock on the back door had been mere child's play for the former leader of the Grove Lords. Hard to imagine a more opportune hideout for a dude with no girlfriend.

Isaac pushed himself up from the floor and noticed that his back was stiff. He'd been hitting the prison gym hard for several weeks before his breakout, trying to get himself into top condition. Still, his thirty-five-year-old body wasn't quite ready for that jump out of a second-story window at the Turner Guilford Knight Corrections Center and the scramble over the nine-foot perimeter fence. Things should have gotten easier after those hurdles, and he probably wouldn't have felt so sore now if the escape had gone according to plan. Deals of all sorts could be cut from inside prison walls, and Isaac had lined up the big items before making his break. A set of wheels with the keys in the glove compartment and a change of clothes in the trunk was supposed to be waiting for him in the parking lot at the 7-Eleven. His new pants were promised with two hundred bucks, small bills, in the pocket.

The car, of course, hadn't been there.

Maybe he'd been screwed by his contacts—which wasn't unheard of in prison commerce. Or maybe some punks just happened by, noticed the unlocked and unattended vehicle, and stole his wheels. Either way, he couldn't go back to his helpers. If it was a screw job, they couldn't be trusted. If something had gone wrong—well, too bad, so sad: it wasn't their fault. The deal was that

Isaac would never make contact with them once he was on the outside. Nobody liked to be extorted twice.

With no wheels, he'd ended up running almost two miles, nonstop, to the Miami River. Had he known the guards at TGK were going to take so long to discover that he was missing, he might have driven the stolen boat all the way to the Bahamas. He wasn't a boater, however, and the prospect of crossing the Gulf Stream alone, in the dead of night, was fraught with problems. Instead, he headed toward the Florida Keys, made it as far as the southern tip of the mainland, and hunted down Sparky's Tavern. Plan B was working just fine until Theo called the cops. Now, law enforcement was all over south Miami-Dade County. He couldn't even risk going into a store to buy new clothes.

Thanks for nothin', brotha'.

Isaac walked down the hall toward the bathroom. A sudden noise startled him, and he dove to the floor. It was the air conditioner clicking on. He rose and checked the thermostat on the wall. The owner had it set at eighty-five, just low enough to keep the humidity under control. The house was obviously being looked after even though it was empty. He was tempted to cool things down a few more degrees, but he decided to leave the setting alone. He used the toilet, and it flushed. He tried the sink. It didn't work, but that was quickly remedied by adjusting the shut-off valve. The city water to the house was still on, one of the many blessings that came with escaping from prison in a state where no one had to worry about pipes freezing. He took a long drink from the faucet and washed his face. It felt so good and made him want more. He could shower and even rinse out the clothes he'd stolen from the homeless guy who was passed out behind Theo's bar last night. He removed the coat, unbuttoned the shirt, and stripped down to the waist. His skin itched. The more he scratched, the more it itched. He checked himself in the mirror over the sink. His chest was covered with welts. He grabbed the shirt and took a closer look. It was infested.

"Bugs!"

His scalp suddenly itched. He rubbed his head frantically with both hands. Tiny insects dropped from his hair and landed as little black dots on the white sink.

A string of hysterical and mostly nonsensical curse words followed, as he quickly kicked off his prison-issue Velcro shoes and ripped off the stolen pants. The socks and underwear were also from TGK, but they too were infested. He pitched all of it into the bathtub, turned on the showerhead, and jumped in. Hot water would have been nice, but that was asking way too much in a vacant house. The cold was more soothing to his insect bites anyway. He rubbed, swatted, and scratched all through his shower, sending one nasty little black bug after another down the gurgling drain. Then he started on the shirt, but it was so threadbare that even mild rubbing risked tearing it to shreds. The pants were more durable, but once they were wet, they smelled like a sewer.

The Grove Lord needed new clothes.

He turned off the shower. Dripping wet and wearing only his prison briefs, he set out to search the house in hopes that something had been left behind. He tried the linen closet in the hall. Empty. He checked the two smaller bedrooms. Nothing. The garage was accessible from the kitchen, but in there he found only a few basic supplies that the maid or the realtor needed to keep the house presentable for potential buyers. He was walking through the living room to the master bedroom when, through the bay window in the front of the house, he spotted an old man and his dog on the sidewalk. Isaac hit the deck.

He wasn't sure if the old man had noticed him or not. The owners had taken the draperies along with the furniture, leaving a clear view into the living room for passersby on the street. Instinct told him not to move a muscle, but Isaac couldn't stop himself from raising up his head just enough to peer over the windowsill. The old man was still standing on the sidewalk. Maybe he hadn't seen anything. His dog, however, was on high alert. The miniature white poodle was barking and bouncing up and down like a Ping-Pong ball, as if to shout, "Run for your life—there's a black man in the house!"

Isaac had to move. On his belly, keeping low, he slithered across the living room floor to the hallway, sprang to his feet, ran to the bathroom, and grabbed his clothes. Soaking wet, bugs or no bugs, they were all he had. He had to get dressed. But then what?

Think, Isaac. Think!

He could still hear that annoying bark. Soon enough, the old man had to realize that his dog wasn't crazy and that something was amiss. Maybe he was the friendly neighbor who'd promised to keep an eye on the house for the owners. Another minute of that high-energy yelping, and he'd probably march straight home and dial 911.

Not good. This was not good at all.

Isaac squeezed the excess water out of his underwear and checked one more time for bugs. Clean. The poodle continued to bark, louder and more aggressively. Isaac had to move fast, but a successful escape was not merely about speed. Once the cops with their dogs and helicopters were hot on his trail, it wouldn't matter if he was an Olympic sprinter. Hiding was the key to his success, and hiding took the courage to do whatever was necessary to keep some nosy neighbor from blowing your cover and sending you back to prison for life. Bottom line: maybe the old man had seen him, maybe he hadn't—Isaac couldn't take that risk.

He grabbed his gun. No silencer. The crack of gunshot in this neighborhood would be suicide.

A quick thought sent Isaac racing back to the garage. Earlier, he'd been searching only for replacement clothes, but there had to be something in that box of supplies that he could use now. He rummaged around and found a mop, a dustpan, and old rags. None of it was of any use to him. Except, maybe, the hammer.

A hammer!

Isaac gripped it tightly as he reentered the house and started toward the living room. From the dark hallway, with his back to the wall, he could see through the bay window. The little white fur ball was still barking, pulling the leash taut, practically dragging its so-called master toward the house. Isaac almost smiled to see that the old man was just about his size. No bugs in those clothes, he'd bet.

He tapped the head of the hammer into the palm of his hand, waiting and watching as the old man continued up the walkway.

This one's on you, Theo. Traitor.

Chapter 7

The FBI had a sighting, and Agent Andie Henning was flying down the turnpike at ninety miles per hour, her unmarked vehicle's removable blue beacon flashing in the early evening darkness. U.S. Marshals and the FBI SWAT unit had already surrounded the house in Homestead. Andie made a mental note of the fact that the address was less than four miles from Theo Knight's bar. The anonymous source in the BOLO—"Be on the Look-Out"—had apparently been reliable.

"I'm five minutes away," she said into her encrypted cell. Police radio wasn't an option. It was well known that fugitives sometimes monitored stolen radios to stay one step ahead of law enforcement.

Andie's adrenaline was pumping, but she was again chiding herself over that awkward conversation with Jack. Not that she would have liked to redo it. She never should have gone there, period. It was just her luck that Jack Swyteck was one of the names on the list of "fugitive's friends and contacts" compiled by the task force. Her boss had jumped all over that in their multijurisdictional meeting.

"Henning knows Swyteck from the Salazar kidnapping case," the ASAC had told the group. "You think he would talk straight with you, Andie?"

"I . . . I suppose."

"I only ask because he is a criminal defense lawyer. I imagine he'd be more inclined to talk to you than just any old cop showing up at his door."

"Swyteck used to be a prosecutor. I'm sure someone at the U.S. Attorney's Office knows him just as well as—"

"Andie, time is of the essence here. Can you talk to him or not?"

No. Absolutely not. Not gonna happen. "Sure," she'd said. "I'll talk to him."

Idiot!

She blew past the last turnpike tollbooth and took the final exit. East-west traffic was heavy on Campbell Drive, but she had to kill her flashing blue light so as not to alert the world—and the fugitive—of the sudden arrival of law enforcement. She weaved her way down the four-lane road as fast as possible without a police strobe beacon. The tires squealed as she cut a hard right turn at the final major intersection. Moments later, she spotted the law enforcement presence in a dimly lit school parking lot. Her car stopped so abruptly that the front bumper nearly kissed the pavement. Andie jumped out and ran toward the SWAT van. Supervisory Deputy Steve Miller of the U.S. Marshals Service was there to meet her. The FBI SWAT leader was with him, dressed in full tactical regalia and toting an M-16 rifle.

"What's the situation?" said Andie.

Deputy Miller was a former marine officer, and he still carried the look so completely that, instinctively, Andie almost wanted to salute him.

"House is two blocks east," said Miller. "We're staging from here to maintain the element of surprise."

"Do you have authorization to breach?"

"Yes. A neighbor spotted a black male inside."

"Have you ruled out that it might be the owner or a repairman?"

"Definitely," said Miller. "The house has been completely vacant. The owner moved to Plant City. I spoke to her by phone myself. Whoever is inside doesn't belong there."

"Is the subject alone?"

"We don't know yet. But now that you're here, any handoff from tactical assault to hostage negotiation will be as seamless as possible."

Andie was one of several trained negotiators in the Miami field office, but the Salazar kidnapping case—where she'd met Jack Swyteck—had firmly established her as the top dog. "I don't want to negotiate for a dead hostage. We need to verify whether he's alone before you breach."

"Techies are snaking listening devices through the attic vents as we speak. We're doing infrared scan, too. Should have the results by the time you suit up."

Andie retrieved her Kevlar vest from her car and put it on. Another SWAT member brought her a helmet, thigh guards, and a bone mike that would link her to the tactical team. She wouldn't be part of the SWAT breach, but preparing for all hell to break loose was part of Negotiation Training 101.

The task force leader was speaking into his bone mike as Andie approached the SWAT van. Miller said to her, "Infrared shows a warm one in the bathroom. No movement. Appears to be sleeping. Good time for a breach."

"Infrared isn't infallible," said Andie. That was experience talking—the Salazar kidnapping case again. *Would all these little Swyteck reminders just go away, please?*

Miller said, "SWAT's going in. If I'm wrong about him being alone in there and a hostage standoff develops, you're here to normalize the situation."

"Pick up the pieces" might have been a better way to put it. Even so, Andie couldn't disagree with the decision. "Let's do it."

THE MOMENT THEO RETURNED from the Keys and his "personal business"—it was about the Prince Albert for Trina—Cy had that unmistakable *Uncle* Cyrus look on his face. Theo knew he was in big trouble.

"In here." Cy grabbed him by the elbow and practically dragged him into the back room. He closed the door and locked it.

Theo wanted to say something, but suddenly he felt like a ten-year-old boy again, and his uncle was ready to slap him upside the head for backtalk of any sort. Uncle Cyrus had been the Knight brothers' one and only source of badly needed discipline.

"What the hell you been doin' with that Isaac Reems?"

"I ain't been doin' nothin' with him." A grown man with balls the size of globes, and out pops the voice of a scared child.

Cy opened the cabinet and threw the orange jumpsuit on the desk. "What do you call *this*?"

Theo knew immediately what it was. "Where'd you find that?"

"Shoved in the corner, behind your big stack of beer kegs."

Theo drew a deep breath, trying not to take the anger he felt toward Isaac and misdirect it toward his uncle. "I know what you must be thinkin'."

"Oh, you got no idea what I'm thinkin'. Why on God's green earth would you help that loser?"

"I ain't helpin' him. Isaac broke into the stockroom, stole my gun and my money.

Tried to make me help him. I told him to get lost. Then I called the cops."

Cy grimaced, as if wanting to believe but not quite able. "I ain't an old fool. The man didn't leave here naked. You gave clothes to a fugitive."

"No way. He came here wearing old rags. We got migrants around here who work the tomato fields. I'm runnin' the homeless out of my parking lot every night. He probably hit one, changed clothes after he broke in, and shoved the jumpsuit into a corner."

"You told all this to the cops?"

"You know cops and me don't mix. Four years on death row for somethin' you didn't do has a way of teachin' you that. Jack met with them. He told them everything."

Cy seemed willing to accept that, or perhaps he just didn't see the point of arguing anymore.

Theo said, "Now that I think about it, Isaac left that jumpsuit behind for a reason. He said if I called the cops, he'd tell them I was the one who helped him escape in the first place. Good thing Jack said no way to a police search inside the building. They would have found this, just like Isaac knew they would. Then I'd really have some explaining to do."

Cy stepped around the desk and stood closer to Theo, a soulful expression on his wrinkled face. His voice no longer had an edge to it, only concern. "Do not reach back into the old 'hood and help that scum," he said. "The past will hurt you, boy. It will cut you open and laugh in your face."

"I ain't helpin' him."

"Swear it." He grabbed Theo's hand and placed it palm down, flat on his chest.

Theo could feel the old man's heart pounding.

His uncle said, "Swear to me, boy. Swear that you won't help that snake."

Even if his life had depended on it, Theo could not have turned away. Never before had he seen that look in his uncle's eyes— such a powerful combination of fear and love.

"I promise," said Theo. "In fact, I'll call Jack now and tell him to hand over the jumpsuit to the cops."

Cy grabbed the jumpsuit before Theo could, then shoved it against his nephew's chest. Their eyes locked for a period of time that seemed much longer than it was, neither man saying a word. Finally, Cy broke the silence, Theo's comment about four wasted years on death row seeming to have carried the day.

"Burn it," he said.

"ON THREE WE'RE GREEN," SWAT leader Michael Penski whispered, his voice breaking the radio squelch in Andie's ear.

Andie was in a cover position behind a coral-rock fence across the street from the target residence. She didn't live and work beneath the SWAT rainbow, but she knew that yellow was code for the final position of cover and concealment. Green was the assault, the moment of life and death, literally. With the aid of night vision, she watched the well-choreographed SWAT movements unfold in a wave of stealth.

Penski counted down in a calm voice that reflected years of training: one . . . two . . . three. The word "three" unleashed a cacophony in Andie's headset, the sound of shattered glass and a blown-out door. She braced herself for the crack of gunfire, but she heard only the shouts of Special Agent

Penski and his team as they swept through the house.

"Down on the floor, now!"

Andie's radio crackled with more shouting. Moments later, the front door opened and Penski gave a hand signal as he announced over the radio, "All clear."

Andie ran across the lawn and hurried through the front door. Penski and another SWAT agent were standing outside the bathroom. Their night-vision goggles were up, and the ceiling light had been switched on. Through the open doorway, Andie saw an old man kneeling on the bathroom floor beside the tub. His hands were untied, though the torn rags that had bound them together were still dangling from one wrist. A saliva-soaked gag lay atop the sink. He wore only his boxer shorts and was apparently unharmed. But he was sobbing uncontrollably, staring down at what appeared to be a small white dog.

It was little more than a blood-soaked stain on the white tile floor.

"He smashed Puffy with a hammer," the old man said, his voice quaking.

Andie could only presume that Puffy had been the "strange noise coming from the house" that the next-door neighbor had reported to 911.

The man continued. "He said he'd do the same to me, if I made a move before daylight."

Andie was a dog lover herself, but no matter how distraught the old man was, she needed to get Reems's photograph in front of him. She carried it with her at all times, as did everyone on the task force. "Is this the man who did that?"

He only glanced at the photograph. "I saw his picture on television this morning. It was the guy who busted out of prison last night. He even stole my clothes."

Andie got a description of the clothing, then asked, "Did he have a gun?"

"I didn't see one."

"How long ago did he leave?" Andie said with urgency.

"Couple of hours ago, maybe."

"Did he steal your vehicle?"

"No. I didn't drive here. I was out walking my—" With that painful reminder of his beloved companion, he broke down.

Andie needed to question him further, but she filled the emotional pause with a quick phone call to the task force leader.

"Talk to me," Miller said over the encrypted cell connection.

Andie gave him the essential details and then launched into her recommendation. "Let's reactivate choppers and canine units. Get MDPD going door-to-door and highway patrol roadblocks on major east-west thoroughfares south of turnpike Exit 11. Reems is wearing a green-and-white madras shirt, khaki pants. Assume he's still armed and clearly dangerous. Estimate he's at most two hours out from our current position, but the timing of the neighbor's 911 call would put it at even less than that."

"Are you certain that the subject left the target residence on foot?" asked the deputy marshal.

"No vehicle sightings as yet."

"What's your recommended containment perimeter?"

"That's your call. But . . ."

"But what?"

She hesitated. Andie *did* like Theo, and what she was about to say would only make it harder to convince Jack that she wasn't out to get his best friend. "We have to deal with the likelihood that the subject will double-back to what he considers safe ground."

"Meaning?"

She hated to say it, but she couldn't ignore the information in the BOLO. "Sparky's Tavern."

Chapter 8

The woman is trying to kill me," said Theo.

He was speaking to Jack, who was seated on a bar stool at Sparky's. Theo was on the working side of the bar, his white shirtsleeves rolled all the way up to his bulging biceps and his Popeye forearms resting atop the Formica. An old Marvin Gaye tune—Jack's selection—played as the Saturday night crowd started to fill the booths and tables.

Jack said, "Trina's crazy about you."

"Stop being fecesish."

"You mean facetious."

"No, I mean you're talking shit."

"Trina doesn't want to kill you," said Jack.

"Maybe not. But she wants to hurt me real bad."

"Let me talk to her. Where is she?"

"Hell if I know. I told her not to come around here no more."

Theo fished a dreaded hazelnut out of the bowl of mixed nuts on the bar and pitched it into a wastebasket thirty feet away. If hazelnuts were the NBA's sphere of choice, Theo would have been a Hall of Fame power forward.

"Exactly what did she do that was so horrible?" asked Jack.

"She told me to get a Prince Albert."

Jack's expression was blank. "I have no idea what that is."

"Neither did I, till she sent me down to the Keys to see this guy named Manny." Theo looked from side to side, making sure no one could overhear. The young women to Jack's left seemed sufficiently engaged in conversation with a couple of guys who— Theo would have bet his liquor license on it—had left their wives at home.

Theo said, "Manny's a body piercer. And a Prince Albert is a metal ring through the head of your penis."

Jack's mouth opened, but the words didn't

come. Finally, he said, "Ouch! Why would Trina want you to get that?"

"Sends a woman into orbit, I guess."

Jack narrowed his eyes, as if trying to imagine how. "Whatever turns you on."

"Don't get me wrong. I dig a woman who's always looking for better sex."

"They put it right through the head?" said Jack. Theo's last remark hadn't even registered. It seemed that Jack's internal pain meter was still processing the procedure, and his brain simply couldn't handle any additional information.

Theo said, "They actually punch a hole on the underside, and they thread it all the way up and out through—"

"Enough!" Jack closed his eyes, as if not comprehending, and then he opened them slowly. "I swear, sometimes I feel like I'm Rip Van Winkle and the whole world flipped out while I was asleep."

"Don't beat yourself up. Turning myself into the Penis Currently Known as Prince is even too much for me."

"So you're not going to get it?"

"Can't."

"Why not?"

"Hey," he said, stepping back as he motioned

toward his crotch. "They don't make rings this freakin' big."

"That's a problem."

"Not to mention the hassle. Imagine setting off metal detectors for the rest of your life and having to announce to the world, 'Calm down, folks, nothing to worry about. It's just my dick ring.'"

"I can see where that would get old."

"And let's not forget, we're talking about a ring, a needle, and the one-eyed monster. You don't go stickin' a needle in the monster's eye."

"You make a strong case."

"Damn straight."

The married guys seated near Jack ordered cocktails for exhibits A and B in their future divorce proceedings. Theo was making cosmopolitans when Uncle Cy tapped him on the shoulder.

"I'm feelin' tired," the old man said. "You mind calling me a cab?"

"That's a thirty-dollar fare," said Theo.

"I can take you," said Jack. He glanced toward the pool table, where Rene was emasculating an unsuspecting biker at a game of eight ball. "Rene and I go right by the Grove on our way home."

"Thanks, but I don't want to cut your night short."

"No problem. There are other bars in Miami."

"No, there ain't," said Theo.

Cy smiled. "I'll just lie down for a while in back. Let me know when you and Rene are ready to go."

They argued about it for a minute, but Cy won out. He headed back to the stockroom adjacent to Theo's office, where Theo kept a cot. Theo was about to go along and help his uncle set up, but Jack stopped him.

"Andie Henning came by my house to see me today."

Theo laughed heartily, glancing toward Rene. "Timing is everything, ain't it?"

"She was asking about Isaac Reems."

"I thought the state attorney promised not to mention my name."

"She kept the promise. They linked me up to Reems another way. But let's be real. Once the BOLO went out and said Reems was last seen at Sparky's, Andie must have immediately thought 'Theo Knight.'"

"I'm surprised she didn't just call me. I got no hard feelings. The two of you didn't work out, but she's still welcome here."

"After what she said?"

"She didn't say nothin', Jack. You two were drinking, having fun. She made a dumb-ass joke about me landing you in jail."

"Getting me disbarred," said Jack, correcting him.

"Whatever."

"Don't dismiss it. It bugs me, the way a cop's mind works. So what if the DNA proved you didn't kill that convenience-store clerk? If you didn't do that crime, you were probably doing *something* when the cops picked you up that night. Or, if you weren't doing something right at that very moment, you've probably done a whole lot of other things in your life."

"I *have* done a lotta other things," said Theo.

"That's not the point."

"You're right. The point is, Andie made a joke, and you jumped all over it."

"What are you talking about?"

"Forget it. Don't make no difference anyhow," he said, pointing with his eyes toward Rene. She was still having her run of the pool table. "There's your woman, right over there. Beautiful. Smart. Rich."

"You know she gave away most of what

she inherited. Tons for AIDS research. I'm guessing she's down to a million or less."

"Down to *a million*? Like I said, she's freakin' rich, okay?"

Jack gave a little smile, but it faded. "She's going back to Africa Monday."

"Lucky you."

"What?"

"That's the way you like it, no? It's easy to convince yourself that you love a woman who's never around. It only gets hard when you have to admit you love someone who's actually here, in love with you, and ready to change your life forever."

"That's such psychobabble."

Rene waved to Jack from across the room.

"If it is," said Theo, "then make her stay."

"I can't *make* her stay. What am I supposed to do, kidnap her?"

"Just make her not want to leave," said Theo. "I dare you."

Jack finished the last of his beer. "All right, I will."

Theo waited, but Jack didn't move. "Well, go on then."

"I'm going. As soon as I finish my brewski."

"It is finished."

Jack took a dry pull from the empty bottle. Theo laughed and gave him a friendly shove, but it was still hard enough to knock Jack off the bar stool and start him in Rene's direction.

"There he goes, ladies and gentlemen: the world's greatest lover." Then Theo lowered his voice and added, "So long as there's an ocean between him and his woman."

Theo watched as Rene stepped toward Jack to greet him, tossing her hair and slipping her arms around his waist as if they were a perfect fit. It made Theo think about Trina—a pleasant enough thought that was quickly interrupted by the imagined pain of a Prince Albert. But he still felt this sudden need to talk to her.

The telephone rang under the bar. No one would expect him to pick up on a busy Saturday night—except Trina. Hell, what did she want him to do now, pierce his eyeball? He let it ring.

"You want me to get that?" asked his cocktail waitress.

"No," he said a little too firmly.

The waitress shrugged it off and went back to slogging drinks.

The ringing stopped. He could have hit star-69 to confirm his instincts, but he was sure it was Trina. She would want to know how it had gone with Manny the body piercer, and then he would have to tell her exactly what he'd just told Jack—that she must be out of her mind, and that it was over between them. There was only one problem. He wasn't sure he could say it.

What's wrong with you, homeboy?

The telephone rang again. Trina obviously wasn't going to take Theo's machine for an answer. He snatched up the phone and said hello. Dead air. It was one of those cheapo cordless receivers that worked about as well as the Batman walkie-talkies he'd stolen from a toy store as a kid. He pitched it aside and hurried to his office. That phone shared the same line, and it was ringing as he entered the room. He closed the door and started toward the desk, but his answering machine picked up before he could get to it. The recorded greeting was in Theo's voice, a throwback to his days as a jailhouse lawyer.

"You have the right to remain silent . . . or you can leave a message at the beep."

The tone sounded, and Theo waited for

the message. He heard only traffic noises, which told him that it was either a cell or a pay phone. He wasn't sure why Trina would be calling from a pay phone—and then he realized who else it could be. Cy was in the next room, and Theo didn't want him to over-hear a message being left. He picked up but didn't answer.

"Theo, you there?"

He recognized Isaac's voice immediately. He was about to speak, but then a thought crossed his mind. Jack had told the cops there would be no search of the premises, but what if they'd tapped his telephone, wait-ing for Isaac to call back?

"Come on, dude. I heard you pick up the phone."

Theo just listened.

"Answer me, brotha'. I need a deal. I know you wanna deal with me, too."

Theo wanted to respond, but the possibil-ity of a law-enforcement tap on the telephone tied his tongue in knots.

"What's the matter with you, boy? Say somethin'!"

Isaac wasn't even trying to sound cool anymore. Sirens blared in the background.

"Knight, answer me already! You hear me? I know you can hear—aw, fuck you, then. That's all I got to say to you. Just—"

Theo waited for a click on the other end of the line, but it didn't come. He couldn't tell if Isaac was still there or not.

The sirens were only getting louder.

Chapter 9

Isaac left the pay phone's receiver dangling from its metal cord. He was off and running with no idea where he was headed—a dangerous place for a fugitive to be. The dark cover of night was his only ally, and even that was betraying him. Moon over Miami—the city was famous for it. Tonight, it was like a spotlight.

Could the damn thing be any brighter?

Thankfully, the sirens had blown right past him. Two Miami-Dade Police Department vehicles were speeding west through the city of Homestead's business district, toward the turnpike. Isaac tried to tell himself that maybe they'd been called to a holdup at a liquor store or a domestic disturbance, but he was certain that the cops were hot on his trail. Choppers whirred overhead, their search-lights cutting like lasers through the night sky. It wasn't just a routine pass. They kept cir-cling back, covering a defined urban and suburban area that included several square miles, but they seemed to be narrowing in on Isaac's present position. The canine units couldn't be far behind.

It was time for a new plan.

He sprinted down a dark alley in a strip mall and found himself at the loading dock behind a grocery store. He had to rest. Months of extra weightlifting in prison could only carry him so far. He hadn't focused nearly enough on cardio training. The side-stitch in his abdomen felt like a knife in his belly. Traces of smoke in the air from those brushfires in the Everglades were starting to bother him. Damn drought. He couldn't even make a run for the wilderness. Not that he would have wanted to go anywhere near that place after dark. It was Alligators vs. Py-thons out there, nature's classic showdown between reptiles for the Everglades' title of chief predator. And the fires worked to the advantage of the police; they didn't waste their time trying to hunt him down in the middle of nowhere.

Exhausted, he stopped and hid behind a towering stack of flattened cardboard boxes. He sat with his head between his knees, searching for a second wind.

"Shoulda' killed him," he muttered beneath his breath. The smart thing would have been to take that hammer and bash the old man's brains in, just like he'd done with that little barking fur ball. Isaac's best advice inside the correctional center had come from a lifer who escaped from a Texas jail and got recaptured less than 300 yards from the Mexican border. "You wanna stay out of prison, you gotta take no prisoners," said the voice of experience. "It's their bad luck if they cross your path, but it's you or them." Isaac couldn't know for sure, but he figured that the old man had wiggled free from the rags that bound his wrists and ankles, run to safety, and dialed 911. The cops might not have thrown every resource into south Miami-Dade County based solely on a tip from Theo Knight, an ex-con. But a second sighting cinched it. All that could have—*should* have—been avoided with just one swing of the hammer.

Fool!

He kicked over a stack of boxes in anger, then calmed himself. None of this was his fault. A measly two thousand bucks was what he had expected from Theo's cash box. He got less then three hundred. That wasn't nearly enough for a new identity and safe transport out of the country. And some Oxy-Contin. Grind those pills to dust and snort 'em. *Oxycotton.* One dollar per milligram on the street. A quick but expensive high, better than heroin.

Gotta have it.

Isaac pushed himself up from the ground. The box he used for leverage had contained produce, and there were still a few grapes inside. He sucked the juice out of them and savored the flesh. Even slight nourishment seemed to bring a much-needed clarity to his thoughts.

Isaac could have come up with any number of ways to get his hands on two grand. Hell, that would have been a bad night's haul back in his days as a Grove Lord. But he'd resisted the impulse to pull off even a simple robbery, save for the relatively risk-free theft of that homeless guy's clothes. His prison sources had warned him that police would be watching crime reports carefully, looking for indicators of a fugitive on the run—stolen cars, weapons, drugs, and cash. He needed to score in a way that would keep him off police radar—like from a girlfriend or a buddy. Even more, he needed a front man he could trust to make all the arrangements on his behalf. Surely a reward was being offered for his recapture, so showing his face in a pawnshop or the like was out of the question.

His thoughts kept turning to Theo Knight. Isaac still had leverage there.

But he was running out of time to play it.

The blare of police sirens again pierced the night. More squad cars were headed toward the Florida turnpike. Isaac counted three this time, a slightly different sound than the last vehicles. Maybe state troopers. The cops had obviously gotten it into their heads that he was fleeing on wheels, which suited Isaac just fine. That was yet another way in which the likes of a Theo Knight could have worked to Isaac's advantage—someone to phone in false sightings to 911, orchestrated confusion.

Gotta take another shot at Theo.

Isaac looked up into the sky. The choppers were back, and it wasn't just the police.

The television media were also getting into the act now. Isaac Reems was no longer the proverbial needle in a haystack. He had to go north, back to where his old friends from the Grove Lords still lived.

Isaac had his wind again. He ran across the loading dock and didn't stop until he reached the chain-link fence behind the building. Intertwined with the fence was a thick ficus hedge, and beyond it was a twenty-four-hour diner. The restaurant was well lit on the inside, but the parking lot behind it was dark. Isaac heard the click of heels near the Dumpster, and he spotted someone walking toward a car. It was a woman—a waitress wearing her powder blue uniform. She was probably just finishing her shift. Tired, no doubt—her guard down. She was headed toward a Mustang. It wasn't new, but it looked fast.

Isaac removed the pistol from his pocket—Theo's gun—and quietly hopped the fence. He made not a sound as he ducked behind another car. She didn't even look in his direction. She continued walking to her vehicle, in the dark, completely unaware. Just a teenager, probably six months out of high school. Too young to think anything bad could happen to her, too dumb to ask the manager to escort her to her car.

Damn, I'm lucky and *good.*

He continued along the perimeter of the parking lot, crouched below the cars to stay out of sight. She stopped. He readied himself. She gave a cursory look around, a woman's obligatory safety check, and then opened her purse. The jangle of car keys got his heart pumping, and he heard the car alarm disengage by remote control. As she reached for the door handle, Isaac sprang from behind the parked van and took her from behind. Before she could make a sound, his hand covered her mouth, and the gun went under her chin with so much force that she was staring straight up at the moon.

"Don't move," he said.

He could feel her fear and the paralysis that came with it. She was no fighter. Isaac was an expert on these things. Quickly but quietly, he took her behind the car and popped the trunk.

"Please," she said, her voice quaking. "Don't—don't rape me."

"Your bad luck, baby. That ain't what I'm after." He stuffed her into the trunk, slammed the lid, and hurried into the driver's seat. The engine started right up, and the gas gauge indicated nearly a full tank. He left by way of the parking lot's rear entrance so that none of the workers inside the diner would see him driving the waitress's car.

He laid the pistol on the floorboard, between his legs.

Plan C, he told himself. *No prisoners*.

Chapter 10

Jack and Rene were cruising north on U.S. 1 with Uncle Cy in the backseat.

Around ten o'clock, a half-dozen MDPD squad cars had converged on Sparky's to make sure Reems hadn't doubled back. Agent Henning wasn't part of the sweep, though Jack wondered if she was behind it. Theo was furious—swirling blue lights in the parking lot were never good for business—and Jack told him to go somewhere and cool off before he took a swing at a uniform. Two hours later, Theo still wasn't back, but Cy was ready for his ride home.

True to his jazz musician roots, Uncle Cy

had the internal clock of a vampire. He seemed to come alive at midnight, which definitely had its drawbacks.

"Say, whatever happened with you and that Andie woman?" the old man asked. He was sitting on the edge of the rear seat, his forearms resting against the back of Jack's headrest. Jack pretended not to hear him.

Rene said, "Uncle Cy asked you a question." The guy really was everybody's Uncle Cy.

Jack tried to catch the troublemaker's eye in the rearview mirror to convey a silent ixnay. Cy didn't take the hint.

"I was just wondering about—"

"Hey, look, Rene: It's a Calvin Klein underwear billboard!"

"—you and that FBI agent," said Cy, finishing his thought.

Jack dismissed it with a wave of his hand. "Oh, I really don't think Rene wants to hear about that."

"She doesn't mind," said Rene.

A red Ferrari flew past them at double the speed limit. "Of course she doesn't," said Jack, barely audible.

"What's that you say?" said Cy.

For some reason, he was not going to let

this drop. It was starting to feel as though the two of them had cooked up this little Mutt-and-Jeff routine for their own entertainment. Jack said, "Andie and I had two or three dates back in January. No big deal."

"January," he said, his face screwed up like a man dividing fractions in his head. "So, how long have you two known each other?"

"A lot longer than that," said Jack.

Rene definitely seemed to be enjoying this, but mercifully she spoke up. "I live in Africa."

"That's a good place to be from," said Cy.

"Well, I'm not *from* there. I've been running a free health clinic for children in Côte d'Ivoire for a few years now."

Cy seemed impressed. "Good for you."

"Thanks. But it's kind of tough on the love life. So Jack and I have this . . . understanding."

"You see other people?" said Cy.

"He sees other people," said Rene. "I'm way too busy for that. I come visit him every few months."

"Say *what*?" said Cy, now speaking to Jack. "Let me get this straight. This beautiful woman comes and visits you every so often. You show her a good time, she gives you lots of lovin'. Then she goes back to Africa and says it's fine and dandy for you to see other women?"

Jack didn't like the way Cy was making it sound. But that was basically it. "It's pretty unusual, I know."

"Unusual?" said Cy, shaking his head. "Man, Theo must hate your guts."

Jack could have explained that Theo wasn't jealous in the least, that Theo was nuts about Rene. But Theo liked Andie, too. And still in the back of Jack's mind was Theo's comment about longing for the woman who makes herself unavailable—the implication that Jack had cut Andie out of the picture only because she was the one who really wanted to be in it. But there he went again, overanalyzing everything.

You done, Swyteck?

"Yeah, Theo should hate me," said Jack.

"Turn here," said Cy.

Jack headed up Douglas Road, the southwest entrance to Coconut Grove. The questionable area near the busy highway was Theo's childhood neighborhood. The worst of the old wooden shacks were long gone—including Theo's old house. They'd been razed and replaced by new single-family homes that were freshly painted in pastel colors. Much of the business district, however, retained the look and feel of the old ghetto. Groups of young men hanging out on the sidewalk with nowhere to go. Drug dealers and whores at work behind the boarded windows of dilapidated buildings. Rap music blaring from low-riding cars with metallic paint jobs and shiny chrome wheels. Bars and package stores marked by crude wooden signs that looked as if they'd been painted by Tom Sawyer on crack.

Cy suddenly fell quiet. He was sitting back in his seat, looking out the window. The dramatic mood swing reminded Jack of the time he and Theo had taken this same shortcut into the Grove. In the span of a single city block, Theo—just like his Uncle Cy—had gone from his usual animated self to staring vacantly out the passenger-side window. It had happened some years earlier, and it was the only mention Theo had ever made to Jack about his mother.

Theo had pointed out where she lay dead in the street.

"You okay, Cy?" asked Jack.

"Mm-hm," he said.

Soon, the ghetto's vapor lights and tall

fences topped with spirals of razor wire gave way to gated streets and oak trees. They were approaching Theo's new neighborhood. Central Grove wasn't crime-free, but the sound of gunshots in this area could just as likely be a doctor shooting his wife's tennis pro as a holdup.

Jack parked in the visitor space outside Theo's town house. Cy thanked him for the lift and climbed out of the backseat. He appeared a little unsteady walking up the steps. Jack got out and helped him to the front door.

"Are you okay?" said Jack.

"It's this damn medicine I'm on," said Cy. "Makes me woozy when I stand up after sittin' for too long."

Uncle Cy had always seemed old to Jack, but he suddenly looked *very* old. "Let me help you up to your room."

Jack sensed that the old man was about to protest, but another one of those dizzy spells came upon him. "I'd appreciate that," Cy said.

At Jack's behest, Rene followed them upstairs to Cy's room. She switched on the lamp as Jack seated him on the edge of the bed. "Rene's a doctor," said Jack. "You want her to check you out?"

"I don't need no doctor. Doctors is what got me all screwed up. All these medicines they give me." The old man lay back against his pillow.

Rene said, "What kind of medication are you on?"

"I don't know. It's sittin' right there on the nightstand."

"He had a mild stroke last summer," said Jack.

Rene read the label. "This is to lower your blood pressure. Your doctor might have to adjust the dose or prescribe something else if you're getting light-headed." Rene took a minute to check his pulse. "Ticker seems fine."

"Of course it's fine. Everything's fine. Now get lost, you two. Go have fun."

The old man's eyes were already closed. Rene pulled off his shoes, and Jack switched off the lamp. Then they said good night and went downstairs. Jack suggested that they hang around for ten or fifteen minutes so that Rene could check on him again before they left.

They sat on the couch in front of the television. Rene snatched up the remote, and Jack was hard-pressed to deny such a pleasure to a woman who was headed back to the primitive corners of Africa's cocoa region in less than thirty-six hours. Jack watched in silence as she switched from Tom Hanks in *Sleepless in Seattle* to George Clooney in *Sisters* to an old episode of *Thirty Something*—again and again.

"You sure you can't stay past Monday?" said Jack.

The question brought her surfing to an end. Jack was apparently stuck with *Sisters.* Not a terrible choice—if you had no testicles.

"I really can't," she said.

"Why not?"

They were seated so close that she was leaning against him, and Jack had both arms wrapped around her. He could feel her body stiffen.

"I'm the clinic's only doctor."

"I understand that. But whenever you come to see me, you always leave sooner than planned. Five days is never five days. A week is never a full week."

"Something always comes up."

"I—" Jack measured his words, but he decided that it needed to be said. "I honestly don't buy that, Rene."

His arms were still around her, but it was

as if their blanket of comfort had been yanked away and thrown to the cold tile floor. They sat in silence, both staring at the television but neither one watching it. Jack wished they were sitting face-to-face so that he could read her expression.

"You're right," she said quietly.

"I am?"

"Yes. I don't really have to get back to the clinic on Monday. I could stay a week. I could stay two weeks."

Jack's chest tightened. It sounded like he was about to get dumped, but he still had to ask: "So why are you leaving?"

Slowly, she broke away from his embrace, sat up, and faced him. "Because if I stayed any longer, I'm afraid I might never go back."

She sounded sincere, and Jack wanted to believe her. But somehow he couldn't help wondering if she was speaking from the heart or saying what she thought he wanted to hear.

Theo's telephone rang. It was across the room on the countertop, and the answering machine picked up. Theo liked to screen his calls, so the message played loud enough for Jack and Rene to hear every word as it was being recorded.

"Yo, Theo! Where the fug' are you, man?"

Jack didn't recognize the voice immediately, and even though he knew he shouldn't listen, he couldn't close his ears.

"Answer me, Knight! I know you got my message. So where are you, dude? I been waitin' here almost half an hour for you."

Jack hadn't heard Isaac Reems's voice in years, and they'd had only one telephone conversation. But he was dead certain that Theo's machine was recording the message of a fugitive.

"Dude, here's the deal," said Reems. "Two thousand bucks. That's all it takes. I'm sure you think I don't know what I'm talkin' about. But trust me, a man hears a lotta shit sittin' in prison as long as I did. So get me two grand, bro'. Just do me a couple of favors. And then I swear, I'll tell you who killed your momma."

The line clicked. The machine stopped recording.

Jack and Rene exchanged uneasy glances.

"What was that all about?" she said.

Rene was a bit of a *New York Times* snob and hadn't read the Miami paper or watched any local news. The first she'd heard of Reems's escape was when the cops showed up at Sparky's and Jack had told Theo to go cool off. She hadn't asked any questions—Jack said the cops were chasing rabbits—but in light of this phone call, maybe it was a good thing she was returning early to Africa after all.

"Excuse me a second," said Jack. "I need to call my client."

Chapter 11

Isaac was getting tired of waiting.

Hours before this follow-up call, he'd left detailed phone messages, one at his home and one at the bar, telling Theo when and where to meet. Not for a second did Isaac worry about Theo calling the cops again. This time Isaac had spelled out exactly what his old friend would get if he showed up.

Finally, the old leader of the Grove Lords had played his ace in the hole.

This was the proverbial offer that could not be refused. Sure, they hadn't seen each other in years, but Isaac still knew Theo. They'd hung out together every day for months after the murder of Theo's mother. Tatum got over it in a day or two. But Theo was obsessed with finding her killer. It seemed that a day didn't go by without Theo vowing to slit that bastard's throat the way he'd slit his momma's. Blood that hot never cools. It was irrational, really, the way Theo had managed to block from his memory all the ways in which his drug-addicted mother had failed herself and her children. In life, she had been nothing to him. In death, she became the score he needed to settle, as if his anger over the way she'd chosen to live her life had no way to manifest itself except in Theo's revenge against the man who had sliced her open and left her dead on the street. Whoever he was. And now, after two decades, Theo had the chance to hear his name.

Where the hell are you, Knight?

Isaac checked the time on the bank marquee on the street corner. Eighty-one degrees at 1:37 A.M.

Theo was more than an hour late.

Isaac had to move. The waitress was still in the trunk, so he didn't have to worry about her reporting the car stolen. But maybe she had a roommate or lived with a boyfriend or her parents. They would expect her home and eventually call the cops, which would trigger a police BOLO mentioning her Mustang. The car had served its immediate purpose. He decided to ditch it in the alley, but first he had to deal with the cargo.

He drew his pistol and popped the trunk. The waitress didn't move. He nudged her. She still didn't respond. He laid his hand on the back of her neck, and she was burning up. It was like the fires of hell in that trunk. The heat had obviously overtaken her. He checked her pulse. She was alive, but he wasn't about to carry her around, dead weight on his shoulders. Wrong place, wrong time, honey.

No prisoners.

He closed the trunk and left her there, then walked around the building to the chosen meeting spot. It was behind a restaurant called Quincy's. Back in the 1980s, it used to be a bar called Homeboy's. "Meet me behind Homey's," Isaac had told Theo in his first message. That was what they used to call it. Even if the cops had tapped Theo's telephones, they had no way of knowing that "Homey's" referred to a ghetto bar called Homeboy's that had closed almost twenty years earlier.

Quincy's restaurant was closed, which made Isaac uneasy about standing around waiting for Theo. Someone might report a prowler. The Dumpster offered the only hiding place. Fugitives had holed up in worse places, he figured. He climbed up and lowered himself into waist-deep trash that soiled his clean clothes and squished beneath his shoes. This sucked in a big way, but it was almost funny. In a wry moment of nostalgia, he wished he'd run to South Miami. Back in the day, the joke among Grove Lords was that you could knock off a bank and clean out a strip mall right under the nose of a South Miami cop—unless your getaway driver forgot to put a quarter in the parking meter. Then you were dead meat.

The good news was that he hadn't heard police choppers or sirens since coming north. But Isaac would be an easier target after sunrise. And the odor of restaurant garbage was getting to him. He had to move soon.

"Come on, Theo," he muttered. "Where's my money, bro'?"

Maybe Theo hadn't listened to his messages yet. But Isaac couldn't let his mind go there. If Theo wasn't coming, that left Isaac in a stinking garbage can with no one to help him thread his way to freedom through a blanket of cops. He was screwed.

Totally screwed.

He heard something. Footsteps? He sat perfectly still and listened. Someone was coming down the alley. He rose up in the Dumpster just enough to peer over the rusty rim. The footfalls grew louder. It sounded like one person, and there was no beam from a flashlight leading the way—pretty reliable signs that it wasn't the cops. A silhouette appeared at the end of the alley and stopped. Isaac couldn't tell who it was, but this was exactly where he had told Theo to meet him, and the outline in the darkness was that of a large man. In silence, Isaac drew his weapon and took aim, just in case. A gunshot would bring the cops, so he had to avoid discharging his firearm at all costs. He wanted to call out Theo's name, but he held his tongue. *Let him speak first*, Isaac told himself.

The man said nothing. Slowly, he reached into his pants pocket. Isaac watched, taking extra care not to make a sound as the man removed something and tossed it on the ground a few feet in front of him. With his other hand, the man switched on a palm-sized flashlight that sent a laserlike beam cutting through the darkness. The light was on only a few seconds—long enough for Isaac to see that there was a roll of money on the ground. Then the man switched it off.

Isaac's pulse quickened. Again, however, he reminded himself not to reveal his position until this visitor removed all doubt as to his identity.

The man said nothing.

Sirens blared in the distance. Isaac was suddenly aware of the sweat beading on his brow. He listened, hoping the man would speak. All he heard were sirens. And maybe helicopters, too. Yes, that was definitely the whir of choppers, and it seemed to be growing louder. The manhunt was coming north—toward him.

The man started forward. Isaac's finger was on the trigger. He wasn't sure what to do about the slow and steady approach of this silent silhouette. Then the advance halted. Isaac could breathe again. But not for long. The man bent down, picked up the roll of bills that he'd tossed to the ground, turned, and headed back toward the dark alley.

He's leaving!

More sirens. Helicopters were closing fast. Daylight was only a few short hours away. If Isaac didn't make this connection, his only option was to use the waitress—but a hostage standoff was the sure-fire end for any fugitive. All the help he needed to complete his escape was just twenty feet away. Twenty-five. Thirty.

"Theo!"

The man stopped and turned.

Isaac rose from his position of safety and concealment in the Dumpster, revealing himself from the chest up. "That you, Theo?"

No answer. The man simply reached inside his pocket and, like before, tossed the roll of bills onto the ground in front of him. Isaac's gaze followed the cash. The diversion was just enough to delay his reaction to the blur of a hand that pulled a pistol and took aim at Isaac's face. The entire motion was completed in a split second, but for Isaac it seemed like an eternity.

He no longer heard the approaching police sirens. The whir of choppers vanished.

He heard only the muffled release of a silenced projectile as his knees buckled and his head jerked back in a crimson explosion—as he left his own body and saw the lifeless shell of Isaac Reems collapse in the Dumpster, trash on top of trash.

Chapter 12

Andie got the phone call as she was preparing for an eight o'clock briefing with her ASAC. She reached the Grove ghetto before 9:00 A.M.

Isaac Reems's body was still in the Dumpster.

It wasn't exactly the answer to her prayers, but it was an answer.

Media helicopters hovered overhead. Television stations from Action News to Telemundo had vans and remote-broadcast crews crammed into the parking lot across the street from Quincy's Restaurant. It seemed strangely Orwellian, this wintry forest of metal towers

topped with microwave dishes. Field reporters were vying for the best position to broadcast the "latest developments" back to their
respective stations. Many of them had been
covering the Reems story from the beginning
and recognized Andie before she could even
step out of her unmarked car. She politely
breezed past the microphones, politely refusing several requests for a comment as she
approached the crime scene.

Uniformed police officers and yellow crime
tape closed off the alley that ran alongside
the east side of the restaurant. The west entrance to the delivery area behind the building was also cordoned off. Andie showed her
credentials and was allowed to pass through
the outer perimeter, but she was stopped before she reached the Dumpster. MDPD was
in charge of the crime scene, and the pe-
rimeter-control officers were determined to
make certain that no one, not even the FBI,
contaminated it. Andie caught the eye of
Lieutenant Dawes, who recognized her from
the task-force meeting. He went to her and
provided an update, the two of them separated by taut yellow police tape.

"You sure it's Reems?" said Andie.

"Positive," said Dawes.

"How long has he been dead?" said Andie.

"Don't know yet."

Dawes had the look and demeanor of a homicide detective who had seen far too many murders. He was tense and angry, his teeth and right hand stained from chain smoking, a clenched fist of a man. Andie sensed that he knew more than he was willing to share, which wouldn't have been the first time in the history of American law enforcement that a homicide detective chose to be tight-lipped around the FBI. Her questions had to be more pointed to draw anything out of him. "Rigor mortis set in yet?"

"Yeah."

"Beyond the neck and jaw?" she asked.

"It would appear that way."

"Full body?"

"Not yet."

"What about lividity? Any blanching to the touch?"

"I'd say it's fixed."

"So, you can set a preliminary on the time of death at six to eight hours." She checked her watch. "Between one and three A.M., roughly."

"That's a fair guess."

"Can you tell if the body was moved here from somewhere else?"

"Not yet," said Dawes. No elaboration.

"Well, what does your ME say about the bloodstains and lividity patterns?"

"No signs that the body has been moved."

Andie said, "So Reems was shot exactly where he was found, in the Dumpster. Are you thinking suicide?"

"Still under consideration."

"Did you find a weapon nearby?"

"Yeah. But it hadn't been fired."

"Blood spray on his hands?"

"Nope."

"Where's the entry wound?"

"Between the eyes."

"Not your typical self-inflicted gunshot," said Andie. "Any powder burns or starburst at the point of entry to suggest a close-contact wound?"

"No."

"Doesn't sound like suicide to me. Any witnesses to talk with?"

"One possibility."

"Who?"

"Reems stole a car to get here. Owner is a nineteen-year-old woman. She was locked in the trunk, semiconscious when we found her.

She's at Jackson now. Maybe she can tell us something."

"Got a name?"

Dawes gave it to her, and Andie wrote it down. Then she glanced toward the Dumpster, where the forensic team was busy searching for fingerprints and collecting other evidence. "Mind if I have a closer look?"

"Sorry. We're doing a footprint and tire-track analysis, and I'd like to keep traffic to a minimum."

"Understood," she said. "Anything of particular interest?"

He seemed to think about it for a minute, as if trying to decide whether her performance thus far had earned an answer to such an open-ended question. Andie hated this game—boy cop tells girl cop absolutely nothing until she dazzles him with her knowledge and lures him into sparring with her. But Dawes was old school, and her persistence seemed to be getting through to him. Whatever worked.

"Hard to say," he said. "There's lots of foot traffic behind a restaurant. But one set of footprints appears to come down the alley, stop about twenty feet away from the Dumpster, and then turn around and head back."

"You're thinking he was shot from twenty feet away?"

"It had to be from some distance. There's no exit wound."

"What kind of ammunition?"

"I can't be sure until the ME extracts the bullet from his head. But the wound looks a little too large for .22-caliber, so I can rule out that much."

"Plus, if it was .22-caliber, the shot probably would have been fired at close range to penetrate the skull. Like the classic Mafia hit, where the .22 is right up against the skull and the bullet rattles around inside the skull, no exit wound, turning the brains to scrambled eggs. That would have left residue."

He seemed surprised that Andie knew that—or at least a little chagrined that he hadn't said it first. "Exactly," he said. "So with a larger wound and no powder burns at the point of entry, I'm saying it's not a .22."

"But if it was a bigger round—say, a .38 or a 9-millimeter—and fired at close range, it probably would have passed right through the skull. You're telling me it didn't do that."

His expression showed less surprise than simple annoyance that Andie was keeping up, or perhaps even a step ahead of him.

"Right. So twenty feet sounds about right to me," he said.

"Did you find a shell casing?"

"Not yet. Shooter may have picked it up and taken it with him."

Andie's gaze drifted back toward the crime scene. She was trying to imagine what it would have been like behind the restaurant after dark. "What's the lighting situation like here?"

"Just that one street lamp on the west end of the building."

"Any stray bullets found in the wall or any-place?"

"No."

Again, Andie turned her attention back to the Dumpster, mentally placing herself at the scene of the crime. "So the killer fires a single round from twenty feet away in bad lighting. Hits Reems right between the eyes. He's so confident that it's a kill shot, he doesn't even approach the Dumpster to inspect his work. He just picks up his spent shell casing, turns around, and leaves the same way he came."

"Are you hinting at a professional job?" said Dawes.

Andie shrugged. "At least someone who knew what he was doing."

"A guy like Reems could know a lot of people like that."

"That's probably true," said Andie.

They watched as the assistants from the medical examiner's office rolled the gurney toward the Dumpster to collect the body. Andie said, "The manhunt is over, and now begins the search for his killer."

"Well, at least your work is done."

"It's never done," said Andie. She thanked him, stepped away from the police tape, and then reached for her cell phone. Their last date had ended with a certain air of finality, but for some reason she still had Jack Swyteck's number programmed into her directory.

Only just beginning, she thought as she placed the call.

Chapter 13

Theo met Jack at the Latin American Cafeteria, a landmark Coral Gables restaurant that specialized in hot pressed sandwiches made on Cuban bread. An early lunch had been Jack's idea, and he was waiting at the busy counter when Theo arrived.

Like every other customer but Jack, Theo wanted to dine in air-conditioned comfort and watch the knife-wielding chef carve up the roast pig and cured hams like a skilled samurai. Jack said he needed to speak to Theo in private, however, so they placed their order inside and endured an isolated table in the sunshine. The outside seating area had lost its shade trees in the last hurricane season, and even though summer was technically a month away, it felt like a sticky August afternoon. The wait for their food came with a view of noisy Coral Way and endless waves of heat rising from the paved parking lot. Theo couldn't stop wiping his brow with a napkin, but Jack seemed content. They were indeed alone, save for a handful of old Latinos who were dressed in their Sunday guayaberas and standing at the takeout window, sipping *tazas* of Cuban coffee and arguing about everything from politics to *beisbol*.

"Where's Rene?" said Theo.

"The mall."

"They don't have one of those in the cocoa region?"

"Yeah, but every time Rene comes to Miami she suddenly feels the urge to barter for something other than live chickens and goats. Go figure."

The waitress came with their order on a tray. "Dos cubanos?" she said. Two cubans? She meant the sandwiches, not the customers. She placed the plates in front of them and handed them their beverages. Materva, a Latin soft drink for Jack. A large mamey milkshake for Theo.

When the waitress was gone, Jack said, "So, what do you think about Isaac Reems? Any idea who would shoot him?"

Theo removed the plastic lid from his milkshake and gulped some down. "You mean other than half the city of Miami?" Theo unwrapped his sandwich. "We gonna talk or eat?"

"Go ahead. Eat."

"First, a tribute." Theo lifted his sandwich from the plate and started singing to it, putting his own words to the tune of Human League's 1986 number one hit, "Human."

I'm just a cuban.
Of cheese and bread I'm made.
I am also ham . . . please forgive me.

He devoured a third of his cuban sandwich in one huge bite.

"You forgot to mention the pickles and sliced pork," said Jack, deadpan.

"Artistic . . . license," he said with his mouth full. It was the same license that turned Madonna's first Latin hit into "Last night I dreamt of some bagels," and Stevie Nicks's "Edge of

Seventeen" into "Just like a one-winged dove"—a true Theo Knight classic, this mental image of a little white bird flying around in circles.

"I got a phone call from Andie Henning this morning," said Jack. "She's looking into the Reems murder."

Theo chewed thoughtfully and swallowed. "I may not have a law degree, but how does the FBI get involved in a run-of-the-mill shooting of a pissant criminal?"

"You're right, local law enforcement does normally have jurisdiction over homicide. So I asked her that question myself."

A bus rolled by on Coral Way, adding diesel fumes to the ambience. "What was her answer?" said Theo.

"It turns out that Andie has been appointed to head up the task force that will be looking for answers about Reems's escape."

"Well, they tapped one sharp agent. But I still don't see how her work on a task force gets her into Isaac's shooting."

"Reems didn't climb out of a barred prison window on a rope made out of bedsheets, hop a nine-foot fence topped with razor wire, and then run to freedom without someone on the inside looking the other way."

"Maybe. But what's that got to do with the shooting?"

"Here's the way Andie sees it. If she finds out who killed Reems, she'll bet dollars to doughnuts that the answer will also point the way to whoever greased the wheels to bust him out of prison."

"Mmm. Doughnuts."

"Focus."

"Sorry."

Jack turned serious. "Andie wants to talk to you."

"Okay. Like I told you before: I got no problem with Andie. I'm sure she's just doing her job."

"And I gotta do mine, too. So tell me something, and don't get cute on me. When's the last time you had anything to do with Isaac Reems?"

Theo didn't answer right away.

Jack said, "When Rene and I dropped off Uncle Cy at your place last night, we heard Isaac's message."

"Dude, don't tell me you were listenin' to my phone messages."

"We were sitting on your couch when he left it. Heard it all."

"Did Cy hear it too?"

"I don't think so. He was upstairs in bed."

Theo nodded, but he was still silent.

Jack flashed his lawyer expression. Theo knew it well—his don't-you-dare-lie-to-me look. "Give it up, Theo. When was the last time you heard from Isaac?"

"Who wants to know?"

"I do," said Jack.

Theo glanced toward the traffic on busy Coral Way, then back at his friend. "This conversation—it's privileged, right?"

"Yup," said Jack. "Attorney-client, all the way."

Theo put down his sandwich. And then he told him.

Chapter 14

On Monday morning Jack took Rene to the airport for a 12:50 P.M. flight to Abidjan via Paris. Jack didn't even try to talk her into staying another day—and it wasn't because he thought she would say no.

"What's wrong?" she asked.

"Nothing."

"It's definitely *something*."

They were walking side-by-side across what was arguably Miami's greatest work of public art—the striking black terrazzo floor at the airport's international terminal. Michele Oka Doner's "A Walk on the Beach" was exactly what the name implied. Thousands of inlaid bronze sculptures reminiscent of the ocean and the artist's native Miami Beach dotted the mile-long concourse. Jack's gaze shifted from two-dimensional brain coral to driftwood to starfish, his thoughts churning.

"Are you mad at me for leaving too soon?" said Rene.

"No—well, yes," he said with a flat smile. "But it has nothing to do with that."

"Are you worried about Uncle Cy?"

"Uncle Cy?" he said, but then he clarified his own confusion. The old man hadn't been himself at all when they put him to bed early Sunday morning. "I'm sure he'll be fine. Like you say, the doctor just needs to adjust his blood pressure medication."

"Then it must be Theo."

Jack tried not to bite. "Why would I worry about Theo?"

"Well, duh. It sounded like someone was trying to extort money out of him for information about his poor mother's murder."

Rene knew about Isaac Reems—even if the cops hadn't shown up at Sparky's on Saturday night, the Sunday morning news coverage of the shooting was inescapable— but Jack still hadn't told her that the phone message they'd overheard at Theo's place had been from Isaac. And he certainly hadn't told her that Andie Henning wanted to meet with him and Theo.

Rene was a smart woman, however. Surely she suspected something.

"It wasn't technically extortion," said Jack. "Just someone who wants to be paid for his information. Kind of like checkbook journalism without the journalist."

Rene stopped and took Jack by the arm. They were dead-center in the rotunda, the crown jewel of Oka Doner's masterpiece. Jack almost felt guilty standing on it.

"Talk to me," she said. "What's going on?"

Jack took a breath and let it out. "I'm concerned that Theo might be getting mixed up with something he shouldn't."

"What kind of thing?"

"I don't know exactly." That wasn't a flat-out lie, but Jack didn't like the feel of it. He sensed that Rene didn't, either.

She said, "Who was that man who left the message we overheard?"

"I—I can't tell you that."

"What?"

"It's attorney-client privilege."

Her look was incredulous. It was almost

as bad as the expression he'd seen on Andie's face—right before they broke up.

Rene asked, "Why are you suddenly his lawyer?"

"Like I said, I'm worried about what he might be getting caught up in."

"Did Theo meet with that caller who left the message for him Sunday morning?"

That information was also privileged. But it didn't seem wrong to get a reaction to Theo's version of events from someone more objective than himself—particularly when she was about to board an airplane to the remote reaches of Africa.

"He says he didn't go," said Jack.

"Then why didn't he answer his cell when you called him?"

"I guess he didn't have it on."

"Which seems odd. You told him to go away for a while till the cops satisfied themselves that Isaac Reems wasn't coming back to Sparky's. You'd think he would have left his phone on."

"Maybe he just didn't hear it ring."

"You called him twice before I finally went upstairs to check on Uncle Cy, and you called him one more time as we were leaving his town house. Don't you remember? You were concerned about leaving Cy before Theo got home."

Jack was thinking like Theo's criminal defense lawyer, and Rene's recollection of his client's unreachability on the night of Isaac Reems's death was a little too vivid for his professional comfort. He checked the departure board overhead. Her flight was right on time. "You'd better get going," he said.

Rene glanced at the board, then back at Jack. She seemed to understand his inner struggle. And thankfully she seemed willing to at least try to work within his constraints and limitations as Theo's friend—and lawyer—even if she didn't have a full grasp of what was going on. Jack wondered if Andie would have done the same.

"Have you talked this out with Theo?" she asked.

"Yeah, yesterday at lunch."

"Did you tell him what's on your mind?"

"Yup."

"Did he answer all your questions?"

"He always does."

"Do you believe what he told you?"

"Of course."

"Why?"

Jack was taken aback. Women always

seemed to ask that one additional question that guys never asked—the one that goes to the core of the relationship. "Because he's my best friend," he said.

"Best friends can still lie to each other."

"They shouldn't," said Jack.

"No. They shouldn't."

Jack suddenly felt as if this conversation was no longer just about him and Theo.

Rene took his hand. "Are we best friends?"

Jack lowered his eyes. "I don't know. Are we?"

"Have you ever lied to me?"

"No."

She smiled, and with a light touch, she lifted his chin until their eyes met. "You just did."

"Huh?"

"Everybody lies, Jack."

"Have you lied to me?"

"Does a pygmy hippo shit in the great Taï Reserve?"

Jack couldn't help giving up a little laughter. Then he turned more serious. "So Saturday night, when you said the reason you never stay longer than a few days at a time when you come to visit me . . ."

"Definitely not a lie," she said, squeezing his hand. "That was the truth."

She kissed him, and Jack held her tight. The smell of her hair was right in his face, and he gave himself enough time to commit it to long-term memory. "I'm gonna miss you," he whispered.

She pulled away and slung her carry-on over her shoulder. "I'll see you. Soon. I'll call you when I get to Abidjan. I promise." She gave him another quick kiss on the lips and then headed toward security. Jack watched from afar as she presented her ticket and passport to security. She turned and flashed one last smile, then disappeared into the maze of international check-in.

Jack tried to catch sight of the back of her head one more time—maybe she'd turn and wave—but he couldn't follow her in the crowd. He stayed put for a few minutes anyway, just watching the endless stream of travelers headed for points unknown. He was sad to see Rene go. He wondered if that was because of his feelings for her—or if he simply dreaded what was next on the agenda.

It was time to meet with Agent Andie Henning.

Chapter 15

The meeting was inside Theo's office at Sparky's Tavern. Jack didn't like the venue, but the idea was Andie's. She got her way—with one notable exception.

"Theo isn't coming," said Jack as he closed the office door.

She wheeled and gave him a look of complete surprise—more like Andie the might-have-been girlfriend than the poker-faced Agent Henning.

"What do you mean he's not coming?" she said.

With a conciliatory wave of the hand, Jack offered her a seat on the couch. She didn't take it. Jack crossed the room and braced himself against the front edge of Theo's desk, half sitting and half standing, his arms folded. The entire room had been swept free of the usual clutter—no papers atop the desk, no Post-its on the computer screen, no receipts and records scattered across the floor and furnishings. Even the wall calendar was gone. Theo had followed Jack's cleanup order to the letter: leave nothing for the wandering eye of the FBI.

Jack said, "Don't read anything into this from a personal or investigative standpoint. He's merely following the advice of his lawyer."

"You and I had a deal," she said.

"And we still do, if you remain willing to share the 'something of interest' that required us to meet in Theo's office."

"You were supposed to let me talk to Theo."

"I can answer your questions."

"That's changing the deal."

"That's the only one on the table."

"You're being a pain in the ass."

"Some things change," he said with a shrug, "and some things stay the same."

She smiled a little, as if to confirm that she

had the energy to butt heads all day long, and he smiled back. Jack had a lot of time and effort invested in Rene, but for a quick moment, a part of him could imagine the fun in sparring with Andie about everything from unreasonable search and seizure to who would end up on top at night.

Her smile faded, and she put on her business face. "Where was Theo on Sunday morning between midnight and three A.M.?"

"He was working at his bar until the cops came looking for Isaac Reems. I told him to go somewhere. He ended up at his girlfriend's and spent the night at her place."

"Would that be Katrina?"

"Trina. She stopped going by Katrina when the hurricane hit."

Again, Andie showed surprise, but it wasn't about the name change. "They're still together?"

Jack wasn't sure how to take it, but her tone almost seemed to ask, How the heck did Theo and Trina outlast us? "Yeah, still together."

"Doing well, I hope."

"Doing just fine." Jack didn't bother with the tale of the Prince Albert.

"Can anyone confirm that he was with Trina that night?"

"Trina can."

She rolled her eyes. "Other than her, wise-guy."

"No, but let me save you a lot of time. Theo didn't kill Isaac Reems."

"I'm not saying he did. I'm not even here on a homicide investigation. Not my jurisdiction."

"It sounds like you're making it your jurisdiction."

"I'm just trying to find out who on the outside was able to get the guards on the inside to look the other way long enough for Isaac Reems to bust out of the TGK correctional facility."

"I hope you find out. But I'd really like to know why you're looking here."

"Because Theo and Isaac were fellow juvenile delinquents back in the 'hood. Because the first place he went when he busted out of prison was Theo's bar. Because the last time Reems was seen alive he was less than four miles from Sparky's Tavern. Because he was found shot on the same street that the Grove Lords used to cruise as teenagers."

"Based on that, you think Theo helped Reems escape from prison?"

"I know Theo, and I have a really hard time believing that he would do something so stupid. But I have to do my job. And there's one other thing in the mix."

"I can't wait to hear it."

"Theo's phone line was tapped."

Lawyer's instinct kicked in: *Confront devastating news with righteous indignation.* "You tapped his telephone?" he said in an angry voice.

"I didn't say *I* did."

"I meant law enforcement."

"Ah, the 'royal you.'"

"The 'totalitarian you.'"

"Hold your horses," she said. "It's not what you think."

Jack hoped not. His deal with the state attorney was no searches of the premises, no taps on Theo's telephone. Things were going to get very sticky if the FBI knew about Reems's phone messages to Theo. *Be cool, Swyteck.* "What are you trying to tell me?"

"There was never an official wiretap of any of Theo's phone lines."

"I'm not sure I'm following this."

"One of the agencies—not *me*, mind you—

sought a warrant, but things don't always move fast on weekends. By the time it was issued and the tech people started acting, it was early Sunday morning. They stopped as soon as they detected an existing power drain on the line."

"Are you saying that Theo's line was *already* tapped?"

She nodded. But it still wasn't clear to Jack if law enforcement had picked up Reems's messages to Theo. "Do you mean his home or his office?" he said.

"The plan was to tap both. The power drain was on his home line."

That was what Jack had feared. "Whose tap was it?"

"That's the big question."

"Some other branch of law enforcement?"

"No official wiretap would be that easily detected. This isn't the old days where telephone exchanges were mechanical and technicians had to link circuits together to route the audio signal from the call. It's digital technology and done by computer."

"So Theo's line was tapped by someone outside of law enforcement?"

She nodded again.

"You never did actually get a wiretap?"

"No. By the time all this was brought to my attention, Reems's body had already been found."

Jack breathed a silent sigh of relief.

Andie said, "I told you I was going to share something of interest."

"You are true to your word, lady."

"I'm glad you feel that way. Now let's see if you are. When was the last time Theo had any communication with Isaac Reems?"

"I'll have to check with Theo. Let me get back to you on that."

"You gotta be kidding me, Swyteck."

"Do I look like I'm kidding?"

"Do I look like I could kill you?"

"Like I said before, some things change." He crossed the room and opened the door for her. "Some things don't."

Chapter 16

Jack and Theo watched as Vinnie Acosta connected a TDR—a time domain reflectometer—to the telephone line outside Theo's town house.

Vinnie was a retired technical agent for the FBI that Jack had worked with during his brief stint as a prosecutor with the U.S. attorney's office. Vinnie had all the necessary toys to operate his own technical countersurveillance company. He was high up on a ladder, accessing a junction box that received the telephone wire from a utility pole on the other side of the parking lot. Jack and Theo waited below in a typical three-men-at-work scenario: one guy actually doing something while the other two stood around watching.

An internal sweep of the town house for a radio tap or an induction coil attached to one of the phones had turned up nothing. They then moved outside to check for a direct-line tap. Jack understood the concept—a slight change in line impedance caused by the introduction of a tap or splice would show up on the screen of the TDR—but gadgets were not his forte.

"How hard is it to get an accurate reading?" said Jack.

Vinnie's focus remained on the junction box. "A TDR is essentially an echo-ranging device. It generates a short, very rapid rise-time pulse that travels along the wire pair at a speed determined by the velocity factor of the wire. When a discontinuity is encountered, the pulse is reflected back along the wire pair to the TDR and oscilloscope. All it takes to measure the actual distance to the discontinuity is a simple calculation on a calculator."

Jack looked at Theo. "What did he just say?"

"He says it's a hell of a lot easier than sticking a metal ring through your johnson."

"That's what I thought he said."

Before meeting Agent Acosta, Jack would never have pictured anyone named Vinnie as a highly intelligent techno-nerd. This was due in part to Vinnie Testaverde's highly skilled but less than cerebral play at quarterback for the University of Miami in the 1980s, but it stemmed mainly from the fact that Rene's old boyfriend was named Vinnie. Once, Jack had even joked that Rene should write a spoof book called *Duh Vinnie Code: A Girl's Guide to Understanding Brainless Hotties Who Talk Like Dis.*

"Got your bug," said Vinnie, checking his calculator. "About forty-three feet from the box."

Theo looked up at the wire and made a rough measurement. "That pole by the Dumpster," he said.

"Good place for it," said Vinnie.

He climbed down and moved the ladder to the other pole. Jack and Theo resumed their all-important positions of standing around and watching. Jack felt as though he should be wearing a hard hat and earning about thirty bucks an hour.

"Yup, it's here all right," said Vinnie.

Theo looked at Jack. "I guess Henning wasn't bluffing."

"Don't touch it!" Jack shouted upward.

Vinnie said, "I can't remove it if I don't touch it."

"It's enough just to know exactly where it is. I want Henning to come out and get it and check for fingerprints."

"I should at least disable it," said Vinnie. "Just one snip of the wire."

Jack gave him the okay. Vinnie took care of it and climbed down the ladder. Jack said, "How sophisticated does the equipment look?"

"Pretty basic. Smaller than a cigarette pack, but not exactly something out of a James Bond movie."

"I guess we're not dealing with the CIA here," said Jack.

Vinnie said, "We knew that when Henning told you about the impedance on the line. That only happens with low-tech stuff."

"Any way to tell how long it's been there?" said Jack.

"Can't pinpoint it. But it looks brand spanking new to me, not very weather-beaten. Two or three weeks, at most. Maybe even a few days. But as soon as you get the FBI out here to remove it and check for prints, that should be the end of that."

Not with Andie on the case, thought Jack.

Vinnie packed his equipment into the van. Theo paid him in cash, and Vinnie was off to another job. Then Jack and Theo went back inside. It was midafternoon on a Monday, an off-hour for Sparky's. Theo was in no hurry to get back to the bar. They stood on opposite sides of the kitchen counter.

"You gonna call Henning?" said Theo.

"Let's sort this out first," said Jack. "Why would someone tap your phone line?"

"If you ask me, somebody put it there after Isaac busted out of jail."

"Vinnie said the equipment looked new, but maybe not that new."

"Maybe they put it up there after finding out that he was *planning* an escape."

"You're making a lot of assumptions there. But if I take what you're saying at face value, why would someone do that?"

"Because they thought he was going to call me."

"But let's assume Andie was telling the truth: law enforcement didn't put it there. Why would anyone else even care if Isaac spoke to you after breaking out of prison?"

"I can't answer that. But whoever it was heard that first call when Isaac said he was

going to be at H-boy's at one A.M. Homeboy's shut down while I was still on death
row. So it's somebody who knew the old
'hood."

"That's my problem, Theo. That makes
you a prime suspect."

"Let's get real, okay? Every cop in the
county was looking for Isaac and they couldn't
find him. So either his shooter stumbled on
him—a random shooting or something—or
he was shot by whoever bugged my phone.
No one else knew exactly when he was going to be where he was."

"But the tap on your telephone could be
completely unrelated to Isaac."

"I might agree with you if it had been there
for a month or longer. But you heard your
friend Vinnie say that somebody just put it
there a few days ago—at most, a couple of
weeks ago."

"That still doesn't mean your eavesdrop-
pers were sitting around listening to your
phone on a Saturday night. Or maybe they
heard it and didn't do anything about it.
The FBI could take the position that you're
the only one who got the message, you
went to see Isaac that night to find out who

killed your mother, and you ended up killing Isaac."

"Except that I have an alibi."

"The jails are full of guys whose only defense was an alibi from a girlfriend."

"They don't have a girlfriend like Trina."

"That's the interesting wrinkle here. As of Saturday night, I thought you didn't either. You told me you were done with Trina because of the Prince Albert."

"We made up."

"Happy to hear that. But if I'm a cop, that's awfully convenient timing."

"What if you're Jack Swyteck?" said Theo.

Jack felt like he was being tested. "I don't doubt you, Theo. But you didn't answer your cell that night."

"Did you call Trina's?"

"Of course not. I wasn't about to dial her number at one o'clock in the morning after you were so adamant that it was over between you two."

"So what's your point?"

"I'd feel better about this alibi if I had talked to you or her the other night."

Theo slid his cell across the countertop. It

hit Jack in the elbow. "Call her now," said Theo.

Jack's gaze was drawn to it. It would have been a betrayal to pick up the telephone and check out Theo's alibi. He slid the phone right back at him. "I don't need to talk to her."

Theo put the cell back in his pocket.

Jack looked away, then back. He wanted to change the subject—but only slightly. "That was one hell of a shot that took out Isaac," he said. "Right between the eyes, dead of night, bad lighting, twenty or more feet away."

"Could be a pro. Could have been lucky."

Jack gave his friend an assessing look. "Sooner or later, Andie or somebody is going to latch onto the fact that your brother was a contract killer."

"Tatum's dead," said Theo.

"But I'm sure he had friends who could hit a shot like that."

"That don't make 'em my friends. I got friends on death row. Does that make 'em yours?"

Funny, but Andie might have said yes—at least that was the way Jack had taken her "bad joke" that led to their breakup. "I guess not," said Jack.

Silence fell between them, and then Theo smiled. He gave Jack a playful punch to the left bicep. It hurt.

"So, nothin' to worry about, right dude?"

Jack rubbed his aching arm. "No," he said. "We're cool."

Chapter 17

Theo's tour started appropriately enough at the Knight Beat—"the swingingest place in the South"—and then moved on to the Cotton Club, the Clover Club, and Rockland Palace Hotel. The night wouldn't end until they reached the Flamingo Lounge at the Mary Elizabeth Hotel. All of these clubs had disappeared years earlier—some before Theo's birth—but Uncle Cy's anecdotes brought them to life.

"The day Miami was born, the official name for this area was Colored Town," said Cy. "Then it was Overtown. I like to think of it as Little Harlem."

They walked side-by-side down Second Avenue, between Sixth and Tenth Streets, once a lively stretch that, back in the day, was known variously as Little Broadway, the Strip, and the Great Black Way. Uncle Cy was dressed like a relic from the jazz and swing era, wearing a three-piece Norfolk suit in natty vintage tweeds, as if defying the fact that it was a balmy evening in May.

"Ain't you hot?" said Theo.

Cy flashed a mischievous smile. "Last time someone on Little Broadway asked me that question it was more like, 'Cyrus Knight— hoo-wee, ain't *you* hot!'"

"Must have been one of the many women you managed to convince that the Knight Beat was named after you."

"How'd you know about that?"

"'Cause it's what I would have done."

They stopped at the corner. A chain-link fence surrounded a vacant lot. A big painted sign promised condominiums "Opening Summer 2003"—a deadline that could now be met only with the aid of time travel. "American Dream Development Ltd.," the sign said, "a Fernando Redden Company." There were a few mounds of gravel and deep ruts from truck tires, but the weeds had taken over. It looked as if the distinguished Mr. Redden's construction had ceased as soon as it had started.

"This used to be a joint called the Harlem Square Club," said Cy.

Theo saw not a trace of the original building. All that remained was the nostalgia in the old man's eyes. "I've heard of it," said Theo.

"Hearing *of* it ain't nothin' like hearin' it. I was sittin' at the bar in 1963 when Sam Cooke did a live recording. I seen 'em all—Cab Calloway, Billie Holiday, Louis Armstrong, Count Basie, Ella Fitzgerald, Aretha Franklin, B. B. King."

"Pretty cool they could book acts like that."

"Yeah, thanks to Glass Killens. A real charmer, famous for carrying around a mystery mug—contents unknown. And one smart promoter. Black entertainers played all the swanky hotels on Miami Beach, but they couldn't stay there. Whites only. So they popped across the causeway to find a room, and Glass would get 'em to play a late-night gig at places like the Harlem Square."

Theo let him have all the time he wanted, but there was no escaping the fact that a community once filled with pride and music was now Miami's poorest neighborhood. More than half the residents lived in poverty, two-thirds of households were headed by un-married women, and only one in ten dwell-ings was owner-occupied. Those cold statistics were borne out by the panhandlers on the streets, the abandoned stores and decrepit buildings marred by gang graffiti, and the virtual nonexistence of trees and green space. Cy's gaze drifted toward busy I-95 and I-395, which intersected in the heart of Overtown. Even at night, the pall of the el-evated expressway was palpable. Ironically, the federal government had started construc-tion of the interstate just as Congress was passing the Civil Rights Act—a fatal blow in a time of great hope.

After a minute or two, Cy shook his head in silence, like a man turning away from the grave of an old friend. "Let's go," he said.

They walked on. Theo's car was parked on the other side of the street, two blocks north.

Theo said, "We're pretty close to where you used to live, ain't we?"

"Not too far. Just a tiny wooden shack on Northwest Twelfth Street." His eyes brightened with another twinkle of nostalgia. "Used to call them shotgun houses, because a bullet fired through the front door would shoot out the back without hittin' anything on the inside."

"You seen many bullets fly?"

"Mostly dope dealers shootin' each other. You got used to that kind of thing. But it was the riots in the early eighties that finally made me move out for good."

A homeless man leveraged himself up from his bed of corrugated cardboard on the sidewalk. His lips were moving, but he was either too weak or too strung out to speak. As Theo and his uncle passed, Theo dug out a ten-dollar bill and deposited it into the dirty paper cup that held a few loose coins.

"Now don't blow it all on food," said Theo. "Be sure to get yourself some liquor."

The homeless man actually smiled.

Theo and his uncle crossed the street. A low-ride sedan rolled past them, rap music blaring from a boom box so big that it filled the entire rear seat. The red metallic paint glistened beneath the street lamps, and a cryptic black-and-gold gang symbol stretched across the hood. The twenty-two-inch rims were chrome-plated with a triple cross-lacing spoke pattern. Three black youths were in the front seat. It reminded Theo of the old days—him, Tatum, and Isaac.

"I lied to my best friend today," said Theo.

"Trina?"

"No. Jack. I told him I got no idea who would tap my phone line after Isaac busted outta prison."

Cy did a double take. "You know who did it?"

"No. But I do got an idea."

The old man was about to ask who, and then he stopped.

Theo didn't say it. He didn't have to.

Cy said, "You ain't serious, are you?"

"You tell me."

His uncle stepped up onto the curb. "You think I bugged your phone line?"

"I ain't makin' no accusations. Just throwin' it out there."

"Well, throw it right in the trash."

"Relax, okay? I never thought you was trying to hurt me. You found Isaac's prison clothes in the stockroom, and I thought maybe you wanted to make sure I wasn't stupid enough to help him."

Cy winced, as if this were the dumbest conversation since the development of human language. "What makes you think I even know anything about phone taps?"

"Jack's tech guy said it was basic equipment."

"So you think an old man who is still recovering from a stroke climbed up on a ladder and spliced a phone line?"

"It's as easy as stealing cable TV. For fifty bucks, you could hire half the people who walk into my bar to do it in ten minutes."

His uncle stepped closer and looked Theo straight in the eye. He didn't look angry. He looked hurt. "I didn't tap my nephew's phone." He shook his head and walked away.

Theo wanted to call out and stop him, but he was momentarily frozen. It was as if the weight of his own stupidity suddenly came down upon him, crushing his heart as completely as the interstate had crushed Overtown.

"Cy, wait," he said, but he wasn't sure his voice could be heard. That same metallic red low-rider was cruising down the street again, the boom box blaring.

Cy kept walking. He went right past Theo's car.

Theo called louder. "Where you going?"

He turned around. Now he *did* look angry. "I'm gettin' myself a cab."

Theo drew a deep breath and let it out. He knew it wouldn't do any good to chase after him, but he wasn't about to let his uncle take a cab home. He watched, hoping the old man would decide on his own to turn around and come back. But he was a block away and showing no sign of slowing down.

"Uncle Cy!" Theo shouted, but the boom box from the passing car was too loud. No way the old man could have heard him. Theo started after him, half walking, half jogging. He was about to call out his name again, but that damn box was blasting even louder.

It was as if the low-rider was keeping pace with him.

Theo stopped and wheeled toward the street. The passenger-side window was half-open, but from Theo's angle it was too dark to see inside the vehicle. "Hey, what the hell—"

The crack of gunfire ended his sentence, and his dive for cover came way too late. He was suddenly down on the sidewalk, his head throbbing like he'd been hit with a sledge-hammer. Theo tried to get up but couldn't.

Something hot was running down his face and neck, but, strangely, the sidewalk beneath him was turning cold.

"Nailed him!" the gunman shouted, and then Theo heard the low-rider burn rubber and speed away into the night.

Uncle Cyrus, he tried to shout, but he couldn't find his voice.

He wanted to wipe the blood from his eyes, but his hands wouldn't move. His vision was a blur, and he suddenly noticed the glow of a street lamp. The lighting, however, was no longer diffused. It was intensely bright in the middle, like a blazing star in the dead of night. Lasers of equally brilliant light shot out from the center at twelve and six o'clock, also at three and nine. Or was it north and south, east and west? There seemed to be a strange confluence of light, time, and direction.

He heard his uncle shout his name, but it didn't sound real.

Then came darkness.

Chapter 18

Jack took the call from Uncle Cy and picked up Trina on the way. Just after 9:00 P.M., they rushed to the emergency room at Jackson Memorial, a public hospital that was a mere hop over the interstate from Overtown and no stranger to gunshot victims. Cy was slumped in a chair in the crowded waiting room. Trina went directly to him and hugged him tightly for support. He was too emotionally drained to stand.

"How's Theo?" said Jack, breathless.

Trina wiped away a tear as she and Uncle Cy broke their embrace.

"Don't know," the old man said. "They

threw me outta the ER so they could work on him."

"Did he regain consciousness?"

"Uh-uh. Not that I saw."

"How did he look when they brought him in?"

Cy's expression was less than hopeful. "Like he been shot in the head. Just so much damn blood."

Jack's gaze swept the waiting room. It was a cross-section of lower-income Miami. An old Haitian woman hung her head into a big plastic bucket that reeked of vomit. A homeless man with no legs slept in the wheelchair beside her. A single mother comforted a crying baby as her four other children played leapfrog on the floor, shouting at one another in Spanish. A drug addict in withdrawal paced back and forth across the waiting room, talking to himself. This was the world of Medicaid and no health insurance. Anything less than a bullet to the head meant a nine-hour wait. Free treatment from some of the best doctors in the world was their consolation.

The whiteboard behind the receptionist showed that Theo Knight was in treatment room number three. Jack approached the counter and snagged the attention of one of the busy nurses. "Any information on my friend in room three?"

She didn't look up from her clipboard. It might have seemed rude, had she not been doing ten things at once. "What's his name?"

Jack told her. She checked the board, grabbed an eraser, and removed his name— which gave Jack a moment of panic.

"They took him into surgery," she said. "We'll let his uncle know as soon as we know anything."

Jack went to the vending machine and bought three bottled waters. Trina remained at Uncle Cy's side, and she was holding his hand when Jack returned. Jack shared the waters and the latest news from the nurse. Through the glass entrance doors, he noticed a City of Miami squad car in the parking lot.

"Did you talk to the police yet?" he asked Cy.

He nodded.

"What did you tell them?" said Jack.

"Not much. Didn't really see the shooter. Black guy is all I can say. Red ghetto car. Drive-by shooting, you know."

Trina rose, clearly edgy. "I need to walk off

some nerves," she said, then headed aim-
lessly toward the whiteboard, as if to confirm
everything Jack had just learned from the
nurse.

Jack stayed with Uncle Cy. "So you see
the shooting as random?"

He shook his head. "Did at first. More I
think about it, more it seems like somebody
from the 'hood. Maybe even an old Grove
Lord. Must've gotten wind that Isaac turned
to Theo for help and Theo went to the cops.
This is payback."

"I could see how you might think that way,"
said Jack. He drank from his water bottle.

"You say that like I'm missin' somethin'."

Jack took a seat directly across from Cy,
then slid forward to the edge of his chair. He
lowered his voice to further convey how serious he was. "I agree that it wasn't random.
But your payback theory doesn't make any
sense."

"Why not?"

"If someone from the old 'hood was ticked
off enough to punish Theo for not helping
Isaac and for calling the cops, why didn't Isaac
go to that person for help in the first place?"

Cy nodded, as if he hadn't thought of that.
"So it ain't payback?"

Jack said, "I think it's bigger than that. Much bigger."

A glimmer of life returned to the old man's eyes. "Talk to me."

ANDIE HENNING WAS IN SUITE 212 at Jackson Memorial Hospital, a private room for Sylvia Peters, the young waitress abducted by Isaac Reems.

Andie had been waiting since Sunday morning to speak with her. Kidnapping was Andie's primary area of responsibility at the FBI's Miami field office. Also, it was possible that Reems had told his hostage something about the prison break, so talking to Sylvia was a key part of Andie's task force review of the escape. Sylvia's parents, however, had refused all requests for interviews until their daughter regained her strength and spoke to a counselor. With Reems dead and the criminal investigation in a postmortem posture, Andie hadn't pushed it. But upon hearing that Theo had been shot, Andie renewed her request with urgency. Sylvia agreed to talk.

Andie stood at the bedrail facing Sylvia. IV fluids dripped into the patient's arm. Sylvia's parents sat in the chairs by the window, monitoring their daughter's words as closely as the bedside equipment monitored her heart rate. Andie took notes and listened to Sylvia's recount of the abduction, asking questions to fill in details. When Sylvia got to the shooting behind the restaurant, Andie slowed the discussion to the interrogator's equivalent of frame-by-frame analysis.

"I blacked out somewhere during the car ride," said Sylvia. "It was ungodly hot in that trunk."

"And you regained consciousness when?"

"I have no idea how much time passed. All I know is that the car wasn't moving any-more. I remember hearing a loud thud. I think it was the sound of the trunk slamming shut."

"So he had actually opened the trunk?"

"I think so. I'm guessing that it was the fresh air that revived me."

"What did you do?"

"Nothing. I was afraid to make a noise. I knew the guy had a gun."

"So you lay there in the dark?"

"Yeah. I was still sort of out of it. It was hard to breathe in there. I just tried to listen."

"Did you hear anything?"

"Not at first."

"Did you eventually hear something?"

"Well, the gunshot, for sure. It was so loud."

Andie said, "The car wasn't far from the scene of the shooting. And I'm sure the alley amplified the sound."

"I knew it had to be nearby. That's when I lost it. This probably wasn't very smart, but I started screaming and kicking against the quarter panel."

"Did you hear anything before the gunshot?"

She nodded and drank from her cup of ice water. "I heard a man's voice."

"Do you know who it was?"

"It sounded like the man who abducted me."

"What did he say?"

"It was just one word. He shouted somebody's name, I think."

"A name?" said Andie.

"Not a common name. It was . . .heck, what was it, now? I remember thinking it was like one of the characters on the reruns of that old Bill Cosby show. The son."

"Theo?" her mother volunteered.

"Yeah," said Sylvia. "Theo."

"Are you sure?" said Andie.

"Positive. He yelled out the name Theo. And then I heard the gunshot. Is that helpful?"

Andie closed her notepad. "It could be," she said. "Definitely could be."

Chapter 19

Jack, Uncle Cy, and Trina rose as Theo's surgeon entered the waiting room. For Jack, it was like trying to read the faces of jurors at the end of a trial, until the doctor removed his surgical mask.

"Your nephew is one lucky man," he said, smiling.

Cy nearly collapsed with relief, and Jack held him up by the arm. "Theo's going to be okay then?" said Jack.

"Fine," said the doctor. "Head wounds always bleed like crazy. Fortunately, the bullet never actually penetrated the skull. Chipped off a small piece of it, but never penetrated."

"So what's his prognosis?" asked Jack.

"Excellent. Full recovery."

"How quickly?" asked Trina.

"We'll keep him here overnight for observation. He has a concussion and should take it easy for a couple of days. The wound needs to be covered for about a week to prevent infection."

"That's it?" said Cy.

"Some scarring. The bullet ripped a two-inch cornrow down his scalp. I used as many subcutaneous stitches as possible to minimize the railroad-track effect, but it won't be perfect. For most guys, that wouldn't be an issue. But your nephew wears his hair very short, so I can refer him to a plastic surgeon to help improve the looks of it."

"Is he awake?" said Jack.

"Should be coming around any minute. We used a mild anesthesia."

"Can we see him?"

"Sure. Normally it's one visitor at a time in recovery, but at this hour you've practically got the place to yourself. Go for it."

They thanked him and found Theo behind a beige privacy curtain in the recovery room.

The bed was adjusted to put him in a seated position, and Theo was noisily sucking down the last few drops of a juice box. The right side of his head was covered with bandages, but otherwise he looked pretty good.

Trina planted a kiss on his lips before he could say anything. She checked out the bandage as she pulled away. "Does it hurt?"

"Not as much as a Prince Albert."

She smiled. "How would *you* know, wimp?"

Cy went around the bed and congratulated him on dodging another bullet—literally. Jack said, "How do you feel, big guy?"

"Like I been drinking cheap tequila all night."

Jack knew that feeling—thanks to Theo. "Police are downstairs," said Jack. "I'm sure they'll want to know if you got a good look at the shooter."

"Not really. Maybe I'll remember more when my head stops throbbing." His gaze shifted to his uncle. "Did you see 'em?"

"Uh-uh," said Cy. "It's like I told the cops. Looked like a drive-by shooting to me. Random, you know? But Jack's got a different take. One that makes pretty good sense to me."

"You know somethin' I don't?" said Theo.

Jack went to the tray table and poured Theo some water. "It's just a matter of deduction. But you have to accept that Isaac was telling you the truth."

"About what?"

"That he knew who killed your mother."

Theo drank his water. "Okay. Let's assume he had some source in prison and found out who killed her. So what?"

"Then you have to assume that the killer didn't want Isaac telling anybody who killed her."

"Logical," said Theo. "So whoever killed my mother also killed Isaac."

"I'm thinking yes."

"And now he wants to kill me."

"Right. Because he thinks Isaac told you who killed her."

"Why would he think that?" said Theo.

"Because he's the guy who tapped your telephone. He heard Isaac call and tell you that he'd give you that information if you helped him beat the manhunt."

Theo grimaced, as if the chain of deduction were suddenly broken. "Some loser killed my momma over twenty years ago. How is that guy suddenly smart enough to tap my telephone right before Isaac calls and tells me he can name the killer?"

Trina groaned, as if perturbed by the microanalysis. "Back up a second. You geniuses are missing the big picture here."

"What's that, baby?"

Trina reached inside his gown and plucked several chest hairs, which made Theo yelp. "Stop calling me *baby*," she said.

"Okay, okay."

The look of concern returned to Trina's face. "What I was trying to say is that maybe Jack's right. This shooting probably wasn't random, which creates one huge problem. Whoever killed Isaac—and whoever *tried* to kill you—won't be very happy to hear that all you ended up with is a concussion and a few stitches."

"You got a point there, ba—"

Her glare killed the pet name. Theo crossed his arms to prevent further chest-hair removal.

Jack said, "Trina's right. He'll be back to finish the job."

Uncle Cy massaged his temples, as if he didn't like the information his brain was processing. "What do we do about this?"

Jack said, "That's something Theo and I need to discuss in private, attorney to client."

Trina looked miffed, but Jack knew that Uncle Cy was the one Theo would really want kept in the loop.

"Why can't they be part of this?" said Theo.

"Lots of reasons," said Jack.

"Give me one," said Trina.

"All right. Because the answer, I think, involves FBI Agent Andie Henning."

Theo looked at his uncle, then at Trina, as if to assure them that Jack knew whereof he spoke. "That's a pretty good reason."

"None better," said Jack.

Chapter 20

Jack met Andie in the hospital's coffee shop. He'd dialed her cell expecting to leave a voice mail message. To his surprise, she answered. To his even greater surprise, she was already in the Jackson Memorial complex.

The coffee shop was nearly empty. Most of the chairs were turned up on tables as the janitor mopped the floor. The only other occupied table was across the room, where a sleepy intern was eating either dinner or breakfast, depending on what time of day she was trying to convince her body it was.

"How's Theo?" Andie asked, stirring a pink

pack of sweetener into her decaffeinated coffee.

Jack told her the good news. "How's the young woman Reems abducted?"

"Fine."

Jack waited for her to elaborate, but one-word answers from Andie usually stood by their lonesome or, at best, were followed by the official "I'm not at liberty to discuss" mumbo jumbo. It was one of the things about Andie that really drove him crazy. That, and . . . *Stop. Focus, Swyteck.*

Andie stopped stirring and, for a moment, put the business expression on hold. "How are *you* doing?"

Jack hadn't given that much thought, and the question forced him to stop and consider it. "It's been crazy, but Theo and I have survived worse."

"You've always been there for him."

"And him for me."

"Old friends are the best friends. You're lucky to have that."

Jack didn't know how to respond—one more pro-Theo plug from Andie, yet another refutation of the basis for his decision to stop dating her.

"What is it you wanted to talk about?" she said.

"I want to deal with you."

"Me?"

"Well, the FBI, actually. And you, specifically, because you're heading a task force that is supposed to find out how Isaac Reems escaped from prison."

Her business face was now firmly back in place. "Are you saying that Theo has information about that?"

"No. He told the police everything he knew the first time, after Isaac came to see him at Sparky's. What I'm offering up now is something we figured out afterward."

"Do you know who helped Reems plan his escape?"

"We think it's the same person who killed Theo's mother in 1986."

"And who is that?"

"Don't know. The crime was never solved."

"Why do you think there's a connection?"

"Not so fast. I said I came here to deal, not to do my singing-canary impersonation."

"Shouldn't you be talking to a prosecutor about that?"

"Prosecutor? For what? Is Theo being targeted for something?"

She paused. Then it came, one of those all-too-familiar sighs. "I'm not at liberty to discuss—"

"Yeah, yeah, blah, blah, blah. Come on. Theo was about an inch away from going facedown on the sidewalk with a bullet in his brain."

"All I can tell you is that the waitress who was abducted by Reems told me something tonight that isn't especially helpful to Theo."

"What does that mean?"

"It means that I'm not at liberty—"

"Will you cut that out already?"

Andie swallowed more coffee. "Take my advice. Talk to the prosecutor."

Jack locked eyes with her, gazing over the rim of his own cup. "A prosecutor won't give Theo the protection he needs," he said.

"Protection from what?"

"The person who killed Isaac."

She blinked. It was hardly noticeable, but Jack seemed to be developing a sixth sense when it came to reading Andie's body language—another one of those strange connections he felt toward this woman. Even more unsettling, Jack's read was that Theo was a likely suspect in Isaac's slaying.

Jack added, "He's the same guy who tried to kill Theo tonight."

She lowered her cup, seeming to collect her thoughts. "I'm open to that possibility."

"You should be. By the way, did your fingerprint analysis turn up anything on the listening device we found on Theo's phone line?"

"Nothing."

"I'm not surprised. In fact, an installer smart enough not to leave prints fits perfectly with my theory. Reems finds out who killed Theo's mother. He extorts the killer into helping him escape. The killer—"

"Wait a second. How does Reems find that out? And how does a prisoner on the inside extort a killer on the outside?"

"I don't know yet," said Jack. "But this is the point I'm making. The killer knows better than to trust the likes of Isaac Reems. In fact, Isaac told Theo—and Theo told the police—that this outside helper didn't deliver the car, the cash, and all the other stuff that was supposed to be waiting for Reems when he escaped. It's possible that somebody stole that stuff before Reems could get to it, but I think it's more likely that the killer played along with the extortion only to a point."

"And then he had second thoughts?"

"I think he had second thoughts all along. So he planned ahead. The only person on the outside who knew exactly when the escape would occur was the man Isaac was extorting. He tapped Theo's phone line right before it was supposed to go down. That way, he'd know immediately if Reems called to tell his old friend who killed his mother."

Andie seemed intrigued. Or suspicious. "Did Reems in fact make that call to Theo?"

"Obviously not. Or we'd know who the killer is."

"Did Reems make any calls at all to Theo?"

This was more than Jack was ready to confirm. "What if he did?"

"Well, I suppose there could be a few possibilities."

Jack studied her expression. "Such as?"

"He could have told Theo to meet him in the alley behind the old Homeboy's."

Her insights were impressive. Then again, maybe it tied in with what the abducted waitress had told Andie. "Could have," said Jack.

"And Theo could have packed his pistol and gone."

"Except that he was at his girlfriend's house. Which leaves only one other possibility. Whoever tapped Theo's phone heard Reems say where he was hiding. He went there, and he killed him."

"Because he feared that Reems was going to tell Theo who killed his mother," she said.

"Glad to see you're with me."

"I follow you. That doesn't mean I'm with you."

"Something you disagree with?"

"I just need to give you fair warning. It's my job to consider more than one possibility."

"Understood. But you have to ask yourself, would Theo have called the cops after Isaac came to see him if he was planning to gun him down himself?"

"That's a fair point. But people do stupid things. They have a change of heart."

"Then you should jump at the chance to protect Theo. If my theory is correct, Theo is the live bait that helps you catch a two-time killer who helped Reems escape from prison. If I'm wrong, or just plain bluffing, what better way is there to keep your eye on Theo the suspect?"

She fell silent, thinking. Finally, she said, "I need a little time to sell that to the bureau."

"But you'll try?"

"I'll try."

"I have your word on that?"

"You have my word."

She raised her cup, and Jack clanked his against it in a silent toast. His coffee spilled on impact, and as they fumbled for napkins to mop it up, Jack got the uneasy feeling that this was a metaphor.

Hard to imagine an alliance with Andie that was anything but rocky.

Chapter 21

Uncle Cy didn't like it one bit.

Just six hours after his release from the hospital, Theo was already trying to sweep his uncle out of the house. "I'm fine," Theo kept telling him. "Take a walk, see a friend, rent some porn. Just go."

The doctors had told Cy the same thing—not the part about the porn, but the fact that Theo was "fine." They'd kept him overnight for observation, liked what they saw, and discharged him with a flesh-tone bandage on his head and a prescription for painkillers. Cy pushed him out of the hospital in a wheelchair—it was hospital policy, undoubtedly implemented after a patient tripped over his own feet and sued the world for failing to remind him that it was left foot, right foot, left foot, right foot—and from then on, Theo was Mr. Independence. "Cy, go away" seemed to be Theo's message. He was a good nephew. He was a really lousy patient.

The phone rang. "I'll get it," Cy shouted.

"No, you won't!" Theo fired back. He launched himself from the couch, muted the television, and picked up before Cy could count another ring.

The old man watched from across the room. It was a short conversation. Cy couldn't hear what his nephew was saying, but Theo had a serious expression on his face. As he hung up, Theo brought his hand to his head, right to the oversized bandage that covered his stitches, and grimaced in pain. It wasn't clear if Theo had touched them because they hurt or if they hurt because he'd touched them.

"Something wrong at the bar?" said Cy.

"No, that was—" He stopped, apparently unwilling to say. "I'm sure everything's fine there."

"You look upset."

Theo was still deep in thought, not at all

focused on the conversation. He went to his computer desk and rifled through a drawer. "I'm not upset."

"You sound like you are."

He slammed the drawer in anger.

"What are you looking for?"

Theo ripped the hospital's plastic ID bracelet from his wrist.

"Scissors are in the kitchen drawer," said Cy.

Theo drew a breath, composing himself. "It ain't the bar. But now that you bring it up, it'd be cool if you popped down to Sparky's to see how Trina's doing. No one in his right mind screws off in front of her, but another set of eyes on those morons can't hurt."

"So that wasn't Trina on the phone?"

"It—it doesn't matter who that was. Can you just go?"

Theo's tone worried him, but there was no denying the anxiety of barely escaping a gunshot to the head—not to mention the added stress of knowing that the killer was probably still gunning for you. "Sure, I can check on things," Cy said. "You want anything while I'm out?"

"No."

"Pizza? Ice cream?"

"No. Really. Nothin'."

Cy noted the tone of voice again. Theo didn't appear angry. It was more a sense of urgency. He was suddenly in a major hurry to get his uncle out the door.

Cy patted his pants pockets. Empty. "You got the car keys?"

"No, you do."

"You drove home from the hospital, not me."

"Yeah, but—"

There was a firm knock at the front door.

"Shit," said Theo.

"Who is it?" Cy called out.

"Go upstairs," said Theo, shuffling his uncle toward the staircase.

"Police," came the answer from outside the door.

Cy shot a look of concern at his nephew. "What's going on?"

"Just go upstairs, all right?"

He shook free from Theo's grip, went to the door, and opened it. Two uniformed police officers, one male and one female, were standing on the porch. Cy recognized them as City of Miami cops. He could see his own concern reflected in the tall guy's sunglasses. "What's this about?"

The male cop answered. "Is this the residence of Theodopolis Knight?"

"Yes. What's this—"

"Is Mr. Knight home now?"

"Yes, he is. But—"

"I'm right here," said Theo as he nudged his uncle aside. He stood face-to-face with the cop, who promptly reached for his handcuffs.

In an instant, the two officers crossed the threshold and had Theo facing the other way, hands behind his back. The lead cop spoke as he cuffed him. "Theodopolis Knight, you're under arrest. You have the right to remain silent, you have the right . . ."

Cy tried to listen as they read Theo his rights, but the voices faded into a whirl of confusion.

"Arrest?" said Cy. "For what?"

Theo said, "Don't say anything."

The cop patted Theo down and found the pistol in his pocket.

Cy said, "That's for protection. His lawyer told him—"

"I told you not to say anything!" Theo said.

The female cop placed the gun in an evidence bag.

The old man watched from the open door-way as Theo went peaceably with the two officers. They took him to the squad car and opened the rear passenger-side door. As he ducked into the backseat, Theo looked to-ward his uncle on the porch and said, "Just call Jack. He'll know what to do."

The cops buckled him in and closed the door. Cy felt like he should do something, but he was helpless.

In seconds, they were gone.

Chapter 22

Theo was arraigned from jail, his court appearance nothing more than a closed-circuit television transmission to the duty judge. Bail was set at $25,000. The charge was harboring a fugitive and a host of related offenses, including the aiding and abetting of Isaac Reems's escape.

Theo uttered just two words at the arraignment: "Not guilty." His lawyer didn't even ask the prosecutor to recommend release on his own recognizance, didn't urge the judge to set a lesser amount. But he did offer Theo some words of encouragement, and he meant them quite literally.

"Watch your back, buddy."

Theo didn't make bail.

It was 10:00 P.M., and Turner Guilford Knight Correctional Center was in lockdown for the night. Theo's mind was elsewhere as the guards escorted him to his cell.

The walk down the long corridor, iron bars on either side, triggered a wave of memories. Prison would always be a part of him, and not even the vindication of DNA testing could erase the fact that he'd lost four of his best years to Florida's death row. Sometimes that seemed like another lifetime. Right now, it felt like yesterday, and the worst of his checkered past was rising up in his throat like battery acid. He'd come within minutes of a gruesome death, saved only by an eleventh-hour stay of execution won by his lawyer from the Freedom Institute, a young idealist named Jack Swyteck. Theo recalled every step of the lonely, final journey from which most men never returned. He'd managed only two bites of his last meal, stone crabs and Key lime pie. He'd refused God's forgiveness, and he would never forget the prison chaplain's frustration at his continued protestations of innocence. He could still smell the tobacco-stained

hand of the prison barber who shaved his
head and ankles so that the electrodes
would connect properly at both ends, ensur-
ing the smooth and efficient passage of ki-
lovolts that would sear his skin, boil his
blood, and snuff out his life. In the Holly-
wood portrayal, a stoic corrections officer
calls out, "Dead man walking." In Florida,
however, it was "Dead man coming," and it
was the refrain of fellow inmates, not prison
personnel, as the condemned man—hands
and feet shackled, dressed in pants and an
orange T-shirt, surrounded by guards—
made his way to the electric chair.

A catcall from one of the inmates caught
Theo's attention. The whistler was deep
within one of the blackened cells, unidentifi-
able. A newbie might have been rattled—the
thought of a horny jailbird liking the looks of
his ass—but Theo was unfazed, keeping his
eyes forward.

You just try it, pretty boy.

They stopped at the third cell from the
end. A black man lay on the lower bunk of a
shadowy, two-man cell. The top bunk was
empty.

The guard rattled the bars with his nightstick. The sweeping beam of his flashlight hit

the sleeping inmate in the eyes. "Up against the far wall," he said.

The inmate rolled out of the bunk and did as he was told. The lead guard radioed the control booth. A buzzer sounded. The cell door slid open automatically.

"It's lights out," the guard told Theo. "Unpack your bag and fill your locker in the morning."

Theo entered the cell in silence. He turned completely around to face the guards, but it wasn't out of respect to authority. It was prison talk between cell mates, Theo's way of saying that he wasn't afraid to show his back to this chump. The electronic buzzer sounded. The door slid closed, the clank of metal echoing off walls and floors of steel and unfinished concrete.

"Welcome to TGK," the guard said. He and the other guard walked away, their footfalls piercing the eerie quiet of prison after lockdown.

Theo turned to face his cell mate. The whites of their eyes met in the darkness from opposite ends of a cell that measured seven feet wide and twelve feet deep. It was bigger than those on death row, but then again, Theo had lived there alone.

"What's your name?" the man asked.

Theo didn't answer. In prison, you didn't give up anything if you didn't need something in return. Theo already knew the man's name: Ricky Baldwin. He knew his prison nickname: Charger. He knew his rap: assault and battery. His victim was a prostitute. Most everyone on the second floor was incarcerated for some kind of sex-related crime. They found a home in TGK, a county-run facility, because they were awaiting trial in Miami or because their lawyer had cut a deal with the state attorney for less than one year of jail time. Most of these guys, however, belonged in Florida State Prison serving much longer sentences. Guys like Ricky Baldwin, aka Charger. And Isaac Reems.

Charger started toward his bunk.

"You're up top," said Theo.

Charger stopped and slowly turned his head, giving Theo plenty of attitude. "Say what, dude?"

Theo gave it right back to him, his most intimidating look. "You're upstairs. That's my bunk."

Charger grumbled and started toward the lower bunk. Quick as lightning, Theo cut him off and grabbed him by the wrist. "Get away from my bunk," Theo hissed, "or I'm gonna end up back on death row."

Charger froze. Maybe it was Theo's tone of voice. Maybe it was the menacing look in his eyes. Or it could have been the way Theo's huge hand fit so easily around Charger's wrist, a strong grip that conveyed his ability to snap a man's bones like brittle twigs. Whatever it was, Theo could feel his strategy working. Nothing short of a shank could have made him back down, because he knew this was the defining moment between him and his cell mate.

The stare-down lasted less than a minute. Then Charger flinched. Theo knew he would. That was the thing about these punks. Sure, Charger was "man enough" to slug a prostitute while her face was buried between his legs. Isaac had even had the balls to sneak through a sleeping woman's bedroom window. But mano a mano, they always backed down from the likes of Theo Knight.

Charger stepped away. Theo took the clean pillow from the top bunk and tossed the used one onto the floor. Charger paused for just a second, as if debating whether to stand up for himself and bitch about it. He didn't. He picked up the pillow and quietly climbed into the top bunk.

Theo slid into the lower bunk and allowed himself a deep, relaxing breath. Mission accomplished. But he still had a long way to go.

He clasped his hands behind his head and stared up at the underside of Charger's bunk. It was dark in the cell, but his eyes had adjusted, and just enough light from the corridor enabled him to see the traces of prison artwork on the metal underside of the top bunk. Some of it was in black marker, some in pencil. There was a calendar, of course. Someone with more talent than taste had sketched a NASCAR race car zooming toward a giant open vagina. There were also gang symbols. Theo recognized some of them. Panthers. Mongroles.

Grove Lords.

Under different circumstances, he might have found irony in the fact that he was in TGK, in Isaac Reems's old cell, in the bunk below Isaac's former cell mate. But there was no irony here. No coincidence.

Everything was going according to plan.

Theo lay in silence, eyes wide open. Sleep was a long way off, and he knew better than to close his eyes any longer than necessary. That was just the way it was in prison.

And prison was where he'd be—at least for a while.

THAT NIGHT, JACK CAUGHT up with Uncle Cy at Sparky's Tavern. The old man was running his nephew's bar during his incarceration, and the place was jumping. Fortunately, Theo's arrest didn't seem to hurt business. Another great thing about Miami: a criminal record was rarely a roadblock to success.

"What are you drinking?" said Cy, shouting over the crowd noise and music.

"Nothin', thanks," said Jack.

"Scotch 'n what?"

It was way too loud. Jack spoke up. "Can we talk in private a minute?"

Cy placed a couple of beers on the barmaid's tray, then with a jerk of his head signaled Jack to follow him into the back room.

Jack had promised Andie Henning that no one—absolutely no one—would know about their arrangement. Jack had also promised Theo that, if his uncle seemed to be taking it too hard, he would make an exception. One look at the old man's face and Jack could see it was destroying him. The worry lines seemed carved in wax. Uncle Cy, however, sounded less than impressed as Jack laid out the details.

"You're saying Theo knew the cops were coming for him?"

"That's why he was trying so hard to get you out of the house," said Jack.

"He should have gone down to the station and turned himself in. Why the big show of having him hauled off in handcuffs?"

"It had to be convincing. We didn't want this to have any markings of an arranged deal."

"Wait a minute," he said, shaking his head. "You asked the FBI for protection from whoever's trying to kill Theo, and the best deal you can cut with Agent Henning is to put my nephew in jail?"

"It was actually our idea," said Jack. "Theo can handle himself in prison. He's probably safer in there than out on the street."

"How about Tahiti? I hear it's nice and safe there, too. And they only use lotion to keep the sun off."

"Running is not the answer."

"And prison is?"

"Not exactly. But it's where we think Theo can *find* the answer."

"Answer to what?"

Jack leaned against Theo's desk, half seated, half standing. "We all suspect there's a chain here. Whoever killed Theo's mother killed Isaac, and then he also tried to kill Theo."

"That's the theory."

"Here's the hole in it," Jack said. "If the guy who killed Theo's mother was so sure that Isaac would reveal his identity even if he bowed to Isaac's extortion demands, why didn't he just have Isaac killed on the inside? Why would he help him escape and then kill him on the outside?"

Uncle Cy considered it, but the best he could do was acknowledge that it was a good question.

Jack said, "Here's the best answer Theo and I could come up with. Any good extortion plan has a safety valve—someone who blows the lid off the secret if the extortionist ends up dead."

"But that's exactly what happened," said Cy. "Reems got shot and killed. Why isn't the safety valve going public?"

"If Reems ends up dead in prison with no help on the escape, the safety valve knows it was a hit. But if the killer helps him escape and then several days later there's a shooting behind the old Homeboy's—well, that's not so clear. Could have been a robbery or just Isaac's bad luck. Theo could have shot him. Cops could have wasted him and made it look like somebody else did it. There are countless possibilities. Once Isaac is outside, no way can the safety valve say for sure that he was killed by the guy Isaac was extorting."

"But then who's the safety valve?"

Jack smiled a little, pleased that Cy seemed to think this made sense. "A safety valve has to be someone the extortionist trusts. If Isaac had someone like that on the outside, he would have run to him for help when his car and cash weren't waiting for him at the convenience store on the night he escaped. He wouldn't have called on Theo."

"So . . . he must be inside."

"Inside TGK," said Jack.

It was as if the proverbial lightbulb had blinked on. Inside TGK was exactly where Theo needed to go.

"How long is he in for?"

"As long as it takes," said Jack.

"Or until it ain't safe in there no more."

"Yeah," said Jack, his expression turning serious. "Whichever comes first."

Chapter 23

Six-thirty A.M. Theo was a half hour away from his first prison breakfast in years, and the harsh lights brightened the entire cell block.

He hadn't slept well; he was wide awake for the 2:00 A.M. head count. The count before that had been between 9:00 and 10:00 P.M., prior to his arrival. Quite a long gap, which he assumed Isaac Reems had noted in the timing of his escape. Theo wasn't sure when his mind stopped racing, and he finally dozed off, but the 4:00 A.M. count had definitely roused him. The mattress was thin, the pillow was lumpy, and the coarse blanket smelled of a detergent strong enough to kill every germ known to medical science. Theo never really fell back to sleep.

Prison life was going to be an even bigger readjustment than he'd figured.

He sat up, swung his legs over the edge of the bunk, and planted his feet on the bare concrete floor. "Dude, whattaya think you're doin'?" he said.

Charger froze. He was standing at the small metal sink, washing his face. He glanced over his shoulder toward his new cell mate. Theo's chilling glare alone was enough to make him realize that there was a new morning protocol and that Charger had broken it. Charger stepped away from the sink, face dripping wet, and made room for Theo.

"Not too smart, are you?" said Theo, as he bumped him farther to one side. Theo didn't enjoy it, but abusing his cell mate was all part of the act. He needed Charger spreading the word throughout TGK that this new guy was a badass.

The noise level within the cell block rose steadily, like one collective stomach growl. At 7:00 A.M. the buzzer sounded, the place fell quiet, and the inmates came to the bars, standing in pairs behind locked cell doors. A team of guards passed from one end to the other and counted heads. The cell-house sergeant signaled to the control booth, another buzzer sounded, and forty cell doors slid open simultaneously. The inmates stepped out into the block to form two lines, one on each side of the corridor. Theo tried not to make his curiosity too obvious as he checked out his new neighbors. Even if he hadn't known that the second floor was mostly sex offenders, Theo probably could have guessed what each guy was in for, just by looking at him. The young Hispanic with jet black hair and a movie-star profile: roofies and date rape. The scrawny white guy across from him: jerking off in school zones. The black guy with arms like an NFL linebacker and a missing right earlobe: beats his wife or girlfriend, or both. Jail was a veritable warehouse of broken lives and useless parts. If Theo looked hard enough, he probably could have spotted one or two old Grove Lords. Maybe Isaac had found them, too.

Theo wondered if his search for the safety valve could possibly be that easy.

"Single file, A block first," the cell-house sergeant announced.

The line was long and Theo was near the

rear, so he butted ahead to get closer to an inmate from two cells down, a brotha' who reminded Theo of his older brother Tatum—someone who looked like a player. He had the body of a weight lifter, the hands of a prize-fighter, and the eyes of a sniper. He was still pulling on his undershirt, half undressed, his briefly exposed back covered with tattoos.

"Hope you like slop," he told Theo, speaking under his breath as he buttoned his shirt.

Theo offered a slow nod—not to express his agreement, just his way of saying it was cool for him to speak without Theo speaking first.

"Yeah, the food really sucks," added Charger. He'd ridden on Theo's coattails to cut ahead in the line.

"Shut up, weasel," said Theo.

Theo was part of the main line, the general prison population, which entered the cafeteria just as the "short line" was leaving through another exit. The short line ate separately—breakfast, lunch, and dinner. It was mostly the kitchen crew, but it also included inmates in protective custody who were isolated for their own safety.

"Snitches," said the big guy, again speaking only to Theo.

The line moved steadily but slowly. Theo grabbed a tray and took everything they offered: toast, diluted orange juice, something that resembled watery scrambled eggs, a glob of oatmeal that stuck together like mastic, sausage patties that could have doubled as hockey pucks.

"Over here," someone said.

Theo turned and saw the Tatum look-alike at the end of the second table, sitting by himself. It was unofficial reserved seating, by invitation only. Theo sat directly across from him but said nothing. He just started eating.

"New?" the guy said.

Theo salted his eggs. "Only to this place."

"Done time?"

"FSP. Death row."

He seemed duly impressed. "How'd you beat that?"

"Good lawyer." It wasn't a lie, his innocence notwithstanding.

"Cool. Maybe I can use him."

"Only one problem," said Theo.

"What?"

"He doesn't defend punks."

He worked a spoon through his fingers like a miniature baton, shooting Theo an angry glare that would have reduced most inmates to gelatin. Theo shot one right back, then smiled. "Gotcha, dude."

It took a moment, but finally he returned the smile—albeit a thin one. A toothy grin wasn't part of prison culture, unless you were a catcher, and this guy didn't roll over on anybody's bunk.

"Moses," he said, extending his hand.

"Theo," he said, shaking prison style.

Charger walked by with his tray in hand. Theo and Moses gave him a collective look that said, "Beat it." He moved on to the next table.

"What you in here for?" said Moses.

"The food."

Another little smile. "Me too," said Moses, and then he stuffed his mouth with the world's lousiest oatmeal.

They invited no one to join them, so they had their own end of the table for the entire breakfast. It was mostly small talk, guarded but mutually respectful, a confirmation that they agreed on certain basic tenets that would ensure their peaceful coexistence: Miami's Duane Wade (not Lebron James) was the best player to go in the famous first round of the 2003 NBA draft; Kobe Bryant never would have made it in prison; and anybody who messes with you, messes with me—and then wishes that he hadn't.

Theo was back in his cell by eight o'clock. Charger had voluntary work duty and wouldn't return until eleven o'clock. Theo had yet to be assigned a job, so he had the cell to himself until lunchtime. He lay on his bunk, thinking. Hooking up with Moses was a stroke of luck. He was definitely an operator, a good contact, the kind of guy who would have latched onto an Isaac Reems. Theo could befriend him on many levels, not the least of which was the fact that Theo had distinguished himself as the Clarence Darrow of jailhouse lawyers on death row, an expert on everything from writs of habeas corpus to a prisoner's fundamental right to chew gum. But Theo knew he had to be careful. Ask too many questions too soon around an operator like Moses and you could end up on the wrong side of the prison balance of power.

Theo's eyelids were growing heavy. The restless night was catching up with him. In fact, he hadn't enjoyed a decent night's sleep since that bullet grazed his head. Weird, but the shooting was beginning to feel like a million years ago. The stitches, however, were a clear reminder of just how recent his latest brush with death had been. He no longer had to wear the bandage, and the scar added to his menacing persona.

He rolled onto his side, but something was poking him in the ribs. Shifting onto his back didn't help. That annoying lump in his bunk was unavoidable. He reached beneath the mattress and found the culprit. It was a tube. Theo read the label. It was some kind of age-spot bleacher.

"No way," Theo said, his words coming like a reflex.

Theo amazed even himself with the knowledge he'd gained in prison, and some things he would never forget, even if he was among the lucky ones who'd managed to keep his pants on. Age-spot bleachers packed a double whammy: an effective lubricant with the added benefit of making the unsexy brown skin that sprouted anal hairs more pink and attractive.

Isaac Reems—badass leader of the Grove Lords—had hisself a girlfriend?

Theo put the tube back under the mattress, still not believing it. No way. Charger had to be getting it from somebody else, not Isaac.

There was just *no way*.

Chapter 24

Jack was in trial all day. The state attorney was determined to make an example out of his client, a high-school valedictorian who should have gone on to MIT, except that he'd already made a cool million selling nonexistent jewelry and sports cars via Internet auctions—always under the stolen identity of other sellers, of course. Jack wasn't optimistic. Predicting jury verdicts was always dicey, but it appeared that this bunch had already left-clicked on Go_Directly_To_Jail.com.

Trial adjourned at 5:00 P.M., and Uncle Cy was waiting for him in the hallway outside the courtroom. Jack wasn't expecting him.

"What's up, old man?"

Cy kept pace as they walked toward the elevators. "You and me are going to Overtown."

"For what?" said Jack, as he hit the DOWN button.

The elevator doors opened, and they went inside. "For Theo," he said.

Ten minutes later they were in Jack's car, cruising past the Miami Arena, the original home of the Miami Heat and one of the more expensive failed attempts to revive Overtown. In theory, fans would shop and dine in the neighborhood before and after events. In reality, they came and left as quickly as possible. No offense to Uncle Cy, but with Theo having dodged a bullet to the head just last weekend, Jack was feeling a similar sense of urgency.

"Turn right here," said Cy.

It was the same street as the shooting. "You kidding me?"

"You think I'd kid about something like this?"

They parked at a metered space at the end of the street, directly in front of a yellow, three-story apartment building called The Landing. The façade was covered with gang graffiti and murals, though some of the markings had been painted over in a different shade of yellow. Security bars covered the first-floor windows.

The meter was broken. Jack put his coins away, said a silent good-bye to his car, just in case, and followed Cy into the building. There was a small vestibule and a sign on the elevator that said OUT OF ORDER. The sign looked as though it had been there since Uncle Cy was Theo's age. Another door led to the stairwell. It was locked. The old man checked the numbers on the mailboxes—there were only numbers, no names—and rang apartment number twenty-two. No one answered. He rang again, and the intercom crackled. It sounded like a woman's voice, but the tinny speaker made it unintelligible. Uncle Cy went to the security door and shouted, "Flo! It's me, Cyrus!"

A buzzer sounded, the lock disengaged, and Uncle Cy opened the door. Jack followed him upstairs to the second floor. The corridor was dimly lit; about half the bulbs were burned out. A brown water stain on the ceiling marked the halfway point of their journey, and the indoor-outdoor carpet smelled of mildew. They stopped at apartment 22.

The door opened a crack, and a woman peered out at them over the chain. Jack met her stare. She had a full face, and her hair was mostly gray. Probably not as old as Uncle Cy, but she could have just looked young for her age.

"Who's he?" she said.

"He's cool. Theo's best friend. His name's Jack."

"Looks like the FBI."

"That's because he just got out of court. He's a lawyer."

She examined Jack through a narrow glare and rendered her verdict. "All right." The door closed, the chain rattled, and then Flo was standing in the open doorway. Her face seemed to light up as Cy greeted her with a kiss on the cheek.

The men entered, Flo shut the door, and Cy poured on a few kind words about how she hadn't changed a bit. She seemed appreciative, even if he was a liar. Flo then led them to an old card table in the kitchenette, which was really just an extension of the living room, which accommodated a TV, a sofa, and a place to eat. On the other side of the table was the kitchen area, still technically part of the same room. Dinner was cooking on the stove, and the entire apartment smelled of boiled potatoes, despite the noisy fan in the window that drew fresh air from the outdoors.

Flo brought a large pitcher of cold lemonade and three tall glasses with ice. She poured for them. Cy assured Jack that it would be the best he'd ever tasted.

"You always did like my lemonade," said Flo.

"A woman of many talents," he said.

Jack tried his and seconded the compliment. "Cy tells me you two have known each other a long time."

"'Bout a hundred years," she said.

"You used to sing in the old jazz clubs, is that right?"

Cy cleared his throat, as if the subject was more complicated than the thumbnail he'd given Jack in the car ride over. "Flo and I were . . . used to . . ."

"Oh, for Pete's sake, Cyrus. Tell him the honest truth. You ruined my career."

"What?" he said.

She looked at Jack, her eyebrow arching. "We started datin', and honey, I didn't feel like singin' no blues."

They laughed, and Jack joined them,

though he wasn't sure that he was supposed to be part of the joke. Cy drank more lemonade, then turned serious.

"Is the boy here?" he asked.

"In the bedroom," said Flo.

"He tell you anything more?"

"Won't talk. But I know he seen something. Maybe you can get it out of him." She rose and called to the next room. "Tyrone!"

It took a minute, but finally the door opened. A thirteen-year-old boy shuffled toward the table, dressed in an oversized Miami Hurricanes football jersey.

Flo returned to her seat and sat the boy down next to her. "This here is Theo Knight's uncle," she told him. "And his friend. Say hello."

"Hey," he said weakly.

"Tyrone's my grandson," she told Jack.

Jack said, "How's it goin', Tyrone?"

"Nice suit. You a cop?"

"Nope."

"Lawyer?"

Jack sensed that it was better to leave that question unanswered. "Theo's my best friend. We met at FSP."

"*You* were in prison? What'd you do, shave strokes off your golf handicap?"

Flo swatted him on the arm. "Show some respect."

Cy gave Jack a little kick under the table, as if to say, "Let me try." "You ever heard of the Grove Lords, Tyrone?"

"'Course I heard of 'em. Ain't what they used to be, but they're still players."

"Both my nephews were Grove Lords back in the eighties. That's how Theo ended up on death row. Jack's the lawyer who got him off."

"Really?" he said, giving Jack another look. "Cool."

"No, it ain't cool," the old man said. "Theo wasted his best years in prison. His brother ended up dead. Their leader spent most of his life in jail and got shot and killed last week. And somebody just tried to kill Theo."

Tyrone didn't say anything.

Jack said, "We hear you might know something about that."

"You hear wrong."

"It happened right here on this street," said Uncle Cy. "Last Friday night."

Tyrone looked away, then back. "I ain't talkin' to no cops."

"We aren't the cops," said Jack.

"No, but if I tell you, then we gotta go downtown and tell it to the cops. You know it, I know it, and that's bullshit!" he said, rising.

"Siddown," said Flo. She had him by the wrist. Tyrone was a big kid and could have easily shaken off the old woman. That he kept his cool and sank back into his chair was a credit to her and the way she'd raised him.

Tyrone folded his arms tightly across his chest. "I ain't talking to the police."

"I know this is tough," said Jack.

"You don't know nothin'," the boy said. "They'll blow my head off. Gram's too."

Jack had seen this many times before—a reluctant witness, a good person caught in a bad spot. Interrogators had many ways of dealing with it. The skill was in choosing the right strategy, especially with kids.

"Let's try this," said Jack. "You don't have to tell me anything, okay? I'm just going to start talking. If I got it right, you just sit there. If I got it wrong, you say 'honky.'"

The kid almost smiled. *"Honky?"*

Cy laughed through a sip of lemonade, nearly spraying it. "'Honky' kind of went out with 'groovy.'"

"Hey, it's my game, okay?" said Jack.

The boy kept his arms folded, but Jack felt

as though he'd cut the tension, maybe even made a breakthrough.

"All right," said Tyrone, "start talking."

Jack glanced at Uncle Cy, who seemed okay with him taking the lead. "Your bedroom," said Jack. "I see it faces right out on the street. And I assume it's got a window."

Jack paused. Tyrone said nothing.

"You were in your room on Friday night. Alone."

More silence.

"Doing your homework."

"Honky."

"He was grounded," said Flo.

"Thanks," said Jack. "But let's keep this between me and Tyrone, okay?"

"Sorry," said Flo.

Jack said, "You were in your room Friday night. And I'm gonna say that about nine o'clock you heard a gunshot out on the street."

Tyrone didn't answer.

"And you looked out the window."

He shifted in his chair, but he said nothing.

"Then you looked over toward Second Avenue. There was a man down on the street. Another man running toward him."

Jack could see the boy swallow the lump in his throat. Tyrone was still in the game, but the tension had returned.

"A car was speeding away," said Jack. "You saw the car. It was red."

Tyrone lowered his eyes, but he didn't deny it.

"Now, you're really afraid of those guys in the red car. Because they're gangsters."

Still no denial.

"You got a look at them, and you recognized them."

"Honky."

The response almost made Jack laugh, but Tyrone's expression was deadly serious: Jack had it wrong.

"Okay," said Jack. "You recognized the car."

"Honky."

"You saw the car again, some other place, after the shooting."

"Honky."

Jack glanced at Cy, who simply shrugged. Jack pondered it, then said, "There was something about that red car. Something about it that told you it was gangsters."

Tyrone was silent.

Jack was definitely on the right track. "It was the wheels—"

"Honky."

"The bumpers or the paint job—"

"Honky, honky."

"The windows."

No reply.

Jack thought about it for a moment, trying to envision something distinctive about the windows on gang-mobiles he'd seen around Miami. "There was a gang symbol etched on the rear window."

More silence. *Bull's-eye.*

"Okay, good. Now, I don't want you to tell me anything, Tyrone. But sometimes I like to doodle when I'm talking to people. Maybe you do, too. Helps relieve the nerves, you know?" Jack took a pen and a small notepad from inside his suit jacket and slid them across the table. "So I'm going to have more of your grandmother's delicious lemonade, and if you want to doodle, you go right ahead."

Jack drank his lemonade. Tyrone stared at the pen and notepad on the table. Finally, he took them. Jack watched as he inked an image onto the pad, but Tyrone's hand covered most of it. He finished in a few seconds and slid the pad back to Jack. Jack didn't examine it. He didn't study it. He didn't want to do anything to make Tyrone nervous. He simply retrieved his pad and pen and tucked them into his coat pocket.

Tyrone let out a sigh of relief.

Flo patted the back of her grandson's hand. "You done good, Tyrone. You didn't tell nobody nothin'."

"No," said Jack. "Not a thing."

Chapter 25

Jack drove Uncle Cy home, and they were in complete agreement: they would do everything possible to keep Flo's grandson out of the investigation, but Jack needed to talk with Andie Henning. A phone call wouldn't do—not if Jack was going to share the boy's drawing with her. Just picking a meeting spot, however, presented real difficulties.

"Let's meet at—" Jack stopped himself, realizing that he was about to suggest the same coffeehouse they'd visited on their second date.

"How about—" Andie did the same thing, maybe even for the identical reason. Weird, thought Jack, the way their minds seemed to work alike sometimes.

Jack said, "There's a McDonald's on Bird Road."

"Perfect," she said.

"No, wait. I can do better than that. Meet me at the gas station on Seventeenth, right next to Casola's pizzeria."

"A gas station?"

"Trust me on this. You'll be pleasantly surprised."

She agreed, but after they hung up, he recalled that she really didn't like surprises, and as he merged into traffic, he wondered why he cared. Rene backlash, no doubt, brought on by the fact that he hadn't heard boo from her since she left Miami. *Oh, Jack, I can't stay more than a few days at a time because I'm afraid I might never leave. Oh Jack, I promise to call you as soon as my plane lands.*

Jack was still waiting for the phone to ring.

The minimart on Seventeenth Avenue was just beyond a part of I-95 that most drivers never saw: the end. It's unclear whether the geniuses who built the interstate simply ran out of cement or actually thought it was a great idea for a hundred thousand cars a day to come barreling down the final exit ramp at seventy miles per hour, straight into the proverbial parking lot that was U.S. 1. Either way, it was the perfect spot for a filling station, and one had graced this location— right alongside the busy highway and elevated Metrorail tracks—as long as Jack could remember. In a recent flash of inspiration, the owner had converted a back room into a small but lively restaurant that served good food and good wine at bargain prices. The décor was reminiscent of a French wine cellar, with long wooden tables and stools instead of chairs, and the wine selection was so good that even the Ritz Carlton's sommelier was a regular. You picked your wine directly from the floor-to-ceiling bins that lined the walls, and the food was served tapas style—appetizer-sized portions to be shared with friends. And on your way out, you could buy Lotto tickets and a pack of Twinkies for dessert. Beat that.

"I never knew this was here," said Andie.

"You like it?"

She surveyed the wall of wines and the waiters dressed in traditional attire. "Yeah, I do, actually. And for you it's perfect. Sparky's used to be a gas station. Your new favorite restaurant still is."

"What can I say? In a Miami-chic world where pretentiousness knows no bounds, a guy has to search pretty hard to find these little gems."

The waiter brought menus, and Jack found himself peering out over the top of his as Andie studied hers. Men often liked a certain type of woman, and if that was true of Jack, Andie had been a complete—albeit brief— break from type. Both Rene and his ex-wife were blondes. Andie's hair was blacker than black, like a midnight blue tuxedo, and her mixed ancestry made her attractive in ways that traditional beauties weren't.

"What do you want?" she said.

"Huh?" he said, averting his eyes.

"What are you ordering?"

"Ah," said Jack, relieved to know he hadn't been caught staring. He made some recommendations, but Andie wasn't very hungry, so he ordered churrasco steak tapas and a small serving of chipotle for them to share. Andie wanted a glass of pinot grigio, and Jack convinced her to share a bottle of Santa Marguerita, since he was buying and it was cheaper here than at the supermarket anyway. That she drank was important. Law enforcement types were always stressed at the end of their day, and he wanted her in a good mood, more receptive to his strategy on how to nail the punks who had shot at Theo.

"I assume you didn't invite me out here to get me drunk," she said.

"No. I have a witness to Theo's shooting."

"Terrific. When can I talk to him?"

"He doesn't want any part of law enforcement."

"Naturally," she said. "That's the problem with drive-by shootings. Witnesses tend to get scarce."

The waiter brought their wine and poured two glasses. When he was gone, Jack showed Andie the drawing that Tyrone had sketched for him and Uncle Cy. It was a menacing-looking knife in an upright position, handle at the top, tip pointing down, and blood dripping from the blade. "There can't be that many red cars with this symbol etched onto the back window."

She examined it while tasting her wine. "I know this gang. O-Town Posse. Started in Overtown about five years ago, but it's grown fast."

"What's with the knife symbol?"

"It's actually a KA-BAR—a military fighting knife made especially for close-combat killing. This is who they are: extremely violent, heavy drug traffickers who would kill you as soon as look at you. They're trying to align themselves with the big leagues—Folk Nation out of Chicago or Crips in L.A."

"So this is a good lead?"

She drank more wine. "Just because we have a red car with a recognizable gang symbol doesn't mean we can peg the shooter."

"Find the car and haul in the owner for questioning."

"I definitely will. But it's not easy to get someone to testify against a gang as ruthless as O-Town Posse, and the owner of this vehicle knows that. He won't crack just because I ask him tough questions."

The waiter brought their churrasco. It was done to perfection, medium rare, and the chimichurri sauce wasn't too oily. "What if I can get the witness to talk? Will you protect him?"

"Did he see the triggerman?"

"No."

Andie finished her wine. Jack poured her more. She said, "I can't sell the bureau on protecting a witness who doesn't know enough to get an arrest, let alone a conviction. I already have my hands full trying to justify protection for Theo."

"He's helping you figure out who helped Isaac Reems escape and who shot him. It's not like he's getting something for nothing."

"But we cut Theo's deal on the assumption that the same guy who shot Isaac Reems also tried to shoot Theo. The more we learn about Theo's shooting, the less it resembles Isaac's."

"You don't need the exact same MO for two shootings to be related."

"No, but now that we know Theo was shot by a gang, the state attorney is going to say, hey, maybe this had nothing to do with Reems. Maybe it was even random. Because the Reems case is looking more and more like a professional hit."

"Gangs do hits," said Jack. "And if somebody wanted to eliminate both Isaac and Theo, what better way to confuse the investigators than to make one of the killings look like a drive-by shooting by a gang like O-Town Posse?"

"But all we have is a theory. *Your* theory. Honestly, it's not entirely adding up for me."

"Why not?"

"There are a zillion holes."

"A zillion?"

"Yes."

"You counted them?"

"Stop being such a literal lawyer. I meant there are a lot."

"Let's hear them."

"I can't name them all."

"You can't name any."

"I can name plenty."

"Plenty? Help me with my math. Is that more or less than a zillion?"

Jack didn't enjoy getting under her skin, but when she wore her FBI hat, that was the only way to make her talk.

She swallowed more wine. "All right, explain this to me. Every arm of law enforcement was out looking for Isaac Reems and couldn't find him. But the killer was able to hone right in on him. I'm curious as to how that works under your theory. How did the shooter know to go to the restaurant that used to be Homeboy's? How did he know exactly when Isaac Reems was going to be there? How did he get such a clear shot at Isaac? Why did Isaac call out Theo's name before he was shot? Why would—"

"What did you just say?"

Andie froze. She'd obviously shared something she shouldn't have. "Forget what I said."

"No way."

"Jack, be professional about this."

"I am being professional. I heard what I heard."

"All right, fine. Now you understand why I'm having difficulty buying your version of events."

He also understood that the only way to change her views was to tell her about Isaac's phone calls to Theo. Only then would she understand how the killer—by tapping Theo's phone line—had heard Isaac tell Theo to meet him behind the old Homeboy's at 1:00 A.M. Problem was, those calls could also prove that *Theo* knew where Isaac was going to be.

"I could fill those holes for you," said Jack, "but I need to protect Theo from any possibility of being charged with Isaac's murder."

"What are you asking me to do?"

"Look at the evidence I'm willing to share with no one else but you. See if it convinces you that whoever killed Theo's mother also killed Isaac—and then tried to kill Theo."

"What if it doesn't convince me?"

"I'll forget that you slipped and told me that Reems called out Theo's name before he was shot. And then you'll show me that you can keep your word."

"Meaning what?"

"Somewhere down the line, if the state attorney ends up charging Theo with Isaac Reems's murder, you can't share this evidence with the prosecution."

"You want me to get amnesia?"

"I want you to make a deal, and I want you to stick to it."

She shifted in her seat, her posture more relaxed, and took another drink of wine. "Let me ask you something. I'm curious. What if we were dating?"

Jack coughed. "What?"

"Assume you hadn't decided that I was anti-Theo and we were now several months into a real relationship. Say I had a slip of the tongue and confidential information about a case popped out of my mouth. Would you be busting my chops like this?"

Jack considered it. "I don't know. That's very hypothetical."

"Very," she said.

"Hypotheticals always make me nervous."

She leaned closer, elbows on the table. "No, Jack. It's *reality* that makes you nervous."

Their eyes met, and her gaze was so penetrating that she seemed to be searching inside him for his response. He had none.

"So, do we have a deal?" he said.

She rose slowly, confidently, his concession of the point having apparently granted her satisfaction—at least for the moment. "I'll think about it. And then maybe I'll give you a call."

She turned and exited through the minimart. Jack drank his wine and watched as he let reality walk away from him. Again.

Chapter 26

Theo needed to buy a guard.

It was a pretty safe bet that an insider had helped Isaac Reems escape. Somebody—namely, a guard—had looked the other way when Isaac climbed out of a second-story window and lowered himself to the yard with a rope made from bedsheets. Part of Theo's "protection" arrangement with Andie Henning and the FBI was to work undercover and find the insider. Theo would honor the deal, but finding a corrupt corrections officer wasn't his main objective. He was more interested in finding out who had killed his mother, who had put a bullet in Isaac's head, and—most important—who had taken a shot at him. He'd be that much closer to answering those questions if he could figure out who had bribed the guard to spring Isaac loose. To do that, he first needed to learn which guards were for sale.

"Your buddy Isaac didn't get too far, did he?"

Theo was alone in his cell when he heard the guard's voice. He turned and saw Mac-Donald standing in the open doorway. They called him Old MacDonald, because he was the youngest guard on the cell block. He'd been a high-school football star, and he still carried himself with the cockiness of a teen-age jock. He was showing signs of going soft around the middle, but his arms and shoulders were enormous. Save for the slight limp from a career-ending knee injury, he looked like he could have gone on to play college ball. Instead, he was a prison guard.

"Say what, dude?" said Theo.

MacDonald stepped inside, serious attitude in his swagger. He stopped about a foot away from Theo, getting right in his face. "None of this 'Say-what-dude' disrespect. It's 'Excuse me, sir.'"

Theo was expressionless. "Say what, dude?"

The stare-down lasted a moment longer, and then MacDonald backed away. He checked the stack of magazines on Theo's bunk, the photograph of Trina taped to the wall. "Who's this?"

In prison, personal information was power, and Theo knew better than to give it out freely. "My grandmother."

"Pretty hot granny."

"She takes vitamins."

"Quite the wiseguy, huh? Maybe I'll stick you in a cell with a real wiseguy. See how you like sucking Italian dick."

"There ain't no Mafia in here."

"How do you know, chump?"

Theo couldn't tell him that he knew more about his fellow inmates than the guards did. Only Andie and her boss at the FBI, the state attorney, the director of the Department of Corrections, and the TGK warden were privy to the special arrangement that had gotten him arrested on sham charges and landed him in Isaac's old bunk pending a trial that would never happen. To everyone else, he was just a regular inmate.

"'Cause I don't smell any garlic."

MacDonald smiled insincerely, then got his ugly face right up in Theo's. "Listen to me, boy. I know Reems was your old buddy. I know you're in here because you helped him after he got on the outside."

"Me and my lawyer say I didn't do it."

He threw a forearm to Theo's throat and pushed him back against the wall. "I don't care what you or your lawyer says. Nobody cares."

Theo wanted to clock him, but he couldn't do his job from solitary confinement.

MacDonald said, "Do you think I enjoy coming to work every day and babysitting scum like you? I had a good record here. I was up for promotion. Then your friend Isaac busts out and makes us all look like Keystone cops. I'm pissed about that. You understand what I'm saying, Knight? I'm *pissed*," he said, thumping Theo's chest for emphasis.

The anger was all over MacDonald's face, but he didn't take that proverbial one step too many—he didn't say "I'm pissed, and I'm going to make you pay for it."

He ripped the photo of Trina off the wall, crumpled it into a ball, and threw it at Theo as he left.

Theo picked it up, flattened out the creases, and put it right back on the wall.

"MacDonald's an asshole," said Moses, as he entered Theo's cell.

Theo said, "You heard?"

"It ain't like I had my ear to the wall, dude. I'm just a couple cells away."

"It's cool," said Theo.

Moses leaned against the wall. "So, you and Isaac go back a ways?"

"Long, long ways," said Theo. "Before I was on death row."

"Isaac was cool in my book," said Moses.

"That so?"

"Yeah. It's a pretty short book, too."

"I'm sure he was honored."

Moses smiled, seeming to like Theo's sense of humor. He started out of the cell. "Walk with me."

"Where to?"

"I got a date. Come see."

Theo followed him out onto the cell block. Free time and recreation lasted until shower time at 8:00 P.M., so the block was abuzz with inmates who were watching television, playing dominoes, waiting in line to use the telephone, shooting the breeze, or just wandering around and trying to shake off the boredom. Theo followed Moses past the bank of telephones and up the stairwell that led to the laundry room and infirmary. Moses took a seat on the third step from the top and peered through the bars that covered the stairwell's only window.

"Right on time," he said. "Have a look."

Theo went to the window and sat one step below Moses. In the distance, beyond a nine-foot-high chain-link fence that encircled the yard, a woman with long brown hair stood beside a car that was parked on the shoulder of the road. She was wearing a long yellow raincoat, even though the sun was setting on a clear and warm evening, not a rain cloud in sight. She unbuttoned the coat, grabbed the lapels, swung open the left side, closed it, swung open the right side, closed it. She continued teasing in this fashion, and it was obvious even from a distance that she was naked underneath her coat, top and bottom, her tan lines highlighting the points of interest. She moved like an exotic dancer to spice things up, bending over and grabbing her ankles every now and then to tempt them with her ass. The show went on for several minutes before she spotted a vehicle approaching, jumped in her car, and drove off.

"Whoa," said Theo. "Who was that?"

"My grandmother," he said. "She takes vitamins."

They shared a little laugh and knocked fists together.

Theo didn't want to move too quickly on Moses, and he definitely didn't want to come across as too hungry for information about Isaac's escape. An indirect approach would test the waters. "Hey, man. How's a guy go about gettin' tits in here?"

He wasn't talking about what they'd just watched; "tits" was code for drugs in prison.

"What kind of tits you like?" said Moses.

"White tits. Fine white tits. Tits so fine and white you can breathe them up your nose, taste them in the back of your throat, and feel them go straight to your head."

"No problem," said Moses. "Just gotta know who to ask."

"I don't think I'll waste my time asking Mac-Donald."

"You don't go wasting your time on nobody."

"For tits, you mean?"

"For everything. You go through me."

"Thanks, dude. But I don't need you for everything. Just certain things."

"You're not listening to me, brotha'. For anything and everything. You go through *me*."

It wasn't an offer. It was an order.

"So, you got yourself the TGK exclusive?" said Theo.

"You learn quick."

Theo nodded. He could have pressed for specifics beyond drugs, but he sensed that he'd already pushed far enough for one sitting.

Moses rose and leaned against the stair rail, looking down at Theo from the higher step. "I like you, Knight. You and me can be cool. But don't even think about muscling in or going around me. 'Cause I'll beat the black right off you."

For the sake of his undercover mission, Theo forced himself not to respond in any way. He simply swallowed what he was feeling and let Moses walk down the stairs and return to the cell block, unharmed and alone.

Theo decided to stay put until his anger subsided. He looked out the window again, his gaze drifting toward the spot where Moses' dancer had been shaking her naked ass. That little display hadn't been about entertainment. It was Moses' way of telling the new guy that he had contacts to the outside.

Theo pondered that for a moment, and it occurred to him that he hadn't really focused on the woman's car—what man would have? But he seemed to recall that it had looked new, and a thought crossed his mind.

He wondered if it was the one Isaac was supposed to have gotten.

Chapter 27

I'm here to see Theo Knight," Jack told the guard at check-in, handing over his Florida bar card. "I'm his lawyer."

In another decade, Jack's mere announcement of his arrival would have triggered only dread and self-doubt. Back in the bad old days, he had been Theo's only hope. Jack's visits to death row were never without news to deliver, and it was rarely good. Had his client believed in killing the messenger, Jack would have been dead long ago. Things were different now, of course, not the least of which was the fact that TGK would routinely allow a face-to-face visit between an inmate and his lawyer, no glass partition and telephone—which meant that Theo could pop the messenger right in the snout if he didn't bring good news this time.

The guard searched Jack's briefcase and patted him down.

"Come with me," he said, and he led Jack to the meeting room.

Attorneys and inmates met in an area separate from the main visitation room, a more private place where they could communicate confidentially. The fluorescent lights overhead were so bright that Jack almost needed sunglasses. The floor was bare concrete, and the cinder-block walls were pale yellow with no windows. Jack was taken to a small Formica-topped table and left to sit and wait. Two minutes later, the door opened, and Theo entered.

"Hey, stranger," said Theo.

The guard said, "You got twenty minutes," and then left the room.

Theo went around the table, and Jack rose to return the bear hug.

"Did you bring the tequila?" said Theo.

"Don't even joke about that."

"Who's joking?"

Jack gave him a reproving look.

"What?" said Theo. "You think somebody's listening?"

"They're not supposed to, but I say you never know."

They each took a chair on opposite sides of the table.

"How's Cy? He hittin' on Trina yet?"

"He's doing fine. I did have that talk with him, though."

"So . . . he knows?"

"I couldn't keep him in the dark any longer. Your going back to jail was eating him up inside. Now he's cool with it. Understands what we're trying to do."

"I wish I could tell Trina," said Theo, and then his gaze drifted off to the middle distance. "Man, I really miss her."

"You do?"

"Yeah. Somethin' wrong with that?"

"No, I—I just don't think I've ever heard those words come out of your mouth before. At least not without some additional reference to the female anatomy."

He put a finger to his temple. "Jail messes with your mind, but it also puts things in perspective. Makes you stop taking things for granted. Maybe *you* should go to jail."

"Me? Why me?"

"I'm talking about women. Makes you appreciate what's real."

"You mean Rene?"

"No, dude. That ain't real. I mean Andie."

"What are you talking about?"

"I seen how you looked at her before, how you still light up at the sound of her name."

Jack averted his eyes, searching for a quick change of subject. "So, you and Trina been talking?"

Only a slight change, but thankfully Theo let him get away with it.

"She wanted to come and visit, but I don't think she's ready to see me like this. I call her every day."

"So do I," said Jack. "She's solid."

"You didn't tell her, did you?"

"About the arrangement? No way. Real undercover agents don't even tell their wives what they're doing, so I'm not about to tell your girlfriend. I try to reassure her, explain enough for her to know that the charges against you won't stick."

"Thanks," said Theo.

"No problem. I'm not just playing Cupid here. Don't forget, she's your alibi for Isaac's shooting."

"You telling me I still need one?"

"For now," said Jack. He told him about Andie's slip of the tongue—how Isaac shouted out Theo's name before the gunshot that killed him.

"How do they know that?" said Theo.

"A witness heard it. Presumably the waitress who was stuffed in the trunk."

Theo drew a breath, then let it out. "I don't doubt it happened. Makes sense Isaac would call out my name. He went there expecting me to come meet him. The phone messages prove that."

"I'm trying to figure out a way to convey that information to Andie without digging a deeper hole for ourselves."

"Meaning what?"

"It's a touchy situation. Isaac tells you he knows who killed your mother. Maybe you interpret that to mean that *he* killed her. You go and blow him away."

"I know he didn't kill her. My brother and me was riding with Isaac in his car the night we found my momma dead in the street."

"I'm thinking like a cop here," said Jack. "Isaac was a gang leader. Your mother was a prostitute and a drug addict. Maybe she owed somebody money. Maybe Isaac *ordered* her killing."

"That ain't what happened, dude."

"How do you know that?"

Theo leaned back in his chair, thinking. Jack could see from the expression on his face that it was a possibility he hadn't considered—one he couldn't readily dismiss. "I guess I don't know. Isaac and me never talked about it."

"And if the cops find out about Isaac's phone messages, they won't believe you never talked to him. They'll say you went there to meet him, he told you the truth, and you blew him away."

Theo rose and began to pace. "Bad enough somebody's trying to kill me. Now if I don't find the bastard, I could be tagged with Isaac's murder."

Jack let him pace a little more, blow off some steam. "That isn't going to happen," he said.

"Says who?"

"We'll find this guy."

"How can you be so sure?"

"There's some good news," said Jack. He told him about Flo's grandson—the gang symbol he'd spotted on the shooter's car and sketched out for Jack.

"Cops been able to locate the car yet?"

"They're looking for it. We don't have a tag number, so they can't just run it through DMV and haul in the owner. Andie tells me it may take some time."

"True," said Theo. "These gangs are smart. They do a drive-by, they might garage the car for weeks, until the heat cools down."

Jack just listened, adding it to the long list of things that he really didn't want to know how Theo knew.

"Can I see the boy's drawing?" said Theo.

"Absolutely." Jack opened his briefcase and removed his notepad. He laid the rough sketch of the bloody knife on the table, facing Theo. "It's a KA-BAR," he explained. "A military fighting knife for a local gang called—" Jack stopped himself. Theo looked as if he'd gone cold. "You okay, big guy?"

Theo didn't answer. He kept staring at the drawing, unable to tear his eyes away from it.

"Talk to me," said Jack. "Do you know this symbol?"

He lifted his gaze and looked Jack in the eye. "Last night," said Theo. "I'm positive I seen it last night."

"Where?"

"In the shower."

"What, like graffiti on the wall?"

"No," he said in a voice so low that it rumbled. "A tattoo. On some dude's back."

Chapter 28

A buzzer pulsated throughout TGK as the guards took Theo back to his cell. It was a sound that Theo hadn't heard since death row, but he knew what it meant even before the voice came over the PA system: "Lockdown. All prisoners to their cells immediately."

A chorus of groans filled the cell block, followed by the shuffling of inmates' feet, like a rag-tag army in defeat, and finally the slamming of cell doors.

Charger climbed up to the top bunk. Theo went to the lower one.

In ten minutes, the place was secure. The

PA system keyed for another announcement: "All prisoners to the bars. All clothing removed."

That triggered further grumbling, punctuated by sporadic shouts of profanity and some clanging on the iron bars in protest. But it was short-lived, quieted in part by a team of guards that swept through the cell block, nightsticks drawn in a show of force.

Theo rolled out of his bunk and began to remove his clothes. Charger jumped down and did the same. There was a protocol to undressing in the presence of your cell mate. It had to do with the eyes: you made damn sure they didn't roam.

"What are they looking for now?" said Charger.

"Hell if I know," said Theo.

But he did know. Theo was looking for the same thing: the O-Town Posse tattoo.

Theo was certain that he'd seen it on somebody's back in the shower, but he remembered nothing more about it. The showers were a steamy, crowded mass of naked male flesh. Looking around too much and making eye contact with the wrong dude was a good way to end up a "catcher"—a daily ticket to taking it up the ass. All Theo had been able to tell Jack was that he'd seen the tattoo, and it was on a black guy's back. Jack immediately passed the information along to Andie Henning, and before Theo returned to his cell the place was in lockdown. They were on a mission to find the guy with the tattoo.

Charger got naked first and walked to the bars. Theo was mindful of the eyes-front protocol, but his curiosity got the better of him. He stole a quick glance at his cell mate's back, checking for the tattoo.

"Like what you see?" said Charger.

For a moment it seemed that the dude had 360-degree vision. "I don't see nothin'."

"It's okay," said Charger, "you can check out my ass if you want to."

"Just shut your mouth."

For more than forty-five minutes they stood at the bars, unclothed and in silence, as a team of guards moved from one cell to the next. Time was something the inmates had plenty of, and the guards wasted it freely. It was a bizarre sight from Theo's perspective, staring out across the block at cell after cell of stark-naked men waiting at the bars. Black, white, and Hispanic. Young and old, fat and slim, many of them cut like bodybuilders, and nearly all of them bearing some kind of tattoo.

Charger spoke softly, his voice barely above a whisper. "Is it true you're in here for helping Isaac escape?"

Theo shook his head, as if losing patience. "You think I'm gonna tell you anything? What are you, an informant?"

"I'm pretty sure you know what I am," he said, his voice still low.

Theo tried to ignore it, but one question had been burning in his mind ever since he'd found the cream under the mattress. "How well did Isaac know what you are?"

Charger scoffed. "That homophobic jerk. He'd beat the living hell out of me just for thinking about him."

Deep down, Theo had figured as much: The bottom bunk and the cream had belonged to Charger, and his boyfriend was from another cell—not Isaac.

"But you seem nice," said Charger.

"Shut it, fool."

"Arms out," the guard told Theo.

Officer MacDonald was suddenly standing on the other side of the bars, and he treated Theo the same as any other inmate. At the same time, a second guard did a visual search of Charger. The beam of a high-powered flashlight swept the prisoners' front side first. The guards ordered them to turn left, right, and then all the way around, inspecting the entire body. Apparently the prison officials did not want the inmates to know that the search pertained only to the back. Or maybe they'd opted for a whole-body scan to account for the possibility that Theo was mistaken, and that he'd actually seen the tattoo on someone's arm or chest.

"Towels on," the guard said. "Showers in ten minutes."

The search team moved to the next cell. Theo wrapped himself in a white bath towel and waited at the locked cell door. Again, he looked across the cell block at the other in-mates—scores of caged sex offenders who had spent the last hour staring straight at his fully exposed equipment.

Shower time, he thought. *Oh joy of joys.*

FLORIDA STATE TROOPER MEL Stratton was twenty minutes from the end of his shift, and he was way below his normal pace for writ-ing speeding tickets. He couldn't figure it out. This was his favorite spot, just east of or-ange grove country, hiding beneath the Min-ute Maid Road overpass on Interstate 95. It was a clear night, no rain or fog to slow down traffic. Still, he'd issued far too few citations for a decent day's work.

It was downright embarrassing.

Suddenly, a car was racing toward him in the northbound passing lane. His radar gun chirped like a parakeet in orgasm. Ninety-five—no, ninety-seven—miles per hour. Didn't slow down one bit as it whizzed past him. Either the Jeff Gordon wannabe hadn't noticed the patrol car in the darkness, or he didn't care. Either way, he'd just made Trooper Stratton's night.

Hot damn!

He tripped the siren and lights. Gravel flew and the engine roared as his car gripped the shoulder and tore onto the interstate. In seconds, he was in hot pursuit, but the target only accelerated. Trooper Stratton radioed in the information, but he didn't have much to say. He had no license plate number, no make or model of the vehicle. It had been a blur in the night flying past him.

In two minutes he was closing in. The speeding car hit the exit at over ninety miles per hour, ran a red light at the bottom of the ramp, and continued down the highway. Trooper Stratton gave chase, lights and siren blaring. It was a lonely road, just a gas station on one side and a fast-food joint on the other. The car was three miles beyond any sign of civilization when it made a quick right turn down a dirt road.

The car had disappeared from sight, but barbed-wire fences lined the road and prevented escape. Trooper Stratton continued in pursuit, his car jumping down the bumpy dirt road like a dune buggy. Then he stopped short, skidding to a stop.

The car was dead ahead, parked—stuck in a rut or ravine, he presumed.

The trooper switched on his spotlight and keyed his public address system.

"Remain in your vehicle," he said.

He reached for his radio transmitter to call in the information, but the license plate was too dirty to read. All he could say for sure was that it was a Florida tag. And that it was a red car. With some kind of gang symbol etched onto the rear window.

It looked like an upright knife.

His pulse quickened; he'd seen the statewide BOLO for a red car with the O-Town Posse gang symbol.

The last sound he heard was a deafening pop and the shattering of glass, as the windshield exploded into a thousand pellets that showered his face and landed in his lap.

Some were clear as diamonds; others, red as rubies.

THE BUZZER SOUNDED. THE announcement over the PA system informed the entire prison population that the lockdown was over. The cell doors opened, and a stream of towel-wrapped inmates moved from their cells to the showers.

Theo exited his cell ahead of his cell mate and walked briskly across the cell block, trying to put some distance between himself and Charger. One man after another hung his towel on a hook and went straight into the community showers. Theo stayed by the sinks, still wrapped in his towel. The only mirror was the dome-shaped security mirror mounted on the ceiling. It was for the guards' benefit, not the inmates'. Theo used it as best he could to check his stitches. The doctor was supposed to remove all of them in a few days. There would definitely be a scar, especially if it was a prison doctor.

The shower area was directly behind him,

and the security mirror offered Theo a panoramic view. Lots of naked bodies, lots of tattoos. Surely the inmate-by-inmate search during lockdown had turned up the O-Town Posse tattoo, but Theo was a skeptic when it came to authority, particularly in prisons. Maybe the guards had missed it. Maybe they'd found one, quit the search, and missed a second or a third inmate with the same tattoo. Or maybe a cool bribe had persuaded some guard to overlook it altogether. Theo couldn't trust corrections officers—not when it appeared that at least one of them had helped Isaac Reems escape. He had to check for himself.

Theo remained under the dome mirror, pretending to examine his stitches. He used the mirror to search for the tattoo. It was more difficult that way, but less risky than prowling through crowded showers and eyeing the backs of naked inmates. He shifted strategically from left to right, working the reflection to his full advantage. No matter how he maneuvered, however, he couldn't quite get a direct view into the deepest recesses of the shower area, where he seemed to recall seeing that O-Town Posse tattoo the other night. He tried standing on the balls of his feet, closer to the ceiling mirror and farther to his right—so far that he almost lost his balance.

"You're doing a lot of looking around tonight," said Charger, as he stopped at the sink beside Theo.

Theo caught himself and quickly resumed the pretense of examining the stitches in his head.

Charger leaned over the basin and splashed water on his face—delicately, the way a personal trainer might spritz a client's face with Evian. Then he removed his towel and said, "You know what they say: The ass is always greener . . ."

Theo ignored him as he sauntered away.

Steam from the hot showers was soon fogging the mirror. Theo's search was turning up nothing anyway, so he abandoned it and took a quick shower, looking at no one. He was on his way back to his cell before 9:00 P.M., but he didn't feel like dealing with Charger. Lights-out was still more than an hour away, so he decided to pay Moses a visit. The cell door was open, and Moses' cell mate was reclining in the lower bunk, alone in the cell when Theo arrived.

"Where's Moses?"

"Gone," he said, never looking up from his magazine.

"TV room?" said Theo.

"Uh-uh. He's outta here."

Theo glanced at the top bunk, and only then did he notice that the bedding had been removed. An image flashed through his mind—the O-Town Posse tattoo on the muscular back of a black man, his identity obscured in the crowded, steamy shower.

"Are you saying they took him away during the lockdown search?"

"Uh-uh. He left this morning."

"So he got reassigned to another cell?"

He lowered his magazine, as if Theo's interrogation was getting on his nerves. "Moses had a court hearing to reduce his bail a week or so ago. Judge's decision came down this morning. He's a free man, dude. Outta here. Get it?"

It took a moment for the words to register. Theo looked away, speaking more to himself than to Moses' old cell mate. "Yeah," he said quietly. "I think maybe I do."

Chapter 29

The orange and yellow swirl of police beacons led Andie Henning through the darkness. Rural crime scenes tended to be large, and this one stretched almost the entire length of dirt road that jutted from the main highway. Andie flashed her credentials to the deputies working perimeter control, ducked under the yellow tape, and headed up the dusty road for a closer look. It was one of those lonely trails to nowhere in the middle of a pasture. On the other side of the barbed-wire fence a herd of cattle slept while standing, which made Andie think of high school and late-night adventures in "cow tipping" back in her home state of Washington. Little mental diversions like that helped her cope with the grim side of her job.

Homicides were always a priority, but even off-duty law enforcement volunteered their services when a state trooper was murdered. Andie also noticed more gray hair than usual, a sign that a few retired officers were kicking in their time as well. They worked in the glow of portable vapor lights that all but turned night into day. A long line of uniformed officers and volunteers paced across the surrounding prairie, searching methodically for a murder weapon or other evidence that the shooter might have tossed or dropped. The suspect's vehicle was long gone, but investigators were making a cast of tire tracks that had been left behind. The center of activity was the Florida Highway Patrol vehicle. The driver's-side door was open, and Trooper Stratton's body was still in the front seat, slumped over the steering wheel. His face happened to be turned away from Andie, which was just as well. Blood was everywhere, telling of a grievous wound, and glass pellets from the shattered windshield glistened beneath the spotlights. An investigator was snapping photographs as Andie approached. The lead homicide detective stopped her before she got too close, introducing himself as Lieutenant Peter Malloy. They had already met by telephone, so he dispensed with the pleasantries.

"You should see the videotape," said Malloy.

All FHP vehicles were equipped with dashboard video cameras, and Andie was eager to see the tape. "Do you have a copy for me?"

"Techies will have some extras ready in thirty minutes or so. You can watch mine."

He led Andie to his unmarked car, took a video camera from the front seat, and held it at eye level. Andie watched the three-inch LCD screen as the action unfolded in silence, the image shaking from the vibration of a high-speed chase up the turnpike. The trooper blew past one car, then another, before making a quick exit. He didn't slow down a bit on the county highway, but the red car was nowhere in sight as the trooper cut a sharp turn onto a dark, dusty road. Suddenly, he came over a small hill and the red car was right in front of him. The patrol car skidded to a halt. In a split second, a gun emerged from the driver's side window, and the trooper's windshield exploded. Tires spun and the red car spit dust as it pulled a one-eighty and sped away.

Lieutenant Malloy turned off the camera.

Andie said, "Looks like the shooter sat there and waited for him with the driver's-side window open. Probably kneeling in the front seat and facing backward when he fired his gun."

"I've watched it half a dozen times, and I agree," said Malloy. "Even so, that was one hell of a shot."

"The file on Moses tells me that he knows how to handle a firearm," said Andie. "That's just one more factor that points toward him as the shooter."

"Unfortunately, as you just saw with your own eyes, there's no clear image of the shooter's face, and the license plate is completely covered in dust and cow manure. I've got our tech people trying to work through that crap, literally."

"I can get the FBI to help with that."

"I'll let you know if we need it," said Malloy.

Her phone rang. She recognized the incoming number. It was Jack. She excused herself and stepped away from Detective Malloy to take the call.

"Where are you?" said Jack.

"In the middle of nowhere," she said.

"You were supposed to call me an hour ago with an update."

"Sorry. I got diverted." She paused to remind herself that all dealings with Jack had to be on a need-to-know basis. This, she decided, was something he needed to know. So she told him.

Jack said, "Any doubt in your mind who the shooter was?"

"We're waiting to confirm some things."

"Did the lockdown search for the O-Town Posse tattoo turn up anything?"

She knew he wasn't changing the subject—just coming at her from another angle to get a response to his original question. "No," she said, just answering his question.

"You mean Theo didn't see what he thought he saw?"

"Not exactly. The warden ordered an inmate-by-inmate search just to see if more than one prisoner had the same tattoo. Somebody who the guards might have missed when they inventoried scars, marks, and tattoos upon each prisoner's arrival."

"So it was in the inventory?"

"Yeah. We pegged it to a guy named Moses Carter."

"I'm confused. If the tattoo was in the inventory, why didn't the guards find it when they searched the inmates?"

"Moses was released this morning."

"I assume you're going to bring him in for questioning."

"That's going to be difficult."

"Why?"

Andie could almost hear the wheels turning in Jack's head, and he spoke before she could frame a response.

"Do you think this Moses shot the trooper?" said Jack.

Again she paused to assure herself that this was something he needed to know. She wasn't sure, but with Theo working undercover, she gave Jack the benefit of the doubt. "I'm thinking bigger than that."

"How do you mean?"

"Let me put it this way," she said. "So far we have Trooper Stratton's videotape of a red car that meets the description in our BOLO from Theo's shooting. The symbol for the O-Town Posse is clearly visible."

"But Moses was in jail when Theo was shot."

"The rest of his gang wasn't. Could have been done on his order."

"A good connection, if you can make it."

Andie was on a roll, her theory continuing to gel, and the words kept coming even though she wasn't certain that Jack was in the need-to-know circle. "I'm not saying there's any connection yet," she said. "But for no reason I know of, just this morning the judge reconsidered Moses' bail, and suddenly the leader of the O-Town Posse is out on the street."

"But he's forbidden to leave Miami-Dade County," said Jack, seeming to follow her chain of thought.

"Exactly. Which means that if Trooper Stratton hauled him back to jail for violating his terms of release, he would have been facing thirty years in prison on charges that are a slam-dunk conviction. Not even a lawyer like Jack Swyteck could help him beat the rap."

"Sounds to me like Moses never had any intention of coming back to stand trial. His only hope was to make a run for it."

Andie glanced toward Trooper Stratton's body, which the medical examiner's team was now pulling from the vehicle. "Yeah," she said softly. "And shoot to kill anyone who gets in his way."

MOSES AND HIS RED car were in an Orlando chop shop before midnight. The O-Town Posse leader had contacts in every major Florida city. Organization was the key to success.

It was difficult to maintain that organization, however, from behind prison bars. Sure, Moses had heard of mob bosses running the Mafia from jail. But O-Town Posse didn't have that kind of structure. Not yet, anyway. Things had been breaking down in Moses' absence, and tonight's run-in with the state trooper was proof of that. Moses' Overtown soldiers had neglected to tell him that they'd used *his* car to carry out the drive-by hit on Theo Knight. This precious little detail came out in a phone conversation with his right-hand man, minutes after Moses shot Trooper Stratton in the forehead.

"How could you not tell me?" Moses had said to him.

"Dude, we—I don't know. You ordered the hit, we did the hit."

"Yeah, and you fucked that up, too."

"The brotha' went down on the sidewalk

like a rock. Blood was coming from his head. Was dead for sure, we thought."

"You just wasn't *thinkin'*, period. Use my wheels? How crazy is that?"

"It seemed to make sense at the time. We figured if somebody spotted the car, we'd tell the cops it was stolen. No way you coulda' pulled the trigger. You was in jail, dude."

Moses knew that was a crock. His soldiers were smart enough to understand that any acts of O-Town Posse would be linked to Moses, whether he was in or out of prison. They obviously realized how stupid they'd been, were afraid to fess up, and were hoping that no witnesses had given the cops a description of the vehicle. That hope had bordered on delusional. Had Moses known that there was even a possibility of a BOLO, never in a million years would he have gone flying up the interstate at ninety-plus miles per hour. Fortunately for Moses, his car was equipped with a police radio (no self-respecting gang lieutenant traveled without one), so he heard Trooper Stratton radio in the vehicle description in response to the BOLO. Moses had reacted accordingly.

Regardless, back in Miami, some idiot's head was going to roll—literally.

"I got about a half-dozen cars you can choose from," the chop shop owner told him. His name was Jamahl, a fat guy who appeared to live day and night in his grimy garage coveralls. "Come out back with me. Take your pick."

The noise inside the garage was deafening. Jamahl's chop team was busy at work on the latest acquisition—pounding, sawing, cutting, ripping—quickly reducing the red car to parts for sale and shipment to Latin America. Moses took one last look at his wheels and followed the owner outside to the junkyard. Five completely intact vehicles were lined up in front of a mountain of quarter panels, wheel wells, and discarded parts from chopped vehicles. Moses zeroed in on the metallic blue 1995 Caprice Classic.

"This one stolen?" said Moses.

"None of these is."

"Right," said Moses.

"I speak the truth, dude. Some of my inventory has to be legit to keep the IRS off my back. And this is it. My five beauties."

Moses walked around the Caprice, inspecting the body, paint job, tires, and rims. It needed a wash, but everything was in good condition. He opened the drivers'-side door and climbed behind the wheel. The keys were in the ignition. The engine started on the first turn, and he liked the sound of it. The odometer posted twenty-eight thousand miles, but Moses figured that the real number was probably double.

"What you want for it?"

"For you? A straight-up trade, brotha'."

Moses nodded. "Appreciate it, dude. But I need to keep my police radio."

"No problem."

They didn't bother with paperwork. A title transfer in Moses' name would only have put the state of Florida on alert and defeated the purpose of his new wheels. He took the police radio from his old car and drove off the lot around 12:30 A.M. The radio told him that the Florida turnpike was crawling with cops, so he followed the back roads out of Orlando, and he would continue on a dark, winding route until he could pick up the interstate.

The police radio was abuzz. They were looking not just for Moses' red car—which was now history—but for him, too. He needed a disguise and a phony ID if he was going to be on the road. A dead cop was a top priority for law enforcement. It was also big news for the media. He couldn't just keep quiet and let it hit the newspapers in the morning. There was one other phone call he had to make.

He dialed the number—he had it memorized—and a man answered in a sleepy voice. In two minutes, Moses told him exactly what had happened since his release from jail. The end of his story was met with stone-cold silence. Moses could sense the anger on the other end of the line.

"Don't worry," said Moses. "I'm still working it the way we planned."

"The plan went out the window when your boys dropped the ball in Overtown. So far, I'm the only one who keeps his promises. You went from no bail to ten thousand dollars bail, thanks to me. Less than twenty-four hours later, a state trooper is dead and you're in king-size trouble. Do you realize how bad this is going to look?"

"Nobody even knows you're involved. It ain't gonna look like anything for you."

"I'm not talking about me. I pulled in a huge favor. That trial judge who cut you a break on your bail this morning is an elected official. The media will absolutely skewer him. I'm going to have one very angry old man on my hands."

"You deal with that end. I'll take care of mine."

"You haven't taken care of shit. Make it right, or don't ever call me again."

The loud click in Moses' ear could only have been the telephone slamming down. Moses simply smiled as he put away his cell. The man's words—*Don't ever call me again*—traveled straight to his funny bone.

"Dream on, dude."

Chapter 30

It was lights out at TGK, and Theo lay awake in his bunk. Plotting his next move was head splitting. There was only so much time he could spend thinking about the O-Town Posse tattoo and Moses' sudden departure, not to mention his search for the man who played the role of "safety valve" in Isaac Reems's extortion scheme. Theo desperately wanted to know the upshot of the cell-to-cell inspection of inmates, but Jack couldn't just stop by to provide hourly updates. Too much contact with the real world (particularly outside of regular visiting hours) would arouse suspicions within TGK and potentially blow Theo's cover. Jack would have to fill him in at tomorrow's meeting. In the meantime, sleep was essential.

Theo was giving his brain a rest, playing one of the many mental games he'd invented while on death row. This one drew on his musical background and was called "Duets You Hope You Never See." He quit when he conjured up the image of Ozzy Osbourne and Keith Richards clad in skimpy Cher wear and singing "If I Could Turn Back Time."

The cell's lock disengaged with an ominous click, and the iron door slid open. Officer MacDonald was suddenly standing over Theo.

"Get up, Knight," he said.

Theo slid out from under the blanket and sat on the edge of the bunk. He was wearing only underwear and a T-shirt. "What's going on?"

"Just get on your feet." He grabbed Theo's orange jumpsuit from the shelf and threw it across the cell. It hit Theo in the chest. "You're coming with me," the guard said.

Theo walked slowly to the toilet and urinated. Charger lay quietly in the top bunk, pretending to be asleep. Theo didn't really need to pee that badly, but taking care of business gave him a minute to evaluate the situation. Pulling an inmate out of a cell at this hour was unusual, and it made Theo wonder if the FBI had decided to make Mac-Donald privy to his undercover status. Maybe MacDonald needed to take him somewhere private to pass along information from Jack or Andie. Or perhaps Jack had come on the pretense of some phony emergency to deliver a message himself.

"Move it," said MacDonald.

Theo pulled on his jumpsuit, a pair of socks, and his prison-issue tennis shoes with Velcro and no laces. "All right. Let's go."

Theo went first, and MacDonald gave him a needless shove from behind as they exited the cell. The iron door slid shut behind them, the ratchet of the lock echoing throughout the dark cell block.

"Where we headed?" said Theo.

"Eyes forward," said MacDonald. "Just do as I say."

The guard gave him another shove, and Theo started walking. Most inmates were asleep in their cells. Some stood at the bars to see what was going on, their hands protruding from the blackened cells. For Theo, it was eerily reminiscent of his predawn walk down death row.

Theo stopped at the guard's command. They were at the end of the cell block, standing before a locked security door. A buzzer sounded, and the door opened. MacDonald gave him another unnecessary shove. If this jerk didn't knock it off, he'd be in serious trouble when inmate Knight returned to his life as citizen Knight. Then again, Theo considered the possibility that it was all an act—that MacDonald was in on the undercover operation, and that he was being rough only to keep suspicions from rising among the inmates.

The security door locked behind them. MacDonald gave a nod and a hello to the guard posted in the short corridor that joined the cell block to the next wing.

"To your left," MacDonald told Theo.

Theo obliged and braced himself for another cheap shot from behind. MacDonald didn't disappoint him. This one nearly made Theo stumble forward. Each shove was a little harder than the last.

"Stop," said MacDonald.

They were standing outside the isolation chamber—not a cell, but a private room in which the guards interrogated inmates, from informants to troublemakers.

"Hands behind your back."

Theo did as he was told. MacDonald bound the prisoner's wrists with metal cuffs, unlocked the door, and pushed Theo inside. He followed right behind him, switched on the lights, and locked the door.

The room was ten feet by ten feet. It had no windows and only one door in or out. The floor was bare concrete, the walls were yellow-painted cinder blocks, and the only furniture was an old oak chair in the center of the room.

Theo had been around the proverbial cell block enough to know that it wasn't standard procedure for an interrogation to be conducted by one guard. This was the moment of truth. Either MacDonald was a player in the FBI's operation and this was going to be something good—or he wasn't, and . . .

A nightstick to his kidneys brought Theo to his knees and his speculation to an end. Theo remained on the floor on hands and knees, keeping his head down. He'd had the holy hell beaten out of him before, both as a child and as an adult, but his body was no longer conditioned for a blow like this one. It took a minute for him to catch his breath. The hot, stale air didn't make it any easier. He was sweating already.

MacDonald circled him in silence, and Theo could hear only the soft step of his shoes and the steady tap of the nightstick in the palm of his hand.

"Isaac was your good buddy, huh?" he said.

Theo didn't answer, which brought MacDonald's boot to his belly. Theo went over on his side, the wind gone from him again.

"You seem to have a knack for making friends with the wrong people, pal."

Theo stayed low, the right side of his face on the floor. Obviously MacDonald wasn't part of the undercover team, but Theo was beginning to think that MacDonald knew why Theo was in jail—and didn't like it one bit.

"Get up," said MacDonald, as he grabbed Theo by the collar. "In the chair."

Theo sat in the interrogation chair, his cuffed hands behind the backrest.

MacDonald faced him directly, boring the blunt end of his nightstick into Theo's chest. He turned it like a screwdriver as he increased the pressure, which hurt like a bitch.

"Nobody sits at Moses' table on his first

trip to the cafeteria," said MacDonald. "Nobody but you."

"He invited me," said Theo.

"Just like that, he decides you're his new pal."

"Yeah," said Theo. "Just like that."

MacDonald bent over and stared straight into his eyes, close enough for Theo to smell the coffee on his breath. The guard said, "I can see this is gonna be a real painful lesson for you, boy."

He jammed the nightstick into Theo's groin, and Theo fell to the floor again. Theo looked up at the ceiling, but he could barely see straight. He rolled onto his side and assumed a fetal position. It had been a long time since he'd felt pain like this.

MacDonald was circling again, taunting him with that tap of the nightstick against the palm of his open hand.

"You and your buddy Isaac Reems stained my perfect record with that escape."

"It was *his* jailbreak."

"But you helped. That's why you're here."

The residual stabbing pain in his testicles was still making it difficult for Theo to form coherent thoughts, but that last remark suggested that MacDonald didn't know anything about Theo or his actual status. This "interrogation" appeared to be about nothing more than a petty correctional officer's bruised ego.

Theo was still lying on his side. MacDonald stepped behind him and pressed Theo's fingertips beneath his boot—slowly at first, then harder, as if trying to mash them into the concrete. Theo grimaced in pain but tried not to cry out, refusing to give MacDonald the satisfaction.

"Lucky for you, I'm a nice guy," said the guard. "I'm gonna give you a chance to help me earn back my superstar reputation."

"Is that so?" said Theo, grunting through the pain.

"Yeah. Looks like your buddy Moses killed a state trooper tonight. Shot him right in the face."

Theo said nothing. Somehow, it didn't surprise him.

MacDonald said, "You and me are gonna work together now. We're gonna catch Moses."

"What're you talkin' about?"

"I kept my eye on you and Moses. I saw your buddy-buddy act in the cafeteria. I watched you two scheming in the stairwell."

"Just jail talk, man."

"My ass," said MacDonald. "Moses blew this county five minutes after he was released. Got in his car and headed north. Police got a BOLO out, but nobody knows where he is now."

Theo's fingers were going numb, which lessened the pain. "Can't help you, dude."

"Yeah, you can. I think you know exactly where Moses was headed when he got out of TGK."

"I don't know nothin'."

MacDonald raised his boot off Theo's fingers and gave him a kick to the kidney. This time, Theo couldn't stop from crying out in pain. He couldn't tell anyone about his undercover status—the deal was that he would take whatever came, like a regular inmate—but he wasn't sure how much longer he could keep this up.

And even if he told him, MacDonald wouldn't believe him now.

The guard knelt at Theo's side and whispered in his ear, his voice taking on the perverse and gleeful edge of a sadist: "I got all night, tough guy. We'll see *exactly* what you know."

Chapter 31

Uncle Cy couldn't sleep.

Lightheadedness had forced him to leave the bar early tonight. It had come on right after Jack called to tell him that a guy named Moses had an O-Town Posse tattoo and killed a state trooper just hours after his release from TGK. Distressing news, but it didn't account for Cy's dizziness. That damn doctor still didn't have his blood pressure medication right. Cy went home and climbed into bed. It felt like the bad old days when he would drag himself home from his gigs, fall onto the bed or sometimes even the floor, and fight with the spins as he tried to find sleep.

Funny thing was, Cy had played his sax so much better when he was high. Or so he'd thought as a much younger man. The owners who fired him from the hottest clubs downtown, the managers who banned him from the big hotels on Miami Beach, the musicians who refused to play with him again—they were all racists or Uncle Toms trying to keep the black musicians down. He kept moving from one gig to the next, drinking, sniffing, snorting, popping, shooting along the way, burning bridges everywhere he went. Eventually he couldn't find work anymore—except in a place like Homeboy's, that dive of a joint where Theo's mother used to hang out. Night after night, he watched her, stoned and stumbling from one bar stool to the next in search of a twenty-dollar trick. When those pockets were emptied, she'd turn to the street. Everyone knew that story's ending.

Except that her death really wasn't the end of anything—especially not now, with Isaac Reems's promise hanging out there for Theo to grasp.

Cy sat up in the darkened bedroom and draped his legs over the edge of the mattress. Things were spinning again. A little blood in his head would sure have been nice. He allowed a minute for it to pass, but the mattress was turning, then the floor, and then the entire room. Slowly at first, but steadily gaining speed. The motion was counterclockwise, as if carrying him back in time and to another place—a snippet from his past that he had all but erased. It was rushing back to him now, and even though his room was a blur, his memories played like a movie in his mind's eye.

A LOUD POUNDING ON the front door woke Cy from a deep sleep. It took him a moment to recognize his surroundings. Not his bedroom. It was the living room. He'd passed out on the couch this time. That was one way for a man of so much talent to cope with playing a hellhole like Homeboy's.

More pounding on the door. He forced himself up and shuffled across the room. The morning sun assaulted his eyes the moment he opened the door.

"Cyrus Knight?" the man on the porch said.

His head was throbbing, and the cotton

mouth was so bad that Cy could barely form words. "What of it?" he said.

The man flashed a badge, as did the younger guy with him. They introduced themselves as Harmon and Kittle, homicide detectives. Harmon was clearly the veteran, teeth stained from years of addiction to coffee and tobacco, his face creased with the lines of too many crimes, solved and unsolved. Kittle looked too young to be a detective, still battling acne and his hair buzzed like a high-school jock.

Harmon said, "We'd like to ask you a few questions about your niece."

Cy scratched his head and cleared his throat. The blinding glare of the sun forced him to keep one eye closed. "It's about damn time you guys come around," he said. "Come in."

"That won't be necessary," said Harmon.

Cy glanced inside his messy apartment, then back at the detectives. A couple of white guys in an all-black neighborhood. "What's the matter? My place ain't good enough for ya'?"

"Seen worse," said Harmon. "This will just take a couple minutes."

"Couple of minutes? This isn't jaywalking. A woman was murdered."

"How can you be so sure it was murder?" the younger detective asked suspiciously.

Detective Harmon rolled his eyes, as if to say, "Rookies." "Kittle, the woman's throat was slit. Let me handle this."

Cy was sobering up quickly. It was clear that the homicide division hadn't put its best and brightest on this case. He directed his question to Harmon. "What do you want to know?"

Harmon pulled a pen and small notepad from his breast pocket. "When's the last time you saw your niece alive?"

Cy thought about it. "Sometime that same day she was killed. I play the sax at Homeboy's. She . . . she sort of hangs there."

"What do you mean 'hangs'?"

"Hangs . . . you know. It's her spot."

The detectives exchanged glances. Kittle smirked. Harmon said, "Did your niece have a job?"

"She, you know, made money as she could."

Kittle said, "We hear she was a prostitute."

Cy shrugged. "Might have been."

Harmon asked, "How well did you know her?"

"Better than most folks."

"And you can't tell us what your niece did for a living?"

"She's got kids, okay? Two boys. Good kids—well, one of 'em is, anyway. I just don't see why you gotta write all this stuff down and put it in the damn newspaper."

"We're detectives, not reporters."

"It's all the same club."

"Sir, I just need the facts," said Harmon.

"Okay, she walked the street. Big deal."

Harmon was deadpan. "She have a pimp?"

"Beats me."

"She do drugs?"

"What do you think?"

"Know anybody who'd want her dead?" said Harmon.

"Not really."

Harmon made a quick entry in his notebook and tucked it back into his pocket. "Thanks very much for your time, Mr. Knight."

"That's it?"

He gave Cy a business card. "Call me if anything comes to mind. Anything at all that you might think is important."

The detectives turned and started down the steps.

"Hey," said Cy.

The detectives stopped, but only Harmon looked back.

Cy said, "You ain't gonna do squat to find the guy who killed her, are you?"

Harmon paused, as if to consider his response. It hardly seemed possible, but Cy would have sworn that the old detective looked even more jaded than when he'd arrived.

"Another black whore gets high on crack and picks the wrong john," he said. "I'll do my best. But we can't work miracles, pal."

THE BEDROOM SUDDENLY stopped spinning. Cy's memories faded, replaced by a pit of nausea in his stomach. This time, it had nothing to do with blood pressure. It was Theo he was worried about, and the memories of police indifference had only heightened his concern. He grabbed the phone on the nightstand and called Jack Swyteck at home, who answered in a sleepy voice.

"Sorry, Jack. Hate to get you out of bed."

"It's okay," said Jack, a frog in his throat. "What's up?"

"I wouldn't bother you like this in the middle of the night, but I just got a bad feelin' in my bones. It's Theo."

"What about him?"

"I been layin' here in bed thinking ever since you called me about this Moses. And it finally just comes to me. Theo got shot while Moses was in jail and Theo was on the outside."

"Yeah, so?"

"Now Moses is on the outside and Theo's on the inside. See what I'm sayin'?"

The line was silent as Jack mulled it over. "Makes perfect sense," he said finally. "A convenient disconnect between the hit and the man who orders it."

Cy's response came from deep inside him, a place laden with emotion. "We gotta get my nephew out of that jail."

Chapter 32

The salty taste of his own blood oozed from Theo's mouth. His ribs hurt, his testicles were swollen, his fingers felt like they'd been slammed in a car door, and the back of his legs still stung from MacDonald's nightstick.

And no end was in sight.

Theo lay on his side, his back to the guard, the concrete floor cool against his face. There was an art to getting through a beating of this sort, and Theo had been reaching inside himself for all the old techniques. The basic strategy was to leave your body and take a mental journey to some other place as far away as possible.

To that end, he'd been thinking a lot about Trina—the passion in her eyes, the softness of her skin, the tingle of her touch. It wasn't working as well as he'd hoped.

"For the last time," he said in a tired voice. "I got no idea where Moses is."

MacDonald was sitting in the oak chair, resting and breathing heavily. Apparently, knocking the stuffing out of a man in handcuffs was hard work.

"Then you have a huge problem, Knight. Because I still don't believe a word you say."

"Why would I protect Moses like this?"

"Because he's your brotha'."

"I hardly know him."

"Doesn't matter. He helped your buddy Isaac. Just like you did."

Theo breathed through the pain. His interest was piqued. "What're you talkin' about?"

"You helped Isaac on the outside. Moses helped him on the inside."

"How you know that?" said Theo.

MacDonald rose from the chair and kicked Theo in the lower back. It must have hit the sciatic nerve, because the pain shot down Theo's leg like a lightening bolt.

"I know it," the guard said, seething, "because you're gonna tell me all about it."

Theo heard a key in the lock, and the door opened. He didn't turn to look, but the sound of footsteps told him that someone else was in the room.

Great. A gang bang.

"What the hell's going on in here?" the other man said.

Theo didn't recognize the voice, but he seemed to have seniority over MacDonald, based on the tone.

"Just a little interrogation," said MacDonald.

The man stepped closer and stopped behind Theo. Theo raised his head to look.

"Eyes forward," the man said, turning Theo's face away with a prod of his nightstick to the chin.

The signs of abuse were all over him, and Theo could only surmise that this officer was smart enough to keep Theo from witnessing the reproving looks he was throwing a fellow guard.

"You can go, MacDonald," the man said.

"But I'm not finished."

"I said *go*."

Theo sensed tension in the ensuing silence, but finally MacDonald crossed the room and opened the door. He stopped and said, "I should have cuffed him sooner. Unfortunately I had to use force after the prisoner jumped me. It'll all be in my report."

"Beat it," the man said.

The door closed, and Theo was alone in the interrogation room with the other officer.

"You all right?" he asked Theo.

"Been better."

"Can you walk?"

"If it gets me outta here, I can."

Theo groaned with pain as the guard took his arm and helped him up. The man was black. Thus far Theo had dealt only with white and Hispanic guards, so he didn't recognize him. He glanced at the name tag. Jefferson.

"Where's it hurt?" said Jefferson.

"Everywhere," said Theo. "My ribs, mostly."

"Come on. Let's get you up to the infirmary."

"Just take me to my cell."

"No," the guard said. "MacDonald packs a wallop. You need to spend the night in the infirmary. Doctor can check you out first thing in the morning and get you over to Jackson if need be."

Jackson Memorial Hospital was where Theo had ended up after the drive-by shooting. If this kept up, they'd be selling him a time-share. "I already got stitches in my head. He bust 'em open?"

"Doesn't look like it," said Jefferson.

With the guard's help, Theo put one foot in front of the other and made it to the door. The guard shut off the light, and they started down the corridor. Theo was shuffling his feet more than walking, the pain in his ribs forcing him to favor his left side.

"Good thing for me you came when you did," said Theo.

"Good thing for everyone."

This Jefferson seemed like an all right dude. It was worth a shot to probe for a little information. "MacDonald tells me Moses killed a state trooper tonight."

"MacDonald talks too much."

"He thinks I know where Moses was headed."

"Like I said: he talks too much."

So much for loose lips.

Another guard looked on with mild amusement as Jefferson and his battered prisoner passed in the hallway. They walked another thirty feet and stopped at the iron bars. The buzzer sounded, the door slid open, and they entered the next wing. Theo's legs were killing him, but thankfully it only took another two minutes to reach the infirmary. The door was made of chain link rather than iron bars. Jefferson unlocked it with his key and escorted Theo inside.

The medical staff had gone home for the night, so Jefferson signed Theo's name into the log book at the registration desk and took him inside. The infirmary was a dormitory-style facility with a dozen beds on either side of the rectangular-shaped room and a wide aisle down the center. A crash cart and a gurney were in the corner, next to a row of IV poles. Only one other inmate was a patient, and he was asleep at the other end of the room, snoring loudly. It was lights-out for the entire jail, but the barred windows had no shades, and the nighttime security lighting allowed them to see what they were doing. Jefferson put Theo in the near bed.

Theo let out another groan as he settled onto the mattress. It was more comfortable than the bunk in his cell, but not even a heated waterbed could have soothed these bruises. That his hands were still cuffed behind his back only made it worse. Jefferson helped him roll onto his side and slid a pillow under his head. Theo asked for water, and the guard brought him a cup to rinse the blood from his mouth. Fortunately, the bleeding had stopped.

Jefferson said, "I'll find MacDonald and see if I can get the keys to these cuffs."

"That would help."

"You okay for now?"

"I think so."

Jefferson left him there. Theo heard his footsteps fade, heard the door open and then close. The noise was loud enough to disturb the other inmate. He snorted twice, smacked like a toddler eating peanut butter, and mercifully his snoring stopped. Theo lay with his back to him, however, so he couldn't tell if the man was actually awake or simply sleeping in a position that wasn't conducive to snoring. Either way, Theo appreciated the silence.

Theo closed his eyes, but they soon opened. Oddly, the silence was almost too complete, at least for a jail. Snoring, farting, puking, grunting, cursing, pissing, howling, sucking, fucking—those were the normal sounds of prison in the dead of night. It felt strange to hear none of it. Beyond strange.

Theo lay motionless in the bed. His left arm was falling asleep from lying on it, but the rest of his body was wide awake. He stayed in that position for five solid minutes. Ten minutes. Almost half an hour. Either Jefferson had forgotten about him or he was having trouble finding MacDonald. He wasn't coming back with the keys to the handcuffs anytime soon. Theo would just have to make the best of it.

He shifted his weight, trying to get comfortable. Then he heard a noise. "Jefferson?" he said.

There was no answer.

He was sure he'd heard something. He remained perfectly still, completely silent.

There it was again—a kind of scuffing noise, but it was so faint that Theo couldn't determine where it was coming from.

"Jefferson, that you?" he said.

The room was silent.

Theo's pulse quickened. Lying alone on death row for four years had taught him to differentiate sounds. He could tell the difference between mechanical sounds and the sounds of the building. The sounds of falling rain and a leaky faucet. The sounds of his cell and another cell. The sounds of an inmate and a guard. The sounds that meant nothing and those that meant trouble.

He heard the noise again—louder, closer, a stealthy attacker's misplaced footfall. Theo sprang into action, but with his hands cuffed behind his back, he couldn't react fast enough. The man quickly overpowered him, burying a knee in Theo's back and pinning him facedown on the mattress. Before Theo could even get a word out, the cord was around his neck. He heard himself groan. His vision blurred. His groaning turned to wheezing. The man pulled tighter, his grip tightening.

Theo kicked and squirmed, but he felt himself weakening. Arterial flow continued in the head and neck, bringing more blood from the heart. The veins, however, were completely compressed, leaving the blood no escape, building pressure on the brain. His head pounded with congestion, like the worst sinus headache imaginable. His eyes bulged, and his face flushed red. He could taste blood, not just from the earlier wounds Officer MacDonald had inflicted, but as additional small bleeding sites erupted in the moist, soft mucosa of his lips and mouth.

Theo felt the man's weight shift. He was leaning forward, and Theo suddenly felt his breath on the back of his neck.

"This is for—"

Before the man could finish, Theo arched his spine and threw his head back like a wild bull, effecting a reverse head butt. It was a direct hit, and the man cried out in pain. Theo seized the opportunity, drawing up his knees, pushing up with all his strength, and sending his attacker flying to the floor. The cord was off his neck. Theo coughed as he sucked in air, but he didn't miss a beat. He rolled off the bed—falling, more than pouncing on his attacker. His arms were useless, but Theo had legs like an Olympic wrestler, and he immediately recognized his serious height and weight advantage over this punk. They were both on the floor. Theo had the guy in a scissors lock, nearly crushing his attacker's skinny neck between his massive thighs.

"Now it's your turn to choke," said Theo. He knew he could have killed him if he'd wanted to. But dead men don't talk. He squeezed tightly, but not too tightly.

"Jefferson!" he shouted into the darkness.

Chapter 33

Just after 2:00 A.M. Jack and Uncle Cy were in the infirmary with Theo, waiting for the on-call physician to arrive. Theo downplayed his injuries, but the evidence of his beating was obvious. Jack got a full recitation of the evening's events while Andie Henning did a physical inspection of the infirmary, and then the two of them went to the warden's office for an emergency meeting. Cy remained in the infirmary with his nephew.

Warden Beth Johnson was the only person at TGK who knew about Theo's undercover assignment. At least she was *supposed* to have been the only one. The abuse Theo had taken at the hands of Officer MacDonald and the fellow inmate's attack in the infirmary raised serious questions. Jack had no intention of leaving TGK without the answers.

Johnson was seated in a squeaky office chair behind a typical government-issue gray metal desk. Jack and Andie sat on opposite ends of an old couch, trying way too hard—as only people trying to deny the attraction do—to put distance between their bodies.

"You two have some kind of contagious disease or something?" said Johnson.

Their responses tumbled out together—"Me? Huh? No." But they quickly took her meaning and relaxed a little.

Johnson was known around TGK as the hard-ass with the great ass, which was basically a handy way of saying that half the inmates wanted to kill her, and the other half wanted to bed her. She was definitely attractive, though the conservative Laura Ashley attire toned things down. Some said that being the mother of three children was the only qualification she needed to become a jail warden, but she was also smart, tough, and savvy, with framed diplomas from Duke, the University of Virginia, and Emory University hanging on the wall behind her desk. Had she taken her law degree and entered private practice, Johnson would have been a formidable opponent for Jack or anyone else on the opposite side of the table.

"Whatever," said Johnson. "To put it in bottom-line terms, I can't tell you how this happened tonight. I'm still trying to figure it out for myself."

"Let's break it down," said Andie. "We have two distinct situations here. MacDonald is an internal disciplinary matter. He abused an inmate as part of an interrogation. Jack and I are both upset about that, but it's not something we need to deal with in the wee hours of the morning."

Johnson said, "Let me assure you, TGK has internal investigative procedures that can adequately deal with Officer MacDonald."

"The state of Florida has a few criminal statutes that also come into play," said Jack.

The warden bristled.

Andie said, "That will all run its course in due time, Jack."

Her tone might have sounded condescending if their past dealings had not taught Jack something about the nuances of her voice. Jack knew she was just trying to keep peace between him and the warden.

"I see your point," said Jack. "But the infirmary is another matter. That was clearly a second attempted hit on Theo. Somebody was trying to finish the job they botched in Overtown."

"Hold on," said the warden. "Before we go riding off into la-la land with conspiracy theories, we need to deal with prison realities. Inmates attack other inmates. That's a fact. It's usually about nothing—one guy doesn't like the way the other one looked at him."

"This one wasn't about nothing," said Jack.

"How can you be so sure?" said the warden.

"Let me talk to the punk who tried to strangle Theo, and I'll prove it to you."

"His name's Holloway," said the warden. "But I can't let you talk to him."

"Why not?"

"He's in solitary and already demanded to speak to an attorney. If I send you down there, some lawyer will claim I used you as my agent to violate his constitutional rights."

"Then bring CO Jefferson in here," said Jack. "I'll show you."

The warden stiffened in her chair. "You expect me to let a criminal defense lawyer interrogate my own correctional officer before I've even talked to him myself?"

Jack said, "You got something to hide, Warden?"

"No, but—" She stopped and looked to Andie, as if expecting the FBI agent to side with her.

Andie said, "It beats having to talk to the *Miami Tribune*."

"Is that a threat?" said Johnson.

"No," said Andie. "It was more of an appeal for a promise from Jack. This stays out of the newspapers, right?"

Jack had to contain the urge to smile broadly and say, "Smooth move, Henning." She *had* threatened the warden, and seeing her pull it off so skillfully, with absolutely none of the repercussions flowing in her direction, served to remind him why he'd been so attracted to her. Before. Months ago. Not anymore.

"Right, Jack?" said Andie.

"Right," he said, snapping out of it. "I have no interest in talking to the press."

"Warden?" she said. "Does that sound fair to you?"

She grumbled, but Andie had left her little choice. "All right," she said. "But if I don't like your line of questioning, I'm shutting things down. Understood?"

"Sure," said Jack.

The warden picked up the telephone and told his supervisory CO to send up Jefferson. It was as if the call had been expected. Less than a minute later, Jefferson entered the warden's office.

The warden made the introductions. The mention of Andie being an FBI agent triggered a twitch in Jefferson's eye. The warden explained that Jack was a criminal lawyer—folks in law enforcement always seemed to omit the part about his being a criminal *defense* lawyer—and that he had a few questions to ask. Then Jack offered his hand, not merely to be polite, but to get a read on just how high Jefferson had raised his defenses. As expected, it felt like two gladiators meeting just minutes before one of them fell in a pool of his own blood.

Jefferson took the wooden chair in front of the warden's desk and sat at an angle, half facing the warden, half facing Jack. His spine was as rigid and erect as the chair back.

Jack asked, "How did you happen to find

Mr. Knight and Officer MacDonald in the interrogation room?"

"I was walking by on my normal rounds and heard a man screaming. It's not soundproof. Thought I should check it out."

Jefferson described what he saw upon entering and further informed Jack that although he wasn't MacDonald's supervisor, he had seniority and told MacDonald to leave.

Jack said, "Theo told me it was your idea to go to the infirmary."

"I suppose you could say that."

"Theo told you he wanted to go back to his cell, but you insisted on taking him to the infirmary."

"If he'd looked in the mirror, he would have agreed with me."

The warden interjected. "If Jefferson had taken him to his cell, I'm sure we would have had a lawsuit on our hands for denying medical treatment."

"You'll have much worse on your hands if you keep interrupting me," said Jack. It annoyed him that the warden seemed less than eager to find out who was behind this latest attempt to kill his best friend.

Andie broke the tension, and Jack decided to let the FBI take the lead for a minute.

"Officer Jefferson," she asked, "how many patients were in the infirmary when you brought Mr. Knight there?"

"Just one. He was asleep, snoring, at the other end of the dormitory."

"Here's something interesting," she said. "I checked the registration log for the infirmary before coming up here to the warden's office. No one was signed in for an overnight stay."

"So?"

"Didn't it strike you as odd that someone was sleeping in there?"

Jefferson pursed his lips, considering it. "I guess I didn't really look at the registration log."

Andie had it on the floor beside the couch. She handed it to the guard. "Somebody signed in Theo Knight, right?"

Jefferson didn't even look at it. "Yeah, I did."

"So it was plain to see that no other inmates were signed up for an overnighter, yet someone was asleep inside, right?"

"Let me see that," said the warden as she reached over the desk and took it from the guard. "There's at least a dozen other names here."

"All from previous days," Andie said.

Jefferson said, "I didn't really focus on the dates. I was more worried about getting Goliath off my arm and into bed before he dropped to the floor."

Jack jumped back in. "Then how do you explain the fact that another inmate got in there before you and Theo?"

"Beats me," said Jefferson.

"Was the door locked or unlocked when you and Theo got there?" said Jack.

"Locked."

"So either the other inmate had a key or somebody let him in."

The warden said, "Probably one of the guards brought him there and just forgot to sign him in."

"Maybe one of the guards *conveniently* forgot to sign him in. A guard named Jefferson."

"Maybe you should have your head examined," said Jefferson.

The warden sat up, glaring. "What are you saying, Swyteck?"

"Jack, ease up," said Andie.

"No," said Jack. "I'm not going to sit here and pretend I don't know what's going on. This was a setup."

The warden rolled her eyes and threw an

arm in the air. "There you go again, getting all conspiracy crazy."

Jack looked at Jefferson, his focus tightening. "You told Theo you were coming right back with the keys to the handcuffs."

"I couldn't find MacDonald."

"Couldn't find him," said Jack, "or didn't look for him?"

"I looked. I didn't see him. I wasn't going to put out an A.P.B."

"So, you were happy to let the prisoner lie there overnight, without being checked out by a physician?"

"The physician wasn't in the building."

"You could have called him in."

"Hey, Knight didn't even want to go to the infirmary. So I didn't push it. I figured he'd be fine till morning." He looked at the warden. "Look, I went off duty an hour ago. Is this going to take all night?"

"No," said the warden. "Go home."

"I'm not finished," said Jack.

"Yeah, you are," said the warden. "Go home, Jefferson."

Jefferson rose and left the room. As the door closed, Jack and the warden locked eyes in a tense stare.

"Don't forget our understanding," said the warden. "No press."

"No problem," said Andie.

"No cover-ups," said Jack, his gaze still firmly on the warden. "I'll see to that."

Chapter 34

Theo received a thorough checkup from the on-call physician. The doctor didn't detect any broken bones, but Theo would have to visit an outside medical facility for X-rays and a follow-up examination. He taped Theo's ribs, gave him an antibacterial ointment for the rope burn around his neck, and wrote a prescription for a painkiller.

"Vicodin?" Theo said hopefully.

"I'm giving you Demerol," the doctor said.

"Good enough," said Theo. "Can't wait to wash it down with a couple shots of Herradura Añejo."

The doctor peered over the top of his

black-rimmed reading glasses, giving Theo a reproving look.

Theo was about to ask where he thought an inmate would get tequila, much less *good* tequila. But lately, just about anything seemed possible in this place.

"Thanks for your help, Doc," said Cy.

The doctor packed his bag, and the guard escorted him to the locked exit door. Theo and his uncle remained behind in the examination room. Theo was seated on the table, transferring an ice pack back and forth from his swollen knee to the fingers MacDonald had stepped on. Cy leaned against a poster on the wall that, appropriately enough, warned of the dangers of hypertension.

"Is all this worth it?" said Cy.

Theo was breathing in and out, trying to get comfortable with tape around his ribs. "All what?"

"Guard beats the crap out of you. Some inmate you don't even know tries chokin' you to death. What're you trying to prove?"

"Ain't tryin' to prove nothin'. Just want to find out who took a drive-by shot at me in Overtown."

"And you think you gotta be in prison to do that?"

Theo inhaled deeply and grimaced with pain. Big lungs were no friend to bruised ribs. "Jack and I agreed that finding the guy who helped Isaac on the inside was the best way to find out who tried to shoot me on the outside."

The guard returned to the examination room. Cy looked at him crossly. "Can I have a minute with my nephew? We're talking family here."

The guard said, "I'm here to keep an eye on him."

"Two minutes," said Theo. "Cuff me if you want."

The guard glanced at Cy, and he backed down out respect for the old man, not any concern for Theo. He cuffed Theo to the rail on the examination table, stepped outside the room, and waited nearby at the reception desk.

Cy had that "Uncle Cyrus" look on his face again—the one that made it impossible for Theo to blow smoke.

"What're you doin' here, Theo? Really. What's this all about?"

"Getting answers."

"You done your part now. Why don't you come home and let the FBI or the warden work over the guy who tried to choke you to death? I'll bet he's got some answers."

"He's a punk who doesn't know shit," said Theo.

"What makes you so smart?"

"Because things don't work that way. Don't you get it? Jefferson bought him off—dope or something—to act like he was asleep and then jump me after we was alone in the infirmary. Dude doesn't even know why he was trying to kill me. He's just a pawn who's got no idea who the real players are."

"And you think you can find these real players?"

"With time, yeah. All I gotta do is work my way up the chain. The guy who tried to kill me killed Isaac. And whoever killed Isaac doesn't want *anybody* to know who killed my momma."

Cy brought his hands to his head, groaning. "After all these years, it finally has to come down to that, does it?"

"Not my choice. That was Isaac's doing."

"And what if Isaac just lied through his teeth when he told you he knows who killed your momma, hoping he could talk you into helping him that way?"

"It's possible," said Theo. "But I don't think

a bluff would have gotten him the kind of help he needed to bust out of jail. He must have had something on the killer—enough for the dude to whack Isaac after he got out and offered to let me in on the secret. Jack and me are on the same page with this."

"Jack," he said, exasperated. "You know I like Jack, but he ain't the one who's sitting in jail with a big bull's-eye pasted onto his back."

"Careful, old man. If I asked him, Jack Swyteck would change places with me in a minute. And not just to get into Trina's pants."

They shared a little smile, and then Cy turned serious.

"I want you out of jail," he said.

Theo didn't answer right away.

"You hear me?" the old man said. "I want you out of this place."

Theo averted his eyes and shook his head slowly. "I can't just—"

"Theo," he said, his voice firm but not harsh. He stepped closer. "I ain't asking you."

"What, you're *telling* me?" he said, scoffing.

Uncle Cy came right beside him and laid his hand on Theo's shoulder. "I'm begging you, boy."

Theo could feel the sincerity in his touch, hear the slight crack in his voice, see the moisture building in his eyes.

"Guard!" he called, still looking at Theo.

The CO entered the room. Finally, Cy lowered his gaze. "It's time for me to go."

Theo said, "Hey, it's gonna be totally—"

Cy raised a hand stopping him, as if to say, "You're all I've got, you're all I've ever had." The words didn't come, but they weren't necessary.

"It's your decision," he said, now looking straight at Theo. "Make it a good one."

The old man started toward the door, and the guard followed.

Theo watched as they left the room, the pain in his ribs worse than ever.

ANDIE SQUEEZED ONE FINAL concession out of the warden before leaving her office. She wanted to see Theo Knight's attacker.

She knew she couldn't question a prisoner who'd demanded an attorney. But both her psychology background and her FBI training in criminal profiling had taught her that some things could never be gleaned from mug shots and criminal records. Sometimes, just laying eyes on the suspect could trigger a thought that filled in another piece of the puzzle.

Duane Holloway was in the hole, one of several small cells in a separate wing of TGK where inmates were kept in solitary confinement. Eager to go home, the warden had no interest in visiting Holloway at 3:00 A.M., and she even allowed Jack to go with Andie, since all they could do was look at the prisoner from outside the cell anyway. A correctional officer escorted Andie and Jack through the maze of corridors and past the security checkpoint that led to the solitary wing. It wasn't underground (basements were rare in south Florida) but it felt like it. The lighting was dim, the concrete walls sweated with moisture, and the air smelled of mildew. Holloway was in cell number three.

The guard stopped at the solid metal door, slid the slot open like the bouncer at a speakeasy, and flipped the light switch outside the cell.

"What the hell?" the man inside said, groaning.

The guard smiled at Andie. "Feast your eyes."

Andie went to the slot and peered inside.

Holloway was sitting on the floor, stark naked. He had an annoyed expression on his face, and Andie couldn't tell if he'd been sleeping or if his eyes simply weren't accustomed to the lights.

He flipped a double bird to Andie, who was nothing more than a pair of eyes in the viewing slot.

Holloway was smaller than Andie had expected. Had Theo not been handcuffed, the attack would have failed in two seconds flat. Like many inmates, however, he had impressive biceps and well-defined abs that came from battling boredom with exercise. He also had a tattoo on his chest, and since Andie was standing less than six feet away from him, she had no trouble identifying it.

"He's Folk Nation," she said.

"What?" said Jack.

Andie stepped away from the door. "He has a tattoo on his chest with a pitchfork and the letters *B-O-S*. That's 'Brothers of the Struggle,' one of the better-known identifiers for Folk Nation. The pitchfork is also one of their symbols."

"I know Folk Nation is a gang, but who are they exactly?" said Jack.

"They're actually not a gang—they're an alliance under which gangs are aligned.

Think in terms of the New York Yankees and Chicago White Sox being part of the American League. Folk's roots are in Chicago, but it has national reach, traditionally aligned with Crips out of L.A. Their rival is People Nation, which lines up with Blood from the West Coast. The big gangs aligned under Folk are extremely violent and have begun to make serious inroads with local gangs in Florida, mostly for the drug trade."

"Why would one of those Folk Nation gangs want Theo dead?"

"They don't need a reason. Random killing can be part of their initiation ritual."

"Hey!" the man shouted from inside his cell. "Is that a woman's voice out there? Come jerk me off, baby!"

The guard smacked the door with his nightstick. The prisoner just laughed.

Jack and Andie stepped farther away from the door. "Is that what you think this was," said Jack, lowering his voice. "A random hit?"

"No," said Andie, her words flowing as fast as her thoughts were coming to her. "I think Folk Nation is in this equation because O-Town Posse wants Theo dead. I think O-Town Posse wants Theo dead because Moses ordered it. And I think Moses was headed north on the expressway tonight because O-Town Posse is trying to cement its alignment with one of the more powerful national gangs in Folk Nation."

"Climbing in bed with the big boys out of Chicago?" said Jack.

"Yeah," said Andie, the picture getting clearer by the minute. "But I have a good feeling about this marriage."

"Why?"

"Moses brings way more baggage than he's worth," she said, cutting him a sideways glance. "Thanks to our Theo."

It was the first time Jack had ever heard her say *our* Theo. Maybe it was innocuous. Maybe it wasn't. But he sort of liked the sound of it.

Chapter 35

Moses was in Atlanta by noon.

His new car was nowhere near as stylish as the one he'd swapped out at the chop shop, but with a dead state trooper under his belt, the last thing he needed while cruising up the interstate was a set of wheels with gang markings. He'd driven all night, keeping his speed at or below the limit, stopping for gas only after he was as far north of the Florida state line as his bladder could stand. His second stop came several hours later at the famous Varsity fast-food restaurant, a greasy-spoon of an institution with irresistible chili dogs and onion rings. It was on Atlanta's north side, directly across the expressway from Georgia Tech, which meant that the lunchtime crowd rivaled that of Times Square on New Year's Eve. Moses ordered his food to go, added a chocolate shake to make his overindulgence complete, used his turn signal as he exited the parking lot, and continued on his law-abiding way up the interstate and into Gwinnett County.

Atlanta's most dangerous gangs weren't only in the city. They ruled from the suburbs.

Compared to Miami's Overtown, the metropolitan area northeast of Atlanta was like a forest. Unlike Overtown, however, developers in these parts didn't make a habit of taking the money from banks or housing authorities and running. They actually built things in Gwinnett County—and built and built. The tree-lined streets slowly gave way to patches of overdevelopment, entire neighborhoods that seemed to be in a state of identity crisis, not sure if they were residential or commercial. To Moses it was all commerce. That was the nature of the gang drug trade.

On a middle-class street behind a supermarket, Moses found the address he was looking for. It was a ranch-style house that needed a paint job and landscaping, but so did most of the seventies-vintage residences around it. He counted nine cars that had arrived ahead of him, four in the driveway and five on the street. This concerned him. He'd thought only one person knew he was coming—Levon Dawkins.

Moses parked at the curb by the mailbox and hit speed-dial number one on his cell phone. He'd been smart enough to stash the phone before his arrest and maintain the service even while incarcerated. No way could he afford to lose his programmed numbers.

Levon Dawkins was inside the house when he answered on his cell.

Moses said, "What's with all the cars?"

"No worries. Ain't here for you, dude." The noise in the background was making it hard for Moses to hear him. Men were shouting, music was blaring.

"Then what you got?" said Moses.

"Two initiations today. You're just in time to see the second."

Moses smiled with curiosity. He'd heard stories about the things young men would do to become a Gangster Disciple, but he'd never seen an initiation rite.

"You're cool with me watching?" said Moses.

"Cool with it? I insist."

"Thanks, dude."

"Don't thank me, fool. You need to see what it takes to become a GD," he said, his tone taking on even more bravado. "And why nobody deserves more respect."

Moses ended the call, stepped out of his car, and headed up the walkway. Not many people could talk down to him and live to tell about it, but Levon was different. Gangster Disciples wasn't just one of the most violent Chicago gangs aligned under Folk Nation. It was also one of the best organized, modeled after a corporation. Cocaine was their mainstay, and Levon was a major player in the wholesale distribution market, supplying mostly retail crack dealers. Lately, the Hispanic gangs had been eating everyone's lunch in Atlanta. Levon was down on assignment from the Windy City to implement Project MAC—Miami-Atlanta-Chicago—and to secure GD's position in the southeast. To that end, building an alliance between GD and O-Town Posse was a top priority, both for Levon and for Moses.

"Who the fugg're you?" said the muscular

black man in the doorway. The front door was only half open, and his huge frame prevented Moses from seeing the source of all the racket inside. He wore a red Atlanta Falcons jersey, but the number—Michael Vick's 7—was nearly covered with the gaudy gold bling hanging around his neck. The rest of his outfit had the telltale right-sided tilt of Folk Nation—black cap with the bill cocked to the right, the right pant leg of his baggy jeans rolled up to the ankle, no shoelaces in the right basketball shoe. He wore a diamond stud earring only in his right ear.

Moses gave the attitude right back to him. "Who the fuck are you?"

The door jerked wide open, giving the doorman a start, and suddenly Levon was standing in the doorway. "Get inside," he told Moses.

Moses entered. Levon shut the door and secured it with the deadbolt and the chain. He and Moses exchanged the symbolic handshake that marked them as gangsters aligned under Folk Nation, and then Levon led him down the hall to a large, windowless media room in the back of the house. Rap music blasted from state-of-the-art surround-sound equipment, and all of the furniture had been stacked against the opposite wall to create a large open space. About twenty young men were standing around in small groups, all dressed more or less like the doorman. They talked and laughed as several vials of cocaine changed hands, each gangster taking a hit when it came his way. Several bottles of coconut-flavored rum were also making the rounds. A movie played on the plasma-screen television mounted on the wall—some hot blonde chick on her knees trying to decide which of three black studs to suck first.

"Do me!" said one of Levon's men, exposing himself to the TV screen.

"Bitch wants a meal, not a snack," said another.

Loud cursing and shoving followed, but it was quickly broken up.

Moses noticed a guy lying flat in the fetal position on the floor beside the couch. He appeared to be breathing, but his face was a battered mess, and his shirt was drenched in his own blood.

"Wannabe number one didn't make it through the initiation," said Levon. He pulled one of the chairs from the stack and climbed up to stand tall above the group. "Listen up!" he shouted.

Conversations faded into silence, and someone lowered the music. The fact that Moses was standing to Levon's right was the first indicator of his importance. Levon said, "This here's Moses. He's my new main man in Miami. He'll be staying with me a while, till the heat cools in Florida."

Hiding from law enforcement in another jurisdiction was one of the biggest advantages of an alliance with a national gang like Gangster Disciples. Most of these guys struck Moses as expendable morons, but any gangster was smart enough to grasp that Levon's reference to the heat in Florida had nothing to do with the weather.

"What's the crime?" asked the doorman.

Levon answered for him. "Murder."

"Killed a state trooper," said Moses.

"Cool," said another.

"Twelve hours after he got outta prison," added Levon.

A guy with a rum bottle flashed a mouthful of gold teeth. "*Very* cool."

Moses' status was established immediately.

Levon said, "Moses has full rights of a Gangster Disciple while he's here. So bring on the next wannabe!"

The men howled like drunken football fans. The rap music cranked up again, and Blondie, the on-screen porn star, was working feverishly on stud number two. A pair of older gang members left the room and returned with a fifteen-year-old black youth who was already blindfolded and stripped to the waist. Crude tattoos covered his chest and arms, and his head was covered with a black-and-yellow bandana. As they led him to the center of the room, it was difficult to tell who was having a harder time walking a straight line, the soldiers or the wannabe. The rum and drugs were kicking in.

Levon went to the wannabe, stood face-to-face with him, and removed the blindfold. The music stopped and the room fell quiet again.

Levon said, "Kenny Butler: Are you ready to become a Gangster Disciple?"

"Yes, sir!" he shouted.

Levon pulled a revolver from his belt and held it in the air for everyone to see.

It was a Russian M1895 Nagant, and the excitement in the room gave Moses the distinct impression that everyone understood the significance of the chosen firearm—everyone except him and the wannabes.

Levon quieted the gang and said, "Bring me Wallace."

The two soldiers walked over to wannabe number one. Wallace was still bloody and lying on the floor, and he groaned with pain as they jerked him to his feet.

"Front and center!" shouted Levon.

The soldiers brought Wallace to their leader and left him there to stand on his own power. His face was swollen from the earlier beating, and he couldn't open his left eye. The blood around his nose was starting to dry a crusty brown, but the big gash on his forehead was still running red. The kid tilted to one side, unable to stand straight, his whole body battered.

"On your knees," Levon said.

Wallace complied as quickly as he could, which wasn't quick at all, his every movement painful.

Levon flipped open the revolver's six-chamber cylinder, which was empty. He took one round of live ammunition from his pocket, inserted it in the first chamber, closed the cylinder, and gave it a spin, Russian roulette style. Then he handed the gun to Butler and guided the barrel of the gun to the base of Wallace's skull.

"You got a choice, Butler," said Levon. "Squeeze the trigger. If the gun don't go off, both you and Wallace is in."

That drew a loud woo-hoo from the peanut gallery.

"What's my other choice?" said Butler.

"You can do the line, just like Wallace did."

The line was a common initiation rite that even Moses and the O-Town Posse had used. The wannabe walks between two lines of gangsters who punch and kick him repeatedly. Only those candidates who walked on their feet from one end of the line to the other are admitted into the gang. If they fall, they have to start over, usually on another day, when the injuries have healed. Wallace had obviously failed in his attempt.

"And if I make it through the line?" said Butler.

"You're a Gangster Disciple," said Levon.

"What about him?" he said, pointing to Wallace, who was still on his knees.

"You walk the line, Wallace is out. The gun is the only way you both get in."

Wallace bit down on his lower lip. Part of him looked as if he wanted to stand up and run, but he remained on his knees.

Butler swallowed a lump in his throat.

"The gun!" one of the soldiers shouted.

"Shit, yeah!" said another, and soon a chant filled the room: "Gun, gun, gun!"

Levon raised a hand in the air, silencing them. "What's it gonna be?"

Butler stared down at the top of Wallace's head. It wasn't hot in the room, but both kids were sweating.

The chant continued: "Gun, gun, gun!"

Levon said, "I need an answer!"

Butler's hand gripped the revolver. The tip of his finger caressed the trigger.

"Gun, gun, gun!"

Still on his knees, Wallace's expression tightened. "Gun!" he shouted.

Butler seemed caught off-guard. It was a ballsy decision for a guy on his knees with a gun to his head.

Levon said, "It ain't Wallace's call. It's yours, Butler."

"Gun!" Wallace shouted again.

The other gangsters cheered.

Butler's arm went straight as a rod, as if he were trying to put as much distance as possible between himself and the target. The gun moved high and then low, left and then right, all around the back of Wallace's skull.

It was obvious to Moses that the kid had

never shot anybody in his life—let alone a friend.

Butler retracted the gun and dropped his arm to his side. "I choose the line," he said.

The gang groaned and booed with disapproval. Levon snatched the revolver from his hand and brought a knee to Butler's groin. The kid doubled over and fell to the floor. Levon kicked him hard in the face, bloodying his nose and mouth. "There ain't gonna be no line, you pussy."

Levon's soldiers grabbed Butler and dragged him away. Wallace was still on his knees, smart enough not to move until Levon gave the order.

"Moses!" said Levon.

All eyes shifted to the man from Miami as he stepped forward. Levon handed him the firearm, saying, "He's all yours, bro'."

The rhythmic chant resumed: "Gun, gun, gun!"

A flat smile creased Moses' lips. He opened the cylinder, and he didn't even have to verbalize his request. Levon knew what he wanted. He handed Moses another bullet.

The gang cheered, loving the way Moses had changed the odds and upped the stakes.

Wallace placed his hands behind his waist, wrists crossed. Moses noticed they were trembling.

Even so, the kid shouted, "Gun!"

Moses inserted the second round in one of the empty chambers, slapped the cylinder closed, and pushed the barrel of the revolver firmly against the back of the teenager's skull.

The room went stone silent.

"What you want, Wallace?" said Moses in a booming voice.

"Do it!"

Without a moment's hesitation, Moses pulled the trigger.

It was almost simultaneous—Wallace falling face-first to the floor and the loud crack of the hammer against an empty chamber. But his head was intact. Raw nerves and emotion had caused his collapse.

Moses popped open the cylinder and let the two unspent rounds drop to his feet.

Levon shouted, "Meet the newest GD!"

The gang went wild. They were suddenly all over Wallace, slapping him on the head and body, screaming and yelling in his face— all a form of congratulations and praise.

Levon pulled Moses into another room,

leaving the gang to celebrate. It was time to get down to business. He closed the door and locked it. They were in a bedroom with no bed—just a table, a few chairs, and a wall of tall metal lockers. Levon opened the one on the far right with a key, removed a packet, and tossed it onto the table in front of Moses.

"Your new ID," he said.

Moses opened the packet and inspected it. There was a Social Security card, a Georgia driver's license and voter registration card, and two credit cards.

"Miles?" said Moses, making a face. "My new name is *Miles* Becker?"

"I set you up in twenty-four hours, and this is the thanks I get?"

Moses grumbled, but he didn't protest. He tucked away the IDs and said, "What else you got?"

Levon opened another locker. It was loaded with weapons—handguns, rifles, even an Uzi. "I assume you dumped the piece you used to waste that trooper," said Levon.

"You assume right."

"What do you like?"

"Nine-millimeter," said Moses.

"How about a Glock?" Levon said, as he

laid it on the table with two ammunition clips.

"Glock is good," said Moses.

Levon went to the next locker. This one had two locks on it. He opened them both and pulled a cardboard box from the top shelf. He placed it on the table and opened it. The inside was lined with green plastic. He punched a hole in it, just big enough for Moses to see the contents.

"This is the best shit we got in six months," said Levon. "We cut it three times and it still kicks ass. Your boys in Miami know their trade."

"We aim to please," said Moses.

"I'm serious," said Levon. "Filthy Mexicans have been killing us in Atlanta. Latin Kings got way too much turf. Eighteenth Street is here, too. Last week I seen two old guys—must have been in their forties—all the way from L.A. Tacos are makin' a push here. But you keep this up, and we'll cut their balls off."

"There's plenty more where that came from."

Levon made the hole in the bag a little larger. "Wanna sample?"

Moses shook his head. "Ain't touched that shit in ten years."

"Twelve for me," said Levon. "Not one bro-tha' I grew up with back in Robert Taylor Homes did the shit and got outta Chicago's South Side alive."

"Guess that's why we're the old men in this business."

The celebratory noises from the media room were getting louder. The two thirty-something-year-olds exchanged knowing smiles, as if to acknowledge that most of those flunkies would be lucky to see seventeen.

Moses' cell rang. He didn't recognize the displayed number of the incoming call, but he answered it anyway. It turned out to be the right decision.

The caller was Jefferson—the correctional officer at TGK.

"Holloway dropped the ball," said Jefferson. "Knight's alive and well."

Moses took the news without any display of emotion, trying not to tip off anything to Levon. "Anything else?"

"Yeah," said Jefferson. "I hear the prosecutor is dropping the charges against Knight for helping Reems escape. He'll be on the street today, tomorrow at the latest."

"Got it," said Moses.

Jefferson hung up. The entire conversation had lasted only thirty seconds. Moses felt his anger rising, but he said nothing as he tucked the phone away in his pocket.

Levon said, "Something wrong?"

Moses thought for a moment, then looked at Levon and said, "I'm gonna need some cash."

"How much?"

"Enough to set me up in Miami for a few days."

"Miami? You going back already?"

"Yeah."

"What for?"

"It's like they say," said Moses, his expression turning deadly serious. "You want something done right, you do it your fucking self."

Chapter 36

Jack spent the night at his *abuela*'s house.

It surprised people that a guy named Jack Swyteck had an *abuela*. Most shocked of all were folks who met him in a bar or at a cocktail party and, tongue loosened, spoke to him gringo-to-gringo about the damn Hispanics taking over south Florida. Jack's mother was born in Cuba. She was a teenager when Castro came to power and her parents spirited her away to Miami under the Pedro Pan program, a humanitarian effort that allowed thousands of Cuban children to escape the dictatorship and live in freedom. The vast majority of families were ultimately reunited in the

States, but Jack's *abuela* couldn't get out of Cuba until Jack was in his thirties, long after his mother had died giving birth to him. Abuela made it her mission to Cubanize her grandson.

The results had been mixed. On their most recent trip to an espresso bar, Jack wanted a *café mocha* instead of a *café cubano*, which was embarrassing enough to Abuela, but then he drove the dagger straight through her heart by ordering a *café moco*—which in *español* meant "coffee booger."

"*Buenos días*," said Jack, as he entered her kitchen.

Abuela was standing at the counter spreading *queso crema* on sliced strips of fresh Cuban bread. The strips were for dunking in *café con leche*, and from the first time Jack had tried it, bagels and cream cheese just didn't cut it anymore.

Jack gave her a kiss and smiled as she called him *mi vida*—literally, "my life"—a term she used only with Jack, and which pretty much summed up the depth of her feelings. He took a seat at the table. Abuela placed his breakfast in front of him and started to wipe down the counter.

"Sit with me," said Jack. "I can clean up."

The way she looked at him, it was as if Jack had said, "I can have a sex change." Abuela was definitely old school.

Jack dunked his first strip of *pan y queso*, trying not to think too vividly about Theo and Trina waking inside his house on Key Biscayne. Theo had been released from jail late yesterday afternoon. Anyone who thought make-up sex was great had obviously never experienced just-got-out-of-jail sex. There was nothing better, according to Theo, even if the term of incarceration was only a few days. Who was Jack to argue? Theo's problem, however, was Uncle Cy in the next room.

"Dude, I need your place tonight," Theo had begged him.

"Find a hotel."

Jack might as well have said, "Buy Trump Tower." For Theo, it was the kind of response that didn't compute between friends. Like an idiot, Jack had handed over the keys and planned to spend the night at his grandmother's.

Abuela had been awake since 5:00 A.M., the radio tuned to a Spanish-language talk show. Jack understood Spanish much better than he spoke it, so he listened. An old woman carried on about *pochos*, a pejorative name for second-generation Mexicans who knew only as much about their heritage as the *George Lopez Show* could teach them and raised children who didn't speak a word of Spanish.

Abuela switched off the radio, and Jack prepared himself for the Cuban version of a well-meaning lecture. But she surprised him.

"You do not mention Rene once since you are here," she said. Her English was roughly on the level of Jack's Spanish, so she often stuck to the present tense.

"I didn't?" he said.

"No. How is she?"

"I don't know. I haven't talked to her in a while."

"Oh? When last?"

"Actually . . . when she was here in Miami."

Abuela looked horrified. "You no call her?"

"We said good-bye in the airport. She said she would call me as soon as her plane landed in Africa. She didn't."

"*Ay, mi vida,*" she said, shaking her head with disapproval.

"Don't worry, your grandson's not that small a person. I allowed for the possibility that something happened, so I called her. Left a message on her cell. Sent her an e-mail, too."

"She no respond?"

Jack dunked another strip of bread. "No. That's just the way Rene is."

Abuela came to the table and sat across from him. "Why you put up with that?"

"That's an excellent question."

"What about that FBI girl?"

"What about her?"

"Why you no call her?"

"Don't tell me. Has Theo turned you into an Andie fan, too?"

"A fan? No. *Pero*, if she is *Cubana* . . ."

He smiled and kissed her hand. The doorbell rang. Jack and Abuela exchanged glances, as if to ask, Are you expecting someone? Neither one was.

"I'll get it," said Jack. He walked down the hall to the front door and checked the peephole. A big eyeball was staring back at him. He knew it could be only one person, so he opened the door.

"Hey, thanks for last night," said Theo, obviously in a great mood.

"I'm not the one you should be thanking," said Jack.

"You got that right. You would not believe—"

"Please, spare me the details."

"No, you don't understand," said Theo. "Some women reach for your joystick like it was a doorknob in the bathroom of a rundown filling station, but Trina, she grabs hold of you and—"

"Okay, okay," said Jack, wincing. He stepped out onto the porch and closed the door. "This is my *grandmother's* house."

"Sorry, man. I just thought you'd be happy for me."

"I am happy."

"You don't sound like it."

"I couldn't be happier. Truly."

"What'd you and Abuela do last night?"

Jack was reluctant to say. "Dominoes."

Theo laughed way too hard. Had they been anywhere but Abuela's, Jack would have flipped him the bird.

"Why are you here?" said Jack.

"I need another favor."

"No, you can't have my place again tonight."

"I wouldn't even think of asking. At least not till you wash the bedsheets."

You mean burn them. "What do you want now?"

"Hey, I almost forgot," said Theo. Jack sensed a little misdirection coming before Theo hit him up for the real favor. Theo started to unbutton his dress shirt.

"What are you doing?" said Jack.

"Check this out," he said, as he pulled open the shirt to reveal what he was wearing underneath it. "You like?"

"It's a T-shirt," said Jack.

"Not just a T-shirt. The idea came to me when I was sitting in jail. I asked Trina to have some samples silk-screened. This is your new marketing angle, a way to build up your criminal defense practice. It's like the advertising campaign for the milk industry—'Got milk?'"

Jack took a closer look. "Got caught?" he said, reading aloud, and then he read the smaller print: "Call Jack Swyteck."

"Good, huh?" said Theo.

Jack just rolled his eyes. "Theo, really—what do you want?"

He buttoned his shirt. "I need you to give me a lift."

"Don't you have a car?"

"Trina dropped me off. Anyway, I need you to come with me."

"Where we going now?"

"My favorite place," said Theo. "Back to TGK."

"For what?"

"Just put on your lawyer face. Come on, hotshot. I'll fill you in on the way."

A TGK CORRECTIONAL OFFICER led them to a private visitation room. Coincidentally, it was the very same cubicle in which Theo, as inmate, and Jack, as lawyer, had met just a few days earlier. This time, however, Jack and Theo sat side-by-side on what Theo called the suit's side of the small conference table, the lawyer and his "investigator." Together, they waited.

Finally, the fortified door opened. A guard entered first. The inmate followed immediately behind him.

It was Theo's old cell mate, Charger.

"Twenty minutes," the guard said, as he left the room.

The empty bunk had been Charger's first clue, and at breakfast he'd heard about Theo's release. The whole cafeteria was buzzing with talk of the attack in the infirmary last night. Charger went to the telephone, dialed Theo's home number, and told Uncle

Cy that he had to speak to Theo—in person and in private. Bringing an attorney along was the only way to ensure privacy, so Theo rounded up Jack just as soon as Cy called and delivered the message.

Charger sat in the wooden chair on the other side of the table, facing Theo and Jack. Theo was about to make the introductions, but Charger didn't seem to care who Jack was. He looked only at Theo.

"I lied to you," said Charger.

"About what?" said Theo.

He looked at Jack. "You got any gum?"

"Actually, I do." Jack offered a stick, and Charger took the whole pack. He tucked a piece into his mouth and chewed. Interesting, but watching him gently work the gum around in his mouth was the first time Theo had so clearly noticed Charger's effeminate side. He definitely worked on his manliness among the general prison population, not one of the obvious prison bitches who enhanced his lips with powdered Kool-Aid from the kitchen as if it were a tube of Hooker Red No. 105.

"What'd you lie about?" said Theo.

"'Bout Isaac."

"I'm listening."

Charger crossed one leg over the other,

again like a woman. "Me and him, I mean. That was a lie."

Theo had little doubt as to Charger's meaning, but somehow it just wasn't registering. "What was a lie?"

Charger looked at Jack, then back at Theo. "Your friend's cute," said Charger.

Theo jumped up, reached across the table, and grabbed him by the inmate number on his jumpsuit. "You little shit, what are you saying?"

Jack pulled him back into his chair. "Easy, Theo. Go easy."

Charger caught his breath and brushed out the wrinkles that Theo had inflicted on his jumpsuit.

Charger lowered his eyes, his hands resting in his lap. "I lied when I said Isaac and me weren't lovers."

"Let's get outta here," Theo said to Jack.

"Wait," said Jack. He leaned forward, elbows on the table, the way he might during the deposition of a witness who was flip-flopping on his story. "Why did you lie about that before?"

Charger leaned forward as well, and suddenly Jack's attempt at intimidation looked more like two people on a date staring into each other's eyes. "Because that was the way Isaac wanted it," said Charger.

Jack sat back in his chair. "He preferred to keep it a secret?"

"Uh-huh. So that was the way we played it."

Theo said, "I got two things to say about that. Number one, I don't believe you. Number two, if this is all you got me out of bed with my girlfriend to listen to, I'm gonna jump over this table and snap you in half."

"Well, then, I'm one lucky boy. Because that's not all I have to tell you. And I can make you believe everything."

"How?"

"Isaac and me shared secrets."

"What kind of secrets?"

"The best kind," said Charger. "Dangerous ones."

"How do you mean 'dangerous'?"

"See, Isaac was a very smart man. Outside our cell, he had to treat me bad. He knew what would happen if he was good to me in front of the other inmates."

Theo said, "Yeah, they'd kick his ass."

"No," he said with a light chuckle. "Nobody kicked Isaac's ass. His concern was for me. He didn't want the bad guys to have any reason to think I knew any of his secrets. Especially, you know, if something happened to Isaac."

Theo and Jack exchanged glances. The same realization had hit them simultaneously: Charger was the safety valve—the person outside the extortion scheme who knew all the secrets and could tell all if the blackmailer turned up dead.

Jack said, "Was there something specific that Isaac wanted you to tell Theo if something happened to him after the escape?"

Charger nodded.

Theo said, "Why didn't you tell me when I was in the cell with you?"

"I didn't think you'd be leaving so soon. And to be honest, I was kind of hoping we'd get to like each other first."

"That ain't gonna happen," said Theo.

"I know. But give me a little credit. I'm sticking my neck out, and there's no Isaac, no Theo, no one at all on the inside to protect me."

"I'm sure we'll read all about it in the next edition of *Profiles in Courage*," said Theo. "So let's hear it."

Charger smiled like a smart-ass, as if he was just now getting to the fun part. "Reality Bitches dot com," he said. "It's a website."

Theo said, "That's all you got? A website address?"

"Yup."

Again, Jack and Theo exchanged glances, both men reconsidering Charger's role as safety valve.

Jack said, "What's on this website?"

"I've never seen it," said Charger, his voice trailing off to a playful whisper. "But from the sound of it, I'd say it has something to do with Santa's naughty list."

Theo narrowed his eyes. "You better not be messin' with us."

"If anyone's messing with you, it ain't me. It's Isaac. Thanks for the gum," said Charger, winking at Jack. He pushed away from the table, walked to the door, and pressed the button on the wall. The door opened, and Charger told the guard he was ready to go.

"See you around, boys," he said on his way out. The door closed, leaving Theo alone with Jack.

"You think he's for real?" said Theo.

"Let's visit that website and find out."

Jack removed his notebook computer from his briefcase and powered it up on the table. The jail made a high-speed wireless Internet connection available to attorneys, and Jack's

Wi-Fi picked up the signal. Theo watched as he typed in the address. Even with a high-speed connection, it took a moment for the page to load. The banner emerged first—"Reality Bitches" in bold red letters. Below it were several boxes, empty at first, and then one by one, the images popped into place.

The first was the face of a pretty redhead who was *maybe* old enough to vote. A string of letters tumbled across the screen and then settled into place to spell "Party Bitch."

Then the second box developed, a brunette called "Head Bitch," followed by "Nasty Bitch," "Latina Bitch," and several others, until the final box emerged. This last image, however, was much slower to come into focus than the others. It also seemed to be a much lower resolution, a little grainy, the color and lighting of much lower quality.

She was "Reality Bitch."

Theo slapped the table and walked away. "Damn you, Isaac!" he said, kicking the wastebasket across the room.

"What is it?"

Theo turned and faced Jack, mad enough to put a fist through the wall. He needed to hit something—or someone.

"Theo, what's wrong?"

"Nothing," he said, trying to breathe in and out, the way Trina had taught him to get himself under control. "There's nothing wrong at all."

"Tell me," said Jack.

Theo walked back to the table, glanced one more time at the screen, and then looked at Jack. "That's her," he said. "That's my mother."

Chapter 37

Theo wasn't handling it well. Uncle Cy wasn't doing much better.

So Jack had to deal with it.

The old photograph of Theo's mother on the website was only the beginning. One click of the mouse set the image in motion, a stream of XXX video. Even if the woman hadn't been Theo's mother, Jack would have had a difficult time watching. He had his own theory as to why Isaac might have wanted Theo to see it, but he needed a profession-al's evaluation before talking it over again with Theo and his uncle.

At one o'clock he was in a conference room

at the FBI's field office. Andie was seated across from him, and his open notebook computer lay on the table between them. Jack typed in the website address and hit ENTER.

The LCD screen blinked, the Reality Bitches homepage lit up—and Andie blinked too.

"You okay?" said Jack.

"Sorry," she said. "I'm trying to be professional, but the existential in me can't help but see the absurd side of surfing porn sites with you."

"This isn't pornography," said Jack. "It's obscenity."

"Oh, well, that makes me feel better already."

There was humor in what she was saying, but Jack knew she wasn't making light of the situation. Few law enforcement officers had witnessed the depravity Andie had as a criminal profiler and hostage negotiator, and everyone had his or her own way of staying sane.

She said, "Does Theo have any idea where this came from?"

"None."

"How about Uncle Cy?"

"He didn't want to see it any more than

Theo did. I asked him if he knew of any hard-core porn films she might have made. He didn't. But he said it wouldn't come as a surprise to him."

"Can Theo put an approximate date on the photo?"

"It's hard to get him to take a really good look at it. But I can tell you that she was thirty-one years old when she died."

Andie studied the photograph on the screen. "She looks like a teenager here. Pretty girl."

"The image is pretty low resolution, so I'm sure that doesn't help."

"Our tech guys can improve that."

"Do the computer enhancements later," said Jack. "Right now, I just want you to watch this. Tell me if you have the same reaction I did."

"What was your take on it?"

"Watch first. I don't want to sway you."

"All right," she said, drawing a breath. "Let's see—no, wait. Tell me her name."

She had reached across the table and grabbed his wrist. Jack didn't pretend to know her every touch—they'd never more than kissed—but he knew instantly that this moment had nothing to do with him. It was between Andie and the woman on the screen—a real person, a human being, not just some pervert's five-minute fantasy in cyberspace.

"Portia," said Jack. "Her name was Portia Knight."

Andie let go of his wrist. "Okay. Let's see what we've got."

"It might be easier to see if we switched off the light."

Andie considered it, then leaned back and flipped the wall switch. The room went dark, and the glow of the screen that bathed them in strangely colored light only added to the eerie feeling of anticipation.

Jack clicked on the photograph with his mouse. The frozen image jerked into motion, and Portia came to life.

Theo's mother was in a dark room, her body illuminated only by the camera's harsh spotlight. The expression on her face could only be described as wary, the nervous smile of a young woman who was beginning to realize that perhaps she was in over her head. Her hair was pulled back tightly, making her face clearly visible.

"Theo got her eyes," said Andie.

She was moving, and as the camera angle

widened, it was clear that she was dancing. Her breasts were fully exposed, and she wore only a red thong, gold hoop earrings, and gold stiletto heels.

Andie said, "Can you turn up the volume?"

"There's no sound."

Even with no music, Portia's movement on-screen seemed smooth and rhythmic, as if Theo's appreciation for all things musical hadn't come entirely from his uncle. Behind her, in a ragged semicircle, a crowd of men stood and watched her dance, all of them smiling, most of them holding large plastic cups in one hand and a smoldering cigar in the other. With such bad lighting, and with the camera's focus entirely on the dancer, the spectators and background images were distorted and obscured.

Andie said, "Looks like this even predates VHS recorders. Probably a handheld sixteen-millimeter."

"I guess that would have been state of the art when Portia was a teenager."

"Yeah, early seventies."

Jack said, "And from the amount of jerky footage, I'd say the cameraman was one of the drunkest guys in the room."

On-screen, Portia showed her back to the camera, and the cameraman zoomed in on her ass. She bent over and grabbed her ankles, knees straight, and slid the thong down her legs, kicking it across the room with a flick of her foot. The cameraman tried to follow the thong as it sailed into the crowd, but it was just a blur.

She continued to dance nude, wearing only her spiked heels. One of the men came forward and started dancing with her. Staggering would have been a better word for it. Portia didn't pay much attention to him, but that only made him bolder. It was a silent video, but the other men appeared to be shouting and egging him on. The closer he came to her, the more she pulled away. He stumbled after her, apparently trying to kiss or lick her breasts, but he managed only to spill his cup all over her.

Portia stopped dancing. From her reaction, the contents of the cup must have been ice-cold. She said something to him. He spoke back to her, clearly angry. Another man tried to pull him back into the crowd. He made some kind of remark to Portia as well. She responded in kind—the same nasty body language—and he threw his drink on her. Another man did the same. Soon, plastic cups filled with beer were flying through the air. Portia was being pelted. She gathered up her white tube top and orange hot pants from the floor, but another man snatched them right back. Suddenly surrounded, she started looking for an escape route. Cups were still flying, and even with no sound it was clear that people were shouting and that things were getting out of hand.

Portia ran.

The cameraman followed.

So did the mob.

The screen was one bouncy frame after another as the cameraman and his drunken friends chased Portia out of the room and down the long hallway. The heels snapped off her shoes, and she gathered speed. She glanced back over her shoulder, tripped on a step, and hit the floor hard. She lay there, naked, sprawling.

Two men grabbed her, their images a blur in the confusion. Portia kicked and punched, but other men grabbed her arms to restrain her. Someone else took her legs. The cameraman zoomed in on her face. Portia was screaming.

Jack looked away from the screen. He'd

watched it twice already and didn't need to see it again. He glanced at Andie, her face aglow with the on-screen events. Even with no audio, it seemed as though Andie could hear Portia's screams. The notepad in front of her had not a single notation on it. Andie simply watched the filmed frenzy unfold on the computer.

It went on for several minutes. Close-ups of the penetration, close-ups of the terror in Portia's eyes. The men's faces, of course, had been carefully edited out. When it was over, the red letters tumbled back onto the screen to spell out a final message in lieu of credits. It read: "Reality Bitches get what they deserve."

Jack closed the website.

Andie was silent. Then she looked at Jack and said, "I'm glad Theo didn't watch."

"So you see it like I do? This is not acting. 'Reality Bitches' means it's real?"

"No doubt about it," she said. "Theo's mother was raped. Before she was his mother."

Chapter 38

Andie ate dinner at her desk. This was becoming a bad habit.

Nearly four months had passed since her last date with Jack. Fifteen weeks since he'd wigged out over her remark about Theo and called it quits. One-hundred-something days without another date of any promise. Two-thousand-plus hours without any hope of . . . "it."

Suddenly, she was counting minutes as the theme song from *Rent* played in her head.

She popped open another diet soda and unwrapped her spicy tuna roll from the local sushi-on-wheels. The bright side was that she was impressing her supervisors and proving herself worthy of advancement to the elite criminal profiling unit at the FBI Academy in Quantico. With every dinner alone at the office, however, the computer dating option seemed less absurd. That so-called cyber expert she'd blown off on Miami Beach had been dead right about one thing: it was hard for a female FBI agent to find love outside of law enforcement. Andie got plenty of interest from men who wore badges. That was one reason she'd been so attracted to Jack. That and . . . "it."

Funny how with certain people you just knew "it" would be good.

She glanced at the phone. Every now and then, she felt the urge to call her former supervisor to see if returning to Seattle was an option. Jack, however, had made that impossible. Even though he was in and out of her life in the span of two weeks, people would have said she jumped on a plane and flew across the country after getting dumped by the former governor's son.

A few more dates with Jack, and maybe it would have been true.

Good thing he wigged out.

Her appetite was gone. The files on the floor called out to her. Each stack was its own case, another investigation, a different victim. Andie had one of those filing systems where the work piled up—literally. Even so, she couldn't stop herself from going back to her computer and that movie again.

The FBI's tech experts had cleaned up the downloadable version of the film and burned it onto a disk, which she now inserted into her PC. It still had its shortcomings—shaky frames, grainy images, poor lighting. The geek masters were good, but they weren't magicians.

Andie let the frames advance in slow motion. It was like laying out the pieces to a puzzle with two parts. One, who raped Theo's mother? Two, why did Isaac want Theo to see it? So far she had the faces of two drunks—the heckler and his friend—in a dark room somewhere in the early 1970s. Those guys were in their fifties now, and it would be impossible to find and identify them if she didn't nail down the location. The answer had to be on this disk, and Andie was determined to dissect it from every angle. Portia's striptease in the darkness. Her argument with the drunks. The ensuing frenzy, the mad chase down hall, the—

Andie hit PAUSE. Something had caught her eye.

She rewound several frames, still in slow motion, and watched even more intently. A flash of light brightened the screen, and she hit PAUSE to freeze the image. The white flash had been the camera's spotlight reflecting in a mirror on the wall. She advanced one more frame—and there he was.

The cameraman.

Whoever had posted this film on the Internet had gone to some effort to protect the guilty, carefully editing out frames that would reveal the attackers' identity. Apparently they'd missed this split-second appearance of the cameraman in the mirror. Andie burned the image to a separate CD and took it upstairs to the tech floor. By definition, these guys had no life, and of course someone was still there after hours.

"Benny, can you help me again?" she said, catching her breath.

Crumpled candy wrappers and empty soda cans littered the work area around Benny's computer monitor. He swiveled in his chair to face Andie, but his mouth was too full to respond. He held a half-eaten Twinkie in one hand and a soda can in the other.

"What . . .now?" he said, swallowing.

Andie showed him the disk. "Can you clean up a still image for me?"

"Right this minute?"

"Pretty please?"

Bennie washed down his Twinkie with a hit of caffeine and sugar. "Okay," he said. "But first: in the television series *Star Trek*, who was originally offered the role of Spock, but declined?"

Andie felt a headache coming on. She liked *Star Trek*, but this was the price she paid for pretending to *love* it just to stay in the good graces of the all-important tech guys. "I don't know. Martin Landau?"

"Corrrr-ect!"

"Really?"

"Yup. And then in a truly interesting twist, after Landau left *Mission Impossible*, Leonard Nimoy joined that show to play the role of disguise expert—"

"Benny, please. The disk?"

He took it and inserted it into the computer. "Sure."

The image popped onto the screen. Benny worked on a monitor much larger than Andie's, and it looked even worse on the big screen. "Well, that could use some work," said Benny.

"Can you fix it?"

"Let's see." Benny zoomed on his face, sharpening the features, darkening the background, adjusting the color. Two minutes and several dozen mouse clicks later, the face was almost as clear as the other two images Andie had pulled from the movie.

"How's that?" said Benny.

"Great. Can you do anything with his shirt?"

"What about it?"

Andie pointed. "There's some kind of artwork on it, I think."

He trained the zoom onto the man's chest, and after another round of computerized adjustments, the shirt started to come into focus.

"It's a frat house," said Andie.

"What?" he said, still tinkering with the image.

"Those are Greek letters on his shirt. This was a fraternity party."

Benny tightened the zoom, and with another series of clicks the front of the man's shirt filled the screen. "That's the best I can do," he said.

Andie studied it. "Pi Alpha Delta," she said.

"Hope that helps," he said.

"More than you know," she said. She thanked him, brought the disk back to her office, and printed out the still images of the cameraman, the heckler, and his friend. Then she called university information to find out if there was a Pi Alpha Delta fraternity on campus.

There was.

Andie tucked the printed photographs into her purse and bolted out of the office.

It took twenty minutes of dodging speeding motorcycles on the expressway and another ten of winding through residential neighborhoods to reach the university's main campus. Pi Alpha Delta was actually located off-campus, one of five fraternity houses directly across from the intramural athletic fields on a busy four-lane boulevard. Andie parked her unmarked sedan in the church lot up the street, walked a half block to the house, and wondered how many frat boys had used the acronym as a bad pickup line—as in, "Come on over to my PAD."

Andie had yet to confirm that the PAD house existed in the 1970s, but from the looks of it, she was betting yes. The unadorned one-story cinder-block construction with low-slung roofline was the typical hurricane-resistant style of the 1960s that only a Florida architect could love. She walked up the sidewalk and rang the bell at the front door. It seemed surprisingly quiet inside. Apparently, even frat boys stopped to recharge their batteries every once in a while.

The door opened, and a muscular young man wearing only nylon jogging shorts and flip-flop sandals greeted her. If Andie had to guess, she'd say he spent more time working on his suntan and his six-pack abs than his studies.

He smiled and said, "Hey, baby."

"Hi. Do you live here?"

"Yeah. Wanna see my—"

"Don't say it," she said. Obnoxious enough, but on some level, she was sort of flattered that he hadn't taken her for the mother of one of his buddies. "My name's Andie," she said. "Andie Henning."

"I'm David. You with a sorority?"

Either David was playing with her, or the darkness was kinder to her thirty-something face than she realized. "Yeah," she said, playing along. "I'm a pledge over at FBI."

He scrunched his face, as if reciting the

entire Greek alphabet in his head, and then it hit him. "You mean . . ."

She nodded and flashed her badge. "Can I come in?"

"Yeah—sure," he said nervously. "I guess so."

He let her inside and closed the door. "How can I do for you? I mean, what—"

"Relax, okay? You're not in any kind of trouble."

"I should probably get our president."

"Is he here?"

"Yeah. But he's kind of—he's with his . . ."

"He's in his PAD?"

He smiled, which softened some of his nervous edge. "You know how that is."

"Look, I'm working on a very old case. It doesn't affect anyone who currently lives here. All I want to know is if you keep any composite photographs of your old fraternity classes around the house."

"Of course," he said. "They're hanging in the chapter room."

"Great. Can I see them?"

"Well, I don't know."

"It will take five minutes. You live here, so all I need is your consent."

"It's just that, we don't really let anyone in

the chapter room. Not even pledges. It's only for brothers."

"Oh, come on. You know as well as I do that there's nothing sacred in there. The only reason you keep it locked is because you don't want anyone looking at those composites and seeing what a bunch of geeks you PADs used to be."

"Yeah," he said with a chuckle. "Those mullet haircuts in the eighties were the best."

"What about the seventies?" she said, soft-pedaling her real interest. "The days of big hair and bad mustaches. Or maybe you don't go back that far."

"Oh, we go back to 1962."

"Wonderful. I love a place with a sense of history. So what do you say? You and me in the chapter room for five minutes? Or do we have to go knocking on the door of your president's PAD?"

"Well, okay. Follow me."

He led her down the hall and through the cafeteria. It was after the dinner hour, but some men were still at the tables, eating and talking, while others were actually studying. They looked up with curiosity as Andie and David passed. Andie followed him to the kitchen, which smelled of some food that

Andie was quite certain she'd never eaten. The final leg of the journey was down a hallway that was too narrow to walk in any formation but single file. The Greek letters πΑΔ were painted on a door that more or less blended into the wall, as if someone had made a halfhearted effort to create a secret entrance. It was secured with a combination lock. David made Andie face the other way as he dialed in the code, and then he took her inside and switched on the light.

"This is it?" she said.

She hadn't meant to insult him with her reaction, but had she endured the living hell that fraternity initiations were in the 1970s and earlier, this first look at the secret chapter room would have smacked of the proverbial crock at the end of the rainbow.

"This is it," he said.

The windowless room had all the charm of an unfinished basement—concrete floor, walls of painted cinder blocks, and shop-style fluorescent lighting suspended from the ceiling. Covering the walls, however, were several dozen framed composite photographs, each with head shots of young men dressed in suits. Andie immediately zeroed in on the composites where the outfit of choice was the powder-blue leisure suit. Andie went straight to them, as she removed her printed photographs from her purse.

David asked, "You know what year you're looking for?"

The composites were arranged in chronological order in columns of three. "Right around here," she said, searching. "Early to mid-1970s."

Andie's adrenalin was pumping. Each head shot had the young man's name underneath it, so if her computer-generated photographs matched, she was home-free. Theo's mother would have been fifteen years old in 1968, so she started there, just to be overinclusive. She compared the cameraman's image first, breezing through the late sixties, and slowing down for more careful examination in 1970, 1971, and so on. She went all the way to 1980.

He wasn't there. She went through it again, just in case she'd missed something.

He definitely wasn't there.

She did the same thing with the image of the heckler and the drunk who had started the war of words with Portia in the movie. She checked each composite, photograph by photograph.

They weren't there, either.

At this point, she was well beyond her allotted five minutes. David said, "Something wrong?"

"I was just so sure that—" She stopped herself and did a double take. "There's a year missing."

"What?"

"Nineteen seventy-two. It's not here."

David took a closer look. "You're right."

Andie walked the entire room, checking to see if it had been mounted someplace else, out of chronological order. "It's not here," she said. "Is there another room where it could be?"

"No. I been living here three years. All the old composites are in this room."

"I need to see 1972," she said.

"Well, I don't know how to help you. The one you want is the one we don't have. Which is sort of an interesting coincidence."

Andie noticed something about the wall. The composites weren't all the same size, and they'd hung so long in the same place that a faint shadow on the painted wall matched the outline of their frame. The composites after 1972 didn't match their shadow— which meant they'd been moved. Rearranged.

Recently. To make it not so apparent that 1972 was missing.

"It's definitely interesting that it's not here," she said, the wheels turning in her head. "But I'd say it's no coincidence."

"Hey, wait a sec," said David. "Pi Alpha Delta does have a historian."

"A historian?"

"Yeah. He's with the national office in Columbus, Ohio. Some old fart who doesn't want to let go of his college days."

"You think he has copies of old composites?"

"He has everything from every chapter in the country. But they'd be little copies. Like yearbook-sized. Would that help?"

Andie smiled. "Immensely. Think maybe I'll visit his pad."

Chapter 39

Jack got a phone call from Andie at midmorning. She had "important information" for him. Before he could ask why she didn't just tell him over the telephone, she beat him to the punch.

"You were nice enough to invite me to dinner at a gas station. How about lunch at a Laundromat?"

Jack laughed, but apparently she was serious. He jotted down the address and agreed to meet her there at noon.

The FBI field office was in North Miami, an area that Jack didn't know well, except to pass by it on his way to Broward County and all-important places like Dolphin Stadium or Fort Lauderdale beach. He was sure they had plenty of good lunch spots up that way. Knowing Miami, however, he wasn't so sure Andie had been kidding about the Laundromat-restaurant. He pulled into a strip mall off North East 163rd Street to see Andie standing in front of the U-Wash-It.

"What do you think?" she said.

Jack checked it out from the sidewalk, peering through the wide-open double doors. The place had no air conditioning; instead, a noisy commercial fan circulated hot air inside. Two sweaty old women shared a bench and yesterday's newspaper as their clothes tumbled in the dryer. A washing machine on spin cycle rattled and shook violently, as if it was about to walk out the door on its own power. That universal and distinctly unappetizing smell of a Laundromat filled the air.

"They really serve food here?" said Jack.

"Yes, but only Chinese."

Jack glanced inside again, then back at Andie. "Chinese, huh?"

She smiled. "Gotcha."

"Funny. But not very politically correct."

"It's okay. I've got my anti-PC license. I'm

half Native American. Come on. We're eating at the deli right over here."

They got sandwiches and sodas at the counter and found an open booth by the window. Another patron had left a Canadian dollar on the table for the busboy, and Jack weighted it down with the saltshaker. Andie squeezed a packet of deli mustard onto her sliced turkey breast, and she was about to start talking business when Jack jumped in and steered the conversation in a more personal direction.

"I'm glad we're doing this," he said.

She looked up from her sandwich. "Doing what?"

It wasn't what she said as much as the way she'd said it, but Jack didn't like the vibe. He could have said what he was feeling—something like, "Getting out together, picking up where we left off last January, giving ourselves a chance to see if we can put aside the fact that I was a total idiot when I called it quits." But something about her body language didn't seem open to it.

"Eating at the deli," he said, "instead of the laundromat."

"Me too." She took a small bite out of her sandwich and looked out the window.

She was tensing up on him. On the car ride over, Jack had come to the firm conclusion that Andie was interested in him again. The playful little ruse at the laundromat had only confirmed that belief. He had yet to hear word one from Rene since her return to Africa, and perhaps it was high time to stop fooling himself into thinking that happiness lay across the ocean. Both Theo and Abuela had told him that Andie was for real, but there was more to it than that.

Jack couldn't seem to stop thinking about her.

"Andie, can I ask you something?"

"Huh? I'm sorry. What'd you say?"

"I wanted to ask you something."

"Uh, sure. Go ahead."

She was beyond preoccupied. Either she'd invited him to lunch for personal reasons and completely changed her mind, or she really did have "something important" that needed to be said face-to-face.

"Never mind," said Jack. "What is it that you needed to tell me?"

She put her sandwich aside. "Good news and bad news."

"Okay. I'll bite. Let's go with the good news first."

"I've uncovered some information that might help us find who raped Theo's mother."

Jack listened without interrupting as she laid out the events of the last sixteen hours. The Internet made a trip to see the Pi Alpha Delta historian in Ohio unnecessary. He'd e-mailed her the 1972 composite, and Andie's tech agent compared the facial images from the movie to the mug shots in the composite. There was no match on the drunk and the heckler.

Jack said, "Probably guests at the strip party but not brothers at the house."

"That was my guess," said Andie. "But we did get a match on the cameraman. His name is Lance Gilford."

"So, when are you going to talk to the esteemed Mr. Gilford?"

"That leads me to the bad news," she said. "I won't be talking to him."

"Why not?"

"Because I can't help you anymore."

"You can't?" said Jack. "Or you won't."

"Can't. It's not my decision."

"Somebody is telling you not to?"

She struggled to put on her business face, the one she always wore when spewing the bureau line. "You have to see this from the

FBI's point of view. I was appointed to head up a task force that is looking into the reasons why Isaac Reems was able to escape from jail. From there, I started looking at who killed Isaac. Then it became a question of who tried to kill Theo. The focus then was who killed Theo's mother. Now I'm trying to find out who raped Theo's mother over thirty years ago. I'm out of my jurisdiction here, not to mention way beyond the scope of my original assignment."

Jack drank from his soda. "You buy that?"

"What do you mean?"

"Do you really believe that 'jurisdiction' and 'scope of original assignment' were the reasons that the powers that be pulled the plug on your investigation?"

"Do I hear another conspiracy theory coming on?"

Jack reached across the table and took a strand of her hair between his thumb and forefinger. The hair was stuck together in telltale fashion.

"I'm not the one who was gnawing nervously on her hair while driving over here," he said.

She lowered her eyes. *Busted.*

Jack said, "I know you better than you think."

"Ditto."

"So, you must know what I'm thinking," he said.

"I might. Tell me anyway."

It could have gone in a couple of different directions from there. Jack thought for a moment, and then he let go of her hair, sticking to business.

"I think you were getting too close for someone's comfort," he said. "Someone who has a very big secret. And just maybe someone with very big friends."

"Big enough to get me pulled off an investigation?"

Jack settled back into the booth. "That's what I aim to find out."

Chapter 40

Jack didn't bring Theo along for the up-close and personal visit with Lance Gilford. Not because Theo chose to stay behind. In fact, Jack had to enlist the help of both Uncle Cy and Trina to keep him at Sparky's. It was only natural that Theo would want to meet the chump who'd filmed the rape of his own mother. The bottom line, however, was that Jack had gotten Theo off death row once already.

He wasn't sure he could do it again.

Gilford still lived and worked in Miami, and it seemed only fitting that he owned a videography company. It was called Memories, and the hand-painted sign on the storefront window proclaimed "Complete customer satisfaction since 1983" in the recording of life events—weddings, bar mitzvahs, sweet-sixteen parties, and quinceañeras.

They left out sexual assaults.

Bells on the door rang as Jack entered the studio. The attractive young woman at the reception desk looked up from the latest issue of *Ocean Drive* magazine. Jack assumed that she wasn't just screwing off, that culling through the local see-and-be-seen publications was a way of identifying prominent families and scouting out new business. Gilford's schedule was booked for the day, but Jack had phoned ahead and persuaded the receptionist to squeeze him in for five minutes before the 2:00 P.M. appointment. Jack didn't say what it was really about, and he was counting on more than five minutes once he, Gilford, and Pi Alpha Delta's dirtiest secret were together in the same room.

Jack introduced himself, and the young woman frowned.

"I'm so sorry," she said. "I know I promised to fit you in, but Mr. Gilford still has some important editing to do before his two o'clock. He can't see you today. But I have something next Tuesday or—"

"This can't wait," said Jack.

"I'm afraid it will have to."

Jack mustered up a smile. "Help me out here, okay? This is a surprise. I've got a blast from the past for him, all the way from his college days and Pi Alpha Delta fraternity. All I need is one minute."

Slowly, she returned the smile, as if she liked being in on the surprise. "He's in the editing room," she said. She led Jack down the hall, knocked on the door, and opened it.

Before she could speak, Gilford said, "Celeste, I said no interruptions."

Gilford had long gray hair that he wore in a ponytail, and that was about all Jack could see of him. He was seated with his back to the door, and his eyes were glued to the LCD screen and the footage from a client's wedding.

Jack said, "That wouldn't be the Portia Knight wedding, would it?"

The tension in Gilford's neck and shoulders was suddenly visible. He didn't move for several seconds, and Jack wondered if he was even breathing. Finally, he turned in his swivel stool to see who had mentioned Portia's name.

Jack did a quick study. The man had

gained a few pounds, the face was fuller and bore the lines of time, and the eyebrows were as gray as his ponytail. But there was no doubt in Jack's mind that he had the right Lance Gilford.

Gilford seemed to be trying to place Jack, but not surprisingly, his expression showed no sign of recognition.

"Who are you?" he said.

"Jack Swyteck. I'm a lawyer for Theo Knight. Portia's son."

Celeste shot Jack a look of surprise. "I thought you said you were—"

"Celeste," said Gilford. "Can you leave Mr. Swyteck and me alone, please?"

"Your two o'clock will be here any minute."

"Tell them to wait," said Gilford.

She seemed confused, but she complied. The door closed, leaving Jack alone with Gilford. He didn't offer Jack a chair.

"What do you know about Portia Knight?" said Gilford.

"I know you filmed her rape," said Jack.

"I have no idea what you're talking about."

Jack leaned against the wall, arms folded. "Do you really want to do this dance, or do you want to hear what I want?"

"I don't know a Portia Knight."

Jack walked toward him, pulled the still image from his coat pocket, and dropped it on the computer table beside Gilford. "This is from the movie that's posted on Reality Bitches dot com. That's you in the mirror filming Portia's rape. And don't tell me that it isn't you, because the FBI has already confirmed that it is."

He stared at the image for nearly a full minute. "Oh, you mean *that* Portia Knight," he said finally.

"Yeah, that one," said Jack. "Interesting thing about the film is that it's been carefully edited. Did you do that work here?"

Gilford leaned back and rested his elbows atop the table. "No, actually. I did it at home."

"So you admit it?"

"Sure. My wife got really sick, and we needed cash. Took a second mortgage on the house, and I even considered selling the business. We were desperate. I don't know what made me think of that old film, but I dragged it out, cleaned it up, and sold it to one of the big Internet porn distributors."

"But first you cut out any frames that would reveal the identity of the attackers."

"Hold on, pal. You need to rewind a second. First of all, there was no attack."

Jack scoffed. "What do you call it then?"

"Damn fine work by a young film student. I wrote the script, I hired Portia to be the lead actress, I got my drunken frat brothers to volunteer as extras, and I filmed the short with a handheld. Nothing is real. Except the sex. Probably could have done the piece with simulated intercourse, but for another hundred bucks, Portia was willing to take it hardcore. My 'extras' were more than willing to cover the added expense."

"I don't believe you."

"I don't really care. That's exactly the way it went down."

"The website says it's real."

"Yeah, and they put twenty-two-year-old women in pigtails and pass them off as teenagers. It's called marketing."

"You can see the terror in her eyes."

"I don't see anything in those eyes but drugs."

The guy was way too cool. Jack said, "You have an answer for everything, don't you?"

"I merely speak the truth."

"Well, let's see if you can handle this truth.

The experts at the FBI have studied this film, and they say it was rape."

"Isn't it against the Florida bar's rules of ethics for private attorneys to threaten people with criminal prosecution?"

"Number one, I'm not threatening you. Number two, it's only unethical if I make the threat to gain an advantage in a civil lawsuit."

"I'm not sure I agree with your interpretation."

"You a lawyer?"

"Went to law school for two years. Then I saw the light."

"That's like two-thirds of a course on how to disarm a bomb. A little knowledge is a dangerous thing."

"I know more than you think."

"Such as?"

"Your threat goes nowhere. The statute of limitations has run."

Jack said, "There is no statute of limitations for rape in Florida."

"Wrong. There's no statute of limitations if the rape is reported within seventy-two hours. If it's reported after that, the statute of limitations is four years."

"Interesting that you know that fact," said Jack.

"You could call it interesting. I'd call it helpful."

He rolled his stool toward the computer screen. "Now, if you'll excuse me, I have some editing to do before my next appointment."

Jack watched him for another moment, but he decided not to push it. Not yet, anyway. "We're going to find out who raped Theo's mother," said Jack, as he opened the door. "With or without you."

He left and closed the door, leaving Gilford alone in his editing room.

Chapter 41

Five minutes after Jack left to meet with Lance Gilford, Theo was on his way to Miami Beach.

South Beach was home to what Theo called the succ-tiful crowd—not merely successful people who happened to be beautiful, but people who found success precisely *because* they were beautiful. They were everywhere. At any time of day or night, it was impossible to cruise Ocean Drive and Washington Avenue and not see a top model posing for a fashion shoot, a film crew shooting a commercial or *telenovela*, choreographers whipping dancers into sync for the making of a music video. They worked the lobbies of famous art deco hotels, on busy street corners, and at popular cafés. It could be in English, Spanish, or Portuguese. They came in all races, men or women, their ages ranging from young to younger. Sex selling everything from Gucci to the Gap, rap to reggae, bling to Cartier. Beautiful meant success, and success was beautiful. Succ-tiful.

"Theo, how you doin', bro?"

Theo hadn't seen Mel Booker in at least a year, right after a failed attempt at rehab. His mood was never predictable, and it was a relief to get the happy "How you doin', bro," coupled with a big hug.

"I'm good," said Theo. "You all cleaned up, finally?"

"Going on eight months now. Nothin' harder than O'Douls. That's why you ain't seen me around Sparky's."

"That's cool. I'm proud of you, man."

Booker worked in a world where sex didn't just sell the product. It *was* the product. He leased a film studio behind an old art deco apartment building on Washington Avenue. It faced the Dumpsters and the rear parking lot, but the windows were boarded over, so it didn't matter. The lighting inside was entirely artificial, mostly from spotlights so bright that Theo left his sunglasses on. He and Booker were standing behind a seven-foot-high divider that cut across the studio. From the working side, Theo could hear the telltale moans and groans of the film stars—Booker's hookers, as they were known in the industry.

"What you got going on?" said Theo.

"Two chicks, one dude. Typical male fantasy shit. Want to watch?"

"Ouch. Quit twisting my arm."

Booker smiled. "Come on."

Theo followed him around the divider to the working side of the studio. Two fixed cameras were in place, plus one guy walking around with a handheld in order to ensure a tight close-up of two beautiful young women getting way too excited over Zeus's big moment. There was something very robotic about porn in progress, with the director barking instructions, the actors responding to his commands, the cameramen struggling for the ideal angle. It certainly wasn't painful viewing, but on some level Theo thought it should be up there with laws and sausages on the list of things not to watch being made.

Booker lit a cigarette. "This is gonna be a great flick."

"Gee, wonder how it ends," said Theo.

They could talk freely, since all the sound would be dubbed in later. Booker said, "Makes me rich. That's how they all end. At least until they ban porn on the Internet, which will never happen."

"If it does, invest every penny in Bring-Back-Porn-dot-com. It'll be the hottest site in cyberspace. What do you pay these people anyway?"

Booker took a long drag, exhaling as he spoke. "Amber's expensive. Twenty grand. But she'll bend over backward—literally—if I ask her to. Rosa gets about half that."

Theo glanced toward the happy guy in the middle. "What about him?"

"Five hundred bucks. And a free blood test."

The director rose from his chair and shouted "Cut!"

Booker said, "You want to meet the girls?"

They were gorgeous, fit, and probably a couple of soap opera rejects. They climbed off the pool table, completely comfortable in their nakedness, and wiped each other clean. It took more than one towel.

Theo said, "Not this time."

Booker removed his cigarette and cupped his other hand like a megaphone. "All right—girls and Tony. The nurse is here. I need two vials from each of you."

They groaned, but not very much. AIDS and other sexually transmitted diseases were the porn industry's biggest threat, and nobody in their right mind worked for a filmmaker who didn't do blood tests.

Theo knew that much about the business of sex, and he also knew how surprisingly tight-knit the porn industry was because of it. Someone like Mel Booker knew everyone.

"So, what brings you here?" said Booker.

"A guy named Lance Gilford."

Booker walked to the coffee machine and poured half a cup, black. Theo declined.

"What about him?" said Booker.

"You know him?"

"Not well, but I know of him. Big-time investor. Mostly edgy stuff."

"How do you mean 'edgy'?"

"He joint-ventures with Reality Bitches, companies like that. It's the kind of stuff I just don't do. Mostly amateur photography. Guys on videotape beating the shit out of their girlfriends. Five punks from a Hialeah gang raping a teenage girl. It's all very low budget but high profit. You put the label 'real' on anything with sex and violence, you get pervs paying through the nose."

Theo reconsidered on the coffee and took a cup. "We talking about the same Lance Gilford? The one I'm after owns a studio called Memories in the Gables."

"Same guy," said Booker. "All his porn is done through offshore banks and some Costa Rican companies. The studio is a total front."

"Money laundering?"

"It's more complicated than that. He married a minister's daughter, so he would shoot a few weddings and bar mitzvahs to convince his family and friends he's legit."

"A man with two lives," said Theo.

"Yeah," said Booker, chuckling. "But it finally caught up with him. His wife moved out and took off for Europe about six weeks ago. Hiding from the media before the scandal hits, I'm sure. This is gonna be one nasty divorce. Anyway, what's your angle? You looking to do some business with him?"

"Business?" said Theo, giving the word careful thought. "Yeah. You could say that. Him and me got *unfinished* business."

* * *

LANCE GILFORD CANCELED HIS two o'clock appointment. He'd played it pretty cool with Swyteck, but he still had plenty to think about. Pretending to care about some bridezilla's $300,000 wedding from hell was the last thing he felt like doing. He went to his computer and pulled up the Portia Knight rape film.

How could he have missed his own image in the mirror?

Perhaps there was some validity to the notion that he had been so careful to protect his friends that he'd failed to protect himself. He'd been so concerned, in fact, that he even paid off the frat boys to destroy the 1972 composite in the chapter room, just in case. The real explanation for his oversight, however, was far less heroic. He'd made the mistake of editing the film at home. The old sixteen-millimeter footage wasn't digital technology, of course, so it took fairly sophisticated equipment to do the equivalent of digital frame-by-frame analysis. His equipment here in the studio rivaled anything the FBI used. The same could not be said about his two-year-old stuff at home.

"Idiot!" he said through clenched teeth.

There it was, his mug and the Greek letters of his old Pi Alpha Delta jersey right on-screen—his momentary reflection in the mirror, visible only with the kind of frame-by-frame advancement that he could never have accomplished at home.

With an angry click of the mouse, Gilford exited the computer program. The LCD screen went blue and turquoise with Caribbean Sea wallpaper, far too calming and relaxed for his present mood.

He drew a deep breath and let it out. No doubt about it: He had trouble on his hands. He hadn't completely lied to Swyteck. Although it wasn't true that his wife had taken ill, the part about dragging out the old film for badly needed cash was no lie. In hindsight, he should have edited out the faces of the drunk hecklers, even if they weren't Pi Alpha Delta fraternity brothers. But the angry expressions of those young men added a certain realism to the overall effect from an artist's point of view—and he was an artist, no matter what people thought about his films. In terms of CYA strategy, however, it was a big mistake.

Gilford picked up the telephone. He dreaded making this call, but he forced himself to punch out the numbers. He reached a secretary and gave his name. She had no idea who he was and asked him to hold. Two minutes later, the voice of an old friend was on the line.

"What is it this time, Lance?"

It was the firm and confident voice of a man of power and position, but it was also the distinctly agitated tone of an old friend who was still ticked off about the release of the Portia Knight rape film.

Gilford cleared his throat to speak. "We have a problem," he said. "Knight and his lawyer got the movie."

"So do a hundred thousand Internet perverts around the globe."

"But Jack Swyteck came to see me today. He knows I filmed it."

"Did you tell him?"

"No. Not at first. But he had . . . proof."

"So you admitted it was yours?"

"Well, you know, it was kind of—"

"Stop blubbering! Just tell me how he knows it's your film."

Gilford started to explain, but he was suddenly afraid. He didn't want to come across as stupid and careless. "I think the FBI helped them."

"That's great, Lance. Just great. What the hell were you thinking when you put that thing out on the market?"

"I lost my ass on that gambling website. I'm sorry, but some of the folks I borrow money from don't fully grasp the legal niceties of a nonrecourse loan. So the movie is out there. Knight and his lawyer know I was the cameraman, and even worse, they've tied it to the PAD house in Miami."

There was stone silence on the line.

Gilford said, "You still there?"

"My face is in that movie," he said in a slow, deep voice.

"I understand that."

"I was angry that you left me in there, but I didn't freak. So long as the film wasn't linked to Miami, I figured there was little to no chance that anyone would recognize me thirty-something years after the fact."

"That was my thinking, too."

"But you thought wrong. So now I'm angry. *Really* angry."

Few things were more chilling than the flat, even voice of someone who was *really* angry. The room suddenly felt hotter. Gilford was starting to sweat. "I—I don't know how many ways to apologize. But we have to stay together on this, right? We need to stay focused. And the question is, Now what?"

"I'll deal with it."

"How?"

"My way," he said, and the line clicked in Gilford's ear.

Chapter 42

It was a big night for Theo's future, and he was trying hard not to let the past spoil his dream of a true jazz bar in Coconut Grove.

Theo had negotiated the business terms of the five-year lease on his own, but he was smart enough to enlist the services of a lawyer, especially since Jack came free of charge. The final lease agreement was in hand and ready for signature in the morning. Theo and his uncle met Jack at the property around 9:00 P.M. for one final walk-through inspection.

Jack looked a little frazzled. He had a trial starting in the morning, and somehow fifteen years of courtroom experience and umpteen successful jury verdicts didn't eliminate the night-before jitters. The mega-cup of coffee probably wasn't helping.

Theo pried the extra-large double latte from Jack's hands and placed it on the bar. "If my well was stocked, I'd give you a drink," he said.

"Do I seem nervous?" said Jack.

"As a long-tailed cat in a roomful of rockers," said Uncle Cy.

Theo and Jack started in the kitchen, and Cy stayed behind in the bar area. The landlord had the propane line reconnected, so this was their first check on the stove and grill, the only major appliance included in the lease. One of the burners didn't light. The room started to smell like gas. Theo pulled a matchbook from his pocket.

"Don't!" Jack shouted.

"I was kidding, okay? You're way too uptight. What's going on, man?"

Jack looked around like a junkie, as if in need of another hit of caffeine. "I need your opinion on something."

"Shoot."

"What do you honestly think of Andie?" said Jack.

Theo looked up from the stove. "Why do you ask?"

"Can you turn that unlit burner off before this place explodes?"

"Relax. It's not like the deal is sealed and we assumed the risk of loss yet."

Jack narrowed his eyes with curiosity. "How does a guy with a rapper's vocabulary spit out legal terms like Clarence Darrow?"

"Prison library. But don't change the subject. What's up with you and Andie?"

Jack offered a schoolboy's shrug. "I'm thinking about, you know, maybe giving her a call."

"You mean for a date?"

"Well . . . yeah."

"Let me get this straight. You're gonna pick up the telephone and ask Andie Henning out on a date?"

"Why is that so incredible?"

Theo said nothing.

"Theo?"

"Sorry, dude. My mind just flashed with the image of pigs flying over a frozen hell."

"Very funny."

"What about Rene?"

"I haven't heard boo from her since she went back to Africa."

Theo tried the faulty burner again. This time it lit right up. He waved his hand, as if it were a sign. "Call her."

"You don't think Andie and I are more like putting a match to a gas leak?"

"Definitely. But what a way to go, huh?"

They finished the kitchen in twenty minutes, and Jack's punch list in progress had only a few small items on it—low water pressure on one of the sinks, some cracks in the tile floor. At that point, Theo hit him with the lease addendum that the landlord had faxed over that afternoon. Jack remained in the kitchen to read it, where the lighting was better. Theo and his uncle handled the bar inspection.

"Tell me somethin'," said Cy.

Theo was on his belly with a flashlight, checking out the beer tap connections. His car keys and cell phone were digging into his groin like a well-aimed jousting lance, so he emptied his pockets and placed them on the shelf. "What?" said Theo, groaning.

"What is it you're trying to find out?" his uncle said.

Theo knew the old man wasn't talking about the inspection, but he played dumb. "What do you mean?"

"What were you runnin' over to South Beach for, talkin' to a guy like Mel Booker?"

He climbed from under the bar and looked at his uncle. "How'd you know I was talking to Mel today?"

"Trina told me."

Theo couldn't really be angry. He hadn't told her *not* to tell Uncle Cy. "Just following leads, that's all."

"Is it all about finding the guy who shot you from that red car? Or who killed your momma?"

"Both."

"See, that's the problem."

"Why?"

"Bad enough someone's trying to kill you. Don't understand why you gotta go looking for a way to kill yourself."

"I'm not gonna get myself killed."

"I didn't say *get* killed. I said kill yourself."

"You aren't seriously afraid I might commit suicide, are you?"

"No, no. That ain't it." He struggled for the right words. "What I'm saying is this. Right now you got your detective hat on, sniffing around like a bloodhound for clues, following this lead and that lead wherever it takes you. I'm telling you to stop for a minute. Stop and think."

"About what?"

"If you want to go looking into who killed your momma, that's your business. But you better prepare yourself to live with whatever you find out."

"Some frat boy filmed her getting raped, and she ended up a drug-addicted hooker who got her throat slit. How much worse can it get?"

"That's a really good question, Theo. All I'm saying is there's gonna be more to the story."

"You know something I should know?"

Cy didn't answer right away. Theo wasn't sure what to make of the silence. "This ain't no time to be keepin' secrets, old man."

"I just knew your momma better than anyone else did. So I can say this without no doubts in my mind: this ain't a story with a happy ending."

"I appreciate that."

He took a step closer, his expression very serious. "I don't think you do. Not entirely. And that's what really worries me."

Theo looked at him carefully, trying to discern his full meaning. His uncle looked right back at him, as if trying to convey something without words. Had Trina been there, she would have kicked both of them in the ass and screamed, "Just spit it out!" But she wasn't there, which left too few X chromosomes in the room for a meaningful conversation.

The old man walked away from the bar and went back to the kitchen to wrangle up a ride home.

JACK GAVE UNCLE CY a lift, and Theo stayed behind. There was more work to do on site, but the old man was tired and Jack still had to outline his opening statement for tomorrow's trial. They were sitting at a red light three blocks away when Cy realized his mistake.

"I don't have my house key."

"You sure?" said Jack.

"I didn't bring one. I rode over with Theo."

"Maybe I can get him to meet us at the town house."

Jack tried Theo on his cell, but there was no answer. "Probably having phone sex with Trina," he said, as he pulled a U-turn and headed back to the bar.

Cy tried peering through the windows as they cruised past the entrance, but the lights were out, and it was too dark to see inside. "Did he leave already?" said Cy.

Jack drove around to the alley. Theo's car was still parked next to the Dumpster.

"Maybe he's locking up," said Cy.

"Maybe," said Jack, but he didn't like the vibe he was getting. He flipped open his cell and speed-dialed Theo.

THEO'S CELL RANG FROM across the room, piercing the darkness. The phone was sitting on top of the bar—right where he'd left it, beside his car keys. Theo was crouched down low behind the U-shaped bar, and the phone was on the opposite leg of the U.

Theo didn't make a sound, didn't dare move from his hiding spot.

After Jack and Uncle Cy had gone home, the first noise Theo had heard was something that sounded like the delivery door opening. "Jack?" he'd called out, but he got no reply. Then he heard a series of quick clicks from the kitchen—the breakers—and circuit by circuit, the lights went out. Instinctively, he dove for cover.

His cell stopped ringing. Theo listened, his ears and inner radar on high alert. He wondered if someone was toying with him, just trying to scare him. Or had someone finally come to finish the drive-by-shooting job they'd botched in Overtown?

He needed to get to his phone. Slowly, carefully, he started crawling on hands and knees, moving along the outside of the bar.

His cell started ringing again—the second time in the past three minutes. Theo kept moving, knowing that the call would roll over to voice mail after six rings. But on the fourth ring, another sound sailed directly over his head—a piercing but muffled sound of a speeding projectile that silenced his phone and shattered it into pieces that flew across the room. Theo froze. His worst fears were realized.

Someone was toying with him

And they had come to finish the job.

"HELLO?" JACK SAID INTO his cell.

It struck him as odd that Theo's phone had cut off after four rings. One ring and then to voice mail meant that Theo's cell wasn't turned on. Six rings meant that the phone was on but Theo wasn't answering.

But four rings and no answer? Weird.

"Stay here," he told Cy. He climbed out of his car and stepped into the alley.

Part of him wanted to dial 911, but it seemed silly to call the cops because a six-foot-five ex-con didn't answer his cell after four rings. Each tentative step down the dimly lit alley, however, made the idea seem less silly.

Jack peeked inside Theo's parked car and tried the door handle. Empty and locked. He continued past the Dumpster, and a sudden movement sent his heart into his throat. A cat jumped down from a stack of crushed cardboard boxes. He gave his pulse a moment to return to mere triple digits—or so it felt—and then he tried the back door. He expected it to be locked, but it wasn't. It creaked open.

"Theo?" he said, calling inside.

There was no answer.

Jack reached around the door frame, found the light switch in the darkness, and flipped it to the on position.

Nothing.

Before Jack could even begin to process what it meant, he heard the quick footsteps, caught a glimpse of the blur in the blackness coming toward him, and absorbed the full impact of what hit him like a charging bull. Jack's feet left the floor, the air fled his lungs, and he landed flat on his back in the open doorway. His arms flailed uselessly in a defensive reflex as the man who'd bowled him over stepped on his chest on the way out.

"He's got a gun!" Theo shouted.

Still disoriented, Jack struggled to roll for cover. Theo grabbed his arm and dragged him behind the open door. Jack tried to keep an eye on his attacker, but in the darkness the man was nothing more than a silhouette racing away from him, down the alley.

Then he heard an engine fire and tires squealing into the night.

"He took your car!" Theo shouted.

Jack's head was pounding, but suddenly he was thinking clearly again. "Your uncle came back with me. He's got Cy!"

Jack's cell rang. The caller ID said it was from Uncle Cy.

"Are you hurt?" said Jack.

"Don't call the cops," said Cy, his voice quaking. "And don't report your car stolen. He says he'll kill me if you do."

Jack could hear the fear in the old man's voice, and he wanted to say something reassuring. But the call disconnected, and Uncle Cy was gone.

Chapter 43

Theo didn't even stop to think. He knew what to do. He got in his car and drove.

Jack had wanted to call Andie. Theo said no. Jack wanted to call the police. Theo said hell no. Jack explained that the cops could run a ballistics test on the bullet that took out Theo's cell, which could be a link to the shooter's identity. Jack asked him to wait. Theo said, "Are you out of your fucking mind?" and bolted out the door.

Jack knew better than to try and follow him.

It was after 10:00 P.M., and Theo figured Lance Gilford would be home. A quick call to directory assistance gave him the address. He parked on the street, walked up the front steps, and pounded on the door.

There was no answer, but Gilford's car was in the driveway, the lights were on inside the house, and Theo could hear the late-night news on television. This time, he beat the door with both fists.

Theo heard footsteps in the foyer, and Gilford announced in a grumpy voice that he was coming. Theo could hardly wait. The deadbolt turned and the door opened as far as the taut brass security chain would allow.

"Who is—" Gilford started to say, but Theo didn't give him a moment to reconsider. With every bit of force he could muster, Theo laid his shoulder into the door. It practically exploded on impact, the chain ripping off a chunk of the wood frame as the door flew open. Gilford was knocked backward and fell to the ground. Theo slammed the door shut, grabbed Gilford with two hands, picked him up off the floor like a rag doll, and shoved him hard against the wall.

"Where's my uncle?" he said, seething.

Gilford's eyes were wide with fright. "Who's your uncle?"

"Cyrus Knight."

"I don't know any Cyrus. Honest."

Theo squeezed him by the throat. "Who are you protecting?"

He gasped for air. "No . . . body."

At that moment, Theo realized that he hadn't come just to find Uncle Cy. He felt himself roiling with the rape of his mother. However far she'd nosedived in life, it had all happened after that rape at the frat house. Portia Knight was a mere teenager in that movie. She was not yet any of the things Theo would later come to hate about her. Not many strippers became nuns, to be sure. But a stripper wasn't necessarily a drug addict, a prostitute, or a horrible mother. Something made her that way. And Lance Gilford was part of that "something."

Theo got right in his face, eye-to-eye. "Portia Knight was my mother. You know who raped her. And whoever it was, he now has my uncle."

"Can't . . . breathe."

"Who was it?" Theo relaxed his grip, allowing him to speak.

Gilford coughed as he sucked in precious air.

Theo said, *"Who was it?"*

"Nobody . . . nobody got raped," said Gilford.

Somewhere in his heart Theo thanked God he didn't have a weapon, but he couldn't ignore the urgency of the situation—not with Cy in danger.

"Where's your garage?" said Theo.

Gilford seemed confused.

"Where is it?" Theo shouted.

"Side door, through the kitchen."

Theo twisted Gilford's arm up behind his back, muscled him into the kitchen and pushed through the door. It was a one-car garage with no vehicle inside. Theo shoved him to the concrete floor, took a long orange extension cord from a hook on the wall, and hog-tied Gilford's wrists and ankles. Then he grabbed his gray ponytail, jerking his head back.

"I'm givin' you one more chance," said Theo. "Who are you protectin'?"

"No one. I'm not lying to you."

Theo wanted to hurt him so badly he couldn't stand it. "Where's your tools?"

Gilford let out a pathetic whimper. "What are you going to do?"

"Fix your car," said Theo, and then he yanked so hard on the ponytail that it stretched the wrinkles out of Gilford's face.

"What do you *think* I'm gonna do? Where's your tools?"

"Over there," said Gilford, "by the workbench."

Theo found a stand-up tool chest and searched quickly through a dozen drawers, not sure what he was looking for, his mind racing with thoughts of creative interrogation. He had a couple of possibilities when he looked up and noticed the power tools mounted on the pegboard. He chose the power drill, plugged it in, and pulled the trigger.

Gilford winced at the mere sound of it.

"Come on, man," said Gilford. "You don't want to do this."

"Where's your bits?"

"Please. Don't hurt me."

"I said where's your damn drill bits?"

"Tool drawer by the light switch. But—"

"Shut up!

The bits were organized by size in a plastic case. Theo took the skinniest one, one-sixty-fourth of an inch, and fixed it into position. He took his time walking back to Gilford, giving him time to think it over. Then he untied one of Gilford's hands, stretched out his arm in front of him, and pressed his hand flat on the floor, palm down. Theo stepped on his wrist to keep it in position, and he placed the tip of the bit on the back of Gilford's hand. It was enough for him to feel it, but it didn't break the skin.

"So you like to film women getting raped, huh?"

"No."

"Does that get you off?"

"It's not what you think."

"How many other rape victims have you plastered on the Internet?"

"Just her. I mean none—not even her." Gilford swallowed hard. "Please, man. Don't do this."

"If my mother had said that, would you have stopped filming?"

"That was thirty-five years ago. You want to hear me say I'm sorry? Okay, I'm sorry. Really, I'm very, very sorry."

"What was his name?"

"Whose name?"

"The guy who raped her."

"I don't know."

Theo pulled the trigger and released. Gilford screamed. The bit was through the dermal layer. A spot of blood emerged. "Last chance," said Theo.

"I swear, man. I don't know!"

"Cy don't have time to waste here, damn it!" Theo twisted the skinny bit from the drill with his bare hand and threw it at Gilford. Then he went back to the toolbox for a replacement—a much bigger bit this time, quarter-inch diameter. He tightened it into place, returned to Gilford, and rolled him onto his back.

He pressed the tip to Gilford's forehead.

"Who is he?" said Theo.

Gilford was about to hyperventilate, his eyes crossing as they followed the bit. "I don't know. Really. I don't, I don't know!"

Theo pulled the trigger, the drill whined, and the spiraling tip of the bit tore at Gilford's flesh.

"Fernando Redden!" he shouted.

Theo pulled back. "Say it again."

"Fernando Redden. That's his name."

"If you're lying to me . . ."

"No, no. That's him. Really, truly. I wouldn't make this up." He was blubbering now, tears streaming down his face.

Theo glared just enough to put the final scare into him. "It's your lucky night," he said, as he put the drill away. "I believe you."

TRINA DIDN'T KNOW WHERE Theo was.

Jack called her at home to explain what

had happened. Theo was up to something dangerous, and if Jack couldn't stop him, the chances that Trina could talk some sense into him probably weren't any better. But she promised to try. She drove to Theo's town house and was inside waiting when he came through the door. The expression on his face was unlike any she'd seen on him before. It scared her.

He said, "What are you doing here?"

It wasn't the warmest of greetings, but it didn't stop her from going to him and hugging him tightly. "Jack told me," she said softly, her lips to his ear. "Do you know anything? Is Uncle Cy okay?"

The mention of Cy seemed to trigger something inside him. She could feel his initial resistance to her touch fading, and he hugged her back.

"I'm just tryin' to sort this out," he said. "Gotta do somethin'."

"Like what?"

He didn't answer. She slipped out of his embrace so that she could look into his eyes. "Where have you been?"

He seemed to struggle, as if debating whether to tell her. Then he looked away and started up the stairs.

Trina followed him to the bedroom. "Theo, talk to me."

He went to the walk-in closet and flipped on the light. Trina stayed behind, sat on the edge of the bed, and waited.

People often thought of her as fearless, or at least rough around the edges. Like everyone else, however, Trina had her demons. The last person she'd let herself care about so deeply was her friend Beatriz—not a romantic interest, but a teenage friend that she loved like a sister. Back before the Soviet Union fell, they went from Cuba to Prague on Castro's factory work program. Their plan was to defect, each pledging never to leave without the other. Only Trina made it, and even after all these years, she still bore the scars of survivorship.

"Theo?" she said.

He didn't come out, but finally he did answer her from somewhere deep in the closet. "Let me take care of this," he said.

Trina didn't know how to get through to him in this mode, but she had to say something. She rose and staked out a position in the closet doorway, arms folded, as if daring him to try and pass.

Theo was kneeling on the floor. He looked

up and stopped what he was doing. The corner of the wall-to-wall carpeting had been rolled back, and the secret hatch to Theo's in-floor safe was open. He was holding a black pistol in one hand and several ammunition clips in the other.

Trina said, "Have you lost your mind?"

"Maybe," he said, as he closed the safe. "But I ain't gonna lose my uncle."

He rose, pulled a leather holster off the shelf, and strapped it on. The gun fit perfectly on his left side for a right-handed draw. He selected a lightweight jacket to conceal his weapon.

He turned and looked at Trina, as if expecting her approval, or at least her acquiescence.

She said, "You think you can solve this all by yourself?"

"Ain't nobody else gonna do it," he said, as he stepped past her and back into the bedroom. He checked himself in the full-length mirror and apparently didn't like the noticeable bulge of his handgun. He went back to the closet to change jackets.

"Jack thinks you should call the cops," she said.

"Sometimes Jack thinks too much."

"I don't like this."

He didn't answer. It was a little too warm outside for a leather jacket, but the bulkier garment seemed better suited to his purposes. He stepped past her and checked himself in the mirror again.

"I'm talking to you," she said.

He turned to face her, his arms extended and his hands resting on her shoulders as he looked straight at her. "You have to trust me on this."

"I don't understand it."

"If it was you instead of Cy, would you understand it then?"

She didn't know how to answer. She just held him. "I love you," she said. "I think."

He smiled a little and said, "Me thinks too." Then he pulled away and retrieved a pen and notepad from the nightstand. She watched him jot something down and fold the paper into thirds. Then he gave it to her.

Theo said, "If something happens, you call Jack, and you give him this name."

She started to unfold it, but he stopped her. "Just give it to Jack," he said.

"What is this?"

"Jack will figure it out."

She hugged him again, this time with a kiss.

"I'll see ya," he said, and he walked out of the room.

Trina sat on the bed and listened to the thud of each footfall on the stairs, the sound of the door opening—and then for a moment there was silence. In her mind's eye she could see him standing in the doorway, maybe rethinking things.

Then she heard the door close, and Theo was gone.

Her eyes closed slowly, and then she opened them, trying to deal with the confusion on every level. It seemed so obvious that Theo was doing the wrong thing, yet she felt certain that there was nothing else he could do.

Her hand shook as she unfolded the paper and read Theo's note. Trying to think through her next move rationally would have been pointless.

She followed her gut, picked up the telephone, and dialed Jack's number.

Chapter 44

Two minutes after his phone conversation with Trina, Jack nailed down one thing for certain: Fernando Redden was no Lance Gilford.

A quick Internet search turned up hundreds of hits. Jack focused on the local media coverage, which was extensive. Redden was the president and CEO of American Dream Development Ltd., a multimillion-dollar company that built housing for low-income families. He was also a south Florida success story, particularly in the Latin community. His name appeared repeatedly in the business section of the *Miami Tribune* and its Spanish-language counterpart, and the society pages couldn't seem to get enough of him and his stunningly beautiful wife. One photograph, in particular, caught Jack's attention. It was from July 1994, just a few months before Florida's statewide elections. Fernando Redden was smiling widely, and the mere sight of the man shaking Redden's hand made Jack's heart skip a beat.

It was Governor Harry Swyteck—Jack's father—campaigning for reelection.

Jack printed the photograph and a couple of other articles of interest, tucked them into his pocket, and grabbed his car keys. Ten minutes later he was at the Coral Gables home of his father and stepmother. Harry answered the door dressed in a terry cloth robe. Agnes was asleep in the bedroom, and it appeared that Harry wasn't far behind.

"I need to talk to you," said Jack.

Harry was halfway into a "not now" sigh, but the expression on Jack's face must have told him it was important. "Sure," he said. "Come on in."

Harry took him to the library, his favorite room in the house. The cherry-paneled wainscoting, floor-to-ceiling bookshelves, and soft leather chairs were all very reminiscent of the governor's mansion. Harry reached for the Russian-cut carafe on the credenza. "Brandy?"

"No, thanks," said Jack. "I'm actually in a hurry."

Harry poured a short one for himself, then settled into the worn leather chair behind his massive desk. As much as their relationship had improved over the years, it bothered Jack that every time he said "Dad, let's talk," Harry still put the old mahogany antique between them—a vestige of the bad old days for a disciplinarian father and his rebellious son.

"Okay," Harry said. "Shoot."

Jack had to stop and think about where to begin. The kidnappers' warning made it best not to say anything about Uncle Cy—at least not until Theo decided to involve the police. Jack didn't have time for all that background anyway. His needs were very specific. He laid the printed copy of the old newspaper photograph atop the desk.

"Do you know this man?" said Jack.

Harry examined it. The recognition wasn't instant, but it finally came to him. "Yeah. That's Felipe Redden. No—Fernando Redden."

Jack did not yet fully understand why, but

it relieved him to see that Redden obviously wasn't one of his father's closest friends. "How do you know him?"

"We've met. That's about all I can say."

"Was he one of your supporters?"

Harry's chest swelled, as if a deep breath would trigger some recollection. "As I recall, he really wanted to jump on board. I talked with him when my campaign was down in Miami. That's when this photo was taken."

"Did you accept his money?"

"Well, let's not be too cynical here. Beyond being a Miami player with plenty of dough, he was the kind of guy you wanted to like. He was born in Cuba in the 1950s—Bejucal, the same town your mother was from."

"Interesting coincidence."

"It got my attention. And his story is a good one. Whole family fled to Miami after Castro took power. Grew up with five cousins in a two-bedroom apartment in Hialeah, worked his way through law school, learned the ropes of local government over the next decade, and eventually landed a job as chief counsel to the mayor of Miami-Dade County—another 'kid done good' from the old Hialeah neighborhood."

"So, you liked him?"

"At first. But my antennae told me to stay away from the guy."

"What do you mean?"

"Can't really describe it. Just my political instincts."

"Had to be something."

Another big sigh. Harry was digging deep into the memory bank. "It was his business dealings. Something didn't add up for me."

"Something illegal?"

"Jack, you're asking me to go way back on a guy I spent maybe a couple of hours with on the campaign trail. As a candidate, you get a feeling about people, and you go with your gut. Redden had lots of friends in county government, which is not necessarily a bad thing. What troubled me was that his development company kept getting fat contracts for public housing projects—one after another, as if Redden was the only developer in town."

"Projects in Miami?"

"Yeah. Mostly Overtown."

Overtown. Mere mention of it hit Jack like an electric current. He wasn't ready to connect the dots in ink just yet, but he had the distinct feeling that things were starting to line up like bullet points on the printed page.

His most recent conversation with Andie was suddenly echoing in his mind—in particular, Jack's "conspiracy theory" about her getting pulled off the investigation into the murder of Theo's mother for "jurisdictional" reasons.

Jack said, "Can I get your honest opinion on something?"

"Absolutely."

"Is Fernando Redden the kind of guy who could get the FBI to back off an investigation?"

Harry groaned. "Jack, that's—"

"I know, it's purely speculation. But you said yourself that you've always trusted your instincts. So I want to know what your gut says about this one. Does Fernando Redden have that kind of pull?"

"Why do you need to know?"

"I just need to."

Harry wrung his hands. Speculating was against his nature, but Jack was giving his father little choice in the matter. "I can't say for sure," said Harry, "but let me put it this way. If Fernando Redden called the White House right now, I'd bet money that his call would go through."

Jack smiled just enough to show his appreciation. "Thanks," he said, rising.

"Where are you going?"

"I wish I could tell you."

Harry followed him out of the library, down the hall to the front door. There was concern in his eyes. "Does this have anything to do with your FBI friend—Andie Henning?"

"It might," said Jack.

Harry nodded knowingly. "Your grand-mother told me about you and Rene. I don't ever get involved in that stuff, but—"

"Dad, this is really not a good time," said Jack, reaching for the doorknob.

Harry held the door shut. "Just hear what I have to say, okay? Thirty seconds of your time. Please."

Jack wanted to fly, but the quickest way out was always just to let his father have his say. "Okay, I'm listening."

Harry glanced down the hall toward the bedroom, then back at Jack. "Your step-mother and I have been together forever, and I love her very much. But once upon a time, I was a young, blue-blooded college student with political aspirations. I was doing every-thing right at UF. Just got tapped into the Florida Blue Key Honorary Society and was lining up support to run for student-body president. Even had my eye on the president of Tri-Delt sorority. Then I came down to Miami on break and met this beautiful Cuban refugee who was working as a waitress and spoke English like a female Ricky Ricardo."

Jack had to snicker.

Harry continued, "She was completely wrong for me. I was night, she was day. This was back in the day when Miami was still called 'My-amma,' for Pete's sake. But you know what? I could not stop thinking about her."

Harry went quiet. Jack said nothing. Over the years, they'd had surprisingly few conversations about Harry's first wife—Jack's mother. As much as Jack's *abuela* liked to tell him that he had the heart of his Latina mother, he was still a Swyteck, and there was no end to the list of things that went unsaid between men.

Harry said, "Do you understand what I'm saying?"

"I—I'm not sure. You think Rene's like that for me?"

"No—*no*," he said, making a face. "I'm talking about Andie."

Jack wasn't sure how to respond. Not since Jack's divorce had Harry Swyteck weighed in on the women in Jack's life. "Did Abuela ask you to say something about this?"

"Not at all. This all occurred to me months ago, when you first dated Andie. I never really got to meet the girl, but Theo told me you were pretty taken with her after just two or three dates. And then you broke it off, apparently for no good reason. I don't know what happened, but here's an old geezer's two cents. Andie's an FBI agent; you're a criminal defense lawyer. I was a police officer before getting into politics, and Lord knows you and I have had our differences over the years. Maybe that . . . that lawyer-cop incompatibility is in the back of your mind. But give some thought to what I'm saying about your mother and me. People don't have to be cut from exactly the same cloth to be right for each other."

Jack was speechless. He and his father were close now, but there was a time—back when Harry was Florida's law-and-order governor and Jack defended death row inmates—when they couldn't even speak to one another. The rift went back much further than that, however, with roots in Jack's childhood and Harry's remarriage to a good woman with a terrible weakness for gin martinis. A lot of history with a sad bottom line: Jack and his father didn't have many moments like this one.

"Thanks," was all Jack could say.

Harry opened the door for him, seemingly pleased that Jack took his meaning. "You're welcome."

Jack went to his car and gave his old man a mock salute as he backed out of the driveway. He was less than half a block away, headed down Alhambra Circle, when he dialed Andie Henning on his cell. He wasn't sure if his father's words had actually prompted him to make the call, but he knew it was the right thing to do. He apologized for the hour but let her know right away how serious this was.

"I need your help," he told her.

"You mean the FBI's?"

"No," said Jack. "Just yours."

"What's wrong?"

He could have started with Uncle Cy, but again he was mindful of the kidnapper's warning about calling the cops. "It's Theo," he said.

"What happened?"

"I think he's on self-destruct."

"What does that mean?"

Jack wanted to explain, but he needed her sworn assurance that he was lining up her alone, not the entire FBI. That was a difficult maneuver by telephone. "I need to meet with you. Tonight. It's important."

She hesitated for half a second. "Okay. We can talk here at my place. You know the way."

That he did. "I'll be there in fifteen minutes. And just to give you a heads-up, you might want to start checking on something."

"What?"

"Dig up whatever you can on a guy named Fernando Redden."

Chapter 45

Twenty minutes later—traffic was worse than expected—Jack was in Andie's Coconut Grove apartment, seated on Andie's over-stuffed couch. It still had the stain from the glass of red wine he'd spilled the first time they'd really kissed, but he held that thought for only an instant. He was about to tell her what happened to Cy, but she had some information of her own for him.

"Redden's quite a character," said Andie.

"In what way?"

"I made a phone call and hit the jackpot. Can't share everything I know. But I can tell you what will be all over the newspapers before long. The guy has taken millions of dollars in public money to build housing projects in low-income neighborhoods, and he's built absolutely nothing. Unless you want to count the four-million-dollar mansion he built for himself in the Ponce Davis area."

"Nice guy."

Andie said, "But I didn't learn anything about him that couldn't wait till morning."

Jack took her meaning and realized that he owed her a pretty full explanation of what he was doing here at almost midnight. "Can you take off your FBI hat for one minute?"

"Only if what you want to tell me isn't illegal."

"Choosing not to report a kidnapping is not against the law," Jack said. And then he told her about Uncle Cy.

She listened without interrupting, and Jack could see that she was trying to show no emotion, though it was hard not to show feelings for Uncle Cy. She remained silent and pensive for at least a minute after he finished. Finally she said, "What would you like me to do?"

"You're trained in kidnappings. I need you to walk me through this. And I need someone to help me keep Theo from getting himself killed."

"You're putting me in a tough spot. You want the FBI, but you don't want the FBI."

"I want the expertise of the FBI. I don't want all the baggage."

"Then you need to hire a retired agent."

"And if I start looking right now, how long after Uncle Cy's dead do you think I'll find the right one?"

She looked away, obviously uncomfortable with the way he'd put it. Jack had struck a nerve.

Andie said, "I'll talk it out with you, okay?"

"Okay," he said with a thin but appreciative smile.

"What do you know so far?"

"Theo's on a mission to find the man who raped his mother. He's convinced it's the same guy Isaac Reems blackmailed to help him escape from jail, it's the same guy who tried to kill Theo after Reems escaped, and it's now the same guy who kidnapped his uncle. He loaded up a pistol and gave Redden's name to Trina before going out tonight. She was supposed to give it to me if something bad happened."

"Do you think Redden was the rapist in that frat film?"

"I think he was more than that," Jack said, as he took a computer-printed copy of a newspaper article from his pocket and laid it on the table. "I went online into the *Tribune* archives before I called you. This is from 1986, about a month before Theo's mother was killed. Fernando Redden was on the front page of the business section. He won the chamber of commerce award for Miami businessman of the year."

Andie gave the article a quick review. "Could Theo's mother have possibly known about this? She wasn't exactly the type to read the business section of the newspaper."

"I'm sure there was TV coverage, too. She could have seen that."

"Are you suggesting that she saw what an upstanding citizen Redden had become and tried to blackmail him about the rape?"

"That's one possibility. But I'm betting that after thirteen years, she saw the face of her attacker on television, she hated the cards life had dealt her, and she simply decided to do something about it."

"She decided to report the assault to the police?"

"Or at least go public with it," said Jack.

"And a guy like Fernando Redden wasn't about to stand for that."

Andie retreated into thought.

Jack gave her a minute. "So, what's your take?"

"I think you may be right," she said, her expression turning very serious. "And I'm afraid Theo is walking straight into a whole mess of trouble."

Chapter 46

Uncle Cy didn't know where they were headed. He didn't know what was going to happen to him. He only knew that he had to pee, which meant that it had to be around midnight. Every night, his aging bladder sent the same signal at the same time. He could have set his watch by it, except that he didn't have a watch. Didn't have a wallet or cell phone either. Not anymore. Cy had surrendered all those things at gunpoint before climbing into the trunk of Jack's car.

The ride was far from comfortable. It was hot, pitch dark, and he was having a tough time breathing. Height ran in the Knight gene pool, but flexibility didn't, which made for a tight fit. The spare tire butted up against his back. Jack's golf bag stole a good chunk of his legroom. His head was propped against the wheel well, and the whine of rubber tires on asphalt was almost loud enough to drown out his thoughts. Almost. Danger pushed the mind in strange directions, and it occurred to him that it had been a while since he'd stared down the barrel of a gun. The first time was a holdup, when he was just nineteen. The last time was during the Overtown riots in 1982. There was one other brush with a Saturday-night special, but he'd been too drunk to take it seriously. Never before, however, had anyone put a gun with a silencer to his head. That changed the equation.

Silencers were for real killers, not amateurs.

Cy felt the car slow and make a hard right turn. The hum of the highway gave way to the crunch and pop of a gravel road. A pothole rattled his bones. Finally, the car came to a stop, the engine shut off, and there was silence.

Cy heard the driver's door open and shut. The jangle of car keys and shuffling of footsteps told him that someone was approaching.

Cy braced himself, expecting to hear the key in the trunk's lock. Instead, he heard a man's voice. He couldn't make out what was being said, but it was growing louder as the man came closer. It didn't sound like the street dialect of the driver, a black guy who'd ordered him to shut his face and get in the trunk. This voice belonged to someone else. Cy was still waiting for the trunk to pop open when, instead, the entire rear end of the car seemed to sink a good six inches. Someone was sitting on the bumper.

"Change of plans," the driver said. He probably thought Cy couldn't overhear their conversation, or maybe he just didn't care. Either way, every word was audible.

"What happened?" the other man said.

"Had Knight all to myself at his new bar. Then, in walked his lawyer and his uncle before I could do the hit."

"Did anyone know you were there?"

Cy wasn't sure, but the other guy sounded white.

"Well, yeah," said the black guy. "I mean, I shot his cell off the bar before his uncle showed up."

The anger in the white man's voice was discernible even through the trunk lid. "So you were playing with him. Is that what you're telling me?"

"A little, yeah. Just enough to keep it interesting."

"Damn it! We agreed to a hit, clean and quick. Just like Reems."

The words hit Cy like an epiphany. Theo had been right: he and Isaac Reems had been in the same man's sights.

The driver said, "Then you should have hired the same guy who hit Reems."

"Then you shouldn't have offered to do it for free."

"Cool down, all right?" said the driver.

"No, I can't cool down. You screwed up the Knight hit twice. At least the first time it had the markings of a random killing, just another drive-by gang shooting gone bad. But this time you definitely went and tipped off Knight to the fact that there's a contract on his head. If he's smart, he's in hiding. It could take weeks, maybe months, for us to get another shot at him."

"Got that problem solved, my man."

"Is that so?"

The driver slapped the trunk lid, and to Cy it sounded as if he were trapped inside a bass drum. "Got his uncle right in here."

"What the hell for? I got no interest in ransom."

"Listen to me."

"No, you listen. All I want is to shut Knight up before he starts blabbering about his mother. We have to assume he knows at least as much as Reems knew. I tried to buy Reems's silence, even paid off that guard to help him skip jail. In the end, Reems had to go. So does his buddy Theo. Period."

"Got it covered, dude. Like you said: Theo probably went into hiding. Which means we gotta lure him out into the open."

"How?"

"Like any fisherman will tell ya, ain't nothin' like live bait." Again he tapped the trunk lid, two quick beats on the metal drum. "And we got all the bait we need."

JACK AND ANDIE PARKED beneath a street lamp in the Coconut Grove ghetto. It was after midnight, but some middle-school kids were still out on the street, jumping the curb on bicycles. A homeless guy was asleep or passed out on the sidewalk. The beat of rap music blared from a pair of giant speakers as a group of gangsters rolled past in their lime-green low-rider.

"I'll wait here," said Andie.

Jack couldn't think of another woman he would leave alone in this neighborhood. He got out of her car, stepped onto the sidewalk, and walked toward the restaurant that had once been Homeboy's Tavern.

He probably could have guessed where Theo had gone, but the LoJack system on Theo's car told him what they needed to know. Law enforcement could access the GPS tracking system, so involving Andie had paid its first dividend.

Jack spotted Theo's car first, and then he saw Theo. He was alone, sitting on a bus bench and staring into the street with unusual intensity. It was as if the chalk line of his mother's body were still there, an unsolved homicide.

A westerly breeze carried a hint of smoke, typical of the late spring fires in the Everglades. The night was far from cool, however, and Theo had to be sweating in his leather jacket. Jack knew why he was wearing it. Trina had told him about the gun.

Jack stopped when he reached the bus bench. Theo was seated at the other end and didn't look at him. He didn't even seem curious as to how Jack had found him.

"Why'd you come?" Theo asked.

"To find you," said Jack. "Why did you come?"

Theo glanced over, and then he looked back at that spot on the street. "Same reason, I guess."

Jack didn't get it at first. Not very often did he hear Theo make allusions to finding himself. He took a seat on the end of the bench, leaving a comfortable space between him and his friend.

"I talked to Trina," said Jack.

Theo showed no reaction.

Jack said, "You can't do this alone."

Theo tapped the bulge in his jacket, the handle of his Glock. "I'm not alone."

"If Redden has done half the things you think he's done, you need a lot more help than that."

"You got a better idea?"

"I do."

"Let's hear it."

"Andie can explain it better."

"No FBI," said Theo.

"She knows."

Theo shot him a sideways glance. "Henning is cool with that?"

"Yeah," said Jack. "She is."

"So the FBI doesn't know shit about this?"

"No. Only Andie."

"Damn," he said. "That's a hell of a woman."

"No kidding," said Jack. "So, you'll talk with her?"

A bus pulled up and stopped in front of them. The air brakes hissed, the doors opened, but Jack and Theo didn't move. The driver shrugged and pulled away, leaving them in a cloud of diesel fumes.

Theo turned to look straight at Jack, his eyes narrowing. "I want you to do two things for me."

"What?"

"Number one, when this is over, don't you dare blow it with her again."

Jack smiled. "Deal," he said, as he extended his hand to shake on it.

Theo shook his hand, but he didn't return the smile. "Two: stay the hell out of this. Both of you."

Theo rose from the bench and walked away.

THEO CABBED IT BACK to Gilford's apartment. He hadn't bothered to ask Jack, but he surmised that it was his car's LoJack system that had had given away his location. It was easy enough to taxi around that problem— literally.

Lance Gilford was right where Theo had left him, gagged and hog-tied in his garage. Coming this close to drilling through the guy's skull had given Theo pause. He knew that Gilford could hold the key to finding Cy, but Theo didn't want to act out of emotion. A little time alone in the Coconut Grove ghetto had given him a chance to clear his head and devise a plan— the kind of plan that could involve neither Jack nor Andie, neither lawyers nor the FBI.

Theo put his gun to Gilford's head. "Time to call Fernando Redden."

Gilford nodded eagerly, as if willing to do anything to avoid a bullet in the head—or worse, a drill bit. Theo told him exactly what to say, and Gilford nodded once more. Then Theo removed the gag, got the number from Gilford, and dialed on Gilford's phone. No one answered at Redden's house. They tried his cell. Jackpot.

"What the hell is it now, Lance?"

"Sorry," said Gilford.

Theo put his ear next to Gilford's so that he could hear.

"Sorry, nothin'. It's one o'clock in the morning."

"I know. I—" Gilford took a breath, and Theo feared he was losing his nerve. Theo glanced at the tool chest—the drill bits—and Gilford fell right back into line, following Theo's script to the letter. "Theo Knight was just here."

Redden was silent. His tone changed dramatically. "Why?"

"He's mad as hell about something. Wouldn't say what. But he gave me something to give to you. It's in an envelope. Kind of feels like a videotape."

"Put it in your machine right now. Tell me what's on it."

"Forget it. I already know more than I want to know. You come here and get it."

"I can't," he said, and the strain in his voice was audible. "I got . . . there's something going on."

"At this hour?"

"Just—yeah, at this hour. I need you to bring it to me."

Gilford looked at Theo. A road trip wasn't in the script, so a little improvisation was in order. Theo nodded his approval. "Okay. I'll bring it to you. You at your house?"

"No. I'm out at the barn, you'll have to come here." Redden seemed to sense how strange that must have sounded in the middle of the night. "I got a sick foal. Can't leave."

"Where's your barn?"

Redden told him. It was in horse country, south Miami-Dade County, not far from Sparky's Tavern. Theo knew the general area. He flashed five digits, four times.

Gilford said, "I can be there in twenty minutes."

Theo gave him the CUT signal. Gilford said a quick "See ya," and Theo hit the END button.

Theo untied Gilford's feet, kept his hands bound, and nudged him toward Gilford's car with his pistol. "Come on," said Theo. "We gotta look after a sick foal."

Neither man needed to ask if its name was Cy.

Chapter 47

Fernando Redden tucked his cell into his pocket and went back inside the barn.

HAPP-Y Stables seemed like the perfect place to keep Cyrus Knight. It was secluded, butting up against a palm-tree nursery on one side and a tomato farm on the other, and it was near Redden's private plane at Tamiami Airport, just in case something went wrong. And there were plenty of places to hide away a hostage. Redden slid open the barn door and closed it. His pupils were adjusted to the night, so he didn't turn on the lights. A horse neighed in the darkness.

"Easy, girl," he said.

The stable had stalls for twenty-four horses, a dozen on each side of the long center aisle. Redden owned a dozen thoroughbreds, with plans to acquire more. He also owned the barn, the paddocks, and the surrounding acres of fenced pasture. He'd purchased the entire package for $7.5 million. Every penny had come from the Miami-Dade Housing Agency, thanks to the contacts he'd built as general counsel to his friend the mayor. Nearly $1.8 million had been approved for the construction of two dozen single-family homes, and another $2 million for an apartment building. The rest was earmarked for assisted-living facilities for the elderly. All of the projects were slated for Overtown. Not one was ever built. Fernando Redden kept every penny of the money. He supposed that he would get around to honoring that commitment. Someday. Maybe. For now, he would just enjoy HAPP-Y Stables—the inside joke being that HAPP stood for Housing Agency Project for the Poor.

Happy was not his mood at the moment, however.

"Moses!" he said, his voice rattling off the barn's tin roof.

Moses emerged from the stablehand's

quarters at the far end of the stable. He was barely visible in the darkness, and it was only the sound of his footfalls on the concrete floor that enabled Redden to discern his approaching silhouette. With horses on either side of them, they needed only the jangle of spurs to look like two gunfighters squaring off at midnight outside the proverbial Gold Dust Saloon.

Moses stopped and leaned against the hitching post. "What's up, my man?"

"An old friend of mine just called," said Redden.

"Who?"

"Doesn't matter."

"Then why tell me?"

"He's on his way over here. Says he has a video for me. It's from Theo Knight. You know anything about it?"

"Uh-uh," said Moses.

Redden went for his gun, but Moses moved like lightening to draw his weapon and pressed the barrel up under Redden's chin.

Redden flashed a stupid, nervous smile. "What . . . what are you doing?"

"You were gonna pull a gun on me, weren't you?"

"No—no, no.

Redden hadn't been this scared in years—maybe ever. But he was also furious with himself. Part of him wanted Moses dead, and he wanted to be the one to pull the trigger. Moses had been so convincing in selling an alliance with O-Town Posse. Unless Redden wanted to go to jail, he would eventually have to pay back millions to the Housing Agency. The drug trade's promise of a 200 percent return on investment would allow him to do that without liquidating his ill-gotten real estate. But Moses and his gang had proved to be nothing but trouble.

"What you want to pull a gun on me for?" said Moses.

"I wasn't—"

Moses pushed the gun up tighter beneath his chin. "Cut the bullshit. You got a problem with me, you spit it out. *Now.*"

"Okay," he said, his voice quaking. "It's just, you know, our arrangement is starting to feel like a one-way street."

"Stop talking like you're on fucking *Oprah*. What's your problem?"

"All right, I'll say it. You and your O-Town Posse have delivered on nothing. I gave you serious money, and I've still got nothing to show for it. I had to eliminate Reems, you dropped the ball on Knight. I got you out of TGK on bail, you went and killed a state trooper. It goes on and on. That's my problem."

Moses gave him a little smile, as if impressed that Redden had the guts to say it. He withdrew his weapon and let Redden stand easy.

"It's coming together, dude," said Moses. "I was just in Atlanta, talking to my contacts. You'll get your return on your money. And I'll personally take care of Knight."

"Good," said Redden, as he massaged away the imprint of Moses' barrel under his chin. "But there's actually something I'd like you to take care of before that."

"What?"

"Lance Gilford," said Redden.

"Who's Lance Gilford?"

"He's a pain in the ass," said Redden. "And it's time he was gone."

THEO RODE IN THE backseat of Gilford's car all the way to HAPP-Y Stables. Gilford drove well for a man with a loaded 9-millimeter Glock pressed against the base of his skull. Redden's instructions were to meet him at the end of the long driveway that led to the barn. The emphasis was on *long*. The final half-mile of winding dirt road seemed to last forever. But Theo knew it wasn't just about distance. The adrenaline was pumping, the anticipation building, like a D-day landing.

The car stopped, and the dust settled all around it. Theo crouched low behind the driver's seat so he couldn't be seen by anyone who might be watching. At Theo's direction, Gilford lowered all the windows and shut off the engine.

Theo said, "Leave the keys in the ignition, get out of the car, and take ten steps away from the driver's door. You stop right there and wait. You move even one more step away from me, I drop you in your tracks. Got it?"

"Yes."

"And you talk nice and loud, so I can hear. Go," said Theo.

Gilford reached for the door handle, but Theo stopped him. "Don't forget the video-tape."

"Oh, right," said Gilford. It was a blank, the pretense for the whole meeting with Redden, so it was understandable that he would forget it. Gilford grabbed it from the console, got out of the car, and did as he was told, stopping at the end of the driveway, exactly ten steps away from the driver's side door. Theo watched from his hiding spot in the backseat, careful not to show too much of the top of his head in the open window. A light breeze carried the dusty odor of straw and horse droppings from the barn. Smoke from the distant Everglades fires was less noticeable this far south, but it created a haze in the atmosphere that made for an unusually dark night.

Gilford waited, shifting nervously from one foot to the other. Finally, the barn door slid open, and a shadow appeared in the doorway.

"Fernando?" said Gilford.

There was no reply. The barn door closed. Through the open car windows, Theo could hear the plodding of footsteps in the dust, but it was too dark to make out the man's features.

"Is that you, Fernando?" Gilford said.

The man kept coming in silence, stopping five yards away from Gilford. From his hiding spot in the car, Theo still didn't recognize him. The darkness was that complete.

Gilford said, "Who are you?"

The man raised one arm and pointed at Gilford. He had a gun. "Give me the videotape," he said.

Theo did a double take. He knew the voice, and before Theo's brain could convince his eyes that he was indeed seeing his uncle, a shot cut through the night. Gilford fell in a heap.

"Get down!" Theo shouted.

Cy dove to the ground. Theo jumped over the front seat, got behind the wheel, and started the engine. As he put the car in gear, another shot rang out from somewhere inside the barn, and the windshield exploded into thousands of glass pellets. It was now obvious that his uncle hadn't fired the shot that had dropped Gilford, but Theo had no time to process that thought. Spinning tires churned up a cloud of dust as the squealing car cut a big arch across the driveway. It skidded to a quick halt, in perfect position to shield Cy on the ground from the shooter inside the barn.

More bullets whistled overhead. Theo jumped out of the car, grabbed his uncle, and pushed him into the rear seat.

"Stay on the floor!" said Theo.

The night crackled with gunfire as bullets peppered the passenger side of the car. Theo drew his Glock and returned fire over the hood, then scrambled on hands and knees to check on Gilford. No pulse. He left him where he lay, hurried back behind the wheel, and punched the accelerator. The tires screamed again, and Theo lowered his head in response to more gunfire. The car finished its sweeping arch into a full one-eighty, facing away from the barn. As it pulled away, the rear tire blew out, possibly from Theo's driving, possibly from gunfire. A second tire exploded, and Theo knew he was dealing with a crack shot. He kept going, but with two flats the car limped away like a gimpy racehorse. And with no windshield, Theo was eating plenty of dust.

Cy shouted, "I heard them talking. They're using me as bait to get you."

"Stay down," he said.

Theo's uncle wasn't telling him anything he hadn't already figured out, and the set of headlights coming toward him only confirmed the fix they were in. A car was fast approaching from the driveway's entrance. Theo was getting boxed in. The bait was doing its job.

"Hold on," said Theo.

Theo threw a hard right and steered the car at full speed off the road. They crashed through a white-painted horse fence and sped into the pasture. The ride was even rougher than expected, and two blown tires didn't help. Theo raced down a grassy slope and hit the brakes in the nick of time to avoid a hood-first dive into the lake.

"Come on!" Theo shouted, as he flew out of the car. His uncle followed, but the old man wasn't moving fast enough. Theo took him by the arm and practically dragged him along as they ran toward a patch of scrub and thick bushes by the lake. They didn't stop until they found taller trees, and they were a good twenty-five yards into a forest. It was ample cover in the darkness.

Cy was wheezing as they rolled onto the blanket of pine needles on the ground. Making a run for it on foot was not a viable option.

"How many are there at the barn?" asked Theo, as he checked his ammunition.

"Two, that I seen," said Cy. "Hispanic guy is in charge. Don't know his name. And a black guy named Moses."

"Moses?" said Theo. "That's the guy I was in jail with."

"He's the one who scares me."

"With good reason," said Theo. His ammunition clip was not yet empty, but he shoved a new one into his Glock anyway, giving himself a full set of rounds. He'd need it with Moses. "I want you to stay here," said Theo.

"Where you going?"

"I got something to take care of."

"What if they see me here?"

"Just lay still. They won't."

"But what if they *do*?"

"You still got that gun they gave you, right?"

"I left it in the car."

"Damn."

"It's got no bullets anyway. It was just a setup, the way they sent me out there and told me to aim the gun at that guy. I think they somehow knew or guessed he was gonna bring either you or the cops with him."

Theo thought for a second. "Okay, here's the plan. I'm gonna run two hundred yards that way and fire a shot or two into the air. That'll get 'em coming in my direction, away from you."

"And then what?"

"Then . . . I don't know. Just stay here, and don't move."

Cy grabbed him by the arm, his voice strained with urgency. "Ain't nothin' you gotta prove here tonight."

Theo didn't answer.

"You hear what I'm sayin', boy? You don't owe your momma nothin'."

The two men locked eyes in the darkness. Finally, Theo shook off his uncle's grasp. "Says you," he said.

He pushed up from the ground and sprinted across the pasture—back toward the barn.

Chapter 48

You need to go after him!" said Redden.

Moses didn't budge. The two men were still inside the barn, standing in one of the empty stalls. The top half of the dutch door was open just enough for Moses to see out into the pasture.

"He'll be back," said Moses.

"I think you're wrong. He's got his uncle, he's got Lance's car. He's gone."

Redden was pacing now, his nerves fraying. Moses was a picture of calm. "Shut up," said Moses.

Redden stopped dead in his tracks. "But you're letting him get away."

Moses glanced out through the opening, then back at Redden. "Have you ever met Theo Knight?"

"No."

"Well, I have. Not for a long time, but I can read people pretty quick. Trust me. Right this minute, he's on his way back here to take care of us."

Redden started pacing again. "I don't see how you can be so sure."

"I was right so far, wasn't I? Didn't I tell you that Gilford's phone call was a setup? Didn't I warn you that if you or me stepped one foot outside this barn to meet Gilford, Knight would shoot us dead?"

"You also said that when Knight saw his uncle he'd do something stupid. You were supposed to take him out."

Moses looked toward the pasture again. "Give him a little time. I can feel it. He's gonna do something real stupid."

A shot rang out from somewhere by the lake. Then another. Redden froze.

Moses smiled to himself. "Told you."

THEO KEPT RUNNING TOWARD the barn. Darkness was his friend, but for maximum cover he moved from tree to tree across the pasture.

Much of the forest had been cleared with the development of the farm, but the biggest oaks remained. Theo stopped about fifty yards from the stable entrance, crouched beneath century-old limbs.

Theo didn't know much about Redden, other than that he'd raped his mother. Studying the enemy before the attack was always a good idea, but somehow a fifty-something frat boy didn't seem that scary.

Moses was another story.

The fit between Redden and Moses didn't strike Theo as natural. Throw Isaac Reems into the mix, and that was one odd-shaped triangle. Crime, as the saying goes, makes for strange bedfellows. Theo supposed that was especially true when the rape of a black teenager in an all-white fraternity was caught on film.

Theo peered out from around the tree trunk and looked toward the barn. He couldn't be certain that Redden and Moses were still there, but two cars had been parked outside the stable earlier. Both were still there. Gilford's body was still lying in the driveway, too. Theo took those as good signs.

He plotted out his next several moves—

tree to fence to stable—and began his final approach.

He was halfway to the fence when a gunshot pierced the silence. A tiny volcano of dirt exploded at his feet, and then another. He dove for cover behind a watering trough and took a moment to make sure he hadn't been hit. He hadn't. But one thing was certain.

Someone was still in that barn.

"IDIOT!" SAID MOSES.

Redden was standing at the dutch door in the empty stall, his gun shaking in his hand. "I thought I could hit him."

"You panicked, moron. Another two minutes and I'd have had a shot I couldn't miss. Now he knows we're waiting for him."

"Then let's get out of here."

"We're not going anywhere," said Moses.

"You were supposed to take care of Knight, not me. I want out of here."

"It's too late," said Moses. "So here's the deal. Find yourself a stall and stay put. Do not move. If Knight sticks his nose inside, you blow his head off."

Redden started that nervous, frenetic pacing again. "No. Absolutely not."

"Who you tellin' 'no'?"

"I need to get out of here."

Moses considered it, then said, "All right. Go."

Redden stopped cold, his face alight. "You mean it?"

"Yeah. You can go. Take the car. I'll cover for you."

He breathed out something between a sigh of relief and giddy laughter. "Okay," he said, giving Moses what most white men thought was the black man's handshake. "You're cool, dude."

"I know. Now get outta here."

Redden opened the interior gate, turned to give Moses a mock salute, and then started running up the stable's center aisle.

He was fifteen feet away when Moses shot him in the back of the head.

Redden fell facedown to the concrete.

Some people would call it cowardice to shoot a man from behind. Others might regard it as cruel. But Redden had disintegrated into a liability that was bound to get them both killed. So Moses saw it not only as a smart move, but as an act of kindness.

Fernando Redden died a happy man. In the HAPP-Y Stable.

One down, Moses told himself, *one to go*.

Chapter 49

Theo heard the gunshot and flattened himself to the ground. This time there was no explosion of dirt around him, and it sounded as if the round had been fired deep within the stable, not out toward the pasture.

Theo took that as yet another good sign—possible dissension, or at least confusion.

He waited a full minute before making another move. Utter silence from the stable made for an eerie darkness, but the cover of night was perhaps his sole advantage. He couldn't count on the element of surprise. The only safe approach was to assume that his enemy knew he was coming back for them.

Why else would they have stayed put? They wanted the showdown as much as he did. The thought made his heart pound.

Left or right? Theo had to choose a path to the stable. There were more trees and cover to the right. He rose up on one knee and took off like a sprinter exploding from the blocks. He made it to the corner of the barn and stopped.

Side or main entrance? Gilford had emerged through the large sliding door just before getting shot, and it was still open. But that seemed like a risky point of entry. If this barn was like others that Theo had seen, the main entrance would lead to a wide center aisle that offered little cover. Much better to try one of the smaller side entrances—the dutch doors that allowed riders to take a horse directly from the stall to the outdoors. Theo counted twelve such access doors on this side of the barn. He steadied his nerves, crouched low, and went to the nearest door. Slowly, as quietly as he could move, he tried the handle. It turned.

For a moment he didn't so much as breathe, expecting even this slight disturbance to draw gunfire. There was none. He turned the handle all the way, and again he waited. Then he pulled the door open about six inches. He stopped and looked inside.

It was a typical square stall with a straw-covered floor. The horse, a beautiful bay-colored thoroughbred, was standing to the side on three legs, the right hind hoof relaxing. The animal appeared to be asleep. Theo was no horse expert, but he knew better than to sneak up behind a sleeping thoroughbred. He pushed the door another six inches, trying to give himself a large enough opening to see if the next stall was empty. It was hard to tell in the darkness. A few more inches of open doorway might have afforded a better view, but this last nudge made the rusty hinges creak like nails on a chalkboard. A shot rang out, the door panel splintered just inches above his head, and the sleeping thoroughbred was suddenly wide awake and kicking.

Theo slammed the door shut and rolled to his left. Another shot rang out from somewhere inside the barn, and the bullet popped through the door behind him. Theo kept rolling, working his way along the side of the barn, but it was as if the shooter knew where he was headed. Rapid gunfire—at least a dozen quick shots—sent shattered pieces of the barn flying at his heels, and he had to roll

as fast as he could to stay ahead of the trail
of bullets. The shooting suddenly stopped,
but Theo wasn't about to wait for it to start
again. He opened a door at the barn's mid-
point and ducked into a stall. This one was
empty, but Theo could hear the neighing and
clamor of startled horses all over the barn.
He immediately drew his weapon, ready to
return fire, but the shooter's gun had gone
silent, which was even more confusing. He
dove through the gap in fencing between
stalls and kept crawling in the darkness, past
horses, through piles of straw and horse
droppings, until he was four stalls away from
where he'd entered.

Theo stopped and listened. Excited horses
in neighboring stalls were settling down, and
he became aware of the sound of his own
breathing. Then, peering out between the
wood struts of the stall, he noticed something
just beyond the gate. On the concrete floor of
the stable's center aisle, a man lay twisted, a
pool of blood surrounding his head. Theo
started, but the body was utterly motionless,
the eyes fixed open. Dead. He went to the
gate for a closer look and saw that the corpse
was Hispanic. Wearing Ferragamo shoes, an
Armani jacket, and a Rolex wristwatch. A

Hispanic with serious money. Theo couldn't be totally certain, but somehow he understood, for the very first time, that he was laying eyes upon the man who had nearly gotten away with the rape of Portia Knight.

And Theo felt only one thing: the deep desire to get the man who'd killed her.

"Just you and me, Knight."

The voice was booming, and Theo recognized it as Moses. Theo was tempted to say something back—to ask if the dead man was indeed Fernando Redden—but it was to no advantage. He kept silent.

Stay or move? It was time for another decision, perhaps Theo's last. He listened. A horse exhaled and fluttered its lips. Another thumped a hoof. The tin roof rattled lightly in the breeze. Every stable had a chorus of normal sounds. Theo drew on his every power of concentration, and he detected the slow and steady click of leather heels on concrete.

It had to be Moses coming up the center aisle.

Then the clicking ceased. Theo strained to pick up the noise again but couldn't. Either Moses had stopped in his tracks, or he had managed to silence his step and was still advancing. Theo couldn't risk the latter.

He had to move.

"Truce?" said Moses, again in a booming voice. It came from the other side of the barn, nowhere near the place that Theo had calculated as Moses' present position. Moses had seen the stable in the light of day and was more familiar with the layout than Theo was. One more disadvantage.

Moses said, "Just throw your gun out into the aisle. I let your uncle go. I'll let you go, too."

Theo didn't believe him for a second. He dug beneath the bed of straw, pulled up a nice-sized rock, and tossed it across the center aisle. The instant it hit the other stall, a shot rang out and shattered the same piece of wood fencing that Theo's rock had struck.

The horses stirred again, and Theo took advantage of the burst of commotion. He crawled through the fence to the adjacent stall, opened the gate, and sent a startled thoroughbred charging into the dark center aisle. He crawled to the next stall and turned another skittish horse loose, and then another. He continued at breakneck speed until ten powerful and magnificent animals were running scared in every direction. Some of them trounced Redden's body—their dead owner—which didn't upset Theo in the least. Moses fired another shot that missed its mark by a good five feet, but the crack of the pistol raised the horses' hysteria to a fever pitch.

Theo began working his way back to the original stall, in the direction of what had sounded like the point of discharge of Moses' last shot. He stayed clear of the center aisle and the horses gone wild, instead climbing through the fencing that separated one stall from the next.

Another shot sent Theo diving for cover. He buried himself in a blanket of dirty straw as he returned fire across the center aisle. Moses was in the stall directly opposite him. Confused horses ran to and fro between the gunfighters, screeching and whinnying as bullets whistled past their delicate legs.

Suddenly, the shooting stopped. Theo tried to listen, but the animals were still too excited for him to hear anything but their hysteria. He was down to his last few rounds of ammunition. He assumed that Moses was reloading, which was perhaps Theo's last chance to make a move. As one of the startled thoroughbreds passed outside the stall, Theo pushed open the gate, grabbed the horse by the mane, and ran alongside it, keeping the animal between himself and Moses.

Moses fired two shots. Theo's horse stumbled to its knees and fell onto its side. Theo fell with the animal and slammed hard against a post. His gun flew from his hand and skidded across the concrete floor, coming to rest somewhere beneath the erratic stampede of the other horses.

Theo thought his horse had been hit by gunfire, but it rose up on its legs and trotted away. Instinct told Theo to seek cover, but he was stunned from the hard fall, and his body didn't respond to his own commands. A rumbling sound echoed above the raucous horses, and Theo saw the main entrance door slide open. The horses ran out through the opening like water through a broken dam. The barn went perfectly still. Theo lay alone in the center aisle, an easy target. His senses were coming back to him, and he rolled for cover. But he quickly realized that he should have been dead, if Moses was still inside the barn—and alive.

He fired a shot at Moses' stall.

All was quiet.

Slowly, and with extreme caution, Theo rose up on one knee. He found a rock and threw it in Moses' direction.

Still no response.

Theo sprinted across the aisle and hid behind a post. From there, he could see inside the stall. Moses lay on his back, looking up at the ceiling, his gun at his side. Theo went quickly through the gate and aimed his gun at Moses' chest.

"Don't move," he said.

Moses merely turned his head, apparently lacking the strength to do much more than that. His shirt was pasted to his chest with blood. One of Theo's shots had obviously found its mark.

"Go ahead," said Moses. "Pull the trigger."

Theo stepped closer, kicked Moses' gun aside, and pointed his gun at Moses' head. It would have been so easy to finish him off, and so deserved. Then a footstep in the aisle gave him a start. He turned and saw Andie Henning.

"Drop the gun, Theo," she said.

He kept the gun aimed at Moses. "Where's my uncle?" he asked Andie.

"Right here," said Cy. He was standing about ten feet behind Andie. "Jack's here, too. Those were Andie's headlights we saw coming toward us before you turned off the road."

Theo said, "Y'all can leave now. This is between me and Moses."

Andie raised her weapon. "I said, Drop the gun."

Theo heard her, but he ignored the command.

Jack said, "Listen to her, buddy."

Theo's attention was solely on Moses. "You and Fernando go way back, don't you? Back to his frat-boy days?"

Moses groaned with pain. "Didn't you hear what the woman said?"

"I don't care what she said," said Theo. "Fernando hired you to slit my momma's throat, didn't he?"

"Theo," said Andie, "this isn't the kind of confession that's going to hold up in any court of law."

"She's right," said Jack.

Theo's focus remained on Moses. "You killed her, and you bragged about it to the wrong guy in prison. To Isaac Reems."

"No way, dude," said Moses.

"Don't lie to me!" said Theo, as he stepped on the wound.

Moses cried out.

"Theo!" Andie shouted.

Theo said, "That's how Isaac found out. It's the only thing that makes sense. No other way for Isaac to be in the picture."

Moses said, "You got it wrong, dude."

Uncle Cy stepped forward. "Theo, stop!"

"Stay out of this," said Theo.

"What're you gonna do?" his uncle said. "You can't kill him here, right in front of an FBI agent. That's cold-blooded murder."

"Your uncle's right," said Andie.

"You gonna arrest me for murder?" Theo scoffed.

"You shoot him, I will," said Andie.

Theo knelt down and pressed the barrel between Moses' eyes. "Do you know how bad I want this?" said Theo.

Andie said, "I can't let you shoot him."

"Then you're gonna have to shoot me," said Theo.

Andie fired a warning shot. "The next one won't miss."

"You're bluffing," said Theo.

"Don't test her!" said Cy.

"I told you to stay out of this," said Theo.

"He ain't worth it," said Cy.

"He deserves to die."

"He's—no, he don't."

"It ain't your call," said Theo.

"Theo, I'm telling you the truth. Moses don't deserve it."

"He deserves worse."

"No, he don't."

"After what he did," said Theo.

"Theo, it wasn't him. Moses didn't do it."

"How do you know?"

"Because I was there."

"What do you mean, you were there?"

"I did it!"

Theo looked at him with disbelief. Jack and Andie looked equally stunned.

Theo said, "I don't believe you."

Cy took a step closer. "She ruined me with her damn drugs. I had a career, a reputation in this town. Until she hooked me on crack. Lost every single one of my gigs. Pretty soon the only joint that would hire me was a dive like Homeboy's. And the only reason they put up with me is 'cause Portia turned her tricks there and gave the manager a cut."

Theo glanced down at Moses, who looked almost as befuddled as Theo felt. Theo didn't want to see his uncle's face, but he finally looked at him. "You lying to me, old man?"

Cy shook his head. "Put the gun away."

Theo looked at Jack, searching for some signal that this was all just a nightmare.

"Do as Cy says," Jack told him.

"Save yourself another useless trip to death row," said Andie, her aim steady.

Theo lowered his gun. He was staring into the darkness, making eye contact with no one. It was difficult to think clearly, but the same thoughts kept swirling in his head—the way his uncle had never been able to tell him a single good thing about his mother, the repeated hints about secrets surrounding her murder, the way he'd pressed Theo's hand to his heart and flat-out warned him: "The past will hurt you, boy. It will cut you open and laugh in your face."

"Hey!" Moses grunted. "Can somebody call 911 already?"

"Yeah," Theo said in a weak voice. "I think I need it."

Chapter 50

Theo wanted to kill his uncle. But not for murdering his mother.

"You were gonna shoot Moses right between the eyes," the old man said.

"You didn't have to lie to me like that," said Theo.

"I couldn't let you kill a man right in front of an FBI agent. No matter how much he deserved it."

The two men were sitting out on the wood deck behind Theo's town house. Venus was rising in the east, and Theo guessed that the sun would emerge in not too many more minutes. Both men were exhausted, but neither one had been able to think about going to bed. Not since the ministroke last summer had Theo seen the old man smoke a cigarette, but tonight was an exception. With everything that had happened at HAPP-Y Stables, Theo cut him some slack.

"Guess I was dead right about Moses," said Theo.

"Mmm-hmm," said Cy.

They'd been over it several times already, each time pressing another bit of speculation into established fact. Moses had been a teenage punk in an Overtown gang in the 1980s. Redden was an Overtown developer who had just been named Miami businessman of the year. Portia Knight saw Redden on the evening news and recognized him as the frat boy who'd raped her fourteen years earlier. She made the fatal mistake of calling Redden instead of going to the police. For far less money than Portia had tried to extort from him, Redden hired Moses to slit her throat and silence her forever. It had been the perfect crime—until all those years later, when Moses and Isaac Reems, fellow inmates at TGK, got to trading war stories about the 'hood.

"Pretty ballsy move," said Theo, "the way Isaac turned Moses' bragging against him and Redden. Isaac got two pretty big players—one inside, one outside—to help him bust out of prison."

"He got hisself killed. Almost got you killed, too."

Cy crushed out his cigarette and lit up another one.

"You gonna smoke that whole pack?" said Theo.

"Mmm-hmm."

White wisps of smoke curled into the night air. Theo watched the leaves move in the huge gumbo-limbo overhead. The breeze was picking up, another sign of the coming dawn. Cy was smoking furiously.

"What's wrong?" said Theo.

"Nothin'."

"You gonna tell me or you gonna make me guess?"

"I said it's nothin'." Cy inhaled so deeply that it made him cough.

"You're lying again," said Theo.

The old man didn't respond.

Theo could have dropped the entire line of conversation, but in his heart he knew that if the sun came up and this remained unsaid, they would never, ever talk about it.

"Something you said before keeps gnawing at me," said Theo. "It was when you and me were alone in the new bar, doing the inspections. I could feel that there was something you needed to say. All you would tell me is to be careful about poking into my momma's murder. And then when I pushed you to explain, all you would say is that it ain't a story with a happy ending."

The ash on the end of Cy's cigarette was nearly an inch long. Theo wanted to walk over and flick it for him.

Cy said, "I don't want to talk about it no more."

"Well, I do." Theo scooted forward to the edge of his chair. "Tonight, when you told me you were the killer, that conversation flashed in my mind. It was like I was hearing your words again: 'This ain't a story with a happy ending.'"

Cy glanced at him nervously, his face clouded by smoke.

Theo said, "When we was in the bar, I figured all you meant was that my momma ended up dead. But the more I thought about it, that's too obvious. No need to say it, right? I knew my momma got killed, so why would you even bother warning me that the story don't have a happy ending?"

"I don't know. Why would I?"

"Last night, for a split second there, I thought maybe I had the answer. The unhappy ending you were warning me about wasn't my momma getting killed. It was when . . ."

"When what?"

"You know."

"When you found out I killed her?"

"Yeah. Like I said: Just for a split second there, that's what I thought you meant."

Cy was staring off toward the trees, avoiding Theo's gaze.

Theo was all the way to the edge of his chair, resting his forearms on his knees as he leaned toward his uncle. "That ain't what you meant, was it?"

Cy flicked his cigarette butt over the fence. Finally, he looked Theo in the eye. "You really want to know what I meant?"

Theo nodded. "Yeah. I do."

His uncle swallowed hard, and suddenly Theo wasn't so certain that he wanted to know. But it was too late to stop it now.

Cy folded his arms and said, "You never was good in math, was you?"

"What are you talking about?"

"Your momma was raped in the spring of 1972."

"So?"

"May 20, to be exact. When were you born?"

The question hit Theo like a punch to the chest. "February 17, 1973."

The two men locked eyes, and it was as if the earth had suddenly stopped spinning. Theo knew it was his turn to say something, but no words would come.

Cy dug a crumpled pack of cigarettes from his shirt pocket. There were just two left. "You want a smoke?" he said.

Theo reached over and took one. His face glowed in the darkness as Cy lit it for him. Then he sat back in his chair and took a long pull.

"Ain't that a two-footed kick in the head?" said Theo, smoke tumbling from his lips.

"Mmm-hmm," the old man said. "With boots on."

Chapter 51

Theo told no one—except Jack.

Of course the media hounded him. They wanted details about the shootings that had left a distinguished businessman like Fernando Redden dead in his barn alongside a guy like Moses, a gang leader who was wanted for the murder of a Florida state trooper. Theo refused all interview requests. He didn't even watch the news on television, except for one short statement from Andie Henning and the supervisory agent in charge of the Miami field office. The FBI declined to comment, saying that details would follow in the forthcoming official final report of Agent's

Henning's task force on security failings at TGK Correctional Center and the escape of Isaac Reems.

Mere mention of a possible connection to Reems's escape was fuel to the proverbial fire, as if an edict had been issued to the media: "Let the speculation begin."

Fernando Redden was buried on the Tuesday following his death. Theo didn't attend the funeral, but over breakfast Trina got so angry at the newspaper that she just had to read him the obituary—a quarter-page fluff piece about the son of Cuban exiles who "personified the American dream." Redden came off like the best thing to happen to housing for Overtown's poor since the Civil Rights Act of 1964. There were even humorous anecdotes about "Fernando el Fantastico"—the compassionate friend, the generous philanthropist, the doting husband. Absent was any mention of the fact that, had he lived, he would have landed in jail for fraud and misuse of public housing funds. That information would not become public until the grand jury concluded its secret investigation and returned indictments against his corporation and shady business partners. It would get even uglier with Moses' three-count indictment for murder—Redden, the state trooper, and Portia Knight, though Moses could probably buy his way off death row by testifying against the corrections officer who helped Isaac escape.

Theo tried not to dwell on any of it. Two o'clock Thursday afternoon, however, brought a flash of renewed anger and a mix of other emotions that he didn't fully understand. According to the newspaper, 2:00 P.M. was the scheduled time for Redden's graveside service. "Family only." *Family.*

Before the burial, Jack had offered to try and get a court-ordered DNA test.

Theo didn't want to know.

Theo had heard before that he was of mixed ancestry, though usually it was said tongue in cheek. When he was on death row, a Native American inmate told him he looked part Miccosukee, which earned him the prison-lawyer nickname "Chief Brief." With a name like Theodopolis, people said he must be part Greek—which now seemed like an ironic ode to his apparent place of conception.

Theo still had his doubts about Fernando Redden being his father. It wasn't exactly a comforting thought, but simply because Portia was raped on film by one frat boy didn't rule out the possibility of another partner that night. She could have been raped again by someone off-camera. She could have had consensual sex earlier that night, that day, that week, that month. Theo liked the latter alternative best. That was the one he would cling to.

Three weeks had passed since the shooting, and it still felt too soon to be celebrating in any way. But Theo had a business to run at Sparky's, the rent still had to be paid on the new property, and it was time to open his *real* jazz bar.

"Place looks amazing," said Jack.

It was early Friday evening, and Theo was on the working side of the bar, mixing a pitcher of martinis. For the past two hours, he'd been so busy greeting guests and putting out fires that he hadn't taken the time to look around. Weeks of preparation and hard work had helped take Theo's mind off Moses and Fernando Redden. Everything from cleaning, painting, and decorating to creating a menu, stocking the bar and kitchen, hiring and training the staff, and booking live entertainment— it was finally paying dividends. The U-shaped bar was killer. The lighting was just right. The twenty small café tables—the exact number Uncle Cy had recommended—were all taken.

The doors were open, and people came. Not just loyal friends. Theo could feel it in the air, and it made his heart swell: he was tapping into the true jazz-lover crowd.

"Want to invest?" said Theo.

"Hmmm," said Jack, as he scratched his head. "Let me think about that. You and me, business partners? I'd say that has about as much chance as—"

"You picking up the phone and asking Andie on a date?"

"I told you I was going to call her."

"And by the time you do, we'll all be playing shuffleboard."

"Look, last time we started dating too soon after the Salazar kidnapping. This time I'm just putting a little distance between the gunfire and the sparks flying, so to speak."

"Well, I invited her tonight. She and Trina are bringing Cy. You got a problem with that?"

Jack tried his martini. He seemed to approve. "I think that's a great idea. Timing's good, too. Rene and I are definitely history."

"I'd say so. What's it been, a month?"

"Actually, she finally called me. Yesterday."

Theo dropped a rack of olives in Jack's

drink. "Really? What took her so long this time? Famine? Tsunami? Swarming locusts?"

"Fear," said Jack.

"Of what?"

"She sensed some chemistry between Andie and me while she was here. Once she got back to Africa, she worked up this fear that I was going to tell her not to come to Miami anymore. That's why she didn't call."

Theo leaned toward him, forearms atop the bar, speaking in an even tone. "That is a colossal pile of crap. You know that, don't you?"

"Maybe." Jack went back to his martini and adjusted his response: "Definitely."

"Good thing," he said, glancing toward the rear entrance. "Because the world's most unlikely ménage à trois has just arrived."

The women were dressed to turn heads, but Theo's gaze fixed on his uncle. Cy had Trina on one arm, Andie on the other, and a huge smile on his face. Of course he was wearing his three-piece Norfolk suit in natty vintage tweeds, as if it were 1956 and he still ruled the Cotton Club, the Knight Beat, and every other famous old jazz club in Overtown. He reached over the bar and gave Theo a huge hug.

"Proud a' you, boy," he said.

The words meant the world to Theo, and he had to close his eyes for a moment to contain the emotion. "Thanks, old man."

Theo broke the embrace, and Trina leaned over to give him a kiss. That left Jack and Andie as the awkward spectators for a moment.

"You look amazing," Jack told her.

"Keen grasp of the obvious there," said Theo. "Siddown, everyone. Got a couple of surprises planned."

Jack offered Andie the stool on his right. Uncle Cy and Trina took the ones on his left. Theo poured martinis for each of them. Then he pulled a tobacco tin from under the counter and placed it on the bar in front of them. It was the fourteen-ounce cylinder, bright red with a white-and-black painted label.

Trina was the first to smile. "Prince Albert," she said, reading the brand name.

"I'm a man of my word," said Theo. "Sort of."

"Pipe tobacco? That's not much better than a roach brooch, bucko."

"Just open it."

She twisted off the lid, and her eyes lit up. "Oh my god! These are amazing!"

Theo said, "Happy belated birthday."

Trina reached inside and removed the diamond earrings. She kissed him and immediately put them on, then stood and checked herself in the big mirror behind the bar. They were shaped like little saxophones.

"Gorgeous," said Andie.

"The earrings aren't bad either," said Cy.

Theo chuckled and said, "Now it's time for your surprise, old man."

"Me? Isn't all of this surprise enough?"

Theo smiled thinly. "Follow me." He stepped out from behind the bar and took Cy by the arm. The others remained seated, knowing that this was about family. Theo led his uncle all the way to the front entrance.

"We can't be leavin', are we?" said Cy, as Theo escorted him outside.

Theo didn't answer. He took his uncle across the sidewalk and didn't stop until they reached the other side of the street. Then Theo squared him around to face the club, offering a view of the main entrance that Trina had denied him by bringing him in through the back door.

The lighted sign above the canopy said it all: Cy's Place.

Cy didn't speak. Slowly he raised his

hands, shaping the left one into an *L* and the right into a backward *L*, framing Cy's Place like a movie director. Theo noticed that his hands were shaking.

"We put it up this afternoon," said Theo. "You like?"

The old man swallowed the lump in his throat. "Don't know what to say. Don't deserve this. Really."

"You want me to take it down?"

Cy pulled himself together and shot Theo a look that said, "You crazy, boy?"

"I didn't think so," said Theo.

He let his uncle enjoy the moment, but Cy probably would have stood there all night, had Theo let him. "Come on," said Theo. "Let's go back inside."

Side-by-side, they crossed the street. Cy stole one last glimpse at the sign as Theo pushed through the front door. Trina hugged and congratulated him back at the bar. Jack and Andie were in a heated discussion that bordered on a flat-out argument as to whether the world's first martini was actually called a martinez, whether it was made with London Dry or Old Tom gin, and whether it came with an olive or a cherry. It was nice to see them getting along as per usual. Theo broke it up before someone got injured, and they all raised a glass and drank to Cy's Place.

Theo gave the old man another hug. "Now you gotta do me a favor."

"Name it," he said.

Theo reached under the bar again. This time, he pulled up the old Buescher 400 saxophone that Cy had passed down to him years earlier.

"Play tonight," said Theo.

Cy's mouth fell open. "You kiddin' me?"

"I couldn't be more serious. Doctor says you're doing great, finally got your blood pressure medicine figured out."

"But . . . I don't have my mouthpiece."

"I already rigged it. Beechler Diamond Alto. Any other excuses you want me to shred?"

"I'm so rusty. I mean, you don't really want this old man to be the first one on your stage, do you?"

Theo pushed the sax a little closer. "You're up, Jazzman."

Cy stood for a moment, expressionless. Then his mouth curled into a sly smile, and he took the instrument—carefully, lovingly, as if it were his baby. "What do you want to hear?"

"How about 'Ko-Ko'?" said Theo.

Cy chuckled. A Charlie Parker classic with dazzling virtuoso technique and complex melodic lines was asking too much. "I'll give you a ballad," he said.

"Cool," said Theo, and then his friends gave Cy an encouraging round of applause.

Cy bowed humbly and then weaved through the crowd, saxophone in hand. From behind the bar Theo cut off the CD that was playing over the sound system and adjusted the overhead lighting. Cy took his place on stage. The room was abuzz with loud talk and laughter, and nobody seemed to pay much attention to the tall, skinny, gray-haired man in the funny suit—until he started playing.

On the intimacy scale, Theo ranked playing the sax somewhere between crying and making love in public, such was the emotional and artistic connection between the musician and his instrument. Capturing an audience was a process, and Cy began with a flurry to grab the crowd's attention. Then he settled into his melody. Conversations quieted, then ceased. The old master was taking control.

Theo stood behind Trina and watched. She leaned back, seated on her bar stool, and settled into his arms. Her shoulder blades felt like wings against his chest, and along with everyone else in the room, she and Theo seemed to float a few inches off the ground as the old man played. Even Jack and Andie were at peace, their fingers interlaced on top of the bar.

After a few minutes, Trina reached behind her and pressed her hand against Theo's face. "I love my earrings," she whispered.

"I'm glad."

"Just one question."

"What?"

"How are you gonna wear these things on your—"

Theo covered her mouth, putting an end to the Prince Albert jokes.

She playfully bit his hand and gently tugged at her earrings, as if to confirm that both he and the jewelry were keepers.

Uncle Cy was in a groove, eyes closed, his body arching as he reached for each high note, a musician's musician playing his heart out.

Theo held his girlfriend tightly, caught up in her, caught up in the moment—spellbound by the timeless magic of Cyrus Knight.

Acknowledgments

After a one-book vacation from the Swyteck series with *Lying with Strangers*, I'm grateful to the team of all-stars who helped me get back into the groove of Jack and Theo: my editor, Carolyn Marino; her assistant, Wendy Lee; and my agent, Richard Pine. I also want to thank my early readers, Dr. Gloria M. Grippando, Eleanor Raynor, and Gloria Villa.

Beth Johnson was the lucky winner of a charity auction that helped me name one of my characters in *Last Call.* I hope she always wanted to be a prison warden. If not, I hope she's at least glad that I didn't lend her name to an inmate. Either way, her generous donation goes to a great cause, the Ransom Everglades School in Miami, Florida.

As always, my biggest thank-you goes to Tiffany. She helps me in too many ways to enumerate, but I want to take this opportunity to assure her that I will never give her a roach brooch, and to assure each and every one of you (especially her friends) that Tiffany had absolutely nothing—zero, *nada*—to do with my research into a Prince Albert.

Finally, I want to thank the many, many pet lovers who wrote to me over the past year. In the acknowledgments to my last Jack Swyteck novel, *When Darkness Falls*, I mentioned the passing of Sam, my beloved golden retriever. *Last Call* was the first novel in a decade that I had to write without Sam at my side. Your stories about beloved pets were a huge comfort on the lonely days. For those of you who had trouble finding the story about Sam on my website, go to www.jamesgrippando.com and click on the menu button that says "Other Writings." But don't forget your Kleenex.